DEATH
&
TAXES

DEATH & TAXES

RICHARD V. RUPP

ARCHWAY
PUBLISHING

Archway Publishing books may be ordered through booksellers or by contacting:

Archway Publishing
1663 Liberty Drive
Bloomington, IN 47403
www.archwaypublishing.com
1 (888) 242-5904

Because of the dynamic nature of the Internet, any web addresses or links contained in this book may have changed since publication and may no longer be valid. The views expressed in this work are solely those of the author and do not necessarily reflect the views of the publisher, and the publisher hereby disclaims any responsibility for them.

Any people depicted in stock imagery provided by Thinkstock are models, and such images are being used for illustrative purposes only. Certain stock imagery © Thinkstock.

Any people depicted in stock imagery provided by Shutterstock are models, and such images are being used for illustrative purposes only. Certain stock imagery © Shutterstock.

ISBN: 978-1-4808-1964-1 (sc)
ISBN: 978-1-4808-1965-8 (hc)
ISBN: 978-1-4808-1966-5 (e)

Library of Congress Control Number: 2015948610

Print information available on the last page.

Archway Publishing rev. date: 08/26/2015

To my patient and beautiful wife, Coleen, who has continually encouraged me to write, and whose editing skills greatly improved this story.

I

IRS Service Center, Fresno, California

He had walked these endless hallways for two years and often wondered why the walls of the largest IRS service center in the country were decorated with Disney characters. What the hell had they been thinking when they designed this place? Did they do it to mock the taxpayers? Was this the IRS's version of Disneyland, or were the powers that be simply implying that the IRS tax rules were akin to *Alice in Wonderland*? This last thought had him laughing to himself. *If not from Wonderland, then maybe from Oz.* They certainly didn't improve the working atmosphere, and they seemed out of place in an IRS office. They made no sense to him, but it seemed that everyone just took them in stride.

He continued walking from the administrative support area at the back of the one-story complex toward the Mahogany Row administrative offices located at the front of the building. He walked through the cavernous Examinations Division bay and strode down the center aisle of mostly empty cubicles. At one point, a colorful Winnie-the-Pooh mural smiled down at him. He was halfway there. *Fuck. This place is big*, he thought.

This'd started out to be such a good year for him. He was living the good life, the really good life. Everything had been going great—and then he'd screwed things up. He was on his way to Shaw's office to fix the problem. *Fucking Shaw is not going to screw everything up. I've got to protect what we're doing.*

He'd planned to go directly to Shaw's office, but as he passed through the cafeteria, he spotted Chris signaling him to sit down. He put change into the Coke machine, waited for the cup to fill, and then sat down next to Chris, who leaned over close to him and whispered, "Are you ready?"

His brain was spinning round and round. He sipped the Coke, wishing it were tequila.

"Yeah," he whispered back.

"You look tired."

"Yeah, still recovering from last night."

He looked up at the big clock, took a final gulp of the Coke, and stood up.

"Got to go."

"Make sure you clean up your mess."

It was just about the appointed time to meet Shaw. *Fuck. Which way is his office? You need a road map to find your way around this place,* he thought. Although he had worked there for two years, he still had a hard time finding his way around. He stood for a moment, got his bearings, and trudged toward Shaw's office.

He'd never delivered mail to this area. Walking down a long, dark hallway, he could see the beginning of the well-lit administrative offices at the front of the building. It was like looking down a long, dark tunnel toward light at its end. Before reaching the well-lighted area, he spotted Shaw's office next to an empty conference room. *I've left Disneyland,* he thought.

He took three deep breaths and looked down at his feet. His brain was still spinning, and he felt nauseous. Finally, he knocked on Edison Shaw's office door and entered. He was startled to see the back of a heavyset man sitting in a swivel chair in front of his desk, facing away from the door he had just gone through. The office was small and dingy. The walls were blank except for a large corkboard mounted on the wall that the man was facing. It was covered with papers and pictures. Next to it was a single three-drawer, gray-metal file cabinet.

"Hello? Mr. Shaw?"

The man swiveled around in his chair to face his visitor.

"Oh, yeah, I've been expecting you. You look just like your photo ID. Right on time. Sit over there. Do you know why I asked you to see me?"

"Not really."

"You've worked in the mailroom for two years now. Is that right?"

"Yeah."

"Straight out of Roosevelt High School?" Shaw asked.

"Yeah."

"We have a lot of people working here from Roosevelt. I bet you know some of them."

"So?"

"Just curious. It's my job to be curious. Exactly what do you do in the mailroom?"

"I sort incoming mail and deliver it. First time I've been up front here."

"Do you deliver mail to the Spanish Language Unit?"

"Yeah."

Shaw reached across his desk, picked up a folder, opened it to a specific page, and turned it around. "Do you recognize this form?"

He looked at the form and knew exactly what it was. "Come on, man. I just deliver mail. I don't know one form from another. Man, this is the IRS. There are thousands of forms."

"You're right there. Just thought you might have noticed this form in particular. Does the Spanish Language Unit get a lot of mail?"

"A fair amount. Maybe twenty or thirty items a day."

"Okay. That's all I need today," Shaw replied.

"That's it?"

"Yes. That's it for today, but I may need to talk with you again in a few days."

"I'll be here." *But you won't.*

As Shaw returned the file to the stack on his desk, the visitor rose and slowly headed to the door behind him. Instead of reaching for the door handle, he bent down as if to tie his shoe. Instead, he lifted his pants leg and then pulled the small Colt .22-caliber semiautomatic handgun from the holster strapped to his leg. In one quick motion, he rose and placed the gun three inches from Shaw's temple, looked away, and pulled the trigger. One deadly shot.

The stack of files fell to the floor as Shaw's body slumped forward. The small-caliber bullet was not powerful enough to go through his skull, but it did the job, lodging halfway in the brain. Blood began squirting out of the hole. A red liquid pool slowly began spreading across the desk.

He felt his hands become sweaty as fear ran through his body. Instinctively, he shoved Shaw's laptop computer away from the growing blood pool. He stood completely still for a moment, listening for several seconds. No one came. *Fuck, that was loud.* The .22-caliber made a loud noise, but not as loud as a higher-caliber gun would have. Luck was on his side. No one had heard the shot.

His hands were shaking. He tried to calm himself. Slowly, he reached into his pocket and pulled out the latex gloves. Putting the gloves onto his shaking hands was challenging. *Fuck these things,* he thought. Finally, he won the battle.

He locked the office door and then picked up the laptop computer from the chair where he had placed it to avoid the spreading pool of blood. With it in his lap, he started typing on the keyboard. It would've been easier to take the laptop with him, but there was no place to hide it in the IRS center and no way to get it past the armed guards at the gates.

He knew the computer's files by heart and searched for specific files that needed to disappear. Each time he found one, he deleted it. Then he deleted them again from the computer's wastebasket file.

Suddenly, Shaw's body jerked upward across the desk. The bloody hand almost touched him. His stomach turned into knots, and his body reacted in a way he had never felt before. He watched as Shaw's body flopped back down on the desk.

"Holy shit! *Madre de Dios!*" came out of his mouth in a muffled scream.

He looked down at his pants, as he felt like he'd pissed. If he had, nothing showed. *Relax; relax. You've done it. It'll work out. Relax.*

The surprise movement of Shaw's body had caused the visitor to rise from the chair. He grabbed at the computer as it slipped from his lap and almost fell to the floor. Stepping back from the chair for a moment, he realized that Shaw's movement was probably a normal reaction for a dead body. At least, he hoped so. *Get a hold of yourself.* He looked down at the front of his pants. *No, you didn't wet your pants,* he told himself.

His hands were shaking worse than before as he struggled to punch the right keys on the computer. He checked the computer's appointment calendar and was surprised that this meeting hadn't been listed. Lucky again. He looked for a paper calendar but didn't find one. He felt relatively safe.

It was time to do the planned cleanup. *What did he tell me to do? Oh, yeah—the bullets don't have any fingerprints on them.* He picked up the spent shell casing, removed the remaining bullets from the gun's clip, and placed Shaw's fingerprints on them. He replaced the shell casing on the floor next to Shaw, reloaded the small handgun, and wiped off his prints. Reluctantly, he gripped Shaw's hand. He closed it on the gun in several places and then returned it to the floor.

He removed the specially designed holster he'd worn on his lower left leg. Raising Shaw's left trouser leg, he strapped it to Shaw and pulled the trouser leg back down.

His eyes scanned the room, and then he took a last look at Shaw. *Just as planned. It should slow down the cops for a while.*

On his way out of the office, he picked up the files from the floor. As he left, he wiped the desk and door handle clean of prints with the Handi Wipes he'd brought with him. Just as he was about to leave, he remembered one more thing. He reached into the inside pocket of Shaw's coat and removed a small, brown notebook, placing it in his own back pocket.

He stepped back into the IRS's version of Disneyland, walking past the Disney characters into the cavernous Examinations Division bay. *Walk normally,* he told himself. He strode down the center aisle of mostly empty cubicles back to the mailroom. He placed Shaw's files into the re-file bin. They would be picked up by clerks in the morning and filed with thousands of other files in the center. He knew it would be unlikely that anyone would remember him walking through, or what files they had re-filed.

The huge, black-rimmed wall clock indicated it was now a little after six. He headed outside and noted the bright-red sunset. It made him think of the pool of blood on Shaw's desk.

His ID card recorded the time of departure. Fortunately, a number of other people had worked late and were leaving at the same time.

He smiled and tried to act normal as he left, but twenty feet from the security gate, his hands began shaking again, and his legs felt weak. A good, stiff drink was in order.

Dos Amigos, his favorite bar, was packed. By the third tequila, his body began to relax and his hands stopped shaking. He had killed once before—an old, homeless guy in a Fresno alley. It was a required killing that allowed him to jump into the Bulldogs. He remembered being scared, but it was pretty emotionless.

He was fourteen when he killed the old man. Six Bulldog gang members stood there, encouraging him to shoot. Killing Shaw in his office in the middle of the IRS service center was different.

Tilting the barstool back, he flipped through the pages of Shaw's little brown book. He picked up the shot glass, licked the salt from the back of his hand, slammed down the shot, and then bit into the lime, finishing the third tequila. Jeff the bartender asked, "What're you reading?"

The notebook quickly disappeared into his jacket pocket. "Oh, it's nothing. Just my little notebook. How about another shot?"

"Sure, but you know what they say: one tequila, two tequila, three tequila, floor. Five tequila, six tequila, seven tequila, morgue!"

Jeff the bartender laughed as he poured the fourth tequila. The regular customer threw out his Bank of America credit card to signal this was the last drink.

2

San Francisco, California

Dick Hartmann grasped the coffee cup his sister had given him in both hands and took a sip. The warmth from the cup felt good on his hands. He looked down at it for the hundredth time and read the inscription:

DICK
MEANING: POWERFUL
It is destined to be
Within your fate
To be a ruler
Both mighty and great.
In all that you do,
You seem to succeed;
You seldom follow.
But take the lead.
You'll always have
The upper hand,
And be the one
Who's in command.

Chuckling to himself, Hartmann said to the cup, "I love you, cup. How could you be so right?" *Get back to the real world. Every* Dick *gets the same cup, you idiot.*

The evening was coming to a close. Hartmann's brain was tiring from reviewing the publisher's proof copy of his *Mastering Criminology 101* manuscript. Each page had been carefully initialed, indicating his approval. He flipped to the back of the manuscript and re-read the last chapter. *Pretty good, if I do say so myself. I'll be able to use it in my next class at Quantico,* he thought. He happily slipped the manuscript into the FedEx box for the publisher. Hartmann enjoyed San Francisco and his job at the FBI. He knew that he'd been lucky in life.

Even though he wanted to climb into bed, the coffee he'd consumed was keeping him awake. He slumped back in his easy chair and thought about his life thus far.

He'd been brought up in an upper-middle-class family in West Hollywood, right on the border of Beverly Hills. From the house on Huntley Drive that'd been built in 1931 by his grandfather and given to his father, he'd witnessed directly, or through stories from his father and grandfather, the transformation of West Hollywood from a neighborhood of families with European ties to an area known as the design district of LA. Since moving out on his own, he'd watched the area become a prominently gay and lesbian community. The kids he'd played with while growing up were from families like his, with German, French, English, or Scottish backgrounds. There were the Eckes down the street; they grew poinsettias in fields along Sunset Boulevard. Toward Fairfax Avenue, there were the Russian Jews, but as he remembered it, everyone seemed to get along.

When he was growing up, West Hollywood was a unique area in that it was comprised of an unincorporated strip of land that separated LA from Beverly Hills, and it was policed by the LA County Sheriff's Department. LA and Beverly Hills cops keep their distance. It didn't become a city until 1984. He grew up in the residential part of West Hollywood, but there was also the Sunset Strip, with its infamous nightclubs, like Ciros and Macombo, and La Cienega, with its upscale restaurants. Oh, the hand-carved prime rib brought out on stainless-steel serving carts at Lawry's, and to have a plank steak surrounded by mashed potatoes and veggies on a wooden platter at Steer's, and breakfast at Norm's, which he walked by every day on his way to Rosewood Avenue Elementary School. *I do like my food,* he thought.

It was before his time, but from the stories of his dad and grandfather, he learned that mobsters like Mickey Cohen, Bugsy Siegel, and Johnny Roselli hung out in West Hollywood, along with many Hollywood stars. As an innocent kid typical of the times, he hadn't picked up on the fact that there was gambling and prostitution in West Hollywood. That's why neither LA nor Beverly Hills wanted the Strip as part of their cities.

He watched as Cedars-Sinai Hospital filled the space that'd once been occupied by the Arden Dairy on Beverly Boulevard. The Pacific Design Center, better known as the Blue Whale, now filled the space once occupied by the Red Car streetcar barn between Melrose and Santa Monica Boulevard. He remembered sneaking around the streetcar storage area with his friends. Those red streetcars actually ran on railroad tracks from West Hollywood down Santa Monica Boulevard toward downtown LA. They were his means of transportation from his parents' house to Hollywood High. *God, I can't believe I went through orange groves near Gardner Junction and rode on a streetcar down Hollywood Boulevard.*

Hartmann remembered seeing changes in his grandfather's and dad's jobs over the years at Warner Brothers. As still photographers, they shot publicity photos, photos during the daily production of a movie, and of course, the final shots of the end of the shooting day as the set was struck. They needed to know the next shooting day that every item on the set was in the same place. His grandfather had worked only with film, but his dad had to move from using the film, which he loved, to digital cameras. This initially befuddled him, but having the good German heritage he had, he mastered the change from the chemical film process to the electronic digital process.

The coffee was wearing off, but he was in a nostalgic mood at this point. He reminisced about taking the Sunday family walks—just the men, of course—from his Huntley Drive home. His father and grandfather would lead; he and his brother would trail as Grandpa, who now lived in Leisure World, would describe memories. They'd go down Huntley Drive to Beverly Boulevard and return on La Cienega. Grandpa would point out that in his day, there was a gigantic, old-fashioned oil derrick that stood in the middle of Beverly and La Cienega that he'd have to drive around. Then Grandpa would tell how he'd put his father up on a pony for the pony ride at the Beverly amusement park. And how he'd watch his father ride the Ferris wheel and merry-go-round. The Beverly Center, with Macy's and Bloomingdales, now occupied the amusement park's location.

West Hollywood and society have significantly changed in three generations. Change seems to be speeding up. I'm not sure I like the direction things are going. I really do want to make the world a better place, but problems seem to be developing faster than solutions, he thought.

He remembered graduating from Hollywood High School. He got a football scholarship to UCLA, and he earned a degree in finance. He wasn't good enough to make the NFL, and Wall Street or commercial banking weren't appealing to him. His mom's dream was for him to become an actor. His dad wanted him to follow the family tradition and join him at Warner Brothers. Neither seemed to be the right fit for him. The Hartmann legacy of studio photographers would end.

Instead, he joined the army. The decision was probably just to get away from the changing world for a while and see what else was out there.

That was an interesting time.

He was never sure why he decided to enlist in the military, but he had, and it turned out well for him, very well indeed. The army gave him one unexpected, exciting, and definitely crazy mission that impacted the rest of his life.

His mind fiercely blocked the memories and images of the tragedy that occurred while he was in the Army. That door was shut. The loss of Diana; he'd witnessed her death, and could have saved her. His excessive drinking and agonizing pain started after that. His world had totally changed and he knew it would never be the same. The boyhood innocence was gone. He needed to do his best to stop such things from happening in the future.

Following Officer Candidate School at Fort Benning, Georgia, he was assigned to the Army Financial Management School in Fort Jackson, South Carolina, where he was officially made a part of the Army Finance Corps. After a year of working in an office, he was asked if he wanted to join a special unit being formed for a specific mission. Apparently, the combination of financial training and the fact that he'd played football at UCLA and was still in good physical condition had something to do with his selection. Before he knew it, he was back at Fort Benning training with the Army Rangers. Following training, he went off on a single mission that had him working closely with a guy who would end up heading up the CIA and would later become chief of staff to the president of the United States.

The army, and particularly, the special mission, made him comfortable with the world he was in. He felt comfortable with himself and found he was smarter than most. He'd also learned that life is more about luck and whom you know than how smart you are. That was proving to be true. From the army, he went directly into the FBI. Following graduation from the FBI Academy in Quantico, the bureau assigned him to a financial-analysis unit in New York.

Shortly after 9/11, the bureau, for some reason, thought Hartmann should become part of their "reengineering" unit at the Hoover Building headquarters in DC. September 11 changed the bureau. Hartmann ended up right in the middle of the change. It caused him to recognize that he was more of a big-picture guy than a detail-oriented, white-collar crimes guy.

Over the next two years, he watched as the bureau began placing a greater emphasis on the concepts of *human capital* and *partnership*—in other words, people with specialized skills working together as a team. He watched as the bureau began to hire staff with language and cyber-technology skills instead of law and finance degrees. He fit into the new bureau better than the old one, even though he was considered old school by many. He wanted to remain in the old-school type job of finding the bad guys who had already committed a crime and taking them down.

As the "reengineering" assignment began to wind down, Hartmann noted an opening in the San Francisco office for a supervisory special agent of the Violent Crime Squad. He applied. He wanted a street assignment. He wanted to go up against the real bad guys. *Must be the same logic that got me into the army,* he thought; however, wanting it and getting it were two different things. The FBI career board had a hard time understanding his logic, but he had more time in grade than the other applicants, and he'd earned lots of cred within the bureau. It also didn't hurt that everyone else was applying for jobs within the terrorism units. Following 9/11, the FBI was challenged by the president of the United States and Congress to double down on their antiterrorism efforts. By growing and reinforcing their ranks, the FBI would position itself to be a more nimble and strategic partner in the war against terrorism. The career board approved Dick's move. Now he'd build his own squad in San Francisco. *I'm going to help change the world for better.*

It was time to hit the sack. As he turned away from the window and headed toward the bedroom, Hartmann noted there was a little Brunello de Montalcino left. It was an excellent red wine he'd brought back from Italy. *Can't let that go to waste*, he thought.

He moved to the table and poured the remains of the bottle into the long-stemmed, large-bowled wine glass. With glass in hand, he strode over to the wall next to the bookcase and gazed at the picture of him and his special mission buddy, Jackson C. Wallace, who was now working for the president of the United States. *What a time we had together. Why they picked the two of us geeks to work with the CIA is still beyond me. Got to train with the Army Rangers at Fort Benning and then visit North Korea. We sure messed up their US-dollar-counterfeiting program.*

The North Korean assignment, combined with two high-profile FBI cases, had quickly moved Hartmann up in the bureau. The bureau cases got him press coverage, and his ego developed a craving for more. This evolved into a rapport with several of the reporters, particularly a couple of the female ones, who often contacted him for quotes, or to help with their stories, or occasionally for other things.

San Francisco readily accepted Hartmann, and he felt it was the best place he'd lived so far. He'd liked his time in New York, but as a smiling, West Coast guy, he had never really fit in. His native LA had become too sprawling and congested. DC was fun, especially the Georgetown bars with all the young congressional and senatorial aides enjoying life to the fullest, but nobody seemed permanent in DC. San Francisco was a friendly, "New York West" kind of town where he could walk everywhere that was important to him, especially to the Le Central bar, his now-favorite watering hole. It was classified as a city, but it still felt more like a small town to him. Although SF was the center of the dot-com world, it still felt like a throwback in time for some reason, where businessmen took leisurely lunches that often included a drink or two.

He sipped the last of the Brunello with pleasure and was headed to the bedroom when the Blackberry on his belt vibrated. He looked down at the screen and read the message marked "Important" from Mark Gambirasi, the field office special agent in charge of San Francisco.

Meeting at 8:00 a.m. New case. See you in the morning.

He acknowledged the message.

See you in the morning.

Hartmann jumped up and grabbed the pull-up bar located just inside the bedroom door. His muscles rippled as he did twenty reps just for fun. Sleep came easily.

3

FBI Training Center, Quantico, Virginia

Coleen Ann Ryan exited Jefferson Hall, the yellow concrete and glass, high-rise, college-like dorm that housed the new agents in training, better known on the FBI Academy campus as NATs. She headed toward the large auditorium through the glass corridors that connected all of the buildings. There wasn't any need to go outside when moving from building to building. The glass hallways weren't there to protect people inside from the elements. Rather, they maintained security from people trying to enter the buildings from the outside.

Coleen stopped in the middle of the walkway and twirled in place. As she turned, she glanced at each side of the glass corridor and looked at the twenty modern buildings carefully secluded in the middle of a woodland area. This had been her home for the past twenty weeks. On her arrival day, Coleen was surprised how this world-renowned law-enforcement training facility looked more like a midwestern university campus, or even Villanova, from where she had graduated, than the grueling training center it really was.

The academy covered 385 acres, but it seemed small in comparison to the huge Marine Corps Base Quantico where it was located. The facility was only thirty-seven miles southwest of bustling Washington, DC, but seemed like another world. In order to get to the academy, Coleen had passed through the Quantico main gate, where marine guards screened her. Then she drove several miles across the base on a rural two-lane road, which was bounded by trees, to the FBI Academy guard post. There, she went through a very intense and serious screening by two FBI policemen. *My God, the FBI has its own police force,* she remembered thinking.

That started the twenty weeks of training. Coleen and the other NATs learned about other critical FBI facilities on campus and came to understand why the academy was isolated from the rest of the world, why security was so important. The glass walkways led not only to the NATs training facilities; they also connected up to the FBI Crime Lab, Forensic Science Research and Training Center, and the Engineering Research Facility. There was a James Bond feeling about those places. She thought, *Where are Q and Moneypenny? Is there a high-tech guy who invents things, like Q?*

She was getting the picture of why this complex, with its information systems, was critical to the protection of the nation.

If you didn't like report writing, the FBI was not the place for you. The NATs quickly figured out that the FBI loved extensive written reports and maintained databases on everything. There were databases upon databases of everything from millions of fingerprints to the tattoos inked onto gang members' bodies—to criminals' DNA, bullet striations, car paint types, national crime patterns, listings of individual dissidents and terrorist group profiles, and on and on.

There was the stand-alone building that wasn't connected to the enclosed walkway. It was rumored that this isolated building was where FBI staff listened to wiretaps originating from across the country.

The campus's isolated nature required the NATs to eat in the dining hall. Of good, Irish stock, Coleen wasn't really into cooking. She had eaten most of her meals out since her graduation from college. She was quite attractive, and most of her meals were paid for by her male friends. The dining-hall food didn't measure up to the standards of the New York restaurants she was used to, but it was free, and best of all, there were no dishes to clean up afterward. Coleen didn't worry about gaining weight because of the rigorous physical activity that was part of their training.

"Coleen, Coleen," shouted Tom Koen. "Why're you standing here?"

Coleen looked up to see Tom and Phil Webster walking toward her. They'd become good friends during the past twenty weeks. The intensive training and mental harassment bonded them together.

"Just thinking back to the day we arrived," she replied.

"Yeah, I'll miss the place, but I'm ready to get back to the real world. Come on. We'll walk over with you. And how is 'Killer Coleen' today?"

"I'm great. Stop calling me Killer Coleen."

"Oh, I'm afraid that one is going to stay with you for the rest of your FBI career. Just think about how wimpy that guy was who you beat in tennis—being beaten by a woman, with most of the class watching. He didn't last a week after that."

"Come on. I'm not the reason he washed out. It had nothing to do with our tennis game. The poor guy was from Wisconsin and had never played before. So, big deal. I play to win. I hit it hard. Of course, his wimpy, uncontrolled hits didn't help him, but that comment proves that you guys are sexist. If he had been beaten by a guy, this wouldn't be a subject of conversation."

"I'm sure you would've driven that ball down any guy's throat, and it's not a sexist thing. Nobody would've paid any attention until he tried to pry your ball out of the chain-link fence and couldn't. Then you walked over and pulled it out with no problem. That did it. Hey, Phil, did you notice she's a pretty good athlete?" Tom asked.

"Yeah, I'm still hurting from hand-to-hand combat with her."

"Okay, you two, enough of that. And thanks for the compliment—I think. Have you guys gotten used to wearing the gun, cuffs, and magazines?" Coleen replied, changing the subject.

"Pretty much so. After awhile, you forget you're wearing them." Tom replied.

"Yeah, but they still feel funny."

"It must be a girl thing."

"Okay. I see you're back to the sexist comments," Coleen said and changed the subject again. "Look at you guys. Suits and ties. You two clean up pretty nicely. You actually look like real FBI agents."

Tom stopped the group and took a step back. "Well, Killer Coleen, you don't look too bad yourself. Miss Businesswoman. It's kind of nice to dress up for a change."

"Tom, forget the 'Killer' thing! You can't nickname an FBI agent 'Killer.'"

"Agent Ryan, you've got a point there." Tom replied.

"I'm not 'Agent' Ryan yet, and none of us will be agents if we don't get moving."

At a fast pace, Coleen led the group down the glassed-in, covered walkway and entered the complex's large auditorium. They each found their family and friends and took their seats with the other new-agent trainees. The class of twenty-five NATs sat in the front rows. Silence fell over the auditorium as FBI Director Robert Mueller walked across the stage and sat down with other FBI officials.

Sitting in the second row between Tom and Phil, Coleen stared down at her hands. They were no longer the soft hands and manicured fingernails she'd had twenty weeks ago. Her nails were cut short. Her hands had toughened and showed signs of calluses. They were no longer the hands of an associate attorney at a prestigious New York law firm. This was a totally different world from her New York law-firm days. After two years at the firm, Coleen had known that corporate law wasn't her calling. There had to be something with a little more adventure—something that helped real people. She considered the CIA but decided that was a little too much adventure. During a deposition of one the law firm's clients, she'd met an FBI agent who'd convinced her to consider working for the bureau. She liked what he had to say.

"Coleen Ann Ryan."

She rose and walked up on the stage. The FBI director shook her hand and said, "Congratulations, Special Agent Ryan."

A man next to the director presented her with an FBI badge and credentials. She was officially a special agent for the Federal Bureau of Investigation.

On the walk back to her seat, Coleen stared at the shiny badge and then at the FBI credential card. She liked her bureau picture. *Girl, you are actually smiling.* To her, the badge and credentials represented a special achievement. *I made it! I made it!* she thought excitedly.

Coleen had had serious doubts during her first week at the academy. A lack of confidence came over her. She wasn't sure if she'd make it through. *What the hell are you doing here?* she had thought. Then a determination had set in that she didn't know she had. The class started out with thirty-two NATs. Seven washed out early on, due to the vigorous academic and physical training. That included her tennis opponent.

Again looking at her hands, Coleen thought of other changes to her body. It was in the best physical condition it had ever been in her life. Tom was right; she was a natural athlete.

Her hands were looking a little unkempt, and her knees still hurt from dropping to the ground during training exercises in Hogan's Alley. She'd chosen a dark-navy suit with long sleeves because it hid the big, black and blue marks on her left arm earned from a stupid mistake she'd made several days ago in the Hogan Bank building.

Why did I dive to the left? That was really stupid, she thought as she recalled the event.

She dove the wrong way in the bank building, tripped over a trash can, and collided with one of the villain actors hired by the academy for realism. Unfortunately, the actor's head was not as hard as hers. She ended up with the headache from hell, but the actor had a broken nose. The instructors stopped the exercise and called for an ambulance to take the actor to the hospital. One instructor made an example of Coleen's decision. She had wanted to crawl in a hole. *I'll be remembered for that one.* Today, both her mind and body felt great. Today, all of the training was concluded.

The graduation ceremony ended and Coleen quickly followed her fellow NATs outside of the auditorium. She sought out her family. Her mother, brothers, and sister were so proud, especially when they had a group picture taken with the director.

"Thank you, Director," she said to him.

"You're very welcome, Special Agent Ryan."

Her mother asked, "Do you know where you are being assigned?"

Coleen had known for a week where she was headed, but she hadn't been in a hurry to tell her mother. She had hoped for New York or Baltimore so she could remain close and see her family on weekends. When she looked at the letter, she'd been startled to see her first assignment was to the San Francisco, California, field office. She was going to be completely on the other side of the country.

"Oh, Honey, that's so far away," her mother replied after she told her.

To which her younger brother replied, "Mom, you knew she was going to go to a warm place. She hates the snow."

4

San Francisco, California

Hartmann opened the front door to his San Francisco Russian Hill apartment building and stepped out onto Leavenworth. The fog was particularly thick this morning. His body shivered for a minute in an attempt to warm up. He could hear the foghorns from the Bay just a few blocks down the hill and the clanging bells from the cable cars on Hyde Street just above him.

He always walked to the FBI office in the San Francisco Civic Center, unless he knew he would need his car for an assignment that day. The forty-four-year-old had finally adopted San Francisco as his city. The politics of San Francisco were certainly different from what he was used to. The first time he voted in an election, he was surprised to see that there were no Republican candidates on his ballot. It was definitely an ultra-liberal city. And there was the gay, lesbian, and transsexual bent, but that was part of its character.

He walked a little faster this morning as he thought about the text message he had received the night before. He was anxious to find out about the new case his squad was taking on. His gait was still like that of an army captain, and his body stood ramrod straight. Down Leavenworth, past Lombard, he marched.

Today, Hartmann was dressed in one of Wilkes Bashford's expensive, Italian, medium-weight wool suits. The store was a famous upscale San Francisco haberdashery. Under the suit, he wore a light-blue, Egyptian cotton, button-down collared shirt with a green and blue striped tie, affixed with a Windsor knot. The suit was really not a match for the cold morning, but he would warm up during the walk. While his FBI salary wasn't bad, it didn't support his lifestyle. He thanked God for his trust fund. It allowed him to afford to occasionally wear a Wilkes Bashford suit to the office. If he was going into the field, he would usually wear one of his Brooks Brothers or Jos. A. Banks suits.

As he did every time he took this walk, Dick chuckled to himself as he passed Lombard Street and recalled the story the bartender told at his second-favorite watering hole, the Washington Bar & Grill (known to the regulars as "The WashBag"). The bartender loved to tell the story of how Lombard's original homeowners purposely designed their street to be a winding road with the idea of discouraging people from using it to get into the main part of San Francisco. Sometimes, great plans have unexpected consequences, as Lombard became one of the most traveled narrow, winding streets in the world. Sometimes people are just not predictable.

Lombard was quiet now, but it wouldn't be on Hartmann's return home. He knew that in about an hour, the tourists would be lining up in their cars at the upper end of Lombard at Hyde Street to travel down the eight hairpin turns of the "crookedest street in the world." Tires would be squealing as cars negotiated the tight turns on this very steep street. Some of SFPD's finest would be posted at either end to control traffic. After the ride down, the tourists would get out of their cars to take pictures. Dick had a fun streak in him, and on his way home, he loved to stand behind a tour group getting their pictures taken. *It's my California personality,* he thought. He was sure that his mug was in pictures all over the world. *Probably a good thing the tourists don't know I'm with the FBI.*

Even though he was in a hurry, Dick made his usual Starbucks stop for coffee. *Have to get my caffeine fix.* Depending on the line, if he knew someone else in there or what was in the paper that day, it would add about twenty minutes to his trip. As usual, there was a line of people waiting to be served. *Not too bad this morning—just four ahead of me.*

The barista greeted him. "Hi, Dick. Usual morning bun and grande coffee?"

"Yeah, the usual, and this paper. How're you doing today?"

"Can't complain. Four seventy."

"Here you go. Put the change in the cup."

"Thanks. See you tomorrow."

"God willing."

Dick took the *Chronicle* newspaper from under his arm and sat at one of the tables near the window. He glanced at an article on the front page about a planned renovation of the Ferry Building. More changes. He liked the looks of the building as it was. It was a landmark building. The clock tower was a familiar and beloved symbol of San Francisco's skyline.

Six sentences into the article, Dick pulled a pen out of the small pen pocket inside his tailored suit jacket. *This world is not changing for the better, and* The *Chron seems to get worse every day,* he thought. He corrected both a grammatical and a spelling error. Couldn't *The Chron* at least afford spell-check? He moved on to the sports section, where grammar was less important.

After gulping down the coffee and bun much faster than usual, he tossed the newspaper in the trash, where he believed it belonged, and headed down to Golden Gate Avenue. He pushed open the heavy, glass doors to the Phillip Burton Federal Building and United States Courthouse, which was located in San Francisco's Civic Center.

Suddenly, he was warm. He wondered why they seemed to always overheat public buildings in the winter.

The security guards at the front entrance recognized him and knew he was an armed FBI special agent. In fact, he was a very well-known FBI agent who frequently made it into the news. He showed his FBI credentials, and they let him pass around the metal detector.

Hartmann exited the elevator onto the thirteenth floor and greeted the receptionist of the San Francisco FBI field office. He passed through the secured door to the interoffice, where visitors were only allowed if accompanied by an agent. Using his access card and code, he entered his private office, hung up his coat, and did a quick check of his e-mails. There was the e-mail marked "Important" from Mark Gambirasi, the field office special agent in charge, asking to see him as soon as he got in.

Mark's first words were, "Here's your five bucks. Your Bruins beat the spread again. I have no idea why I bet against them. How was your extended weekend?"

"Not bad. Watched my Bruins beat your Cougars on Saturday. Took my usual Sunday jog across the Golden Gate Bridge to Sausalito. Had lunch at Scoma's and took the ferry home. Slept and watched golf in the afternoon. Monday, I played golf at the Presidio. It was a perfect three days."

"Oh, to be a bachelor again. I spent the weekend repainting my daughter's bedroom a lighter pink color. I hate painting."

"Sorry to hear about your painting project, but I know you love your daughter and the family life. Other than to collect my five bucks and exchange niceties about our weekends, why am I in your office?" Dick asked.

"Well, first, Coleen Ryan, your new squad member, is with Molly in HR getting her paperwork done. She came in early and I gave her the grand tour. Apparently, she went apartment hunting over the weekend and struck out. See if you can help her locate a place. The dot-com boom has made it impossible to find an affordable place to stay."

"I'll see what I can come up with."

"Second, I know it's unusual, but I want you to personally be the case agent on a new case, rather than assigning it to one of your squad members. It's high priority. Justice, with the approval of Treasury, has assigned us as the lead on either a suicide or murder case at the IRS service center in Fresno. You'll be working with the IRS Criminal Division."

"Okay. Sounds interesting," Dick replied.

"As I understand it, an IRS special agent at the service center either committed suicide or was murdered. Either way, we need to find out what happened. The IRS is concerned that their agent discovered someone messing with their computers. The Fresno IRS Center is the largest in the country and processes more than 25 million tax returns each year. More than $200 billion—billion, with a B—in taxes are collected there annually. That's a lot of motivation for suicide or murder. The IRS is sending a whole team of special agents from their criminal investigation division to try and figure out if their computers have been compromised. As you know, their agents are basically auditors with guns. The chief of the division told me they're not trained to investigate murders, so we've got that part of the assignment."

"Who's the contact at the center?"

"Here's what I have. The head of the center is Doug Smith. He contacted DC for help. There's also another senior IRS special agent at the center who had been working an undercover assignment there. Because he was already there, he's been assigned to the case. His name is Robert Larson. Doug called him, and after Larson had talked with his bosses at the IRS, they decided to seek our help. He'll introduce you to Larson and the head of the security unit in Fresno," Gambirasi explained.

"I won't need an introduction to Larson. He actually lives here in the city and works out of the IRS office in Oakland. We've worked a couple of other cases together. He's a fellow sports nut. Went to Cal Berkley."

"That's great. It'll make things run smoother. Go see Ruth about getting a plane out of San Carlos. Oh, and don't forget your new squad member. She's probably finished in HR and hunting for you."

"I'll track her down."

"And Dick, there is tremendous interest in this case in DC. Keep me advised on your progress at least daily, and more often if you feel anything significant is happening."

Dick peeked into the HR department and didn't see a new face. When he opened his office door, he was surprised to see a young lady seated in front of his desk. She stood up from her chair and faced him.

Oh, my God, I don't need this. Why can't they send me an ugly broad who would scare any subject into submission—or a nice kid who likes to have a beer and bet on sports? No. They have to send me a young gal with a great face that looks better in person than the picture in her bureau personnel file. She has great pins that go all the way up to her ass and is well endowed upstairs. I don't need this distraction at work, he thought.

Coleen was wearing a tailored black pantsuit—and not the kind worn by the former first lady, Hillary Clinton. She had on a light-green blouse that matched her eyes. Small, single pearl earrings matched a single-pearl ring on her right hand. A very preppy, yet young, businessperson's look. Definitely Irish ancestry, medium-dark hair with a tinge of red. Nice package.

"I suspect you're waiting for me. I'm Dick Hartmann."

"Hi. I'm Coleen Ann Ryan. I hope you don't mind my sitting in your office. Molly let me in. As I understand it, you're my first bureau boss."

"Welcome to the San Francisco office, Agent Ryan. Do you always go by three names?"

"No. Just call me Coleen."

"I'll do that, and you can call me Dick. By the way, is your first name really spelled with one L, or is your personnel file wrong?"

Coleen thought, *Oh, I like his voice. Sounds like a radio announcer, but Dick? Shit. I can't work for a Dick! God, I hope I don't slip and call some subject a dick or dickhead, or even worse, say, "You're nothing but a big dick!"*

"The personnel file is correct. My name is spelled with one L. My guess is that my dad thought it was a cool spelling when he chose it. I'll admit that the spelling has been a hassle all my life. Even spell-check will change it back to two L's. My dad must have known I was going to be one of a kind," she replied and then thought, *Well, if this is going to be my first boss, he's not too bad. I like his crew cut, blond hair, and great blue eyes. Wow! Nice clothes. I bet there are some great abs under there.*

"Okay. I'll remember to spell it with one L. I understand Mark gave you the grand tour of the office, so with that done, I'll show you your home away from home and introduce you to the other squad members."

As Coleen sat in her assigned cubicle, Dick shouted to a group talking together in one of the adjacent cubicles. "Okay, Animals, we have a new assignment. We're off to wonderful downtown Fresno."

Daniel, one of the team members, spotted Coleen. "Hey, Boss, who's the girl? She's a looker."

"Everyone, this is Coleen—with one L—Ryan. She's now one of us. Just graduated from the academy. A Villanova graduate. Got a law degree, but got past our screeners because of her language skills in French and Italian. Don't ask me the logic in assigning her to us."

Well, at least he read my file before I got here, Coleen thought.

Laughingly, Dick continued. "With any luck, maybe our next assignment will be in France or Italy, but in the meantime, we'll be speaking English, maybe some Spanish."

The squad, now including Coleen, headed to the basement garage and piled into one of the FBI's Chevy Suburbans. They headed for the San Carlos Airport, twenty miles south of San Francisco, where the San Francisco FBI office maintained its fleet of aircraft.

During the trip, Dick's team members introduced themselves to Coleen. Daniel, who was sitting next to Dick in the front seat, turned his head back toward Coleen.

"Hi, Coleen. Welcome to the squad. I'm Daniel Lee. I'm originally from LA and graduated from USC, just like my dad. I'm the team's computer geek. You'll find our boss here is a sports fan with a strange sense of humor. He's from UCLA and hates the USC Trojans. Despite our number-one standing, he likes to refer to my Trojans as the 'Condoms.' We don't have a good animal name like the Bruins or your, I believe, Villanova Wildcats, but my team seems to be able to handle the Bruins very well. Dick refers to our squad as the 'Animals,' but he generally leaves the condom reference out unless he's pissed with me."

Coleen replied, "Great to meet you, Daniel. Thanks for the info, but I'm going to forget about the USC condom reference. I take it my new boss has a warped sense of humor."

Dick, with a smug look on this face, turned his head so all could see the smirk he was displaying.

Daniel responded, "You've got that right, but you'll hear him make the condom reference over and over again. He thinks it's funny."

"Hi there, Coleen. I'm Brian, Brian Brooks from Salt Lake. I'm a graduate of BYU and the team's specialist in accounting. Staying with the apparent theme going on here, my school team mascot is the Cougars, a good animal name like the Wildcats. Unfortunately, my team keeps getting beaten by both the 'Condoms' and those baby bears."

Sitting in the third row of seats next to Coleen, Harriet followed with her introduction. "I'm Harriet Foster. As you can tell by looking at me, I'm the double-minority team member, being both black and female. I keep the team hiring statistics in balance, which is more than you can say for the rest of the FBI. Actually, I keep the team in balance."

Sticking out her hand and shaking Coleen's, she added, "I'm glad to welcome another female member. Maybe we can keep these characters straight. My credentials for being on the team are that I'm a former army intelligence officer and graduate of LSU, the Tigers. Fellow cat lady, welcome to our team."

Shortly after boarding the FBI twinjet at San Carlos Airport, Dick reviewed with them what he knew about the case at the IRS service center in Fresno.

5

Fresno, California

The twinjet FBI aircraft touched down at the Fresno Yosemite International Airport. It traveled along the taxiway toward an isolated area at the far end of the field and pulled up in front of the Fresno Air National Guard hangar. The plane doors opened, and it was beyond hot. It was like stepping into a blast furnace. Fresno was having a record September heat wave. It was over one hundred degrees with 60 percent humidity.

Hartmann and his team began sweating almost immediately as they descended the plane's stairs in their wool San Francisco suits, dress shirts, and ties. Their clothing was designed for a summer day in the foggy, windy City by the Bay, not for California's Central Valley, where Fresno was located.

Robin Carlen-Murray, special agent in charge of Fresno's FBI resident agency, greeted them at the bottom of the stairs. "Welcome to toasty Fresno."

The team split up, with Dick riding with Robin and the rest of the team following in a bureau-provided SUV. As Dick glanced out the window, he recognized the flat, dry landscape. He'd been in—or maybe it was better described as "driven through"—Fresno a number of times over the years.

"Robin, I can remember coming through Fresno when I was a kid. Our whole family would spend a couple of weeks in the summer camping in the Yosemite or Sequoia national parks. My dad would drive the Dodge up with the tent trailer in tow, and we'd set camp up in one of the national-park campgrounds."

"A lot of people are still doing just that."

"Those were great summers. We'd swim or ride an inner tube in the cold Merced River and at night warm up next to a campfire. God, I can still remember singing 'Ninety-Nine Bottles of Beer on the Wall,' over and over again."

"Oh, God, don't get me started thinking about that song. I'll have in my head all day," Robin replied.

"You know, when I was really young, they were still doing the fire falls. We would watch the hot, burning embers spill from the top of Glacier Point to the valley three thousand feet below. From where we were, it appeared as a glowing waterfall. It was a shame they were stopped, but it's probably not a good idea to dump burning embers off the side of a mountain. Boy, how times change. Hopefully for the better."

Suddenly, Dick spotted a familiar sign.

"Welcome to Fresno
All-American City & Raisin Capital of the World"

"Robin, when I first started coming to Fresno, it was just a modest-sized farming community. Now look at that skyline ahead."

"I joined the Fresno office a couple of years ago. Fresno was, by then, a metropolitan area with a population of more than a million people. Most people don't realize how big it is because of LA and San Francisco, but Fresno still has a small town vibe."

"From what I recollect, Fresno is like most of California's farming communities—Reagan country, with a strong conservative Republican base," Dick said.

"I suspect that's true, but it's changing with the increasing Hispanic population, and a lot of Bay Area transplants are moving into the area. I'm not sure why the Bay Area folk are moving here—two totally different worlds. I suspect it's an economic thing. They're moving from one economic extreme to the other. The cost of living is pretty cheap here, and I know San Fran is one of the most expensive places to live in the world."

"Tell me about it," Dick responded.

Dick glanced over at the speedometer. Robin had a lead foot. They were hitting eighty-five miles per hour as they sped down Highway 41. Robin slowed as she turned east on Route 180 and exited on Peach Avenue. They went a few more blocks. Just past a community park, they turned right onto Butler Avenue, a tree-lined, middle-class, residential street. Halfway down the block, there was what looked like a very large park with mowed lawns and full-grown oak trees.

"That's our destination. Doesn't look like the IRS's largest processing center, does it?"

"Sure doesn't. This thing is in the middle of a residential district. You'd think it was a school or some sort of recreational facility, except for that twelve-foot-high, chain-link fence topped with barbed wire," Dick said.

"Wait till you see the inside," she replied.

Robin pulled up to a security gate, where the guard confirmed that they were expected. After giving them parking passes, he directed them to pull up in front of the administration building and park in the visitor's area near the front entrance.

As they got out of the cars, they faced a very plain-looking building that had gray concrete walls decorated with small rocks. There were no signs or markings on it announcing that this was an IRS service center. The only marking was the address, 5045 East Butler Avenue, which was carved into the concrete of the front wall. At the front desk, the entourage was greeted by Doug Smith, director of the center.

"Welcome to the IRS Fresno Service Center. Sorry the circumstances aren't better. To get things started, I've arranged a conference room down the hall."

As they entered, Smith introduced them to two men seated at the table in the middle of the room. "This is Mark Stevens, who heads up the center's security, and this is Robert Larsen, special agent with our Criminal Investigation Unit."

Hartmann greeted both men and turned specifically to Larsen. "Good to see you, Bob. It's been awhile since we've worked on something together."

"Dick, I heard they'd assigned you to this case. It is great to see you, too. First time we've worked on a murder. In fact, now that I think about it, this is the first time I've ever been involved in a murder case. Not part of my IRS job description. That's why you're here."

"Can you clue us in on what happened?"

Mark Stevens took the lead in responding. "At nine fifteen last night, our security office received a call from one of the center's custodians that there was a problem in one of offices in the Criminal Investigation Unit. Two of our security people checked it out and found one of our auditors, Edison Shaw, dead at his desk. It appeared to them that he'd committed suicide. They secured the room and called me. I arrived a little before ten and checked out the room and then called Doug. He, in turn, called Bob, who, as you know, is a senior IRS special agent. He's here on an undercover assignment.

"They both arrived at about ten thirty. Bob asked me to contact the local police and arrange for their Crime Scene Investigation Unit to go over the room. We're suspicious of it being suicide because there was no suicide note, and because of the nature of Shaw's work. Our suspicions were confirmed when the CSU's analysis concluded that Shaw didn't have any gunpowder residue on his hands.

"At this point, we jointly made the decision to contact the bureau and not to involve the Fresno police any further. We didn't want them to look at, or take, Shaw's computer or any of the documents in his office. We have a lot of sensitive information in this complex of buildings that must be kept confidential," Stevens finished.

Dick said, "I get the picture. Do you mind if we use this room while we're conducting our investigation?"

"Of course. You're welcome to use it," Bob replied.

Mark added, "All of the security tapes and premises' entry data from yesterday have been secured in my office."

"Do you want to see Shaw's office?" asked Stevens.

Dick responded, "We'll take a look in a few minutes, but first, Bob or Doug, do you have any idea what Shaw was working on?"

Doug responded, "Not personally, but Bob may have a better idea. At some time, we should also contact his supervisor. I didn't want to contact her until we'd eliminated her from suspicion."

Bob chimed in, "I know he had just finished an assignment involving a tax-examining assistant who'd accepted a two thousand dollar bribe to erase a tax liability for a friend. I don't think that case is the basis for his murder. The lady involved has been terminated from the IRS, and it is highly doubtful that she could get back into the facility.

"He'd just started working on something else, but he was keeping it close to the vest. An IRS special agent is like an internal auditor in private business. We're pretty much left on our own to do our jobs. We don't like to share anything big that we're working on until we're sure it's for real. Shaw also liked to get the proper credit for his findings. Unfortunately, historically, the IRS is very competitive that way."

We have to be concerned about what happened because of the volume of transactions and amount of money running through this center. We're very concerned about white-collar crime. Though a lot of paper flows through this center, we're basically a paperless facility, with everything being maintained on computer. Our computer system is considered the crown jewel of the IRS." Continued Bob.

Dick thanked the men for their help, turned to his team, and said, "Okay. Let's get started. Doug, do you mind introducing Agent Brooks here to Shaw's supervisor? Brian, see what you can find out about Shaw's current projects, and see if you can get Shaw's computer. I want to know everything that's on it."

As Doug and Brian left, Dick asked Mark to take him and the rest of the team to Shaw's office.

Robin begged off joining the group. "Dick, I think I'll leave things in your good hands. I need to get back to the resident agency. My desk is already loaded with cases. I'll catch up with you later today."

6

IRS Service Center, Fresno, California

The resident IRS Criminal Investigation Unit was located at the front of the building near the conference room. It didn't take the team long to arrive at Shaw's office.

Two security officers from the center's Security Unit were standing in front of Shaw's office, which was sealed with yellow crime-scene tape. The team noted a group huddled together in a quiet discussion across from Shaw's office. They quickly determined that this group consisted of a Fresno PD Crime Scene Unit (CSU) supervisor and a couple of guys from the Fresno Coroner's Office waiting to take the body.

Dick first spoke to the security officers to determine what they knew. They informed him that because this was an auditor's office, it was locked all the time. The auditor and probably his supervisor would have a key. Security and the janitorial staff would have master keys.

"Thanks for the info. We'll take over from here, but we would appreciate it if you'd block off this section of the hallway," Dick said. Then he turned to the head of the Crime Scene Unit and asked, "Have you finished processing the scene?"

"Not completely, but I suspect the FBI will want to pick up from here."

"Yes, we're assuming control of this case. It would be helpful if you'd stick around and provide a briefing of your investigation to our FBI team. But for now it would be appreciated if you'd give me a basic idea of what you did determine," Dick responded.

"My initial conclusion is that the death was at the hands of another. It clearly wasn't a suicide. There's no GSR on the victim's hands, no suicide note, and the scene was wiped down to remove prints," the head of the CSU replied.

"Did you have to disturb the crime scene much?"

"Did it by the book. I took photos of everything before we really went to work on Shaw. Everything is pretty much intact, except I sent the gun to the sheriff's crime lab."

Dick glanced into the office and made a mental note of what he saw. "Harriet, you've been elected to photograph, inventory, and bag items from the scene. When you're finished, let the coroner's office take the body. And Harriet, make sure Brian gets Shaw's laptop as quickly as possible to process."

Larsen quickly interrupted Dick. "I know that laptop is important to your investigation, but it is an IRS laptop and may have sensitive info on it. I want one of our people to monitor what your guy finds on it. It may tell us if the IRS computer system has been compromised or if files have been improperly used. That laptop could be significant to both of our investigations."

"Agreed. Now let's find out what the security-camera tapes and card-scanning data can tell us."

The security office was located in the middle of the complex, and what a complex it was. They walked down hallway after hallway, through a huge, open bay, where hundreds of data-entry clerks were entering tax information. There were also hundreds of empty desks and cubicles.

Coleen couldn't control herself as they passed a mural of Winnie the Pooh—just one of several Disney characters they'd passed that adorned the walls of the center. She blurted out, "Who came up with the decor for this place? It had to be a kid."

Mark responded, "No it wasn't a kid. I'm sure Uncle Sam paid someone a fortune to pretty-up this complex. As I understand it, back in the 1970s when this place was built, Disney characters were at the height of their popularity."

When they arrived at the security office, the agents were further surprised by its size. There was a glass-walled room. It must have had fifty monitors with recorders that covered all segments of the center. There was office space for eight people, a lunchroom, and a changing area, which included showers. There was a gun locker and hangers full of bulletproof vests.

Dick commented to Mark, "You have quite an operation here."

"Yeah, we do, but it's needed. This center is like a small city. There are about 1,900 permanent workers at this complex. During tax season, the IRS hires more than 2,700 additional clerks, data transcribers, and tax examiners that work for two to four months. We're just winding down now from the current tax season.

"We have to process all of the full- and part-time clerks for clearance to work here. We fingerprint everyone and send the prints and other info to you guys for background checks. We maintain security over billions of taxpayers' dollars. On occasion, we fend off a disgruntled taxpayer or a protest group that doesn't believe Uncle Sam should collect taxes. Now we even have to worry about anthrax in the incoming mail."

Dick asked, "How big a staff do you have?"

"There are thirty-one security officers and four support staff. All of our security officers are armed. We operate on a twenty-four hour, seven days a week basis," Mark replied.

"I'm impressed."

"How do you want to handle the tapes and security card records?"

"If it's okay with you, I'd like Daniel to work with one of your security guards to view them. Daniel has done this type of work before and will get the information from the cameras that we need," Dick replied.

"No problem."

Mark introduced Daniel to Jeff, who, being one of the new security guards, got the assignment of viewing forty-seven monitors that were connected to cameras located throughout the complex.

"Mark, I understand that Shaw was married. I'd like to interview the wife. I assume she's been notified about what's happened?" Dick asked.

"She has. Doug Smith and I did the notification in person late last night. I'll give her a call and let her know you're coming. What time do you want to go over?"

"Agent Ryan and I'll head that way right now. Here's my cell phone number. If the timing won't work for Mrs. Shaw, just give me a call. Oh, it would help if you'd give me the address and directions."

Before taking off, Dick went over and opened the door to the monitor room and shouted in at Daniel, "Coleen and I are going over to Shaw's house! Tell everyone we'll be back around four thirty. It looks like we'll be here overnight."

He then asked Mark if he could make hotel reservations for his team. "That'd be five rooms for one night."

"Will do. Everyone seems to stay over at the Piccadilly Inn. It's close, and they offer government rates."

7

IRS Service Center, Fresno, California

Daniel knew he'd been given one of the most monotonous jobs in law enforcement: reviewing hours and hours of security-camera discs. He also knew that with today's technology, viewing images from cameras like those at the IRS service center could solve many crimes. He followed Jeff into the monitor room. They pulled up chairs to begin the process.

Within a few minutes of conversation, they figured out that they had a number of things in common and would enjoy working together. They were about the same age, were computer geeks, and liked the same video games and music groups. This was a good thing, since they were going to be spending many hours together over the next couple of weeks.

Jeff pointed toward two plastic containers on his desk. "Here are the forty-seven discs from yesterday. Our digital surveillance system records the actions of people throughout the facility in color."

"Jeff, this system is unbelievable."

"It needs to be if we're going to protect the people's tax dollars, and their identities. There are billions of dollars that flow though this center. We have social security numbers, addresses, phone numbers, and who knows what else on millions of taxpayers. You should see this place around April 15. In fact, I'll show you this place on April 16."

Jeff went over to a large, fire-resistant metal cabinet that was designed to store six months of discs from the security system. He pulled out a disc and inserted it into a video player.

"Look at that monitor sitting next to the operating security monitors. This will give you an idea of how chaotic this place is during the tax season."

Jeff narrated what was on the screen. "There are tax returns piled nearly four feet high on hundreds of carts. Each of those returns is tagged and scrutinized. The data on them is then typed into computers by thousands of clerks, including a whole crew of temporary workers. This place is a zoo. We have to make sure all of that information is kept safe."

"Well, let's see if the data has been kept safe."

Quickly, Daniel mapped out a plan of action. He told Jeff, "The first thing we have to figure out is the timeframe we want to view on the discs. Where's the ID security-card system with the entry and exit data located?"

"It's on that computer right over there."

"Okay. What time yesterday did Shaw enter the premises?"

Jeff typed some info into the computer. A listing of the times people entered the center the previous day came up on the screen. He then modified the search to include arrive time and people's last names.

"Shaw entered at 7:18 in the morning."

"Okay. So we're going to need to look at all of the discs from seven in the morning yesterday to, let's say, midnight."

"Are you kidding? That'll take us months."

"Actually, by my calculation, working eight hours a day, it would take about eight hundred hours or a little over three months for one person to go through them."

"So for the two of us, it will only take a month and a half?"

"Don't worry. I have a plan. It'll be done by the end of the week. We're going to set some parameters for a group of my friends at the FBI Information Technology Center in Butte, Montana, who are going to help."

Daniel continued, "First, I want you to go into the ID security-card system and provide me with a copy of Shaw's ID picture. Can I assume you have cameras that pick up the images of people that enter and leave the center?"

"We do. Camera one picks up people when they enter, and cameras two and three pick up the images as they leave."

Curiously, Daniel asked, "Why do you have one camera on people when they enter and two on them as they leave?"

"Simple. We aren't that worried about what people bring into the center, but we're very concerned about what they may be taking with them when they leave."

"Understand. That's perfect. Then I want the segment of yesterday's disc where Shaw entered the Center at 7:18, and I want the segment where Shaw is leaving the center the day before yesterday. With his ID picture and the images of him front and back on the discs, my people in Butte should be able to zero in on when he appears on any of the forty-seven discs from yesterday. We may be able to determine where he went yesterday, and to whom he may have talked.

"The last thing I need from you today is a listing from the security-card system of all the people who left the center between 7:18 and midnight last night."

Jeff printed out a list of 319 names and then commented, "God, you FBI guys are good."

In a humorous tone, Daniel responded, "Yeah, we rock."

After Daniel had downloaded the discs to his computer, he sent them via Internet to Butte, with a detailed request of what he wanted.

Just as they were finishing up, one of the security guards entered the monitor room with his lunch bag and a Coke and asked, "Who's your friend?"

"Ed, this is Daniel with the FBI. He's one of the agents investigating Shaw's murder. Daniel, this is Ed Abramson. He's one of the security guards here. Former marine. I'm teaching him to play chess."

Ed walked up to Daniel and they shook hands. "Nice to meet you, Daniel. FBI, huh. Investigating Shaw's murder? I thought he committed suicide."

"Apparently not."

"Well, that probably means you're not going to be able to play chess today. I'll head for the lunchroom."

Jeff turned to Daniel. "You going to need me for anything else at the moment?"

"No. Thanks for your help. I've got plenty to work with, but I'm sure I'll be back tomorrow. Get on with your chess game."

"Thanks. We do this just about every day at lunch. I'm upgrading Ed's chess skills. He still has a way to go. I'm ahead twenty-seven games to twelve."

As Daniel was leaving, he noted that Jeff pulled a folding chessboard out of a drawer in his desk. He and Ed placed the chess players on the board as Jeff continued to view the monitors.

8

Fresno, California

After grabbing a bite to eat near the IRS center, Dick and Coleen followed Mark's directions and arrived at Mrs. Shaw's house at two in the afternoon. It was a traditional California frame, stucco house with a red tile roof, located in an older, tree-lined section of Fresno. The house and yard were well kept.

As they were getting out of the car, Dick commented, "See that guy getting into the gray Chevy over there? I've seen him someplace recently."

"I don't recognize him."

"Coleen, I suspect you haven't done anything like this before. Follow my lead in interviewing Mrs. Shaw. Keep in mind her husband was murdered yesterday."

"I'll definitely follow your lead. The academy doesn't prepare you for this. I must admit, my stomach is in knots," she replied.

"If it helps, my stomach is also in knots. You never get used to this. At least she already knows what happened to her husband."

They could hear the doorbell ring in the house. A very nice lady in her late forties answered. "I assume you're the FBI agents Mr. Stevens called me about. Please, come in."

They both entered the house, putting their FBI credentials away without even bothering to show them. As Mrs. Shaw beckoned, they sat down on the living room couch.

Mrs. Shaw asked, "Is there anything I can get you? Water? Juice? I'd offer coffee or tea, but, being Mormon, we don't drink either."

"Oh, nothing," Dick and Coleen responded, almost in unison.

"We're sorry for the loss of your husband, Mrs. Shaw," Dick said in a soft voice, "but as you can imagine, we need to ask a few questions because of the nature of his death."

"Yes, I understand."

"Do you know of anyone that would want to hurt your husband?"

"Not really. He occasionally was disliked at work because of what he did, but I can't think of anyone who'd murder him. And I'm positive it wasn't suicide, as some seem to think! Ed wouldn't do that."

"Did he recently talk with you about anything that was happening at work or what he was working on?"

"Edison brought some of his work home, but I seldom paid attention to it. He would go on his computer a lot, but he never mentioned what he was working on, and I never paid much attention to his work."

"Does he have any files or records here that we may look at?"

"We did convert one of the bedrooms into an office after our son left for BYU. You're welcome to take a look if you want."

"Thanks. We'd like to. We'll try not to disturb anything."

Mrs. Shaw showed them into the office, where Dick and Coleen spent several hours looking through the neatly stacked papers. There were books about computer programming, computer fraud, general accounting and bookkeeping, auditing techniques, and several IRS manuals. There were Sunday school class teaching lessons and the usual office reference books, such as a dictionary and a Spanish/ English language dictionary. There was a laptop computer docking station connected to a large monitor and an HP printer.

Two of the desk drawers were locked. Dick asked Coleen to see if Mrs. Shaw had a key. When Coleen returned, she went over to a curio box on the bookshelf and took out a key. With it, she opened the drawers. The agents discovered dozens of little notebooks filled with writing.

After going through everything, they decided, at least on first blush, that nothing there seemed tied to the murder or what was happening at the IRS center.

Dick and Coleen returned to the living room. Mrs. Shaw wasn't there. They found her in the kitchen cleaning dishes.

Dick remarked, "Thanks for your time. We've finished up for today. It seems like your husband was a very orderly person."

"Oh, he was. Everything had to be in its place. I think that's why he made such a good auditor."

"We went through the collection of little notebooks in the desk drawers. They seem to contain some sort of notes about the cases your husband was investigating. Each entry was dated, but the last date we noted was about two months ago. Do you know where the most current notebook is?"

"I know exactly where it would be: the inside breast pocket of Edison's jacket. He always had one of those journals with him. He was a fanatic about them. He used to say that he solved most of his cases by the notes in those books. When he'd just about filled up one of the books, we'd have to go to Staples for a new one. He got different colors but always the same type of little journal book, with an elastic band attached that would hold it shut. The cloth bookmarker in each book was always set to a random page in the middle of the book where he kept his computer passwords. He could never remember them. As an auditor, he had three different passwords that allowed him access to different computer systems. Ed always complained that the IRS's IT people made him change passwords every month. He said it would have been okay if he could use something like one of our grandchildren's names or dates of birth or something like that to remember the passwords. But the IT people had a bunch of rules that made it impossible to set up any sort of pattern that you could remember."

Mrs. Shaw looked remorseful as she said, "I'm sorry. I can see him now writing in that damn little book. Sometimes he would just stop while we were shopping, or eating, or even discussing something. He would often take that book out and write in it. The notebooks were actually called 'Markings by C. B. Gibson'—the printer, I suppose. Sorry to run on like this."

Coleen put her arm around Mrs. Shaw. "That's all right. That's all right. I'm sure you're overwhelmed with grief and shock."

Dick asked, "Sorry, Mrs. Shaw, but I do have just a couple more questions. Do you know if he transcribed the information from his books to his computer?"

"I'm not sure, but I doubt it. He was very competitive at work. He didn't want the other auditors to know what he was working on. He was a very private person who sought, or probably needed, credit for what he did. As you probably noted, he used a lot of shorthand in his books that would make it difficult for someone to figure out what he was writing about."

Coleen responded, "We noted that, but I don't remember seeing the password page you mentioned. Dick, do you remember seeing a password page?"

"No, I don't."

"Oh, my dears, that's because Ed would rip the page out and run it through the shredder when he had to start a new book. He was very meticulous about such things."

"Well, thank you again for your time."

As Dick was just about to exit the front door, he looked back and asked, "Did you happen to see a man driving a gray Chevy in front of your house earlier?"

"No. Why do you ask?"

"Oh, just that I noticed a man pulling away from the street as we were coming in."

"Probably visiting a neighbor. As you can imagine, my mind is elsewhere. I haven't really paid any attention to what's been happening on the block."

As they got into the car to head back to the IRS service center, Coleen looked at Dick and asked, "What was that about?"

"Just a hunch."

"Well, your hunch may be right. She was lying about not seeing someone in the neighborhood. On top of that, there seemed to be more dishes in the sink than would be used by one person. Even in her grief, she doesn't appear to me to be the type to leave dishes sitting in the sink for very long, and it sure didn't look like she had cried much about losing her husband. Maybe it's a Mormon thing?"

"I know. Coleen, it appears you can read people. I predict you're going to make a good addition to the squad."

"Dick, what do you make of his little notebooks?"

"I'm convinced that the current one would be a help to our investigation. Hopefully, Harriet found it in his jacket pocket, but for some reason, I have the feeling it won't be there. If not, we're going to immediately let Mark Stevens know to make sure he has disabled Shaw's passwords."

9

IRS Service Center, Fresno, California

Daniel was still talking with Jeff in the monitor room. Dick stuck his head through the door. "How's it going?"

"Oh, hi, Boss. Going great. I downloaded data from the security discs to my computer and sent it off to my buddies in Butte for analysis, using some parameters I set up. We should have something to work with early next week."

"Great."

Dick walked over to Mark's office and stuck his head in. "Mark, do you have a minute?"

"Sure do. How'd it go with Mrs. Shaw?"

"It went well. We didn't turn up anything that seemed significant, at least at this point in time, but you never know. I have a favor to ask."

"Anything you need."

"The security guard at the gate this morning. I saw his picture up on the wall outside. What's his name?"

"I'm not sure who was on the gate. Show me the picture."

They walked over to a wall that contained pictures of all of the security staff. Dick pointed to one of the pictures and Mark said, "That's Ed Abramson. He's been with us for a long time, a fellow

Leatherneck, NCO. I believe he left with the rank of first sergeant. Why your interest?"

"Just a hunch. Can you provide me with a copy of his ID photo and home address?"

"You're not thinking Ed had something to do with Shaw's murder, are you? He's one of the nicest guys around here."

"As I said, just a hunch."

Mark went into his office and opened a locked filing cabinet, from which he removed the file on Edward Abramson. He returned and gave it to Dick, with the stipulation that Dick should make photocopies of whatever he needed and return the file.

"Mark, by any chance, do you know anything about the notebooks Edison Shaw used to keep information on in regard to his audit cases?"

"Only that he was always pulling one of those little notebooks out of his inside coat pocket. He would flip off the elastic band and open it to the proper place using the attached bookmark. I'll tell you, if you asked him a question about a case, he had the answer someplace in his notebooks. It was an obsession with him."

"You aren't the only one who got that impression. We heard exactly the same thing from his wife. Oh, that reminds me. According to Mrs. Shaw, her husband kept his computer passwords in those notebooks. I'm going to check with Harriet to see if she found the notebook on him or in his office. You should make sure his passwords are deleted from the systems, just in case."

"Thanks for the suggestion. I'll make a phone call right now to make sure they're deleted. That may be the reason he was killed."

Dick and Coleen latched onto Daniel. They all headed out to find the rest of the squad. Harriet was just coming out of Shaw's office as they walked up to it. The coroner had already removed the body, and Harriet had gone through everything in the office.

Dick asked, "Did you find anything of interest?"

"I further confirmed it wasn't a suicide. The lower right-hand drawer to his desk was locked. Security had a master key that opened it. Guess what I found: a shoulder holster with a 9mm Beretta in it. I suspect it was his service weapon. I can't see him using the piece of junk indicated in the CSU's photos to shoot himself. Other than that, if I found anything else of value, I don't know it yet. There wasn't a lot to look at. I suspect whoever murdered him took any incriminating evidence with them," said Harriett.

"Okay. Let's see what Brian's come up with. Any idea where he is?"

"As a matter of fact, yes. I took Shaw's computer to him. He set up shop at that IRS agent's desk. Follow me."

Harriet led them over to a cubicle in the big bay. It was where IRS Agent Larsen had been working undercover. Brian was with him, and three other people were looking at Larsen's computer screen.

Brian looked up at them. "Hi, Boss. These are three of Larsen's pals from the IRS Criminal Investigation Unit. They've been sent in to help analyze what this may be all about. We're all trying to figure out what's on Shaw's computer and what he accessed on the IRS's computer network. It's interesting that he never saved anything on the network, but he sure looked at and downloaded a lot of info from it. It also looks like some files were deleted from his computer."

"Figure anything out?" Dick asked.

"Nothing that ties together yet. No question something is fishy. We'll figure it out, but at the moment, my brain is fried."

"Well, you confirmed something we learned from Mrs. Shaw. Mr. Shaw was a loner."

"That explains why he didn't save files to the network," Brian replied.

"That'd be my conclusion. Did you get a chance to interview Shaw's supervisor?"

"That I did, Boss. It's my impression she doesn't know anything of value. Shaw had hinted to her that he'd stumbled onto something that could be of interest but didn't supply any more info than that. I have a listing of his cases, but nothing seems to jump out. I'm having my new IRS buddies here review them."

"Good work, Brian. Okay, everyone. Let's check into the hotel. Larsen, where're you and your crew staying?" asked Dick.

"The Piccadilly Inn."

"Looks like we're all staying at the same place. Nothing like a murder to start a bonding process. Excuse me for a minute. I need to speak to Harriet and Brian."

Dick motioned to Harriet and Brian to follow him into a cubicle across the way. He said softly to them, "Sorry to do this to you guys, but your day isn't finished yet. Here's a picture of one of the security guards by the name of Edward Abramson. Here's his home address. I want you to stake out his house until eleven tonight. Follow him if he leaves, and let me know by cell phone who he meets or where he goes. You'll be relieved by two of the local agents, assuming I can work things out with the local special agent in charge. I'm afraid your dinner tonight is going to be take-out."

They both looked at him a little quizzically but indicated it would be no problem.

10

Fresno, California

The Piccadilly Inn University Hotel was located on Cedar Avenue, about eight miles from the IRS service center. It was more like a motel than a hotel, with parking areas located adjacent to rooms around the complex. There was a main building with a covered driveway in front of it for checking in. This building housed the hotel's front desk, bar, breakfast dining area, and six meeting rooms. The hotel's guest rooms were situated in three, three-story buildings, which surrounded a garden courtyard, swimming pool, and spa.

Fresno was home to several Piccadilly Inn Hotel properties. This one was named the University Hotel because it was just a block north of the Fresno State University campus, whose mascot was the Bulldog. The campus took up several square blocks, with the hotel being located a block and a half away from the Fresno Bulldogs' baseball complex and football stadium.

The squad let Brian and Harriett check in first so they could head out for their stakeout. At five thirty, Dick, Coleen, and Daniel met with the IRS agents in the lobby. On the advice of the desk clerk, they headed next door to Marie Callender's for a government expense account dinner.

Just as they were being served, Dick's cell phone rang. It was Brian. "Hey, Boss, your security guard is on the move. It looks like he's headed out of town."

"Okay. Keep me posted when he stops. If he doesn't stop, give me a call."

"Will do."

After dinner, the whole crew went to the hotel bar for a beer before heading up to their rooms. Dick's cell phone rang again a little after six thirty. It was Brian. "Boss, we're in the town of Oakhurst, about forty miles north of Fresno. He pulled into a place called Erna's Elderberry House. Looks like a very fancy spa with a restaurant in the front. He's parking his car."

"Does it look like a place where you can follow him in without being noticed?"

"I think so."

"Okay. Call me back when you know something further."

Following Brian's call, Dick explained what was happening to the rest of the team. They decided they'd had enough beer, but they wanted to stay together for Brian's reports. They situated themselves at an empty table in the lobby, watching CNN news as they waited.

Brian parked. He and Harriett walked up the steps leading them to the entrance of what looked like a European country estate. The front door was open. They could see the security guard meet a middle-aged woman. The two greeted with a kiss. The FBI agents watched as the maître d' approached them. He spoke with them for a while and then escorted them out to the patio area just outside the main dining room.

Brian took Harriett's arm. They went through the front door as if they were a couple.

The maître d' asked, "May I help you?"

"We're from Fresno and heard good things about your restaurant. We wanted to take a look."

"Unfortunately, we're booked for this evening; however, we could offer you drinks in the bar or out on the patio, if you would like."

"Harriett, what do you think?"

"Brian, the weather is so nice up here in the mountains. I think a drink on the patio would be very nice."

"Then, Monsieur and Madam, please, follow me."

They walked through the main dining room and out a French door onto the patio. They were seated under a tree at a small table with a white tablecloth, next to a water fountain.

"Would you like to see the wine list?" the maître d' asked.

"Yes, please."

There were several tables on the patio. Other couples occupied four of them. There was a flirtatious young couple at the closest table. They suspected the couple was on their honeymoon. Based on their dress and accents, it appeared that European couples occupied two other tables. The security guard and his lady friend occupied a table at the other side of the patio. They seemed to know each other quite well.

The maître d' returned. "Have you made a selection?"

Pointing at the wine list, Brian indicated a wine. "Yes, we'd like a bottle of this Jordon Cabernet Sauvignon."

"Fine choice, sir. I'll have the waiter bring it right out."

As the maître d' walked away, Harriett asked, "Do you have any idea what you just ordered?"

"None whatsoever. There were no beers on the list."

"You know we're not supposed to be drinking on the job."

"Harriett, we're following people. We have to fit in. Besides, I'm not dumping that wine. The bottle cost sixty-eight dollars."

"What? I'm glad it's your expense account. I want to see the explanation you use."

"Oh, relax. Dick will love it. I just have to remember the name of the wine to tell him."

"This is an impressive place."

The waiter returned with the wine and a bowl of smoked almonds. He displayed the bottle to Brian, who indicated approval by a nod of his head. The waiter opened the bottle sniffed the aroma and then poured a small amount into Brian's wine glass. Brian swirled the wine in the glass, sniffed it, took a sip, and said, "Yes, that'll be fine."

As Harriett was being served, Brian asked, "By the way, what is that building up there above the patio?"

As the waiter filled Brian's glass, he responded. "It's our spa. Many famous people frequent it—mostly Europeans. Our owner is a lady from Austria. That's the reason for the European flavor. She's well known in Europe."

Harriett was impressed. She thought to herself, *Boy, this place is magnificent. Great for a romantic evening. I have to return with someone other than Brian.* It appeared to her that the rooms were decorated with antique French provincial furnishings and magnificent tapestries and original oil paintings hanging on the walls.

Abramson and his lady friend had ordered a bottle of champagne. They seemed to be having a great time while they were enjoying it.

Guests from the spa building periodically strolled down the hill to enjoy the restaurant and bar. Hummingbirds were flitting from tree to tree between the bushes on the patio.

After a half hour, Abramson and his lady friend had finished their bottle of champagne. They apparently had reservations in the dining room and were escorted there by the maître d'. From where they were now seated, the FBI agents could no longer watch their subjects. They needed to make a change.

Brian waved to their waiter. "My friend is getting cold out here. I wonder if we might be able to move into the bar area?"

"But of course, sir. Please, follow me."

The FBI agents settled onto barstools that allowed them to see anyone who left the restaurant, but they didn't have eyes directly on

Abramson's table. This time, they both ordered cranberry juice with soda water. Brian picked up his cell phone and called Dick.

Dick answered his cell while the rest of the team listened attentively to what he was saying. Brian reported, "He met some lady at this restaurant. They shared a bottle of champagne and are now being seated for dinner."

Dick commented, "I'll bet I know who the lady is. Describe her."

Brian described Mrs. Shaw to a tee.

"Okay. You and Harriett enjoy yourselves at the restaurant and follow Abramson home. I don't think he'll try to run, but we better not take any chances. The locals will relieve you at his house, and then head for the hotel and get some sleep. We will visit with Security Guard Abramson and Mrs. Shaw first thing in the morning. I'll arrange with the residence agent for babysitters for Mrs. Shaw until we meet with her again tomorrow. Both are possible flight risks."

After Dick explained Brian's side of the conversation, they all headed up to their rooms for the evening.

Back at Erna's Elderberry House, a waiter from the adjacent dining room was apparently assigned as the bartender. He asked if they would like anything to eat. It would be possible to serve them a cheese plate or something from the dessert menu. Brian thanked him and indicated that they hadn't realized that the restaurant only had a prix fixe menu. He added that they worked for a company in Fresno. They'd been sent to check out the place for the company's tenth anniversary party.

The bartender left but returned a few minutes later with a folder that contained the restaurant's catering information, including menus, wine list, bar drink pricing, and costs for special decorations.

Harriett picked up the cheese menu and noted that a cheese plate included six cheeses for twenty dollars. "Brian, by any chance, do you like cheese?"

"I can take it or leave it."

"I'm starving and happen to like cheese. Will you share a cheese plate with me?"

"This is starting to sound like a date, but of course, I'll share a cheese plate with you."

When the waiter returned, Brian ordered the cheese plate and another round of drinks. As they had nothing to do but wait, for laughs, they priced out a company anniversary party for twenty people. This also gave them a reason to stay on until the security guard and Mrs. Shaw left. When they'd finished pricing out the party, Brian looked over to Harriett and said, "I'm definitely sticking to the keg and pizza parties I have on my deck. A party here would cost me at least a month's salary."

Harriett changed the subject. "What do you think of Coleen?"

"She seems sharp enough. From what I've seen, the bureau usually sends the sharpest ones to tutor under Dick. After all, they picked us to train under him."

"A little ego showing there, but you're right. We probably have the best squad in the bureau. I think Coleen will fit in with the rest of us 'Animals' well. She seems to have a good personality, but she definitely is a northeastern gal, the way she dresses and speaks. I think Dick likes her."

"I won't disagree with you on that."

As they continued to wait, they went back to the restaurant marketing materials. They learned from the kit provided by the waiter that the restaurant was named for the elderberry bushes that covered the rolling property and that the restaurant was part of a five-star spa hotel named Chateau du Sureau. They periodically traded off going to the restroom, so they could make sure the couple they were following didn't skip out on them.

To make conversation, Brian asked, "How do you like living in the Sunset?"

"It's great, but boy, it's cool and foggy out there. I can walk to the beach or jog through Golden Gate Park. I found a great local Irish pub where I've made some friends. During the summer, I go with friends to Stern Grove to hear the free concerts. You know, it's hard being a single FBI agent. Especially when your date finds out you're packing."

"Oh, God, I can remember my dating days. Some of the gals were impressed that

I was carrying. Others, I never was able to contact again after they found out."

"How's the family and living on the Peninsula?"

"We love the Peninsula. It's warmer than the city, and the schools are better than in San Francisco. Mary is working close to home as a claims adjuster for a major auto insurance company. She likes helping people and really enjoys what she's doing. Both the kids are in day school. It's a little hard being in Dick's squad, as we are on the road so much. I like our cases, but we do get the unusual, time-consuming assignments."

Finally, Brian and Harriett decided they'd overstayed their welcome in the bar and were becoming obvious, particularly as they were drinking cranberry juice and soda water. They could've ordered a drink, or wine, and milked it for a while but decided against that. They mutually decided the couple was not a flight risk from the restaurant and finished the assignment in their car.

At eleven, the couple left Erma's Elderberry House. They kissed romantically, and then got into their own cars. Both turned onto the highway back toward Fresno.

As Brian drove the car following Abramson, Harriett called Dick on the cell. "Date night's over. Abramson and Mrs. Shaw are headed back to Fresno."

"Okay. Follow Abramson home and let the locals take over, and then get some sleep."

11

San Francisco, California

It was the last Friday of the month, the day they all somehow managed to take off work together. They'd done it every month for almost two years now.

Chris Martinez, Jimmy Sanchez, and their girlfriends, Adriana Escobedo and Liz Gonzalez, were in Jimmy's classic, customized Chevy heading west for San Francisco. It was still early morning as they left Fresno, and as with every other time, they arrived around ten in the morning at the Park Hyatt Hotel in the Embarcadero Center. The valet parking attendant welcomed them back. He was well aware of how Jimmy wanted his car treated, which was all right with him. Jimmy would give him a fifty-dollar tip every time they checked out. The two couples checked into their rooms.

At eleven, they met in the lobby and headed back upstairs to room 912. That was the room of Victor Farajian, the US representative of a Hong Kong tailor. Some guy in the hotel bar had introduced them to him two years before. He came to San Francisco once every six months to market his upscale tailored suits and monogrammed shirts. He always set up shop in a Park Hyatt Hotel room.

Chris and Jimmy had each changed into one of Victor's suits from a previous purchase, as Victor always requested. It made their fittings easier. As always, Victor measured them and made notes on their record sheets. The suits and shirts they selected would arrive from Hong Kong about six weeks after their purchases. In a parcel-post package, they'd be all wrinkled up in brown paper wrapping and tied with cord. But once the garments were cleaned and pressed, they fit their bodies perfectly and looked absolutely fantastic. They stood out in Fresno when they were wearing these suits, as opposed to the baggy pants and untucked shirts worn by their gang-member friends.

With Adriana and Liz, they looked at and touched the fabrics spread out on the bed in the hotel room. Each selected two light wools for new suits. Chris and Jimmy sat down next to the desk in the room, with Adriana and Liz looking over their shoulders. Victor showed them drawings and pictures of the latest styles and helped them select the way in which their next suits would be tailored.

When that was done, they looked at the shirt fabrics Victor had in a folder. Each selected fabrics for a dozen new shirts.

Victor asked, "How do you want your shirts done? Button-down collars? French cuffs? Monograms?"

Chris responded, "Same as last time. Italian spread collars and monograms on the shirt pocket. I want these six fabrics with French cuffs, and these six with buttons."

"Same for me on the collars, but I want my monogram on the shirt cuff. French cuffs on these six, and buttons on these six," Jimmy replied.

Victor totaled their bill, which was more than six thousand dollars each. Out came the credit cards to settle the bill.

With the guys' shopping done, Ariana and Liz walked from the hotel to Union Square for some shopping with their guys' credit cards. They loved these trips. They loved their guys. They loved their credit cards.

The girls walked around Union Square, stopping in at Postrio for lunch. They reminisced about their lives.

"Liz, do you remember when we all graduated from Fresno State? We had no idea what we were going to do."

"Yeah. Remember that IRS recruiting booth on campus? They were desperate for people, especially those with computer skills. Then they found out we spoke and read Spanish. They were just starting the Spanish Language Unit. I think that cinched it."

"Uh-huh. We lucked out there. It's unbelievable. Chris has got to be one of the smartest people alive. He's a computer genius. He came up with the idea of how we could improve our lifestyles by working in the Spanish Language Unit. Now look where we are."

"Yeah. We're headed into a haute couture store in San Francisco's Union Square to buy those Prada purses we saw in the fashion magazine. What a life," said Ariana.

"Do you think we will ever get married to Chris and Jimmy?"

"I have no doubt about it. We're perfect together."

"You know we're going to have to leave Fresno at some point in time."

"I can't wait. Chris has it worked out. We're going down to LA for a few weeks. He has some friends that have a boat docked in Marina Del Rey. We'll live on it for a while, stay out of sight. Maybe even sail down to San Diego or up to Santa Barbara. Then we'll find a place to live here in San Francisco. I love it here. It's so much fun."

12

San Francisco, California

While their girls were on their shopping spree, Chris and Jimmy walked over to a high-rise office building on California Street in the Financial District, where there was a Bank of America branch on the ground floor. They took the elevator up to the eleventh floor, where two years before, they'd made arrangements for executive office space. They used the space every last Friday of the month.

Chris said to the very attractive, blonde receptionist at the big, curved reception desk, "Hi, beautiful. How's it going?"

"It going fantastic. How are you guys doing? Haven't seen you in awhile."

"We're doing awesome. Any mail for us?"

"Let me look."

She returned with a handful of envelops and handed them to Chris.

"Thanks. Which office can we use today?"

"Take 1107. It's vacant and has a great view of the Bay."

Once in the office, Chris opened the mail. After throwing out the junk mail, there were only two letters left, a bank statement from the Bank of America branch located downstairs in the lobby of the building and a B of A bill for their business credit cards.

Jimmy opened the briefcase they always brought with them and began endorsing 136 checks with a rubber stamp that read, "Ira Roth Silverstein and Associates, LLC dba The IRS Guy." When finished, he completed a deposit slip for the amount of $372,047 and took it downstairs and deposited it in the bank.

Chris sat at the office table and wrote a single check in the amount of $86,547 to pay the credit card bill for the seven company credit cards.

When Jimmy returned from the bank, Chris shouted at him, "Jimmy, what the fuck is Jorge doing? He went over the limit on his card with more than twenty-five thousand dollars in charges last month."

"I don't know, but we'd better find out when we get back. We need to keep him in check. I'm never sure if we have him under control."

Chris and Jimmy met up with the girls in their hotel rooms. After a little respite, they headed down California Street toward the Ferry Building and picked out a table at the Market Bar. Jimmy and the girls ordered margaritas, while Chris ordered a Bud Light. They enjoyed watching the Friday afternoon bustle with the businesspeople running to catch ferries to places such as Alameda, Vallejo, Sausalito, Larkspur, and Tiburon.

They tilted their heads back to enjoy the little sun San Francisco had to offer on this day. They all agreed that this was a great city, particularly when you had almost unlimited money to spend. Another year in Fresno and they were out of there.

Chris looked at Jimmy and commented, "Remember when we opened the bank account for The IRS Guy with the forged corporate documents and the corporate seal your brother got made someplace? All that lady at the bank wanted to do was open that account for us. It must be our good looks. I don't know how banks stay in business."

"Yeah, dude. That was fantastical. Did you see the balance on the bank statement? We're really going to celebrate tonight!"

"Fuckin' right, but first we have one more thing to take care of for Gomez. What type of home entertainment system should we order?"

They walked back to the bank building on California Street. When they got out on the eleventh floor, they asked the blonde at the reception desk, "Is there a computer available?"

"Let me check the book. You can use number three. You guys know where the computer room is located?"

"Yeah. Thanks. We know."

There were eight computers and several printers in the room. Three of the computers were being used. They found number three. Chris sat down, signed in, and opened up the Internet browser. He typed in *www.sears.com*, clicked the button for "Sears Online," and went to "Electronics & Computers."

"Here's a Sharp fifty-inch LCD full high-definition television on sale for $1,439. You think Gomez would like that for his crib?"

"Yeah. I'm sure of it. Is it eligible for store pickup?"

"Yup."

"Perfect. Buy it."

Chris added three DVD movies and a Panasonic 5.1 Channel Blu-Ray Disc Home Theater System. He clicked on "Store Pickup."

"It's asking for a zip code. What zip code should I use?"

"Use the one for the office here."

Chris typed in 94111 and completed the section for payment by credit card. He filled in his personal e-mail address for a confirmation of the purchase and then opened up the Spider Solitaire game on the computer and played while Jimmy went out to talk with the blonde at the reception desk.

After he lost two games, Chris opened up his e-mail account and found the Sears confirmation notice with an indication that the items he purchased were in stock and could be available for pickup at the San Bruno store, near the San Francisco Airport, in twenty-four hours.

Next, he looked for a U-Haul truck rental facility located close to San Bruno. He arranged for a truck to be picked up the next day and returned the same day in Fresno.

Now it was really time to party.

13

San Bruno, California

Hungover, Chris, Jimmy, Adriana, and Liz ordered Bloody Marys and breakfast from room service. At noon, they checked out of the hotel.

Jimmy tipped the parking attendant. They headed down Clay Street and turned south on the Embarcadero. Just past PacBell Park, the Embarcadero turned into Interstate 280. They headed south and transitioned onto 101 South. Jimmy took the Third Street Exit into Brisbane, passed the Cow Palace, and then pulled into the U-Haul facility where they'd made a reservation.

Twenty minutes later, Chris had completed the paperwork and was driving the U-Haul out with Adriana at his side. They followed Jimmy's Chevy back onto the 101 South and in a short distance got off in the town of San Bruno. They pulled into a shopping center and parked in front of the Sears store entrance. Chris pulled a note out of his pants pocket and dialed the number on it.

"Hello."

Chris responded, "Is this Ralph?"

"It is."

"Al Gomez said you'd be expecting my call."

"Oh, yeah. I'm on break right now. I'll be back at the pickup desk in twenty minutes. Wait until then. I'll be standing in the lobby of the pickup area. Just walk in and wait. I will come up to you to ask if you need any help, okay?"

"Sounds cool to me. See you in twenty."

After window-shopping in the mall to kill time, the group headed to the Sears pickup lobby.

A man approached them and said, "Hi, I'm Ralph. Can I help you?"

Chris replied, "Hey, man, good to meet you. We ordered some merchandise over the Internet to be picked up here."

"Do you have the pickup order?"

"Sure. Here it is."

"Wow, man. You fuckers picked out some fantastic equipment. Do you have a vehicle that it will fit in?"

"We have a rental truck. I'll bring it around."

"Okay. Bring it over to the loading dock on that side of the building and I'll get you squared away with the merchandise. As I understand it, this is just the start of big things to come."

"Gomez has really worked this out. It should mean more money for all of us."

"Will you guys be doing other pickups?"

"I don't know, man. We'll have to wait and see. Gomez will let us know."

Chris pulled the truck over to the loading dock. With the help of Ralph and Jimmy, they loaded the boxes of electronic equipment into the back of the truck, securing it with straps. Al Gomez's house in Fresno would be their next stop.

14

Fresno, California

The squad was sitting at a table in the hotel's complimentary continental-breakfast room as Dick gave out the assignments for the day.

"Harriett and I will interview the security officer at the IRS center. Mark has already set up the meeting in one of their conference rooms. Coleen, you go with Brian to interview Mrs. Shaw again at her residence. Daniel, you come with Harriett and me to the Center and see if the IRS special agent auditors have come up with anything."

Mrs. Shaw answered the door in her bathrobe and was surprised to see Agent Ryan standing there with another man.

"Good morning, Mrs. Shaw. This is Special Agent Brian Brooks. We have some additional questions to ask you. May we come in?"

Mrs. Shaw held the door open for them. This time, she didn't offer any refreshments. Her intuition told her this visit was going to be different from the first.

Brian began the conversation. "Ma'am, you probably don't know this, but we were at the same restaurant last night."

"Oh, my! Then you know who I had dinner with."

"Yes, ma'am. We do."

The tears flowed and the words came blurting out. "Oh, my God. I knew we couldn't keep it a secret. Ed Abramson and I have been seeing each other for quite some time. My husband and I just kind of fell out of love, and he was spending more and more time at work. Ed and I met by chance at the library, and things just seemed to click between us. Agent Ryan, you know what I mean?"

Coleen's response was somewhat delayed. Then she said, "Mrs. Shaw, I'm not sure I do know, but knowing or not makes no difference. Your husband was murdered, and it very well could have been by the man you've been seeing."

"Agent Ryan, Ed did not kill my husband. I am absolutely sure of that because when the murder happened, he was here with me."

"Mrs. Shaw, are you telling us that you are Edward Abramson's alibi for the time of the murder?"

"Yes, I am."

The questioning of Mrs. Shaw went on for some time. Just before leaving, Coleen advised, "You may or may not have noticed that there are two FBI agents parked in front of your house. They will stay there until we get a better handle on this. Understand?"

"Yes, yes. I understand."

Before getting into their car, the agents leaned into the open window of the Bucar parked in front and advised the agents inside what had happened.

Coleen commented as they headed to the IRS center, "Let me get this straight. We have the widow of the murder victim as an alibi for our most likely suspect?"

"I think that's a perfect summary. Dick will love it."

Dick and Harriett went directly to Mark's office in the security section when they arrived at the IRS center. Mark invited them in and advised Dick that he'd done as requested. "Edward Abramson is waiting in the conference room. I didn't clue him in as to why I wanted to see him, or that you'd be with me."

"Thanks, Mark. I need to make a call before going in."

The call only lasted a couple of minutes as Brian filled Dick in on the visit with Mrs. Shaw.

"Okay. Let's do this." Dick, Coleen and Harriett followed Mark into the conference room. Dick opened the door unannounced and found Ed sitting in one of the chairs at the conference table drinking a cup of coffee.

He looked surprised. "Who are you?"

"Special Agent Hartmann with the FBI, and this is Agent Coleen Ryan."

Dick opened with, "How was your dinner last night?"

After he uttered, "Shit," Ed related basically the same story as Mrs. Shaw.

After listening, Dick said, "Ed, first I'm going to ask you to give us your service weapon. Is that all right, Ed?"

"It's okay. I understand."

"Ed, I think you're telling the truth, but now we need to try and corroborate your story. That's not going to be easy, as your only alibi is the murder victim's wife, with whom you're having an affair. Agents Foster and Brooks are going to take you to the FBI resident agency here in Fresno and have someone give you a polygraph exam. Do you understand?"

"Yes, and I actually look forward to the test. I didn't kill that auditor, Shaw."

Brian was delighted when Dick called and asked him to join Harriett in taking the security guard for the polygraph test. His meeting with the IRS special agents indicated to him that they hadn't progressed any farther than they had yesterday in trying to figure out if the IRS computer system had been breached.

It was early afternoon when the team met up back at the hotel. Foster and Brooks advised everyone that Edward Abramson had passed the polygraph test. They all concurred that unless they were fools, Abramson hadn't murdered Shaw.

Dick called Mark and Robin to advise them that his squad was returning to San Francisco for the weekend and would return on Monday or Tuesday. He also made sure Robin had a couple of agents tail Abramson, just in case they were fools.

The FBI plane arrived back at the San Carlos Airport at one thirty. Dick headed for the city to see an unusual sporting event. Well, not really a sporting event. He hoped it wasn't over.

15

San Francisco, California

It was late Friday afternoon when Hartmann arrived at Le Central Bistro on Bush Street, near the entrance to San Francisco's Chinatown. It is the oldest French bistro in San Francisco and head-quarters for the "Mischievous Irregulars" group, of which Hartmann was a member. They met there every Friday afternoon.

Dick had three favorite watering holes in San Francisco. They were points in a triangle. Point number one was Le Central. The other two points were the Washington Bar & Grill, better known as the WashBag, and Moose's, which was situated directly across Washington Square Park from the WashBag. All three were in walk-ing distance from Dick's Russian Hill bachelor pad.

Well, we're honored today, he thought. Parked in front of the bistro in a no-parking zone was the hydrogen-powered, green Hummer H1, with unmarked California Highway Patrol cars parked in front and back.

As his eyes adjusted to the muted lighting in the bistro, Dick spot-ted most of the Mischievous Irregulars sitting at the bar. He hadn't missed the game.

The seating was not totally "Friday normal." Ron, who was not a member of the group, was sitting on the first barstool near the front entrance drinking a cup of coffee. That meant the governor must be on the premises. *Yup. There's Arlene, standing by the kitchen door.*

The governor was well protected by his CHP bodyguards. Ron's ever-watchful eyes checked out everyone who entered, and Arlene made sure no one came through the kitchen or got close to the governor's table.

Dick sat in his usual spot next to his best friend Gordy, who, as usual, had a glass of Cote de Rhone in his hand. The barstool between Gordon and Dan had been reserved for him with the placement of a glass of the red house bordeaux covered with a cocktail napkin. Dan was on his right drinking one of Toni's Blood Marys. The Irregulars usually were wine drinkers, but on occasion, they would have a hard drink depending on how the day was going. You could tell if someone had been out the night before because he would order one of Toni's Bloody Marys, made from scratch and guaranteed to wake you up.

"How're you doing, Toni?"

"Can't complain. You're late today."

"Just got off a plane. Had to come and cheer you on."

"You just made it."

"I see there's a prestigious audience today."

"Yeah. Screwing up my Friday."

Toni took very good care of her Mischievous Irregulars. God forbid if a woman should try to sit at one of the guys' spots at the bar. Toni felt that the guys tipped far better than the gals, and besides, they followed her rules. Today, she had to stare at Ron's back as he watched the front door. He was taking up the front barstool. There was nothing she could do about it. Stares and rudeness did not work in this case.

Dick took a sip then turned his head toward the back table, which, as he suspected, was occupied by California's movie star "Governator."

Schwarzenegger was sitting with "da Mayor," Willie Brown. *They're either talking about politics or women,* he thought.

The back table was often Willie's private office on Fridays. He held fort there when there was business to be conducted; otherwise, he sat at his usual table at the front of the restaurant. Willie had been termed out as speaker of the California State Assembly, so he ran for mayor of San Francisco and easily won. Politicians on both a state and national scale would frequently consult with him at Le Central.

With "da Mayor" on the premises, at least Wilkes would have one supporter for today's game. Most of the bar supported Toni, as she had control over the pour of their drinks.

San Francisco's best-known upscale haberdasher, Wilkes Bashford, was standing next to the floor-to-ceiling mirror that was on a wall at the back end of the bar. His San Francisco clothing store was located just a couple of blocks from Le Central near Union Square. He had other locations in the upscale Palo Alto and Carmel communities.

When Willie was not holding forth in his Le Central "office," Wilkes, Harry De Wildt, and "da Mayor" would dine at the table next to the open front window in the bar section of the restaurant, weather permitting. They would play boss dice at the table to see who picked up the lunch tab. The two had been buds going way back, and their pictures at Bay Area events were frequently seen in the *Chron*, *Examiner*, or the *Nob Hill Gazette*. Hartmann occasionally appeared in the *Chron* or *Examiner*, but it wasn't in the society section of paper. His name and sometimes a picture would appear in an article about one of the cases he was working on.

Today, the mirror at the back of the bar had printed on it, with various-colored marking pens, "Our Cassoulet has cooked for 12,092 days." Recently printed with a red marking pen under that was "Toni—9 days."

James, another Irregular, was sitting to the left of Gordon with a glass of white wine in front of him. He was giving odds on the event.

Toni, the female bartender, had set a record of beating Wilkes for nine days in a row at rolling boss dice. Dice rolling is a way of life in San Francisco that dates back to the tented saloons of the Gold Rush.

Originally from Southern California, Dick learned from his San Francisco friends that boss dice is taken seriously in their town. The stakes are usually a round of drinks, but in some cases, it may be played for lunches or money. The game is usually played by males, unless the bartender is female. Strangers are virtually never invited to participate, and even someone who would like to play would not do so unless he was known to one or more players. On this day at Le Central, the big-boss dice game was being played by two players only: Bartender Toni and Wilkes Bashford. They would initially each roll five dice simultaneously. The player who rolls the higher poker hand is the boss. On the second roll, the boss must use, or leave showing on the bar top, those dice that made him or her the boss. The boss then picks up his or her unmatched dice and rolls again, being careful to conceal the second roll from the opponent. Was Toni going to make it ten wins? If she did, it would match the record set long ago by Wilkes.

The lunch specials for the day were on the chalkboard. Dick selected the old-fashioned beef stew with a side of macaroni. Not exactly the fare you expected in a French restaurant, but it fit the Irregulars and the rest of the upscale, older business crowd that frequented the bistro. In fact, today, the "Governator" ordered the stew as well.

James was giving fifteen-to-one odds on Toni and five-to-one odds on Wilkes. None of the Irregulars could figure out how James arrived at these odds, but they weren't complaining, as they were all winning money from him. Dick handed over his buck to James, betting on Toni.

As he usually did, Wilkes took off his jacket, hung it neatly on a nearby peg, and was ready for action. The Irregulars were suspicious when Wilkes produced a new dice cup. Toni filled a couple of dining room drink orders and then wandered over to a spot at the bar directly across from Wilkes. They both rolled, and Toni won the first roll. Wilkes won the second roll.

It was now down to the last roll. Toni rolled three sixes.

Wilkes loudly banged his dice cup on the bar and raised it carefully with both hands. He had rolled four twos and called out, "Pick them up!" as he believed it to be unlikely he would win with the hand he'd thrown. This meant that both players had to start all over again and the round was thrown out. Apparently, Wilkes decided on a reroll, worrying that Toni would get another six. Wilkes's reroll was a total disaster, with only one pair of threes.

The Irregulars decided he'd rolled against the odds. Toni won again, and drinks were being refilled along the bar. The Irregulars all congratulated Toni. The game would continue for another day.

With that over, Dick started a discussion with Phil, another Irregular who lived in the same apartment building on Russian Hill. Dick remembered that Phil had told him he was getting riffed by Bank of America following their purchase by some bank in North Carolina. San Franciscans were up in arms over the sale. *What was this world coming to?*

"Are you still planning to leave the city?" he asked.

Phil confirmed, "I am. The bank gave me a good severance package, and there's nothing for me in banking here. Lots of former bankers are looking for jobs in the city now. I'm going to invest some of my severance to buy a video rental store up in Clear Lake, north of here."

"Boy, that'll be a change of life for you. I thought you liked the city scene?"

"I do and I don't. It's time for me to give something else a try."

"Are we still on for golf at the Presidio tomorrow?"

"We are. I'm looking forward to taking some of your money."

Dick hesitated before asking his next question. *The best thing that could happen would be for Phil to say no,* he thought. Dick didn't always have good judgment when it involved women, and this idea involved a woman that had just started working for him.

"Phil, when are you planning to head up to Clear Lake?"

"As soon as possible. The current owners of the video store want to leave ASAP, and I want to get some training from them before they go."

"What're you going to do with your unit in our building?"

"I'll probably just turn it over to the building owner. I'm on a month-to-month basis now, and they'd love to see me leave. Because of rent control, my rent is half the going rate."

"Can I pitch a plan to you? If it doesn't work, I'll take care of any problems."

"A plan that could generate problems. I can't wait to hear this one. Pitch away, old boy," Phil said.

"We have a new, single agent in our squad. In today's environment, it's doubtful she could find an apartment, and she probably couldn't afford it, even if she did. She's a good kid, and her bureau life would be a lot easier if she lived in the city. How about subleasing the apartment to her?" Dick asked.

"Dick, you know that's risky in this town. All of the landlords want the older tenants out so they can double or triple their rents with the dot-com crowd. However, I owe you, and actually, I'd like to keep the unit, just in case my Clear Lake plan turns out to be a stupid idea for a guy who likes to live in the city. You make sure I get paid my rent every month, and we have a deal. I know you. She must be a winner or you wouldn't be doing this."

"Well, she is a looker, and she'll definitely bring down the average age in the building. I'll invite her to meet us for lunch at the Presidio following our golf game tomorrow. You up for that?"

"Works for me."

"And you seem to have forgotten my connections with the building owner. It'll work out," Dick said confidently.

"Now that I think about it, doesn't this deal end up costing your uncle money?"

"He can afford it, and if he found out, I suspect he'd like my motives. At least I hope so."

Dick called Coleen on her cell phone and explained what he was trying to do. She agreed to meet him at twelve thirty the next day at the Presidio Golf Club.

Conversations between the Irregulars continued over Gordys, which Toni poured for everyone. The Gordy was named after Hartmann's friend who'd been frequenting the bar since the day it opened. It meant a free half pour of whatever wine you were drinking.

16

Presidio Golf Club

Dick and Phil returned their pull carts to Presidio Golf Club's storage room and headed upstairs to the bar. They sat at a window table in the bar and added up the scorecard.

"Phil, looks like you owe me ten bucks," said Dick.

"God, I played terrible. Too much on my mind, the move and all."

Dick spotted Coleen as she was getting out of a cab. He headed to the club's front door to greet her.

"Coleen, this is Phil."

"Hi, Coleen. Welcome to the Presidio Golf Club."

"Thank you. This place is beautiful."

"That it is."

"Dick, how long have you belonged?"

"My uncle is a member and sponsored me when I moved to San Francisco. So it's been three years."

Dick provided Coleen with some background on the club. "This club has a unique history. Its structure and atmosphere are more like that of a European golf club. The club doesn't own or maintain the golf course. Rather, this building is located adjacent to the Presidio public golf course. We have an arrangement for our members to play on the course."

"That is a unique concept."

"Now for the history lesson. The course was first laid out in 1895. For many years, it operated as a joint venture between the US Army, which occupied the Presidio, and the private club. The army redesigned the course in 1962 as the Presidio Army Golf Course and vacated the property in 1989 when the Presidio was closed as a military base. The course is now part of the National Park Service."

Phil joined into the conversation. "Coleen, see that green down there? That's the ninth hole. It's named the 'Hole of Fame or Shame.' As you can see, the dining-area windows overlook the hole, and everyone here can see exactly how you played it."

"I suspect that hole would have a bad effect on my game."

"You play golf?"

"I do. My dad was a pretty good golfer, and I shamed him into teaching his girl how to play." Suddenly, Coleen's head turned and then lowered as she turned back to the guys. In a low voice, she said, "Isn't that Nancy Pelosi over there?"

"It is, and that's her husband, Paul."

"I'm impressed."

The three chatted for a while longer. Then Dick commented to Coleen, "This may be a bad idea, but let me tell you why you may want to consider it. Because of the dot-com growth in the city, it's impossible to find an apartment. If you do happen to find one, it'll probably be unaffordable on a special agent's salary, even with the bureau's San Francisco housing allowance. Phil here is moving out of a unit in the same building where I live, but he wants to keep it in the event things don't work out for him in his new venture. He's willing to, in effect, sublease it to you for what he pays in rent, which is half the going rate."

"What's the place like?" Coleen asked.

"It's a one-bedroom in an older, but well-maintained, high-rise building on the top of Russian Hill. It's clean and airy and has a view of Lombard Street. There's a closet and it includes parking, which is impossible to get in this city. What else could a girl ask for?"

"All right, guys, I'll take a look. How far is it from here?"

"It's only a couple of miles. I'll take you there now."

"Why not?"

17

San Francisco, California

When Hartmann transferred from DC to San Francisco, his dad suggested he look up his uncle George, who proved to be a godsend. The dot-com era had made living space in the city impossible to find, and if you did find something, it cost a fortune. Dick had no desire to relocate to the 'burbs and was determined to live in the city.

His visit with Uncle George solved his living arrangements quite nicely. Uncle George had retired from his executive vice president position with Pacific Gas and Electric Company several years ago. He was making good money, so he invested in an apartment building up on the top of Russian Hill. Upon his retirement, Uncle George and Aunt Martha decided to move into the city and live in the building that was part of their investment portfolio. Prior to their move, they decided to combine two of the building's units into one and remodeled it so that was more reflective of their lifestyle. Against Aunt Martha's wishes, Uncle George decided to act as the building manager, since the manager they had inherited had proven to be a disaster. Uncle George now had plenty of time on his hands. It gave him a chance to get away from Martha's extensive "honey do" list.

Just as Hartmann was about to move into a small unit in the

building, his aunt passed away. At the funeral, his uncle advised him, "Well, Dick, with Martha gone, I have no desire to stay in San Francisco. The city and this building remind me too much of Martha. I'm going to go out playing golf every day. I just bought a smaller condo unit on the sixteenth tee at Ironwood Country Club. It's in Palm Desert, down near Palm Springs. There's a great clubhouse and two fantastic golf courses."

"I certainly understand your decision," Dick replied.

"Kid, I've always liked you, so here's the deal. You know the Russian Hill building is owned by a family trust that your aunt and I set up. I've made arrangements with a firm to manage the building now that I'm leaving. They've hired a single guy as the onsite manager. There's no way I'm going let that guy have my unit. I'll let the management company know my unit is to be leased by you at the family rate."

Dick learned that the family rate was half the current dot-com rate. He now had a unit on Russian Hill with a large living room, a separate dining room, two bedrooms, and a full kitchen.

He later learned from his dad that not only did his uncle like him; he also liked the idea of an FBI agent who was part of the family being located in the building. It made him feel comfortable about the home he and Aunt Martha loved.

Dick pulled into the basement garage, where Phil was waiting for them.

"Phil, how 'bout showing Coleen your unit and see if you two can strike a deal."

"Will do. Just don't tell your uncle that I'm not living here anymore."

"My lips are sealed."

"Come on, Coleen. My unit is located on the third floor at the back of the building. It has a great view of the Crookedest Street in the World."

"What's the deal about Hartmann's uncle?"

"Oh, he didn't tell you?"

"Tell me what?"

"His uncle owns the building."

"Nice."

In the elevator, Phil filled Coleen in on his plan. He was moving to Clear Lake, one hundred miles north of San Francisco, where he had purchased a video store, but he wanted to keep the apartment just in case things didn't work out. He planned on leaving most of the furniture there, and the unit would remain in his name in order for her to keep the current rental rate, which was well under market value.

"As you see, the unit is small. It's a one bedroom, one bath, with a combined kitchen, living, and dining area."

"It's bigger than the studio I had in New York. Everything was combined into one room, and there was no view."

After viewing the apartment, and considering that Dick Hartmann lived in the building, the deal was sealed. Coleen would be able to move in on the first of the month, which was just a week away. Having settled that, they both headed for Dick's apartment.

"Well, it looks like you're going to have a new neighbor. Coleen's going to take my place," said Phil.

"Welcome to the neighborhood," Dick replied to Coleen.

"Thanks. Wow! You have quite the place here."

Coleen looked out the living room bay windows at the view of San Francisco Bay. One set of windows looked out toward Alcatraz, the infamous federal prison, and the other toward Coit Tower, across the city on Telegraph Hill.

"The neighborhood looks great. You have an unbelievable view."

"I do. Have to laugh about the Alcatraz view. Reminds me of work. The bureau put a lot of people in that place."

"This seems like a convenient location," Coleen remarked.

"It is. It's close to North Beach and Chinatown. One day, you can eat great Italian and the next, great Chinese."

"Now, that's my style of dining. Eating out."

"You went to Villanova and are Irish. Can I assume you're Catholic?"

"Can't fool you, Mr. FBI agent."

"Just wanted to let you know; you can walk to Saints Peter and Paul Catholic Church on Filbert Street. It's on the north side of Washington Square Park. It's where I go to mass."

Dick opened the door to a built-in wine cabinet located adjacent to a kitchen that rivaled that of a small restaurant. Dick perused his wine collection for a moment, selecting one from the third shelf.

"How about an Italian red? I have an idea you'll like my selection. I know Phil certainly likes it."

Phil responded, "Is that the Brunello di Montalcino you bought in Italy?

"It is."

"Coleen, you'll love this wine. I can tell Dick likes you. He only offers that wine to special friends."

"It's to reward you for allowing Coleen to take your unit." Looking back into the wine cabinet, Dick thought to himself, *I'm going to need another vacation in Italy to replenish my wine supply.*

After taking a couple of sips, Coleen commented, "I agree with Phil. This is absolutely a great wine. I love it."

Continuing to enjoy the wine, Coleen wandered through the apartment, making mental notes as she went. Dick's shoes were neatly lined up along one wall in the bedroom. Nothing was out of place. The kitchen was designed for a gourmet chef. All stainless steel and gray granite. There was a gas-fired Viking range with a smaller testing oven and a large regular oven. It had a huge stainless steel vent overhead. The built-in refrigerator was a Sub-Zero to match the Sub-Zero wine cabinet in the adjacent dining area. Two conclusions were reached by Coleen: he was a type-A personality, and he couldn't be living this lifestyle on an FBI salary.

During a bathroom visit, Coleen observed everything was clean and neat, unlike the bathrooms in a number of other bachelor pads she'd seen. On returning to the living room, the survey continued. On the wall across from the couch were two floor-to-ceiling bookshelves separated by a computer desk. Mounted on the wall above the computer was a flat-screen HDTV. She suspected the TV was tuned to sporting events most of the time.

Moving on, Coleen stood in front of a picture of a group in military uniforms. "I see you were in the army."

"Yeah. Actually the army finance corp. We paid the army's bills."

"Sounds like a tough job," she said humorously.

"It did get exciting at points."

"Who's the gal next to you? She looks pretty."

Dick wandered over to look at the photo. Coleen did not notice the couple of little tears well up in his eyes. His mind started to remember something, then went blank. "Oh, that's Diana. She was a unique person and quite attractive."

One of the bookcase shelves housed two rows of college beer mugs. The front row held mugs for USC, Brigham Young, UCLA, and LSU. The back row held two UCLA, two USC, and six mugs from other colleges.

The remainder of the shelves on the bookcases held books. There were two volumes titled *The Complete Sherlock Holmes* and *The Annotated Sherlock Holmes*. There were a number of Agatha Christie's murder mysteries, as well as books by other popular mystery writers. More serious books in the other bookcase included such titles as *The Anatomy of Motive*, which looked like a textbook, *Canadian Criminology Today*, *Crime Scene Investigation*, *Essentials of Reid Technique: Criminal/Interrogation and Confessions*, and *Investigating a Homicide Workbook*. Then there was a whole set of finance books.

Finally, Coleen's eyes drifted to several copies of the same two books lying on their sides. Turning her head to read the titles, she noted, *Hartmann's Glossary of Criminology, Second Edition* and *Criminology – Past, Present, and Future* by Richard A. Hartmann.

"I knew you lectured at the academy, but I didn't know you were a published author," she said to her new boss.

"Oh, those. When I'm not working, or when there aren't any sporting events on TV that I like, I write. Keeps me out of trouble. Seems I've gotten pretty good at it. You can take one if you want. Guaranteed to put you to sleep at night. I don't recommend trying to read the glossary from cover to cover. Not much of a plot."

"Thanks! I'll take them if you'll sign them, and I'll remember your advice on the glossary."

While Dick was signing the books, he said, "I'd like to ask for something from you in return."

"You can ask."

"I'd like a Villanova beer mug to add to my collection."

"Done. I suspect it's to add to your collection over there. Let me try some Sherlock Homes deductive reasoning on why you want the mug."

"Go for it."

"The front row of mugs represents you and your current squad members, excluding me. The back row represents former members of your squad."

"Doctor Watson—I mean, Doctor Ryan—astute observations, as Holmes would say. You're well on your way to becoming a fellow criminologist."

"Thank you, Professor Hartmann. Do you have a hat and pipe like Mr. Holmes?"

"Not yet. Nor do I take drugs or live a bohemian, messy lifestyle. I just happen to like Sherlock Holmes. I also like 007, but I don't live his lifestyle either."

"From what I've seen of your place, your lifestyle is closer to 007 than Holmes. Now, Sherlock, tell me about the back row of mugs."

"Well, first, I can say that no one on my squad has been killed in the line of duty. In fact, they are all alive and well. Jim Mead (UCLA) and Vivian Marr (Brigham Young) are back at headquarters in DC. Matt Fremont (LSU), you probably met at the academy. He's teaching interrogation techniques back there."

"Oh, my God. Yes, I do know him. He scared me to death when he interrogated me in an exercise."

"That's got to be him. He's very good at what he does. I used to watch him interrogate people while he was working in my squad. Some people just have a natural knack for it. Bob McMillan (USC) left the agency. He's teaching history at a private college outside Santa Barbara. The rest are working in various field offices across the country."

"Just curious. How'd you and Phil meet?"

"Here in the building."

"Yeah," Phil said. "I'm going to miss this place. It's been my home for eighteen years."

They bantered back and forth over a second bottle of wine, and then Coleen asked Dick to call her a cab and Phil headed off to his unit. It was still fairly early in the afternoon, but they had to do their weekend chores and get ready for another week of work. Dick thought about asking Coleen to stay for a while, but he decided there would be plenty of time to get to know her better.

As Dick washed and dried the wine glasses, he thought to himself, *God, she's good-looking.*

18

FBI Field Office, San Francisco, California

Most of the cubicles were still empty as Hartmann walked from the lobby of the San Francisco FBI Field Office to his office. He'd scheduled an early meeting on this Monday morning with the special agent in charge, Mark Gambirasi, to bring him up-to-date on what'd happened in Fresno and how the investigation was going.

Following the meeting, he returned to his office and called Daniel to see how the security-system analysis was going. Daniel was still half asleep. He explained that the FBI Butte, Montana, Information Technology Center (ITC) must have worked over the entire weekend on its part of the project. The edited edition was ready for review on his laptop.

A text message from Dick requested all of the Animals to meet in one of the large conference rooms at 9:00 a.m. to go over what Daniel had learned.

Dick's commanding voice announced, "Okay, ladies and gentlemen. Let's start the show. Daniel, tell us what you have."

Daniel started with, "Here are the parameters I gave our techs in Butte. First, I set a timeframe of the past three months. Then I indicated that I only wanted images with Shaw in them. Based on those parameters, the techs came up with an hour and three minutes of video for review."

Dick responded, "Okay, everyone. Let's watch the movies. Sorry, no popcorn. I want everyone to keep your eyes peeled and note anything you spot that might help us solve this case. Daniel, can I assume there'll be a time stamp indicated on the surveillance pictures?"

"There will be, Boss."

"Everyone should use the time-stamp reference when making your notes. Daniel, roll it."

Dick leaned back in his chair with his hands clasped behind his head. This was a tedious, but important, part of detective work. You're looking for some little thing that will break the case. He was really interested in what he'd notice in the surveillance pictures versus what his Animals might spot. Multiple eyes and brains were important and picked up different things.

It took more than two hours to view the video, with numerous segments being looked at over and over again. Following a break, they compared notes. Between the five of them, there were eighteen segments they wanted to look at in detail. From these, they agreed to narrow it down to eight segments.

"Boss, Shaw seems to have an interest in a particular section of the mailroom," noted Daniel.

"That he does, and in the March 1 through March 4 segment, he seems to be taking some mail out of one of those plastic mail cartons. It also looks like the station or position where the box is located belongs to just one guy."

"Does anyone have any other thoughts about the material we've looked at this morning?" asked Dick.

All agreed that there didn't seem to be anything else that popped out.

"All right. Clean up anything you have on your desks. Tomorrow, we head back to Fresno. I'll drive my car. Who else wants to drive?"

Brian volunteered to drive and said he'd pick up Daniel. Dick planned to drive Harriett and Coleen.

Dick asked Daniel to call his new buddy Jeff at the IRS center to have him get copies of the discs from the past three months.

"When you get the discs, have Butte look for Shaw on them. Okay, people, at five tonight, I'll buy you a drink at Harrington's. Then we are off for a very sober week or two in Fresno. Any questions?"

Coleen asked, "Where's Harrington's?"

"Just latch onto one of the other Animals at five. They won't lead you astray."

19

Harry Harrington's Pub, San Francisco, California

Harry Harrington's Pub is located adjacent to the San Francisco Civic Center, directly across Polk Street and the Federal Building. It's basically an Irish pub that isn't trendy or flashy. Rather, Harrington's has plenty of seating, a jukebox, and a blue-collar look. Not the place where you'd expect the lunchtime and after-work clientele to consist of city, state, and federal civil servants of all types and ages. After the white-collar civil servants leave, it becomes a working man's bar, with stiffer drinks and friendly regulars.

Harrington's had been there longer than any of the agents at the San Francisco FBI Field Office could remember. Dick was introduced to the place shortly after being transferred to San Francisco. It wasn't his favorite place, but it was the closest bar to his office, and it was frequented after work by a number of the other agents.

Doc, the bartender, had, over time, developed a group of loyal customers, some of whom were there the day it opened. If you believed the old timers' stories, Harrington's had changed little since opening day. In fact, the walls probably had the same paint as they did on opening day. Display cases contained police department badges from across the country, and old-time boxing and baseball pictures covered the walls. On a ledge just below the ceiling directly across from the bar was a collection of old-time cars and a train set. A picture of Michael Collins, "The Lost Leader," was located above the back of the bar, and a statue of Saint Patrick holding an American flag sat on the bar. There was a single pinball machine on which you could play a baseball game called Triple Play—when it worked.

Dick was standing at the bar talking with Doc about the weekend college basketball games when his Animals arrived en masse. They headed directly to Dick, who welcomed them and Coleen to Harrington's, and then introduced her to Doc.

Doc, in his gravelly, low, quiet, Bronx voice, asked, "What'll you have, Miss Coleen? I understand Dickey here's buying."

Coleen immediately responded with, "Doc, do I detect a New York accent? God, that's music to my ears. Since I'm in California now, what kind of wine do you have?"

Hearing Coleen's question, the rest of the squad smiled and quickly looked down, waiting for Doc's reply.

"Miss Coleen, thank you for the compliment. As respects the wine, we have some white shit." With that, he pointed to a well-aged box of chablis that apparently had been sitting on the back of the bar for some time. "And, sorry to say, we have been out of the red shit for some time. Want some of the chablis, or do you want to try something else?"

"Well, I'm thinking about the chablis. What's the expiration date on that box? Oh, I mean the vintage date on that box?"

"Oh. I can see you're a lady of taste."

"That's right. Now that I've thought about it, chablis is really not to my liking. How 'bout a cosmopolitan?" Coleen replied.

The squad started to really chuckle now. They'd heard the line that would be coming several times before.

"Miss Coleen—a good Irish name, by the way—for your

information, this is a bar. It's not a magazine stand. We don't sell no fuckin' cosmopolitans here."

"Doc, I think over time, I might get to like you. How about a Jameson's on the rocks?"

"Miss Coleen, you've got it, and I'll make it a double on the house. Good choice."

Once the initiation harassment was over, the rest of the squad ordered their beers. Coleen commented to Dick, "You seem to spend a lot of time in bars for an FBI agent."

Dick thought for a while and then responded, "Hadn't really thought about it. San Francisco is probably a lot like New York or DC. People want to get out of their apartments, or condos, and be with other people. I have my bachelor pad up on Russian Hill with its great view, but it's nice to get out and meet people. As you may have noted, I have a lot of friends at my watering holes, and often, the discussions get pretty interesting."

Daniel, overhearing the conversation, chimed in, "Coleen, I don't know if you know it, but Dick is called 'The Professor' by many at the bureau. He periodically teaches an advanced criminology course at the academy. He's known for solving unsolvable crimes. I suspect you were selected for his squad because of a combination of your IQ and how you scored on those psychological tests they gave you back at the academy. You've been assigned to be trained by a master."

Dick stopped Daniel by saying, "Okay, Daniel. That's enough. Coleen, don't believe everything Daniel says—just some of it. I do know that you have a very high IQ. Can't comment on the psychological tests. I also know you're quite athletic. Heard something about you getting the nickname of 'Killer' at the academy."

"Okay, *Pro-fess-or*! And, how in the hell did you hear about the 'Killer' thing? I'm not even going to respond to that."

"Understand perfectly. As you've already figured out, I keep my lines open to the academy staff, and I do thank you for the honor, Ms.

Coleen, of being called 'Professor.' I like to be called 'The Professor' and instructing at the academy. Not only because of the satisfaction teaching gives me, but also because being at the academy gives me access to other instructors who clue me in on the best recruits and their attitudes—something you don't find in personnel files. Then it's just a matter of lobbying with the right people in DC to get them assigned to my squad of Animals. I love it. Screw the system."

Dick turned and called for Harriett to come closer. "Harriett, I want you to clue Coleen in on how to pack for quick travel. You know, the duffle bag that can be grabbed in a moment's notice, packed and ready for a quick, multiday trip."

"Will do."

With that, Dick closed out the tab. Looking at his team members, he said, "Get a good night's sleep. We're headed back to Fresno in the morning. We need to be sharp."

20

Dogg Pound, Fresno, California

It was late in the day, but still warm, as Ed Abramson drove west from his apartment. He pulled the visor down to protect his eyes from the blazing sun. He turned onto East Jensen Avenue and then left on South Walnut Avenue, venturing into the southwest Fresno neighborhood the locals called the "Dogg Pound."

Fresno's Dogg Pound neighborhood was the city's low-income area, heavily populated by Hispanics. It was comprised of dense, run-down housing units and large apartment complexes, surrounded by vacant lots and fields. The area suffered from physical neglect—a true sinkhole. The driveways were unpaved and lined with old tires. Garages were dilapidated, and the houses were usually protected with steel bars bolted to the front of the windows. The Dogg Pound looked more like a desert, with houses and unattached garages scattered around. The only vegetation consisted of native cactus. Lawns with grass were not part of the landscape.

Abramson chuckled to himself as he spotted a large, unleashed dog of questionable breeding pooping in front of a house. Yes, he was back in the Dogg Pound.

The area got its name from the Bulldog Gang, who had controlled the neighborhood for years. The Dogg Pound belonged to the Bulldogs. Even the Fresno police had given up trying to control crime on its streets. The cops were seldom called to the area because the gang members retaliated against anyone who called the cops in. Civilians who unknowingly ended up living there cowered in fear. If the Fresno PD did respond to a call, no one would tell them anything. They seldom patrolled the area, particularly at night. It wasn't even safe for them. In their place, the Bulldogs established their own form of order and protection, so a rough quiet prevailed over the Dogg Pound. This is where Alejandro Gomez lived.

Ed was just about to turn onto Gomez's street when he spotted a 1980s Chevy Blazer coming toward him with no apparent driver. There was a young Mexican girl dancing alongside. Music was blaring from the vehicle and several gang members were laughing from the porch of a nearby house. Ed slowly worked his way around the vehicle, and the girl, as she was running to get back into the driver's seat. He watched in the rearview mirror as the girl regained control of the Blazer with a big smile on her face.

He turned the corner and pulled up to Alejandro's house. Compared to the rest of the houses on the block, Alejandro's house was reasonably maintained and much bigger than the others. Three cars were parked on the front lawn, or what would've been a front lawn, if it wasn't used as a parking lot. Ed parked his car next to a blue, two-seated Jaguar. He knew this car was out of place. It would've been jacked in a minute if it belonged to anyone other than Al Gomez.

Ed walked up to the group of husky gang members that were hanging in front of the house. They had that gangbanger look about them, with their baggy shorts or pants and red "Bulldog" gang shirts. Because of the heat wave, some were bare-chested, proudly displaying their gang-identifying tats. All of them had Bulldog tattoos—some on their arms, some on their chests, others on their shaved heads.

He was first greeted with barking from the group. Joining in on the barking was a leashed bulldog. Barking was a fellow Bulldog greeting, a scare tactic to strangers, and a taunting to police. The barking stopped, except from the dog, when Ed was recognized by the leader of the group. He was waved forward and greeted at the front door by Al's current girlfriend, a stunning, lightly tan-colored Mexican girl with a nice ass and long, black hair. Al seemed to have a new girlfriend every time Ed came over.

Ed had met Gomez in the marines during a tour in Okinawa. He was in his brigade, but he ran into trouble with the locals. Gomez had spent a year in the brig and was then dishonorably discharged from the corp for raping a fourteen-year-old girl. Ed had done his best to protect his young Hispanic corporal, but to no avail. There was no question he'd raped the girl, and there was no excuse for that. If there was any excuse, it was that no one was paying attention to what'd been happening on the island since the US military established bases on it during World War II. Young US troops with high testosterone levels and too many drinks trolled one of the many wild and crazy island bars. They couldn't tell the hookers from the flirting schoolgirls who hung around the area—which was a recipe for disaster.

Gomez was in the wrong place at the wrong time. A new base commander, in conjunction with the local police, ended up making an example of Gomez to satisfy the Japanese people's ire. They were up in arms about the rapes occurring on their island. Al was one of the first to be prosecuted and convicted for what he did. There were plenty before him that had done the same thing, but their crimes were ignored.

He changed in the brig, which was a breeding ground for gangs. If you were Hispanic and came out of the brig with a dishonorable discharge, there wasn't a lot waiting for you in society when you came home. You joined with others like you to fight a different type of war and live in a different type of society.

Al always remembered Ed favorably because of what he'd tried to do for him in Okinawa. Unfortunately for Ed, over time, Al's power and the money he had to spread around brought him under Al's control.

"Hi, my gringo friend. How's it going?"

"Damn fuckin' great, *amigo*."

"Good to see you, Sergeant. Come on into the entertainment room and see my new fifty-inch, high-def TV. You should hear the sound. It's hooked up to the home entertainment system. It's like being in a theater," said Gomez.

"By the way, thanks for the entertainment."

"What entertainment?"

"The dancing girl running next to the Chevy Blazer with no driver," Ed replied.

"Oh, that. Had nothing to do with it. It's kind of weird, isn't it? It's something that got started over in Vallejo by some rapper named E-40. It's called 'ghost riding.' See it all the time now. Carlotta, get Ed a beer!"

"Mr. Sergeant, what kind of beer would you like?" Al's girlfriend asked.

"I suspect you have a Dos Equis."

"My friend, you remember our favorite beer. Of course we have it. Carlotta, bring me another one too," Al interjected.

Swigging their beers from the bottles, Ed and Al walked through the living and dining room areas. Ed noted a change in décor. The rooms were set up like offices, including several computers. Three gang members sat at the computers. One appeared to be working on some sort of list. The other two were playing Internet computer games.

"What's with the layout?"

"Oh, that. We've expanded our operations. I'll explain later. Come. Let's check out the entertainment room."

The first bedroom off the hallway leading to the back of the house had been converted into an entertainment room. Facing the new TV was a white-leather couch and two leather, theater-type chairs with armrests and cup holders, or rather, beer-bottle holders.

The couch was occupied by one of the gang members and his girl-friend. As they entered, the couple quickly separated themselves from each other. She put her blouse and bra back on and turned around to look at them. Apparently, they weren't that interested in watching the movie playing on the big screen.

Al shouted, "Diego, zip your pants up. We're all going down to Dos Amigos to show my friend Ed here how we have a good time. You drive everyone down in the van."

"Fucking right on. Come on, bitch."

"Al, before we go I need to make a head call," Ed said.

Al responded, "You never could hold your beer. You know where the head is."

As Ed passed Al's bedroom, he glanced in. Nothing had changed since his last visit. Unlike the rest of the house, everything was neatly arranged. It looked like a senior NCO's room in a barrack. There was a standard-size bed, but it was covered with a tightly pulled brown blanket that he was sure you could bounce a quarter off. In front of the bed was a military footlocker. There was a dresser with a mirror above it. Al's marine dog tags were hanging on a nail on the wall next to the mirror. The wood floor was swept clean. There was no carpet. *I guess this makes Al feel comfortable. The Marines had taught him well, except for his stupid mistake,* Ed thought.

Ed found everyone in the front yard waiting for him. He jumped into Al's Jag. Beers still in hand, they tore their way through the streets of Fresno to Dos Amigos, down on Martin Luther King.

Al was a silent partner in the Dos Amigos restaurant with a middle-aged couple who had not wanted to leave the neighborhood. It was a good partnership for them. Nobody ever hassled them, and they did a great business.

From past experience, Ed knew that this was going to be a long night. A hangover was guaranteed in the morning. But he also knew that if past experience were any predictor, he'd end up in one of Al's houses with a horny Mexican gal, or maybe even two from the restaurant. The odds were pretty good, because he was a friend of Al's and no one wanted to cross Al. No one in Fresno challenged the "Big Dawg" of the Bulldogs.

Al parked the Jag right in front of the restaurant. The spot was vacant because of the fire hydrant and the fact that it was Al's spot.

Ed followed Al to his usual booth in the alcove between the bar and the dining room. As soon as they sat down, a very attractive waitress came from behind the bar. She was well put together and had jet-black hair. She was wearing an enticingly low-cut, black dress, which just managed to keep her breasts from popping out. It was short and showed plenty of leg.

"Ed, meet Heather."

She bent over the table and said, "Hello, Ed."

Great view. Great tits. Bet she gets great tips.

As was tradition, Al ordered two depth charges. As the drinks were being served, Diego showed up with the rest of the gang. He and Carlotta started to join them in the booth, but Al waved them away. "Give Sergeant and me some time to talk in private. I have a bar tab running. Diego, make sure everyone gets whatever they want, and have Heather send over an order of nachos."

Once they left, Al leaned toward Ed and said, "My friend, you're the only person I can talk to."

"Come on, Al. Look around. You have all kinds of friends."

Laughingly, Al responded, "Ed, those aren't my friends. Those are gangbangers. They're members of what has ended up as my dysfunctional family. I'm their really bad-guy father figure. I learned well in the brig how to be a very bad guy. Now that I'm in this position of power, I love it. I really love it. Society doesn't want me, and I'm living a pretty good life in this other world by being a fuckin' miserable dick.

It's a whole other world, you know. We're not far from being animals. Our behavior is lowered to the most basic level, without the emotions a human being is supposed to possess. Most people in society don't want to know about this seamy world, nor admit to it."

"My friend, you're right about that."

"I'm a fuckin' A-hole and enjoy being one. I have really learned to play the role. I'm this gang's fuckin' drill sergeant. That's the model I use being their leader."

Al paused and stared at the group at the bar. "Look at them. Most of my soldiers are on parole. The younger recruits have been in a juvie home, and most of the older ones have served hard time. All of them have assaulted, knifed, or shot someone. That's how they've proven themselves—even the young ones."

"You know what six of them did last week? They cleaned up our neighborhood. Some stupid black family moved in just three blocks from me. Can you believe that? You know what I had them do? I had them do a drive-by. They ended up shooting into the house and killing the twelve-year-old daughter. They moved out the next day. Some newspaper reporter referred to it as a new form of ethnic cleansing. We're just protecting our neighborhood."

"I thought you got along with the blacks in our unit?"

"We tolerated each other. Had to, to work as a unit. Needed to protect each other's backs if we went into combat. But, in the brig, there are the blacks, the whites, and the Hispanics. You learn quickly to stay with your own."

Al looked again at the group. "You see Garcia over there? He left Fresno at sixteen to check out San Francisco. He hustled drugs on the streets and was picked up by the SFPD. The juvie court, with the blessing of the San Francisco district attorney, sent him to a group home in Visalia. He simply walked away from the home after a couple of weeks and returned here. No one bothered to come after him.

There are too many of them. He became a member of our gang by shooting a homeless man."

Heather returned to the table with the nachos and set them in the center of the table between Al and Ed, again bending over to display her tip-improvers.

Ed took a nacho and dipped it into a section of the plate that was overflowing with cheese, beef, and sauce. After eating several of them and wiping his mouth with his napkin, he responded to Al, "I'm sorry the corp didn't work out for you. You were a good marine until you got screwed."

"You're right, you know. I was actually proud to be a marine. The corp was structured. That was good for me. It was exciting and it consisted of mainly a great group of guys, mostly like me. Of course, there were some assholes. It fit me well, but that's history that can't be fixed now. But, I've taken what the corp taught me and I'm applying it here in Fresno. I'm taking a disorganized street gang and turning them into a well-run criminal enterprise. We're the best at selling PCP, Mexican tar heroin, methamphetamines, and marijuana on the streets of Fresno. Now we are getting into identity theft."

"So that's why you have all those computers back at your place?"

"Yeah, that's why."

"Well, you're right that neither of us can go back now," Ed replied.

"How did the cleanup at the center go?"

"Shaw's dead. From what I hear, it went smoothly."

"Good job. What effect will it have on our operations?" Al asked.

"I love your calling them 'operations.' Sounds like we're back in the military."

"You know, I watched a show on PBS the other night. Yes, PBS. On that big-screen TV of mine. It was about the old mob. When they started, they were a lot like today's gangs. Then one of them decided they should get structured like a business and even get involved in legit businesses. That's what I'm doing, except with a military flavor.

Did you realize the US military is the largest business in the world? I got that from PBS too."

"Al, I love your dreams. To answer your questions, of course, with Shaw gone, we have no way of getting any more files with the data we need. It's unlikely I could find another Mrs. Shaw."

"How was the sex with her?"

"Not as good as the sex with one of your girls. Any chance of my getting some tonight?"

"You know I always take care of you. How about Heather over there?"

"You're on."

"Okay. What about the Spanish Language Unit operation?"

"It's still up and running, but I understand there are some asshole auditors all over the joint. We should back off for a while."

"Okay. I'll tell them to close up shop for a while. We have plenty to do processing of the files we have from the other operation. It looks like we need to speed the processing up. What're you going to do about Mrs. Shaw?"

"I may need your help on that. She's now a major problem for us. She knows too much."

"Understand. I'll arrange for the problem to go away."

With the business over, Al shouted to Carlotta, "Carlotta, get your ass over here. I'm lonely, and tell Heather to join us."

21

Fresno, California

Dick and Brian picked up their passengers in their Bucars (cars issued by the bureau) and headed out on the three-hour drive to Fresno. A group conversation was held between the cars by cell phone. The decision was made for everyone to meet at the Fresno Resident Agency Office and then have lunch together. After that, they would head for the IRS center.

Robin Carien-Murray, the special agent in charge, had a meeting room reserved for them. As some of her agents were involved in the case, Dick asked her to sit in on the beginning of the meeting. Once everyone settled in with their coffees, Dick asked Robin, "Did your agents babysitting Mrs. Shaw and Ed Abramson have anything to report?"

"Not in regards to Mrs. Shaw. From what they told me, she was acting like a perfectly normal person. She never left the house. As for Abramson, that was a different story. He went into a section of the city pretty much controlled by the gangs. They didn't follow him into the area, because they would've been immediately spotted as outsiders. They did see him coming out of the area riding in a different car with a local gang leader. They ended up at a nearby Mexican restaurant that is frequented by local gang members. Abramson left with a girl from the restaurant. They went back into the same gang-controlled area of the city."

"Interesting. We're going to have to find out more about Mr. Abramson. Thanks for the update, Robin. We're going to spend some more time looking at the surveillance pictures from the IRS center."

"The room is all yours. See you later," she responded.

Brian attached his computer to the monitor in the room. "Okay, my fellow Animals, here's what the techs in Butte have come up with."

The edited video showed Shaw in various areas in and around the mailroom. He seemed to be concentrating on the same area as they'd seen in the previous pictures. In some of the earlier shots, he could be seen taking some items out of a specific mailroom carton in the early evening and then returning them twenty or thirty minutes later.

After a period of time, Dick said, "Hey, Brian, check with your newfound buddy Jeff at the Center Security Office and determine what type of mail goes into the carton Shaw showed so much interest in. Retrace Shaw's exact steps and actions. Go down after working hours and take the mail out of that carton and copy it. Then return it back to the same carton. Also, find out who the person is that has control over that mail carton."

Robin stuck her head in the door. "How're things going?"

Dick answered, "Perfect timing. We just finished. Robin, would you have one of your agents work with Agent Foster to see if they can figure out who the people are that Abramson was talking with at the Mexican restaurant? It may or may not be useful, but it needs to be checked out."

"Would be happy to. Why don't I see if the agent that'll be working with Agent Foster is in, and then we can all grab a sandwich?"

"Sounds like a plan."

22

Fresno, California

Dick looked down at his cell phone. "Hi, Robin."

"Hi, Dick. Harriett is on the line with me. We just reviewed the most recent report from the agents following Abramson. They identified the person he went to the restaurant with as a local gang leader, Alejandro Gomez. The person he left the restaurant with was one of the restaurant's cocktail waitresses, Heather Johansson. Abramson apparently stayed overnight in the gang area and was seen driving his car out of the area the next morning. I have some pictures from surveillance."

"Interesting. I'm fairly convinced that Abramson didn't directly kill Shaw, but he may've been involved in setting it up. Do you think the local gang has anything to do with what's happening at the center?"

"God, I hope not. If they do, it could prove to be a major disaster. We need to talk with Doug Smith and let him know what we've found out."

Dick and Robin agreed that they should try to find out more about what had happened at the restaurant. Harriett from Dick's team and Agent Andrew Marx from Robin's team were assigned the task. They picked up copies of the restaurant surveillance photos and headed out.

It was now two thirty, and the lunch crowd was gone. Dos Amigos Restaurant was just about empty. Harriett and Andrew went up to the bartender, who was talking with one of the cocktail waitresses.

In a soft voice, Agent Marx said, "Hi, I'm Special Agent Marx with the FBI, and this is Agent Foster." As he spoke, they both slid their credentials across the top of the bar for viewing. "We'd like to ask you some questions about a patron who was at this restaurant yesterday.

Foster then slid one of the surveillance photos that showed Abramson across the bar top. "Did you see this person here yesterday?"

The bartender appeared to be reluctant to say anything. "Look, guys, we get all kinds of people in here every day. I don't really pay any attention to them." He looked again at the picture and said, "That looks like it was shot in the evening. I get off work at four-thirty in the afternoon."

Marx noted an expression of recognition on the cocktail waitress's face and said, "Miss, you look like you recognize him."

Reluctantly, she said, "No, I don't recognize him. Uh, but the guy in the back of the picture is Jorge."

"Who is Jorge?"

"Jorge used to work here. We went to the same high school, Roosevelt High. I used to date him. Great kisser! Lots of fun!"

"Can you tell me anything else about Jorge?"

"Is he in some sort of trouble?"

"No. Not at all. We're just interested in the guy he was with."

"We don't date anymore, but we're still friends. He's a great guy. As I said, he used to work here as a waiter. He comes in all the time and meets with a bunch of his friends, including this other guy in the picture. He and his friends are nice to me and are great tippers."

"Interesting. Do you know where Jorge works now?"

"The same place most of his friends work; that IRS building over on Butler," the waitress replied.

"Do you know what he does there?"

"I'm not sure. I know his friends got him the job. Most of them graduated from Fresno State. They took the special IRS courses over there, which, in this town, just about guarantees you a job in the IRS building. Everyone likes him. He would talk with those guys a lot, and they helped him get the job over there."

Harriett, noting the cocktail waitress's name on her badge, asked, "Grace, the other guy in the picture that comes in sometimes, do you know anything else about him?"

"Sure. Everyone knows him. He owns a part of this place. That's Mr. Gomez."

"And you have never seen the other guy before?"

"I don't think so, but he looks somewhat familiar. I'm not sure why. He may have come in a long time ago. Can't really say."

"Can you give us Jorge's last name?"

"Sure, it's Jorge Garcia."

"Thanks, Grace. You've been very helpful. Can I get your last name?" Harriett asked.

"Sure, it's Ocampo. Grace Ocampo."

As Harriett and Andrew returned to their car, Andrew said, "Well, I can certainly fill you in on Mr. Gomez. He's a well-known gangbanger in Fresno, with a rap sheet a mile long. Jorge Garcia is another matter. We need to find out more about him, particularly as he works at the IRS center."

As the Bucar pulled away from the restaurant, the bartender picked up the phone and made a call.

23

IRS Service Center, Fresno, California

Agent Brian Brooks found Jeff in the IRS center's security office monitoring room and asked, "Hey, Jeff, ready for some more sleuthing?"

"I sure am. This is a lot more fun than just sitting here watching monitors. I can't believe I'm working with the FBI."

"Well, you are, and what you're doing is truly of great help to us."

Brian set up his laptop on the desk in front of Jeff. "Jeff, I want to share some of what our techs in Montana came up with. There's Shaw in the mailroom. Do you have any idea what that particular mail carton that Shaw keeps looking at each day is for?"

"No idea. Why don't we go over there and take a look?"

"No. Let's wait until after the shift to do that. I don't want to tip anybody off that we're interested in them."

"Okay with me. I have nothing to do this evening, and I'm really interested in what's happening."

"One more thing. We noted that the mail carton is picked up each day by the same person. See there on the video? Do you know who he is?"

"No idea."

"Okay. The Montana techs enlarged the picture of the guy. While we're waiting, we can go through the ID pictures of the mailroom staff and see if we can identify him."

"Good idea. How many people work in the mailroom?"

"About two hundred, which is a lot better than looking at the entire two thousand two hundred photos we have on file. We can narrow it down further by eliminating all of the photos of females."

"Okay. Let's get to work."

An hour and twenty minutes later, Jeff shouted out, "Isn't this the guy?"

They both looked closely at the picture from Montana and the one on the screen and agreed that it was the same person.

"His name is Jorge Garcia. I'll pull up his file."

With Brian looking over his shoulder, Jeff brought the Jorge Garcia employee file up on his computer screen.

> Jorge Rodrigo Garcia
> Date of Hire: 03.01.02
> Position: Term Mail Clerk
> Born: 06.07.82
> Sex: Male
> Place of Birth: Villahermosa, Mexico
> Citizen: Yes. Naturalized along with parents in 1994
> Background Check: Approved 02.17.02
> Education: Graduated Roosevelt High School
> Address: 671 S. Cedar Ave., Fresno, CA 93702
> Home Phone: 559-555-8961

Armed with this information, Brian called Hartmann's cell phone.

"Interesting. That's the same name Harriett came up with during her visit to the restaurant. Looks like we have our first break."

Dick concluded the cell call with, "It's almost four in the after-noon. What time can you and Jeff look at that mail carton?"

"Jeff says about five-thirty. There's only one shift in the mailroom, and they leave at five. Probably be back to you about six-thirty."

"Okay. Just keep me posted. Coleen and I are with the IRS audit crew. They still haven't come up with anything. Based on the infor-mation you and Harriett got, I'll get the assistant US attorney up to speed. We'll need approvals for some wiretaps, and hopefully, we'll have some warrants in the near future."

"I'll call Daniel and Harriett. Let's all plan to meet in the security office at six-thirty to compare notes and see what we have."

Hartmann and his team situated themselves in a corner of the security office, away from the security personnel on duty. After Harriett filled them in on what she'd learned at the restaurant, Brian showed them a printout of Jorge Garcia's employment information. They now had a lead that might take them somewhere.

Dick indicated, "I've been in touch with the assistant US attorney, and we have approval for wiretaps on both Jorge's and Abramson's phones. Plus, we have a warrant for their financial records. Daniel's working on getting wiretaps in place and copies of their financial records."

"Brian, how did you and Jeff make out with the mail pickup?"

"Here're the copies of what we got. They came out of a mail carton labeled 'Spanish Language Unit.'"

"Looks like most of this stuff is letters to or from Hispanics."

Brian said, "Notice anything similar about these letters?"

Harriett responded, "Yeah. They all seem to involve Hispanics who are paying additional taxes. Many of them indicate a check for the owed taxes is enclosed."

"You've got it. Jeff, what's the Spanish Language Unit?"

"From what I understand, it's a unit initially formed about twenty years ago to assist Spanish-speaking taxpayers on the telephone. Over time, it was expanded from just telephone assistance to include Spanish language forms and correspondence because of the increased number of Hispanics filing tax returns. The unit is located over in the north side of the building. It's called the SLU for short. There's a separate office with about twenty Spanish speaking people in the unit."

Dick asked Jeff, "In the morning, can you get us a list of the employees in that unit, along with their pictures and employee information?"

"Sure can."

"All right, everyone, it's been a long day. Let's head to the hotel and get some grub."

Dick drove the bureau SUV out of the IRS center driveway, and just as they reached the street, his cell phone rang. He said hello, listened for a moment, and then slammed on the brakes and hit the dashboard with his fist.

He looked at Brian sitting next to him and said, loud enough for everyone to hear, "Mrs. Shaw's been shot. That was Robin Murray. The agent following Mrs. Shaw saw the shooting and fired at the suspects. Brian, look at the Fresno map and get us to the Vons Grocery Store on Blackstone Avenue, between Shaw and East Ashland Avenue."

24

Fresno, California

As Dick turned the corner, they could see the flashing red lights several blocks ahead. He pressed the accelerator pedal down to the floor and then hit the brakes and screeched to a stop in front of the yellow police tape that'd been strung across the street.

They showed their credentials to the Fresno PD officers on the scene and then walked over to Resident Agent Robin Murray. She was standing with the two agents who had been conducting the surveillance on Mrs. Shaw. They were talking with the two Fresno PD detectives who were assigned to the shooting investigation.

"Detectives, this is Agent Hartmann from our San Francisco Field Office, and these are members of his squad. Do you mind if I go over what happened one more time to bring our San Francisco agents up to speed?" Agent Murray asked.

"Not at all."

Robin explained, "We had surveillance on Mrs. Shaw because of an ongoing FBI case. My agents watched her go into the supermarket over there. About a half an hour later, she returned to her car with a basket full of groceries. Suddenly, a white Ford Taurus with four young Hispanics in it pulled out of a parking spot across from her car. One of them shouted something at her, and then two of them fired at her with handguns. The Taurus squealed out of the driveway of the parking lot and headed north on Ashland. My agents called the incident in and then went to check on Mrs. Shaw. She was still alive. They performed first aid on her. Detective, do you know how she's doing?"

"The last we heard is that the EMTs were working on her, so as of a few minutes ago, she was still alive. As to her condition at this moment, I have no idea," the detective replied.

"Agents, we just got word that one of our patrol cars located the Taurus. It was abandoned about two miles from here. They must have had a backup car." One of the patrol offices commented.

25

It was a little after eleven in the evening when Grace left the Dos Amigos Restaurant and walked to her car, just down the block. She was surprised to see Jorge sitting on the hood.

"Jorge, what're you doing here?"

"I was just thinking about you."

"Oh, that sounds nice."

"How 'bout you giving me a lift?"

"Sure. Get in."

Grace turned the engine on and put the car in gear. "Where to?"

"A house on South Walnut in the Dogg Pound."

"Jorge, you're kidding. I'm not driving into that area."

"Grace, I'm afraid you have to. There's someone there who wants to see you."

"And who would that be?"

"Al Gomez."

"No, Jorge. I'm not going to go there."

Jorge pulled a knife from his jacket pocket and held it next to Grace's side. "Grace, I don't want to hurt you, but we are going to that house now."

Grace shouted, "Why are you doing this to me?"

"Grace, I like you. I like you a lot, but this has to be done. The reason you have to come with me is that Al heard that you may have talked to the wrong people about the Bulldogs."

"No, Jorge. No. You know he'll kill me."

"Sorry, Grace." With that, he pricked Grace in the side with his knife. Her body jerked away from the knife blade and the car swerved, almost going up on the sidewalk. A small amount of blood appeared on her blouse just above her waist. Grace now realized how serious this was.

"Jorge, what the fuck are you doing? You don't have to stab me with your fuckin' knife. That hurt."

"Look, Grace. You don't mess with the Bulldogs. I really didn't want to do that, but you're so fucking stubborn. Let's just get to Al's place."

Following Jorge's directions, Grace pulled up in front of Al's house. The ever-present Bulldog bodyguards in their red shirts started barking. Jorge took the car keys out of the ignition and walked to the other side of car, where he grabbed Grace by the arm and forcibly took her up to the front door. The barking got louder as she screamed. Jorge dragged her through the living and dining room. Three of the Bulldogs playing Grand Theft Auto on computers didn't even bother to look up.

Grace stopped fighting as she was led into the entertainment room. Al, his girlfriend, and three of the gang members were watching a soccer match between the Los Tricolors, the National Soccer Team of Mexico, and Costa Rica on the big screen TV. There were open pizza boxes on the table, and beer and soda cans scattered everywhere. Everyone was shouting for the Tricolors. Al rose from the couch, and suddenly, the party stopped.

Al shouted, "Mute the fucking sound! We have serious business to conduct." Looking at Grace, he spoke in a calm voice. "Hey, bitch, get over here."

Grace slowly walked over to where Al was sitting as Jorge quickly left.

"I understand you talked to some cops. What did you tell them? And don't lie. I already know most of it."

"I didn't tell them anything."

Al leaned over to his girlfriend, Christine, and asked, "Do you believe her?"

"No way. That bitch is lying."

"See if you can convince that bitch to tell us the truth."

With that, Christine got up and grabbed Grace by the hair and pushed her to the floor. She sat on her and slugged her in the chest and face. Grace was smart enough not to throw a serious punch at Al's girlfriend. All of the gang was watching the one-sided catfight that ensued. Finally, Al had the gang separate them.

Al got up and grabbed Grace by the neck with one hand. He leaned close to her face and whispered into her ear, "Who were they?"

Grace looked up at him with her bloodied face covered with tears. In a whimpering voice, she said, "They weren't local cops. They were FBI."

"You've got to be shitting me. What'd they want?"

"They had a picture of some guy. I didn't know the guy. But I recognized Jorge. He was standing in the background."

"What did you tell them?"

"I told them that I used to date Jorge."

"Anything else?"

Grace hesitated with fear of speaking, and then she couldn't stop herself from blurting out, "His last name and where he worked."

"Shit. You bitch. Why couldn't you just shut up? You have no idea what you've screwed up."

"I'm sorry. Really, I'm sorry."

He had to make an example of her. "You're going to have to pay for what you've done. Bulldogs, we're going to have a party! Bitch, let's see your tits."

Grace thought for a moment, and then, fumbling, took off her blouse and bra.

"Nice hooters you've got there. Check out those hooters, boys."

"Come over here." Al played with her breasts. "Nice nipples. You know you have to pay for what you've done."

"Yes, yes, I understand."

Al unzipped his pants. "Suck my cock. I'm sure you know how to do that, going out with Jorge."

In a few minutes, Grace knew she was done. She leaned back and said, "Did I do a good job?"

"Yeah, but let's get some more opinions from the guys. I can tell they're jealous. Ben, bring the dice cup over here. Let's see how many of you are going to be lucky tonight."

Al handed the dice cup with two dice to Grace. "You know what to do?"

"I can pretty well figure it out. I roll the dice and that's how many guys I have to give a blow job to."

"You're a smart bitch."

Al nodded, and Grace rolled a seven.

"Who are the lucky ones?"

"Whoever you want, bitch."

Al unmuted the TV and went back to watching the game with Christine sitting next to him.

Grace picked Ben first. She knelt down in front of him, unzipped his pants, pulled out his cock, and put it into her mouth. While she was working at it, she thought to herself, *Okay, I can do this. It's not that bad a punishment. He probably doesn't know I've done more guys than this at a rainbow party. The other gals hated me because my lipstick ring was always highest on the guys' pricks. The bad thing here is that to do this right, I'm the only one to make them all come. God, what a thought. It sucks. At least they are not all going to fuck me. Or are they?*

Grace played a guessing game as she selected the seven guys. *Is this going to be a big cock, or a peewee cock? How long will this guy take?* Two of them lay back on the couch with smiles on their faces, while others would grab her hair and push her face in further. Some grabbed her tits.

She knew the drill well as she stroked each penis for a few seconds to get it hard before she started. She used her hands as well as her mouth and looked up at the guys periodically and watched their faces. They all looked happy.

She finished, just as the Tricolors won. Everyone except Grace was shouting the Tricolor chant, "Jeeeh pute! Jeeeh pute!"

Grace was just a lonely fixture in the midst of a crowd of celebrating Bulldogs. The celebration continued with the gang chant: "I'm from the pound, Dogg Pound, and up to no good."

When things quieted down, she went over to Al and simply asked, "Can I go home now?"

"Sure, bitch. Wash up in the bathroom at the end of the hall. Ben here will drive you home."

She picked up her blouse and bra from the arm of the couch and walked down the hall to the bathroom, where she threw up. Grace hoped her payback was over, but why was Ben driving her home? She could drive her own car. That didn't make sense.

After Grace left, Al leaned over to Ben and said, "You need to make sure Grace doesn't talk to any more cops. You drive her in her car, and pick three of the guys to follow you in the van. Take Daunte. He hasn't been initiated to be part of the Bulldogs yet."

"I understand, Al."

Grace looked at her face in the mirror over the sink of the bathroom. The right side was starting to swell from where Al's bitch girlfriend had hit her. Her side had blood on it from Jorge's knife prick.

Her ribs hurt. Her whole body hurt. She washed her face and wiped her body with a damp towel. She found some Listerine in the cabinet under the sink and rinsed out her mouth. She thought, *They're not going to let me go. When Al said, "You don't know what you've done," his expression indicated it was something really bad. This nightmare isn't over. I've got to get out of here.*

Grace put on her bra and blouse, went over to the bathroom window above the toilet, and slowly raised it. She was able to climb out and drop softly to the ground.

One of the guys who was sitting on the edge of the porch after too much Tequila Pong spotted her crossing the yard. He shouted at her in a drunken voice, "Hey, bitch. What the fuck are you doing?"

Grace knew she had to get away. She started running toward a spot in the backyard where the wooden fence had missing slats. She heard shouting coming from the back of the house.

"Get that bitch! She's ratted out the Bulldogs. Nobody does that. Get her!"

Grace slid through the slats of a wooden fence that ran across the backyard and then through the field behind the house. She could hear the Bulldogs making a barking sound behind her.

"Arf! Arf! Woof! Woof! Arf! Arf!" The Bulldogs shouted.

She ran, but not fast enough. Three gang members who'd been playing video games in the house caught up with her and threw her to the ground.

"Arf! Arf'! Woof! Woof!" One of them stood over her, making a howling sound like a coyote.

This time, she fought back with all her might. One of the gang members kicked her in the side while the other two held her down, and then her will to fight was gone.

They hauled her back through the missing slats. Al was standing on the porch.

"What do you want us to do with her?"

"Just get her out of my sight. Ben knows what to do," Al replied.

They shoved her into a van and drove to an empty field in the Dogg Pound, where they stopped. They spread out an old sleeping bag next to the van and then cut her clothes off. The combined rape mentality of the gang members moved them to do the unthinkable. When one gang member finished, another took his turn. Grace recognized each of their faces from either school or the restaurant.

The last was Daunte, just fifteen years old. Grace looked into his face and said, "Daunte, what're you doing here? You're friends with my little brother."

Almost crying, Daunte responded, "I'm so sorry, Grace. They're watching."

Grace just spread her legs and pleaded, "Daunte, not you. Why you? You're so young."

He was the last to rape her. When he was done, the gang stood around Grace. Their emotions were in a different world. Ben walked over to Daunte, handed him a gun, and said, "You want to Jump-In? Here's your chance. Shoot the bitch. You're going to be one of us."

Daunte wasn't sure what to do. He didn't want to shoot Grace, but he wanted to Jump-In. He pointed the gun in an awkward way and fired five shots in her direction. His aim was not that good, and the gun's recoil didn't help. He hit her with three of the shots, but not in any vital areas. Grace got to her knees and then stood, looking like some kind of a monster out of a movie, with all of the blood and dirt on her. The adrenaline had kicked in, and her face had a scary, determined look about it. Then she fell with a thud. She was still alive but unconscious.

"Man, you Jumped-In. You're a Bulldog."

The gang rolled her up in the sleeping bag, not realizing she was still alive. They put her in the van and drove to a junkyard several miles from the site and tossed her into the back of a junked pickup truck. She landed on her back with the sleeping bag still covering part of her.

Grace used her bloody hand to move the top of the bag away from her face. It was a warm night, but the air felt cold on her face. As the blood drained from her, the cold feeling moved over her entire body. She died with pain that only she would know.

Ben walked over to the pickup truck with a spray can in his hand. With red spray paint, he wrote, "Don't Rat on a Bulldog" on the side of the truck. A piece of bent pipe was used to prop up one of Grace's arms to make sure she was found.

When the gang members returned in the van to Al's house, he told them to get some cleaning supplies from under the sink in the kitchen and clean up the inside of the van. "Vacuum it first, and use a lot of bleach to clean it up. Don't leave a spot on it. You understand? Not a spot. You get rid of that bitch's car. Torch it!"

Al turned to Ben. "How did Daunte do?"

"Daunte did fine. A little scared. Not too accurate with a gun, but he did fine. He's ours now."

"Okay. Now we need to see if we can slow down those federal cops like we've done with the Fresno cops. You know they're close to discovering our operations. We need to teach them that Fresno belongs to the Bulldogs."

"How're we going to do that?"

"We are gonna fuckin' kill a bunch of 'em. That should get 'em off our backs," Al replied.

"Fuck'n right. When?"

Al knew this was a bad plan. The feds were like the marines. They wouldn't back off, but no other plan came to mind.

"Tomorrow afternoon. You can't be involved, but I want you to set it up. Use Diego as the lead; he's got some experience in this type of operation. Get seven of the new guys to go with him. They'll need to steal two cars."

26

Fresno, California

It had been a long day for them. Hartmann and his squad were tired and hungry as they piled into the two Bucars and headed out of the IRS service center. They paid no attention to the boy with the red shirt sitting on his bicycle across the street.

The cell phone call was made quickly. "They just left the center and are headed your way."

"Gracias," was the only response.

The cars headed toward the hotel. Just as they started turning left into the hotel driveway, the front vehicle's windshield burst into a million pieces. Dick and Daniel were covered with shards of safety glass. Fortunately, both were wearing sunglasses that protected their eyes from the glass splinters. There were bursts of bullets hitting the vehicle.

"What the hell?" came rolling off Dick's lips.

In an evasive move, Dick swerved the car toward the hotel driveway and shouted, "Get out! Use the car as a shield. Somebody's shooting at us!"

Their instincts took over. They responded just like they'd been taught at Quantico. Each agent rolled out the left side door and slid down behind the car.

Coleen's mind raced as she hit the ground. *I just went through this at the academy.* But she wasn't at the academy. Someone was firing real bullets at her, not colored paint bullets. She looked at the two holes in the car above her head. *Those are real holes in the car. The windshield actually broke.*

Daniel, who was sitting in the right rear seat of the front car, felt a bullet hit his right shoulder. The force of the bullet had moved his body backward into the seat. Blood was spreading over his shirt. He felt an adrenaline rush as he bent down, moved across the seat, and rolled out of the car. His right hand was useless, but as he'd been trained, he got his service weapon into his left hand and started firing.

The gunfire continued both ways. Bullets were coming in rapid fire. They just kept coming, hitting both Bucars. The windows were gone, and the tires on the right sides went flat. There was at least one automatic weapon, maybe a shotgun, a couple of semiautomatic rifles and handguns firing.

After peeking over the hood of the car, Dick shouted, "The shooters are in those two SUVs across the street. Cover me!"

As the squad rapidly fired their weapons, both Dick and Brian managed to crawl to the trunks of their Bucars, where the heavy artillery was stashed. They pulled out MP5 semiautomatic rifles and shotguns. Thank God they had their Bucars. Then the fireworks really started.

It was a busy street. Cars started swerving and brakes were screeching as vehicles came to a halt and either turned around or emptied. People on the streets were running for cover.

In order to get better firing positions, Brian and Harriett ran across the street, using parked cars on the street as shields. From behind one of the parked cars, they started returning fire, Brian with the semiautomatic rifle and Harriett with the shotgun and then with her service revolver.

The IRS special agents staying in their hotel had heard the gunfire below. They came running out of the hotel with their handguns drawn. They started firing at the two SUVs from behind a wall at the end of the hotel driveway. They had the shooters in a crossfire.

Between the loud popping of gunfire, police sirens could be heard coming from all directions.

The Bulldogs figured it was time to ditch the scene. Two of them ran from the rear SUV and jumped into the one in front. The bullet-ridden SUV took off with its tires squealing. Gunfire was still coming from the vehicle's windows. As it turned right at the corner, it sideswiped a responding Fresno squad car and sped out of sight.

Suddenly, there was dead silence, except for distant police sirens coming from all directions. Within minutes, the scene was lit up with a sea of red lights. There were police vehicles everywhere. Within seconds, several of the vehicles took off at high speeds down the street where the SUV had turned, their lights flashing and sirens going.

Dick checked on his Animals. Everyone seemed all right except for Daniel, who'd been hit by a bullet in his upper right arm. It appeared to be just a flesh wound, but there was a lot of blood. Coleen had bruised knees from crawling out of the car and hitting the street. They'd been lucky.

Dick got a first-aid kit out of the trunk of what was left of his Bucar.

Coleen, in a somewhat shaky voice, called to Dick, "Give me that. I was known as the nurse in my family. I use to patch up my brother and sister all the time."

A Fresno police officer ran up and said he'd called for ambulances. Then, turning to Dick, who seemed to be the person in charge, the officer asked, "Who in the hell are you guys? I assume from the way your cars are rigged, that you're law enforcement?"

Dick flashed his bureau credentials and said, "You're right on that. We're FBI special agents."

Putting on their FBI badges, Dick, Brian, and Harriett walked over to the remaining SUV, which was surrounded by several Fresno police officers. The driver was slumped over the steering wheel. He'd been shot several times. One shot went through his head. Outside, at the back of the vehicle, was another body. He'd also been shot several times. There was no question that they were both dead.

Dick looked over at a sergeant who appeared to be in charge and asked, "Any idea who they are?"

"Based on the red T-shirt and bulldog tattoo, I'd say he was a member of the Bulldog gang. That's the largest gang here in Fresno."

"Yeah, I see the tattoos on both of them. That one is just a kid. He can't be over sixteen."

The sergeant responded, "He's probably younger. I suspect this was part of his initiation into the Bulldogs. They use young kids as shooters. If they get caught, they end up in juvenile court. No death penalty and they get short sentences. The driver is probably in his twenties. He was here to make sure the kid did his job."

Dick was talking further with the sergeant when his cell phone rang. It was Special Agent Carlen-Murray with the resident agency.

"Dick, I understand you managed to create a reenactment of the OK Corral in the middle of my town. Are your agents all right?"

"Daniel took one in his right arm, but it appears to be just a flesh wound. Everybody else appears to be okay. How'd you find out so fast?"

"It's not that big a town. I'm on my way over. Expect a Lieutenant Rosy Peria of Fresno PD to track you down. I'm also forewarning you that the press are on their way, including the local TV stations."

"I'll let you handle the local press."

"That's why I'm on my way. As the resident agent in charge, I already have a rapport with them."

"Who's Lieutenant Peria?"

"She heads up the Fresno Police gang unit. It's actually called the Bulldog Tactical Team. The gang problem is so bad in Fresno, there's a multiagency gang taskforce formed to handle it. Both Rosy and I are on it, along with representatives from the sheriffs, the CHP, and the US marshal's office. The Bulldog Gang comes close to controlling Fresno. See you in fifteen."

As Dick was closing his phone, he spotted an attractive Hispanic lady wearing a badge headed his way.

"You must be Rosy."

"Robin acts fast. You must be Agent Hartmann."

"That I am."

"Nice to meet you."

"Likewise."

"Do you mind gathering up your team and meeting me in the hotel lobby? I need to talk with all of you."

"No problem, but I suspect that two of them are headed to the hospital. Let me go check on them, and then I'll meet you at the hotel."

A number of ambulances had arrived. Dick found Daniel and Coleen standing at the back of one of them. Daniel had his right arm wrapped with bandages and looked a little pale.

"Daniel, how's it going?"

"Just a scratch, but they want me to go to the ER. Boss, can you talk them out of it? I hate hospitals."

"No way. That looks like more than a scratch. You need to get it checked out properly. Nurse Coleen, would you mind accompanying Daniel, and make sure he stays out of trouble with the other nurses?"

"Will do, Boss."

Daniel responded, "Cut it out, you two. It hurts to laugh."

"And Nurse Coleen, have those knees checked out when you're at the emergency room. They don't look all that great at the moment."

Coleen responded, "In case you haven't noticed, your pants don't look that good, either."

Dick looked down at his ripped pants and thought to himself, *Coleen is fitting in with this crew.* He then located Brian and Harriett. The crime area was now cordoned off with yellow crime scene tape. The Fresno PD CSIs were starting their work.

Lieutenant Peria and Agent Carlen-Murray were waiting for them in the lobby. They all sat down on lobby sofas. Dick explained that two of his agents were headed to the emergency room, but that they seemed to be all right.

Robin introduced Rosy, who then took charge of the meeting.

"Robin, I'd like this case to be handled by our gang joint task force. With your permission, the Fresno Police will take charge. Is that all right with you?"

"Rosy, I'll have to check with Washington, since federal agents were shot at and one was wounded. But I suspect it won't be a problem. Dick, what do you think?"

"I don't have a problem with Fresno PD handling the case, but I do need to find out why a gang was shooting at us. Rosy, if you do end up handling the case, and I think you will, I would like an update daily. My gut tells me that they were shooting at us because of the case we're investigating."

"May I assume that case has something to do with the murder at the IRS center?"

"It does."

"Okay. I won't ask you anything further about that at the moment, but because of what has just happened, I'm going to have to ask you to surrender the weapons you fired tonight. You'll get them back in the morning, but I need the sheriff's lab to fire them so we can determine whose bullets are in the corpses out there.

"I suspect each of you will have to draft a report for your agency. I'll accept copies of those reports for my investigation. In regards to your accommodations at this hotel, I'll arrange for all of you to be on the top floor with a police guard. I met some IRS special agents while I was waiting for you, and they'll be housed on the same floor with you. For some reason, the Bulldogs don't seem to like you. I know you're FBI agents, but my advice is, don't go out tonight. As you may have heard, the Bulldogs have more power than they should in this town. Have a good night's sleep. I'll be back to talk with you further in the morning," Rosy directed.

Hartmann and his crew went over to the front desk to pick up keys for their new rooms. As the keys were handed to them, they could see Rosy and Robin talking with the press outside the hotel. They also noted that several of the reporters were trying to talk their way past the police guards at the hotel entrance.

Portable lights had been brought in to light the crime scene. They were supplemented not only by the streetlights but also by those of the local TV camera crews. Fresno PD CSIs were taking photos of the bodies, the cars, and the shell casings. A coroner's truck was just pulling up as they got into the elevator and headed upstairs. They were greeted on the third floor by two of Fresno's finest, assigned to protect them.

As they were looking to see where their rooms were located, Brian said, "I know this's been a rough night, but I'm hungry. We haven't eaten dinner."

Dick replied, "So am I. How 'bout some pizza?"

"I'm drooling just thinking about it."

With that, Dick pulled out his cell phone and used the autodial to call Coleen. "How are you and Daniel doing?"

"I'm doing fine. They're going to keep Daniel overnight for observation. He lost a fair amount of blood. It was a through and through, so he's got a lot of stitches on the front and back of his shoulder. I was with him when the doctor sewed him up. They had to clean out some cloth and glass. I suspect he's going to be in a sling for a while. They told him he was lucky and that it would hurt for a couple of days, but it should heal just fine. He'll probably be released in the morning. I was just getting ready to come back to the hotel."

"Great news. This may sound strange, but on the way back to the hotel, would you mind stopping by a liquor store and picking up two cases of cold beer? One Bud Light and the other Beck's. Oh, and get some wine for yourself, and we probably should also have some soft drinks. We're going to have a floor party. You'll figure it out when you get here."

"Will do, Boss. Sounds interesting."

Dick then called a local pizza-delivery service. He ordered enough pizzas for his crew, the two Fresno PD guards, and the IRS special agents who were now also housed with them. After all, they'd come to the FBI's rescue.

Forty-five minutes later, Coleen arrived at the floor with a bellman. His cart was loaded with the requested cases of cold beer, soft drinks, and a bottle each of chardonnay and cabernet. Twenty minutes later, the pizza was delivered.

As they had the floor to themselves, most of the agents propped the doors to their rooms open. They were glad to blow off a little steam after what'd just happened. Dick's and Brian's rooms were next to each other and became party central. Both their bathtubs were overflowing with ice, beer, and soft drinks. Dick's tub included the bottle of chardonnay. The pizzas were spread out on the beds in both rooms.

Everyone sat in chairs from their rooms, or on the beds, to watch what was happening just outside their hotel. The local TV stations had canceled their regular broadcasts to air new developments of the shooting. The local anchors and reporters were constantly updating what they'd learned. The speculation was that it was a gang shooting by the Bulldogs against law-enforcement officers. Maybe the gang was revolting against the gang taskforce that'd been established by a number of local, state, and federal law enforcement agencies. The FBI was mentioned by the reporters. Rosy and Robin were interviewed, and they implied that local FBI agents were involved. No mention was made of Dick's squad.

The mayor and police chief held a press conference. The mayor declared a state of emergency, which included a citywide curfew until seven the next morning.

Dick was washing down his pizza with a Beck's beer when Bob Larson from the IRS Criminal Investigation Unit pulled a chair over next to him.

"Well, you guys certainly know how to liven up a town."

"Not intentionally. By the way, thanks for coming to our aid out there," Dick replied.

"No problem. First time I've ever had to fire my weapon on duty."

"Bob, have you guys been able to figure anything out yet?"

"Not really. I feel sorry for Doug Smith. Basically, we're doing a full-blown audit of his Center. One thing for sure: you don't want a murder occurring at an IRS center. We're now auditing everything at the center. Anytime you do that, you find something. So far, we've discovered that two of Smith's audit staff members were changing file information for payoffs. The Collection Department has a whole bunch of misfiles that need to be corrected. Stuff like that, but nothing that seems to tie to Shaw's murder."

"Well, now that they're fed, we probably should get our troops into bed. They should be as relaxed as they're going to get tonight. See you in the morning, and thanks again to your guys for coming to our rescue. It really was appreciated."

27

Fresno, California

It was early in the morning, but you could tell it was going to be another hot, humid day in Fresno.

Hartmann used the hotel phone to contact each of his team members to let them know he'd made arrangements for everyone to have breakfast in one of the hotel conference rooms downstairs. From the way they answered their phones, he could tell he was their wake-up call. He called Robin to see if she and her friend Rosy could join his crew for breakfast.

Dick and his squad sat around a large conference table with Robin and Rosy sitting at either end. After the table was cleared of the breakfast dishes, Robin asked Rosy to open the discussion.

"As a little background for the agents from San Francisco, Fresno has a major gang problem, and it's growing. We have our homegrown gang called the Bulldogs, but other gangs are moving up here from LA because of the crackdowns there. It's been building for several years. Some time ago, the mayor implemented a gang-prevention initiative to retake Fresno from gang control. When he did that, we requested help from the highway patrol and county sheriff's department. Jointly, we'll do a major sweep, and things'll be quite for a while. But the gangs just go underground for thirty or sixty days and reemerge. Thus far, our efforts have not worked that well. My department, even with the outside support, has been overwhelmed by them."

Rosy thought for a moment and then added, "The crackdowns are a good thing as far as they go, but they turn out just to be Band-Aids. The press attention helps, and everybody feels safe for a few weeks, but then we're right back where we started. The violence and killings return. The gangs not only have time on their side; they're also well financed from the methamphetamine and other drugs they sell. They're heavily armed, have a hair-trigger mentality, are very proud, highly motivated, and are a crazy force. It's becoming a culture unto itself. We're now arresting second- and third-generation gang members. We have both father and son gang members in jail at the same time. Fathers, grandfathers, and even great-grandfathers count themselves as part of the gang."

Robin took over. "Somehow, Dick, your investigation at the IRS service center triggered last night's shootout. So far, we've been able to keep your names, and why you're here, out of the press. Last night's shooting has prompted action by the Fresno mayor. Rosy'll fill you in on what's going to happen. Rosy, you're back up."

"Thanks, Robin. First, we've confirmed that it was Bulldog gang members who were shooting at you last night. We located the SUV that took off from the scene. It was abandoned a couple of miles from the shooting, and the occupants evaded us by going across a ravine, where another car was waiting for them. This was a well-planned event. Both SUVs were stolen yesterday morning. Bullets from the guns of FBI Special Agents Daniel Lee and Harriett Foster killed the two gang members at the crime scene."

Robin interrupted. "Harriett and Daniel, I've contacted the attorney general's office. A deputy AG has been assigned to any shooting hearings there may be. You'll probably be required to attend the hearings. I suspect they'll be concluded quickly and quietly. It may not be possible for us to keep your names out of the press, but we'll do our best. Sorry for the interruption, Rosy."

Rosy continued. "Fresno PD has been trying to suppress the Bulldog gang for some time. I head up this effort. To give you a little background, the Fresno Bulldogs are the city's largest street gang. They're named after the Fresno State University mascot. They are mainly a Hispanic gang, with more than four thousand documented members and six thousand "wannabes" and associates who wear red Fresno State clothing as their trademark. There are more than five hundred validated and another five hundred associate Bulldog gang members currently in prisons statewide. Another 650 occupy our local jail. The Bulldog gang is active in all areas of Fresno, and they're continually connected with assaults, robberies, and drugs. We understand their latest criminal endeavor is identity theft. What's scaring our citizens the most is that the Bulldogs suddenly have gotten web-savvy, showcasing illegal exploits, making threats, and honoring killed and jailed members on the digital turf."

Rosy continued, "What happened last night sent the mayor into a tirade. To him and the chief, it was the last straw. It's not just the shooting you were involved in. Last night, there was also a terrible e-mail sent to our chief from a Bulldog member, taking credit for the gruesome gang rape and murder of a local waitress. All hell has broken loose.

"As Robin knows, both the FBI and Fresno PD have tried to get undercover officers into the gang. In fact, one of your FBI undercover agents was almost killed within two weeks of trying to get into the Bulldogs. The young agent was identified by the Bulldogs but was able to get out when he signaled his handlers that he was in trouble. They moved in and had to kill three gang members to extricate him."

Robin continued. "Dick, he was a new agent just out of the academy. Looked young for his age and was Hispanic. He received severe stab wounds and resigned from the bureau. I understand he's now teaching high school."

"I remember him from the academy. His class attended one of my lectures, but I had no idea what'd happened to him," Dick replied.

"We kept it quiet, for obvious reasons."

Rosy continued her explanation of the Bulldogs. "We've had a number of Bulldog locations under surveillance for some time. Two days from now, the mayor and chief of police will be giving a press conference to update the public on what happened last night. During the press conference, we're going to raid five of the Bulldog locations."

Robin again interrupted, "We'll all be involved in the raids. I requested SWAT's help last night. FBI SWAT teams are being flown in from both San Francisco and LA to support the mission. It'll be a major effort. Yes, Harriett. You have a question?"

"Yes, Rosy. You mentioned a waitress was murdered. Can you tell me more about that?"

"Sure. Her name was Grace Ocampo. She was a waitress—"

Before Rosy could finish, Harriett finished her sentence. "She was a waitress at the Dos Amigos Restaurant. I interviewed her yesterday about Ed Abramson. What happened to her?"

"Her body was found in a tow yard in southwest Fresno. It appears she'd been beaten and sexually assaulted. Probably gang raped and then murdered. Her body was stuffed into a sleeping bag and put it in the back of a pickup truck in a tow yard."

"Oh, my God. She was just in her twenties. Seemed like a sweet girl. Somebody must have seen me interview her. I feel terrible."

"Harriett, I understand how you feel. I know it doesn't help, but the Bulldogs have their own rules. One of them is 'snitch and die.' They were enforcing that rule. The truck she was found in had 'Don't Rat on a Bulldog' written on its side. That's their way of intimidating people. They do that well. Listen, this isn't going to help, either, but Ms. Ocampo wasn't the first. The same gang murdered a pregnant seventeen-year-old a year ago and dumped her body in that same junkyard for the same reason. She was going to testify in a federal court case about some gang drug dealers. The feds lost the case because of her death."

Dick broke in, hoping to redirect the conversation, mainly to change the topic. With a voice of authority, he stated, "Rosy and Robin, I'd like one of my team members to participate in each of the five raids. I'm not sure what we're looking for, but we may find something that'll help us with Shaw's murder investigation."

Rosy nodded to Robin and replied, "I have no problem with that."

"Thanks. By the way, what was in the e-mail to the chief?"

"It was like a threat to the city," Rosy responded. "It read something like, 'I think the chief is wasting his time. He can't get rid of the Fresno Bulldogs. We're too big. You can't take the color away or the Dog. Real dogs don't claim either one. It's the city we claim. We claim Fresno!"

Robin then advised them that a briefing on the raid would be held at Fresno PD headquarters tomorrow. "Since you no longer have any transportation, I'll arrange for you to be picked up for the meeting."

"Oh, yeah," Rosy chimed in. "Except for the two weapons that killed the gangbangers, I have your weapons in the trunk of my car."

As they left, Rosy returned their weapons. She shouted back at them, "I've got some work to do at headquarters, but if you want, I can return for lunch."

Since they were without their own means of transportation, the lunch offer was accepted. Weapon inspections and cleaning kept them busy until lunchtime.

28

Fresno, California

Rosy joined the visiting FBI agents for lunch at Marie Callender's next to their hotel. Everyone had ordered when suddenly, out of nowhere, Harriett, who was seated in the booth between Daniel and Brian, burst out with, "You guys stink."

Brian raised his arm, took a sniff, and responded, "It's not me. It's my clothes. This is the third time I've had to wear this outfit, and in this heat, I sweat a lot. My travel bag has three changes, and I had to throw out my pants and shirt from yesterday after rolling around in the street."

Harriett said, "Brian, I'm in the same boat, but at least I wash my underwear and blouse out each night. Dick, how much longer before we get a break and go back to San Francisco?"

"My guess is a couple more days."

Coleen chimed in, "Time out! Time out! Harriett, shopping opportunity!"

"Girl, you're right. Shopping opportunity!"

Brian, known to be the cheap one, shouted, "Coleen, have you ever heard of hotel laundry services? You take it down in the morning and it's back in your room at night. And best of all, the bureau pays for it."

Dick chimed in, "Guys, I can't believe I'm saying this, but I think Coleen's right. I need some replacements for my wardrobe. We're all starting to really smell like animals."

Everyone laughed and mutually agreed that some shopping appeared to be in order. The Animals shouldn't smell like animals.

"Rosy, I know you're busy, but could you direct us to some clothing stores?"

"I'll more than direct you; I'll join the 'shopping opportunity.' It's the break I need. What kind of stores are you interested in?"

Coleen quickly responded. "Is there a Macy's, Bloomingdale's, or even better, a Ralph Lauren around here?"

"I can tell you have northeastern tastes."

Harriett chimed in. "Rosy, I don't care about the northeastern fashion tastes, but Ralph Lauren sounds like expensive taste to me. The first two stores would work for me. Coleen, what's the starting pay at the bureau now?"

"I'm sure it's about the same as when you started, but I got this $2,200 travel allowance, with not that much to ship, so I might as well use some of it on clothes."

Harriett responded, "It sounds to me like we're going from a 'shopping opportunity' to a 'shopping spree.'" Staring at Coleen, she added, "At least for one person."

Coleen didn't want to say something bad about shopping in Rosy's town. The best she could come up with was, "I'm saving the spree part for Union Square in San Francisco. This is just a shopping preview with the possibility of minor acquisitions."

Daniel offered, "I'm getting the impression there is West Coast shopping, and then there is East Coast shopping."

Turning to the guys, Rosy asked, "I think that I've figured out where the gals want to go. What're you guys looking for?"

Dick suggested, "How about a Brooks Brothers or a Jos. A. Bank store?"

Rosy sarcastically commented, "I can tell the FBI dresses differently than the Fresno PD. Now that I think about it, you talk differently, too."

"Rosy, are you looking for a job transfer?"

"That's okay, Dick. I like my hometown, and they need me. Back to the shopping spree, or should I say, shopping preview? The best we have to offer in the way of a department store is Macy's. Let me make a phone call on the men's stores."

After a couple of minutes, Rosy said, "There's a Jos. A. Bank store near the Macy's, so everyone's is in luck. This should be an interesting day."

They all piled into the Suburban, with the Fresno PD escort behind them. Within a few minutes, they pulled into a shopping center parking lot where Macy's was located.

Harriett and Coleen started going through the racks in one of the women's sections. Rosy volunteered to help. After ten minutes, the guys decided to find the men's department and told the gals they'd be back in twenty minutes.

When the guys returned, the gals were gone. Brian, who was the only married one, said, "Welcome to the world of women's shopping. My wife does this to me all the time."

Dick spotted a sales clerk and asked, "Have you seen three young women shopping in this section?"

"Seen them? I sure have. They're back in the dressing rooms trying on just about every item in the store."

"Do you mind telling them we're here?"

"No problem at all. Your wives seem to know how to enjoy themselves."

"They are not our wives. We all work together."

"Oh. I'll tell them you're here."

Five minutes later, all three of them came out wearing low-cut, black cocktail dresses. They strutted around the guys with flitting eyes. Then they put their arms around each other and said in unison, "What do you think?"

None of the guys' minds were working too well. They couldn't believe what they were seeing. Basically, all their thoughts went something like, *They all look great. Really great.* Then, coming back to reality, Dick replied, "Ladies, you look great, but I don't think our assignment today had anything to do with the vice squad. By any chance, did you find any practical, law-enforcement-type clothes?"

Rosy responded, "By that comment, do you mean we look like hookers?"

Dick thought to himself, *Oh, God, I've done it again.* "No, No. Not in the least. Not even close."

"You mean hookers look better than we do?"

"Harriett, get me out of this. You know how I can stick my foot in my mouth."

"Ladies, he's right. He has a serious habit of sticking his foot in his mouth."

"Thanks for the help, Harriett. Did you find some replacement clothes?"

"Yes, we did."

With that, they withdrew to the dressing rooms. Coleen called between dressing rooms to Harriett, "Is Dick always this much fun? He doesn't seem like a typical FBI agent."

"He can be a lot of fun to work for. His philosophy is that our job shows us the worst of society, so we need some humor. While we're working, though, he tends to be very serious."

"What's your impression of him?"

"As you've already noted, handsome. In regards to personality, he's smart, intuitive, honest to a fault, funny, and uncomfortable around fools, which makes him cranky."

"Does he ever get mad?"

"Girl, you don't want to be around him when he does get mad. It doesn't happen often, but when it does, watch out. The good thing is, he doesn't stay mad for very long, and he doesn't seem to hold a grudge."

"God, he sounds too good to be true. Thanks for your insight."

"Girl, I've a hunch you'll be providing me with info on Dick in the near future. You know he likes you."

"He does?"

"Yes, girl. He does."

The girls returned with their selections, smiled as they passed the guys, and found the saleslady.

The next stop was Jos. A. Bank, which was located in a shopping complex across the street. They parked and as they were walking up to the men's store, the girls spotted a shoe store. Coleen shouted ahead to the guys, "We'll catch up with you."

The guys went into the men's store, found a clerk to help them, and within twenty minutes had what they wanted. Once they'd all paid for their purchases, Dick made a suggestion.

Ten minutes later, the shoe shoppers walked into the men's store looking for the guys. A salesperson near the store entrance pointed them toward the men's suit department toward the back of the store. They walked over and suddenly Dick, Daniel, and Brian sprang out from the dressing-room area, each wearing Speedo swim trunks and muscle-man underwear shirts.

Everyone broke out into laughter.

You can't say I don't know how to bond a team, Dick thought.

29

Fresno, California

It was nine in the morning as the squad looked out the hotel lobby window. The sun was up. It was going to be another hot day. They wondered if Fresno would ever cool off.

The San Francisco agents noted that the people on the streets of Fresno seemed to be going about business as normal. The ride to police headquarters was quiet and uneventful.

After the usual greetings, everyone gathered in a large conference room. Robin and Rosy stood at the front of the room.

"Everyone, this is Commander Harold Wyndom of the Fresno Police Department," Rosy announced. "As soon as you fill your coffee cups, he'll fill us in on what's going to happen tomorrow."

Dick and the squad wandered over to a table at the side of the room. They poured cups of coffee, selected doughnuts, and sat at an unoccupied table. The room was designed for videoconferencing with a large screen on the wall behind the front table, where Robin and Rosy now sat with Commander Wyndom.

Once everyone had settled in, Commander Wyndom pulled the microphone closer. "I thank you all for coming and showing your various agencies' support for our effort to take back Fresno from street gangs. Your agencies have all agreed to assist us in serving warrants to members of the Bulldog gang.

"Our raid will commence sharply at six tomorrow morning. Usually, the gang members are asleep at this hour, and many will be hungover from partying the night before. We've identified five houses in the Dogg Pound area of Fresno where the warrants will be served. History tells us the gang doesn't like Fresno PD entering this area, so we can expect strong resistance from them. They're armed and might even have automatic weapons. That's why we've asked for your assistance. For all of our safety, we need to go in quickly, and with an overwhelming force."

Clearing his voice, Wyndom continued, "We have the commitment of seven SWAT teams with armored vehicles, in addition to our department's SWAT unit. They'll act as a strike force for each of the houses where the warrants are being served. As soon as they enter the Dogg Pound, a perimeter will be established around the area by other police units to prevent gang members from entering or leaving the area. Streets to the area will be blocked off with barricades by the Fresno Road Maintenance Department. Our Skywatch helicopter will hover overhead to monitor what's happening. A temporary jail will be set up at the Fresno State College football field.

"Now, let me take a roll call of the participating units and agencies so that everyone knows the players. Captain Reynolds with our SWAT unit?"

A face appeared on the video screen, "I'm here, Commander."

"Sergeant Black with our air support unit?"

From the screen again came "Here."

"California Highway Patrol?"

"Right here. We have two SWAT teams and three patrol officers."

"Thanks. FBI?"

Robin said, "Here. We'll be providing two SWAT teams, twenty local agents, and four agents from our San Francisco Field Office."

"Fresno Sheriff's Department?"

"Right here. We'll provide our SWAT unit and thirty officers."

"Sacramento Police Department?"

"Here," came from the screen. "Our SWAT unit is committed."

"And last but not least, LAPD, which is used to similar gang problems."

"Commander, thanks for that comment. From what I understand, our gangbangers in LA are migrating to Fresno. Sorry 'bout that. Our SWAT unit is ready."

Wyndom wrapped up. "That completes the roll call. I'll go over a brief explanation of the operation, and then one of my staff will fill you in on your specific assignments. There will be two staging areas. One is a remote hangar at the Fresno Yosemite International Airport. The FBI SWAT units are being flown in there this afternoon by air force aircraft. Also, the LAPD unit will be flown in by an Air National Guard aircraft. Our SWAT unit is already in there getting things ready.

"The other location is a field off Highway 99 at Avenue 7. That's where the highway patrol, Fresno sheriffs, and Sacramento units will all assemble. The CHP will have their mobile command center located there as well. Exactly at 6:00 a.m. tomorrow morning, we'll all move out. Any questions on the overall operation?"

The LAPD representative asked, "Who'll have overall responsibility for coordination of the operation?"

Commander Wyndom responded, "I will be responsible for the operation. We'll have a command-center vehicle, which'll be located at the airport. I'll coordinate things from that location. The highway patrol will set up their support command center at the Highway 99 and Avenue 7 location. You'll be provided with communication frequencies to contact me. All units are to be at their designated locations at three thirty tomorrow morning. Any other questions? If not, let's get down to the individual assignments."

After the logistics were reviewed, Dick and the Animals headed out to lunch and rested for their early-morning start.

30

Fresno, California

It was three in the morning and still hot when Hartmann's squad was picked up at their hotel. The drive to the Fresno Yosemite International Airport took only ten minutes. They checked through special security at a remote gate and drove to an older, remote hangar, where one of the bureau's big, blue-and-white mobile command center trucks was parked.

An agent exiting the command truck spotted Dick getting out of the car. A sarcastic voice announced, "Good morning, Agent Hartmann. I brought your replacement vehicle. It's the blue one over there. The keys are in it. See if you can keep it in one piece for at least a couple of months."

"Try my best, but I suspect the odds are against that today. It'll probably take a couple of bullet holes. Better the vehicle than me."

"Can't argue with that. Sounds like you've had an exciting time the last couple of days. The Fresno PD guys say today will probably be like the Fourth of July, with lots of fireworks. I'd like to join you guys, but I'm stuck here at the command center for this one."

As they talked, two air force C-130 Hercules aircraft taxied over to the hangar and began unloading the FBI SWAT vehicles, which were then driven over to another parking lot full of SWAT vehicles from other agencies. *This* is *going to be like the Fourth of July,* Dick thought.

"Hey, guys, the briefing is starting," came a shout from one of the SWAT team members.

The hangar was filled with folding chairs. Commander Wyndom and Rosy were on a temporary stage with a whiteboard and large map of the city on either side of them. A video screen was above them, connected to a closed-circuit TV, which was connected to a second staging location.

"Ladies and gentlemen, we're going to serve warrants to individuals in the Dogg Pound this morning. Our previous experiences with the Bulldog gang tell us that this probably won't go down easily."

Rosy continued the briefing. "All of the locations where we're serving warrants are located in southwest Fresno on the very edge of the city. It's known as the West Side neighborhood. It's made up of dense housing tracks and apartment complexes, which are separated by vacant lots and open fields. The Bulldogs have lots of members and friends in the area. When you go in, don't trust anyone to help you.

"Surveillance at one of these houses indicates that some of the gang members involved in the shootout two days ago are located there. We don't expect them to surrender easily. In addition to the warrants, ICE will be checking for individuals who are in the country illegally.

"There'll be units surrounding the streets bordering the area we're raiding. They'll arrest anyone trying to leave and will also prevent others from entering. The plan is to seal off the streets leading into the area before the SWAT vehicles enter.

"We'll approach the Dogg Pound from two directions. A member of Fresno PD will lead each raiding party. Just FYI, your cell phones won't work in the area. We're jamming all cell phone transmissions in the area during the operation. This should give us an advantage, as the gang members communicate by cell phone. There are very few landline phones left in the area."

Commander Wyndom ended the meeting with, "It's time to clean up Fresno. Play it safe out there. This operation is now a go."

Dick had divided his squad so that he and each of his four agents were assigned to different locations. They weren't part of the initial raiding party. They were assigned to locate items that could assist them with the FBI's investigation into Shaw's murder or gang member activity somehow linked to the IRS service center.

Dick assigned himself to the house where the participants in the recent shooting of their vehicles were believed to be located.

Exactly at six, the two convoys of vehicles were on the move.

The raid got off to an ominous start, as Jorge Garcia was just returning from his new girlfriend's house when the convoy of SWAT vehicles passed him. He guessed where they were headed and immediately got on his cell phone. The call was cut off in mid-sentence as the FBI cell phone blocking system went into effect, but the Bulldog in Al Gomez's house heard enough to warn those in the house to prepare for a raid by the cops.

The SWAT vehicles rolled into the Dogg Pound. They had entered the Bulldog gang's 'hood.

Fifteen minutes into the mission, a special TV news broadcast went on the air, originating from the mayor's office. His speech began. "Today, we begin taking back Fresno from the gangs that have plagued our city for all too long. Today's operations will have far-reaching effects on curtailing gang activity throughout Fresno. Citizens of Fresno, because of today's planned law-enforcement activities, you are advised not to enter the area of our city known as the Dogg Pound."

Al's instincts told him this wasn't a normal raid. *Bad plan, bad plan, but the only one I could think of,* he thought. He'd prepared for this day. He swung his feet out of bed, quickly pulled on this pants and shirt, and grabbed the backpack that hung on a peg in his bedroom. He used the key that hung around his neck like a dog tag to open the footlocker at the foot of his bed. He filled the backpack with a number of the neatly stacked hundred-dollar bills. He unplugged his laptop computer and slid it into the money-filled backpack. Making his escape, Al took the same route through the broken slats in the backyard fence that Grace Ocampo had used to try to make her unsuccessful escape.

As he ran across the field toward the street, Al noticed the CHP cars parked every half block along the streets. *Shit.* He found a clump of brush and lay down quietly to wait, just as he'd been taught when he was a marine. After a few minutes, he tried to use his cell phone but couldn't get a signal. He looked back at his house and watched as the SWAT vehicle pulled up.

There were ten members of the Fresno Police Department SWAT unit standing on its running boards as the vehicle pulled up to Al's house. They had to quickly scatter, as the alerted gang members were firing various types of weapons at them, including some that were fully automatic. Ready for battle, the gang had barricades in place at the doors and each of the windows. This wasn't going to be the surprise raid they'd hoped and planned for.

The teams at the other locations were having better luck. The Bulldogs were surprised and no match for the SWAT teams. There was the occasional "pop, pop" of weapons being fired and the louder "flash-bam" sound of grenades going off, but the teams managed to get to the front doors and break them down with battering rams. Things quieted down within a few minutes.

Dick, as an observer, followed the SWAT team to Al's house and stopped half a block away. He noted the surprise plan of attack hadn't worked. As team members jumped off the armored vehicle, they used it and a concrete block wall to the left of the house for cover. A major firefight ensured. "Pop, pop, pop."

One of the officers at the back of the vehicle had been hit as he ran for cover. He was lying on the ground in front of the house across the street. His fellow team members attempted to reach him when gunfire started coming from that house. The raiding party was now caught in a crossfire.

A heavy stream of bullets was coming from the house across the street from Al's. *That's a fucking fifty-caliber machine gun. Where in the hell did they get that?* Dick wondered.

Dick thought to himself, *This is a stupid idea*. He adjusted his seat belt so he could duck down below the dashboard and gunned his new Bucar's engine. It jumped forward and gained speed as it headed straight for the window where the gunfire was coming from. The car plowed three feet into the frame house and had enough impact to send the machine gun and the two gang members operating it flying against the far wall. From the body parts and blood splattered on the wall, there was no question that they were both dead. The rest of the gang scattered toward the back of the house. After a few minutes, they were either dead or had surrendered to the SWAT team.

Dick sat in what was left of his new Bucar for a few seconds and then started pushing back on the inflated airbag that was hampering his movement. Gunfire from Al's house was now focused on his car. The SWAT team continued to return fire while Dick crawled over the seat into the back of the car and was able to open one of the rear doors. *God, another destroyed vehicle; how I hate paperwork,* he thought. He initially used the door as protection as the gunfire continued. He was able to crawl to the wounded officer and started pulling him to safety. Two SWAT team members ran out and helped to get them both to a protected area at the side of the house.

Within minutes, they were joined by several officers from other raid sites that'd been secured. A secure perimeter was established around Al's house as the gunfire lessened. Now it was "waiting and negotiating" time.

After a two-hour standoff, the decision was made to mount a

battering ram on the front of one of the SWAT vehicles and storm the house. *A much smarter idea than what I did,* thought Dick. Sharpshooters were positioned around the perimeter to cover every window and door. Tear-gas canisters were launched, and several made it through the already shattered windows.

The use of the battering ram on the front of the house was rejected. There were cars parked in the front yard of the house that the SWAT vehicle would have a difficult time maneuvering around. In addition, the width of the front porch protected the front door and windows. They decided to drive the SWAT vehicle across the field at the back of the house. As the vehicle was getting into position, it passed within six feet of Al's hiding spot. It gained speed and demolished the already broken wooden fence and then raced across the backyard, demolishing the gang's Ping-Pong table and the sliding glass door.

SWAT members inched their way through the tear-gas-filled house, firing their weapons as needed. One of the gang members decided to make a name for himself by running out the front door and opening fire from the porch. He was quickly taken out by one of the sharpshooters. The few remaining members either left their weapons inside the house or dropped them as they came out.

Dick counted eleven bodies strewn across the dirt in front of the house. Most sported very apparent Bulldog tattoos. He guessed that they ranged in age from twelve to one man in his late forties. The older one had that hardened, menacing, muscular look that one gets from spending time in prison.

Suddenly, the house across the street burst into flames. A back bedroom, being used as a small meth lab, exploded. Bullets from the gang's stash of ammunition, including the remaining rounds from the fifty-caliber machine gun, began flying in all directions. The fire department arrived but moved back for safety reasons. The gang members on the ground who were still alive were handcuffed and moved away from the burning house.

Dick was startled when his cell phone rang. The FBI cell phone jamming system had been turned off. He heard Daniel's voice. "Hey, Boss. How's it going where you are?"

"It didn't start well, but it's under control now." *I'm not going to mention what happened to the Bucar.* "Apparently, someone tipped the gang off that we were coming, and they were ready and waiting for us. One of the houses involved caught fire and blew up. We've been showered with exploding bullets for the past half hour. There are a number of gang fatalities and apparently one wounded SWAT member. Other than that, not much happening here. How about at your location?" Dick added facetiously.

"Nothing like what you went through. I heard the explosion and gunfire from your location. Actually, the raid here went fairly smooth. Boss, I think you should get over here. You should see what I found next to a computer here."

"It's going to be awhile. I need to go through this place and see if there's anything of interest. I'll head your way as soon as I figure out how to get a ride."

"Why do you need a ride? I thought you had a car."

"It's a long story. I'll explain later."

Dick carefully walked through Al's house, stepping over demolished furniture, fallen walls, and dead bodies. He noted a number of computers that seemed to be set up as part of a network. He took a particular interest in Al's bedroom, with a footlocker filled halfway up with bundles of hundred dollar bills. He called the command center and requested a team to analyze the contents of the computers. He also requested a replacement vehicle.

Dick headed over to Daniel's location and found him sitting in front of a computer located in the dining room.

"Dick, look at this."

It was a printout with an IRS heading at the top that listed hundreds of names, addresses, employers, social security numbers, ages, earnings amounts, and in some cases, credit card numbers.

Wearing latex gloves, Daniel pulled a flash drive from the computer. "The information on the screen is from this memory stick. If you were looking for information for identity theft, this would be a gold mine."

"Pack up that computer and all of the pages on this table and take it to the resident agency office. I'll call Larsen, the IRS agent, and have him meet you there. See what else you can find on the computer. Were those files sent anywhere? Are there more of them? You know what to look for. I'll check with the command center to see who was picked up at this house. We'll want to talk to them."

Dick called the rest of his team to see what, if anything, they'd found at their locations, and to advise them to meet him at the resident agency office.

It was early evening when the CHP cars guarding the Dogg Pound were called off. Shortly after they left, a figure crawled across the field. When Al got to the street, he stood up, adjusted the straps on his backpack, and made a call on his now-operating cell phone. His old marine sergeant picked him up twenty minutes later.

31

Fresno, California

The large-screen television at the front of the room was the center of attention. It was tuned to KFSN, the local ABC affiliate. A breaking news banner was stretched across the top of the screen as Fresno's mayor and police chief were giving a press conference.

Hartmann and his squad sat eating a late lunch as they watched in the hotel meeting room that was now assigned to them as an office. They could see both Robin and Rosy in the background with several other law-enforcement officers who were involved with the raid.

The police chief gave the statistical results of the raid. "Early this morning, we arrested nearly three hundred people in a massive operation targeting what is referred to as the Dogg Pound area of Fresno. This area contains a high concentration of Bulldog gang members, which are Fresno's most violent criminals. We're not done. We're going to continue to conduct further operations citywide until we get the violent crime back down to where it should be: nonexistent!"

The mayor's next statements ended the press conference. "We have to stop the gang activity in our community. Gangs have made the conscious decision to be violent—to kill, to rob, and to rape. They have no redeeming value, in my eyes.

"Crimes involving gang members have simply become too common and too violent to ignore. The numbers of gang members are multiplying each day. They're coming to our community from Southern California, and many of our own youth are joining their ranks.

"I'm here to tell the citizens of Fresno that this morning's police activity was just the start. We're going to eradicate gangs in Fresno."

When the squad had enough of the politicos, they started working on a makeshift storyboard with pictures of the suspects and the crime scene. Dick started a timeline with the others assisting him in remembering things. A bellman arrived with two flip charts for their use.

At Dick's request, Robert Larson and two other IRS special agents showed up to help with the brainstorming session. Everyone knew each other, having lived in the same hotel on and off for what was now going on three weeks.

Dick shouted to the entire group, "Okay, Animals!" and noted the quizzical look on the IRS agents' faces. "Oh, sorry about that!"

Then, thinking about what he'd just said, Dick looked over to the IRS agents. "Sorry, guys. That's what I call my squad. I'll explain it to you some other time."

Dick started over. "We need to take some time to see what we have and if we can make any sense out of what's happened in the past three weeks. Daniel, why don't you start us out?"

"Well, we definitely know that Shaw was murdered. His murderer has to be someone who either works at or has access to the IRS center."

Harriett added, "From what happened yesterday, we can assume that the local Bulldogs had something to do with it. Otherwise, why shoot at out-of-town FBI agents?"

"I agree. My gut says they're tied together. Now, where does that lead us? What do we need to do?"

Dick looked toward Larsen. "Have you guys identified anything in your audit?"

"There's nothing obvious in regards to access to the computer or any anomalies we can identify in any of the programs to-date. We think it's time to start questioning people about what you found."

Daniel chimed in. "I have two ideas. First, I'll go back to the security office and see if there are cameras that would show us who was around Shaw's office around the time of this murder. Second, we need to see if there's any way to determine if any gang members work at the Center. Boss, I hate to profile an ethnic group, but I think we should interview all of the Hispanics who work at or have access to the Center."

"I like your ideas. Go ahead and see what you can do with the discs from the cameras. Robert, what do you think about screening the Hispanic staff at the Center?

"That's going to be a delicate one. Let me talk with Doug Smith and see what he thinks. If he agrees, we'll need to add to the number of agents we have here. I don't want to use the Center's security staff, based on what we know at the moment."

"Okay. You'll get back to me on this one?"

"Will do."

"Now, what else do we have?"

32

Fresno, California

Hartmann sat in the hotel conference room with his hands behind his head, mentally going through Shaw's death, Abramson, and the Bulldog Gang. How did they fit together? And then there was the terrible rape and murder of a young girl, which was probably triggered by their investigation. Harriet had taken that hard. It was late afternoon on Friday. His brain was fried. With what had happened and where they were on the case, he realized that he and his squad were stuck in Fresno for the weekend. In law enforcement, there are no weekends.

It was doubtful that they'd learn a lot over the weekend, but you never knew. This was still a new case and one where time was of the essence. He didn't want his squad to have to restart thinking about the case after two days off, but his experience as a law-enforcement officer told him it was once again time for the squad to blow off some steam. By the very nature of law enforcement, street agents see the worst of society, and once in a while, they have to get it off their minds.

Dick thought to himself, *Sports are a great release. I love sports, and I know all the Animals love to follow sports.* They were always fighting over which one of them got the first shot at the sports page of the newspaper.

Dick called Rosy, whom he knew was single, on his cell phone. "Hey, Rosy, I was wondering if you know a good sports bar in the city. We need to blow off some steam, and going to a sports bar on a Friday night sounds like just the ticket. By the way, you're welcome to join us."

"I do know a great sports bar, and the answer is yes. I'd love to join you guys."

"You're going to be way outnumbered tonight by feds. My bet is the IRS guys'll be joining us.

"How about five thirty at your hotel bar?"

"Sounds good to me."

Dick called out across the room. "Anyone interested to joining Rosy and I at a sports bar tonight?" He didn't want to seem to be pressuring anyone, which was sticky for him, since he was the boss. They all seemed to really want to join in and blow off some pressure, even the IRS guys.

Coleen was with the IRS guys at the hotel bar listening to their war stories when Dick arrived and joined in. Ten minutes later, the rest of the squad completed the group. The new arrivals were just about to order drinks when Rosy walked in.

Coleen called out to her, "Rosy! Rosy! Over here. I don't know if you've met the IRS agents yet."

"Great to meet you guys. Is everyone ready for a James Bond?"

IRS Special Agent Robert Larson responded to Rosy before anyone else could get out a word. "Rosy, what the heck are you talking about?"

"The sports bar we're going to has a drink called the 'James Bond.' Only appropriate for this group."

The hotel bartender joined the conversation with, "You guys must be going over to The Silver Dollar. Hate to lose your business here, but you're headed to a great spot. Should I cancel the last orders?"

Dick responded to the group, "Is that okay with everybody?"

All were in agreement. Dick charged the bill to his room and added a good tip. They were all talking together as they headed out to the hotel parking lot.

Dick and Coleen rode with Rosy in her car, and the rest piled into the bureau-provided SUV. They turned left onto Shaw and drove a little less than two miles, just past the Fresno Fashion Fair shopping mall, where they'd last blown off some steam. They turned into The Silver Dollar Hofbrau parking lot.

Upon entering, it was apparent that Rosy was a regular. She was greeted by a number of the staff and a couple of regulars as they walked along the lengthy bar. A very attractive blonde bartender dressed in a tight, low-cut, black dress was taking orders. Because of their numbers, a petite blonde waitress, also dressed in a nice black dress, walked over to assist in taking their orders.

Dick looked around and noted all of the waitress and the bartender were petite blonds wearing black dresses. *Who does the hiring? Where do they find all of the petite blonds? They certainly aren't an equal opportunity employer,* he thought. The crowd was casually dressed. Many were in Bulldog attire. Most were just Fresno State students or supporters in to have a beer, but some were gangbangers. You couldn't get away from them in this city.

Rosy introduced the waitress to the group and asked her to make sure she took good care of her friends.

Brian started out by asking, "Rosy tells me you have a drink called a James Bond. What's in it?"

With a smile on her face, she responded, "Bombay Sapphire Gin, Stolichnaya Crystal Vodka, vermouth, and your choice of an olive or an onion. Of course, it's shaken, not stirred. Think you can handle that, big boy?"

"I'll take a pass on that one. Make mine a Bud Light."

"You've got it. What does everyone else want?"

Wanting to last the night, they all ordered beers ranging from Bud to Foster's. Dick ordered a stein of Warsteiner, a good German beer.

"I'll put in your drink orders while you look at the menu. There are a couple of empty booths over there. It may be more comfortable for you."

Rosy asked the waitress to bring appetizers with the drinks for each booth. She ordered sides of calamari, mozzarella sticks with marinara sauce, and onion rings to get them started.

Coleen spotted a jukebox and headed toward it with Dick in tow. Rosy followed them over. They agreed on five songs: "Get the Party Started" by Pink; "Complicated" by Avril Lavigne; "Soak Up the Sun" by Sheryl Crow; "Jenny from the Block" by Jennifer Lopez; and "Where Are You Going" by Dave Matthews Band.

Coleen grabbed Dick and began dancing. He joined in as best he could. As they were dancing, she shouted over the music to Dick, "How about a bet on the game tomorrow?"

"What game?"

"You're out of touch. My Wildcats are playing your Bruins."

"My God, how did I miss that? Villanova and UCLA. That should be a great game."

"Should be."

"If I can get tickets, you want to go?"

"It's in LA."

"Easy trip from here," he replied and then thought, *So much for my "we're stuck here," importance of the case" philosophy.*

"Why not?"

Dick left and got on his cell. Fifteen minutes later, he told Coleen, who was now group dancing with Rosy and Harriett, "Got the tickets for the game and flights to LA and back."

When they returned to the table, the waitress was delivering the various beers in frosted mugs, along with the sides ordered by Rosy. They each ordered carved meat plates ranging from roast beef and corned beef to pastrami. Dick ordered what was billed as genuine Chicago knockwurst.

As they were eating, a well-dressed, middle-aged man walked over to the table. "Hey, Rosy, how's the FPD treating you these days?"

"Andy, how you doing? The department is treating me great. How's the car business?"

"Can't complain. The economy is good and people are buying cars."

"Everyone, this is Andy Kelly, the local Dodge dealer. This is pickup truck and SUV country, and Andy does quite well. Andy, careful what you say. These are FBI and IRS agent friends of mine."

"Nice to meet you all. Were you involved in what happened yesterday?"

Rosy responded for them. "Yes, they were. They're helping me clean up our town."

"Rosy, that's great. Speaking for Fresno, I thank you all. There's no question we have a drug and gang problem and can use all the federal help we can get."

The table thanked Andy for his comments. As he was about to leave, he turned back toward them. "You guys interested in joining me in my box at the Bulldog football game tonight? I'm headed over there now, and there's plenty of room for all of you."

Rosy looked at Dick for comment.

"Why not? Everyone interested?" he asked.

The five songs they'd selected were over and The Silver Dollar was filling up with a younger crowd. They all agreed going to a football game would be better than spending the night in an out-of-town sports bar filled with a bunch of drunken young party "Animals."

33

Fresno, California

It was easy to follow Andy, as he was driving a fire-engine red Dodge Durango. The two cars filled with law-enforcement officers followed the red vehicle back down Shaw, and everyone in the cars laughed when Andy pulled into the Piccadilly Inn and parked his car in the lot. The two cars parked next to his.

Andy stepped down from the running board of the Durango and opened the passenger-side door for an attractive lady. A man and a lady exited from the backseat of the vehicle. "Meet my wife, Lydia, and my sales manager, Ralph, and his wife, Judy. It's safe to park here. I'm friends with the owners."

Dick responded, "Were not worried about parking here. This is the hotel where we're staying. I'm not so sure how safe it is around here. We were shot at right over there, across the street."

"Short memory. I saw it on TV the other night, but I didn't know this is where you guys were staying. This is where all of the excitement occurred the other day. Well, hopefully it's safe tonight, with all of the Bulldog football fans around. It's just a short walk over to the stadium."

"We know. Generally, our workout is to do a few laps around the stadium every morning."

"You guys do look fit. I guess it's part of the job."

"That it is. We need to be in as good a shape as the bad guys."

"I have to respect you for what you do. It's not something I could do."

"Hate to tell you, but I would have a hard time being a car salesman." Quickly changing the subject, Dick said, "Who are the Bulldogs playing tonight?"

"We're playing the San Diego State Aztecs. Should be a good game. The last spread I saw was almost even for the game. I do feel sorry for any team coming into Bulldog Stadium. You'll see why during the game. The Bulldogs' fans are considered some of the noisiest in the country."

Dick could hear the noise coming from the stadium as they continued walking from the hotel parking lot. It was a perfect Central Valley evening for football. The temperature was in the mid-seventies and, thank God, there was little humidity tonight. They walked down North Cedar Avenue and turned onto Bulldog Lane, a tree-lined concourse that led to the stadium. Andy got them through the ticket gate. They headed up the stairs to Andy's sky suite.

Dick looked down at a sea of bright red in the stands.

"We pride ourselves in providing the Bulldogs with a home field advantage. They seldom lose home games because of what we call the 'Red Wave.'"

"Andy, how big is this stadium? From the outside, it doesn't look that big, but you get inside and this is a major stadium."

"It holds more than forty-one thousand people and is usually filled to capacity for each football game. The reason you don't think it's that big from the street is that the field down there is thirty feet below grade level, so the stadium has a very low profile."

Dick sat between Coleen and Rosy. He loved sports, but this

evening, he was more curious about the crowd than the game. In walking over and up to the skybox, he'd noticed a lot of people sporting bulldog tattoos.

"Rosy, this is going to sound strange, but am I looking at close to forty thousand gangbangers down there? This is like a gang in San Francisco being called the Giants or in LA being called the Dodgers."

Rosy responded. "It's unfortunate that the gang decided to call themselves the Bulldogs, but it's a fact of life here in Fresno. My department estimates that there are ten thousand Bulldog gang members in Fresno. This is out of a population of eight hundred thousand. I'm sure some of them down there are gang members."

"Do you think you'll ever get them under control?"

"I honestly don't know. From a law-enforcement perspective, we hope to contain and isolate them from the law-abiding civilian population. My chief says my unit's mission is to eliminate the Bulldog gang in Fresno, but he adds, 'It's like going into Iraq, in some respects.' Unless the economy changes to where they can get educations and jobs, and Americans stop buying billions of dollars in drugs, which support the gangs, then containment is all, I believe, we can hope for. I read a report just yesterday that sixty thousand Fresnoans live in high-poverty neighborhoods. For those neighborhoods, the principal commodity of trade is drugs. I'll bet that out of the forty thousand people down there, two thousand are buying drugs from gang members. Unfortunately, it's the way of life here."

Dick sighed and replied, "Well, I guess we have job security."

Dick and Rosy were interrupted from their sober conversation by a roar from the crowd. The Bulldogs had just scored a touchdown.

34

Westwood Village, California

Their bodies were in great shape, and they needed to be, as Dick and Coleen continued their sports weekend. They caught a Saturday morning flight from Fresno to LAX. Dick had arranged for a rental car, and they drove to the W Hotel near the UCLA campus in Westwood. They checked into their rooms and agreed to meet in the lobby in half an hour.

Dick, who was a die-hard UCLA fan, having graduated from the school, changed into a UCLA jersey and khaki cotton pants and headed back downstairs. As he sat in the lobby watching the elevator for Coleen, he noted a lot of people wearing Villanova jerseys exiting from the elevators. One of the elevator doors opened, and there was Coleen with her arms around two other people. They were all wearing 'Nova jerseys.

"Hey, Dick, meet my friends from 'Nova. Guess what? You're invited to the 'Nova alumni party. It's here, in this hotel. By the way, nice outfit."

He was going to a rival team's party wearing a UCLA jersey. This was going to be interesting. He would have to be gracious and keep his mouth shut—neither of which he was necessarily good at.

"Nice Villanova jersey you have there. At least our pants match."

"Let's go to a party."

"You think they'll let me in?"

"Don't count on it, but I'll do my best. I'll even pay for your ticket."

The entire Villanova crowd was nice, and many of the staff from campus seemed to know Coleen. She had a way with people and worked the crowd like a politician. He met the president of Villanova, an Augustinian priest, the basketball coach, and the director of alumni affairs, who volunteered to give him a 'Nova jersey in exchange for his UCLA one. He politely declined, but he did think of going back upstairs and changing into a white golf shirt. *No. No way.*

He was surprised in talking with the Villanova folks at how many of them were in the military, or in law enforcement. Dick met a fellow FBI agent and a DEA agent. Several were in local law enforcement, and there was also a parole officer. He had no problem carrying on a conversation with this group.

The food at the reception was interesting. It definitely had a Philly bend. There were cheesesteak hoagies, with or without Cheese Whiz. The Cheese Whiz thing seemed to create a lot of discussion between the alums. The hoagies were on Amoroso rolls brought in by the campus staff. They also brought Tastykakes from Philadelphia for dessert. The bar included Rolling Rock Beer.

Not exactly a UCLA party. Where's the sushi? The tacos and margaritas?

After the party broke up, Dick, Coleen, and several of the alumni walked over to the Westwood Brewing Company on Glendon. When Dick was at UCLA, it was called the "Brewco." The group, including the DEA agent and the parole officer, sat at the outside patio drinking microbrews and eating fries. The Villanova stories were flying like crazy, and they didn't even mind a few of Dick's UCLA stories.

After a few brews, Coleen asked Dick, "How'd you end up as a special agent in the FBI?"

"I got out of the army and decided that I was a patriotic person, and law enforcement seemed like a good place to go. The top law-enforcement agency in the country seemed to be the FBI. I wasn't the CIA type, and local law enforcement didn't seem attractive to me either. Not for publication, but I was in the army finance corp. Basically, we paid the army's bills. There were payroll checks to the troops and bills for rent, eggs, tanks, artillery shells, and research projects. You name it, we wrote checks for it.

"Some money laundering and counterfeit-currency problems cropped up that involved a foreign government. I got involved in that project. The project required a liaison with our Treasury and State Departments. For some reason, I was selected as the Department of Defense liaison. I liked this type of work. When I'd built up enough brownie points with the right people, I easily got into the FBI. I like what I do.

"You'll learn there is a bad side to the job as well. This is a terrible way to put it, but we clean up our society's garbage. Sometimes the garbage is just shredded paper from financial institutions' trash bins, and other times, it's rotting garbage from trash cans in alleys. What we do has meaning, but it's hard on us. You'll see what I mean over time. Many law-enforcement people end up leaving because they can't stand the trash they're dealing with."

Suddenly, Dick thought to himself, *This is getting complicated. How did I get into this mess?* They couldn't take their eyes off each other. His was an awkward stare. Hers was—one of interest?

"You sure know how to romance a girl. Just kidding. I liked what you had to say. It provides a good perspective for me on what I've gotten into."

"Sorry about that. Probably why I've stayed a bachelor all these years. Let's see if I can improve on the conversation."

Dick was saved by the 'Nova crowd. "Hey, you two, it's time to head over for the game."

Hand in hand, they all walked together over to Pauley Pavilion, the famous house that John Wooden built. A CBS-TV van was parked next to it, with black cables running inside. This was a nationally televised, nonconference game.

Every time before, Dick had sat behind the Bruins' bench. This time, in his UCLA jersey, he was sitting way upstairs in corner seats behind the goal post at the west end. The seats were about as far away from the game as you could get. Dick was getting a better understanding of home-court advantage. *Visitors, welcome to Pauley. Good luck having your team hearing you cheer them on.*

"First time I've been up here."

"I see UCLA treats the visiting team well," Coleen replied.

"It's called home-court advantage. I have a sneaking hunch that 'Nova does the same thing."

The UCLA band started playing, and the cheerleaders were revving up the crowd. The arena was just about full—full of Bruin fans who knew how to taunt the visiting team. The Villanova cheerleaders were doing their best to see their fans, let alone hear them, up in the second deck. It appeared that the Pauley Pavilion setup had an impact on the Wildcat players. The game ended up child's play for the Bruins. They ran their transition game and full-court press to near perfection, driving Villanova to distraction. The Bruins were up by thirty-one points at the half. The Wildcat fans realized the game was out of reach. They made their points about the Pauley effect, but they praised Dick's team. The final score ended up being ninety-three to sixty-five. The Wildcat players had twenty-six turnovers. It was a real shellacking.

On the way back to the hotel, Dick asked Coleen if she wanted to go out to dinner that night. She agreed to meet in the hotel lobby at six o'clock.

Upon returning to his room, Dick called one of his favorite restaurants for reservations. He took a nap and showered. He was anxious for the time to pass quickly so he could be together with Coleen again. *What is this all about?*

They met again in the lobby. Dick drove down Wilshire Boulevard toward downtown LA. They entered Beverly Hills, passed Rodeo Drive, and he turned left onto Canon Drive. He turned right on the next block and parked the car on the street.

"Sorry. I don't use valet parking. I'm so used to having weapons in the trunk, I just automatically park on the street."

"I could use some walking. Where're we going?"

"Oh, a little restaurant right around the corner."

They walked around the corner, and on their left was Spago's.

"Oh, my God. You have got to be kidding. We're eating here?"

With a grin on his face, Dick responded, "Yes, we are."

"Good evening, Mr. Hartmann. Good to see you again. How are you this evening?" the maître d' asked.

"Just fine. Is my table ready?"

"Of course. Follow me."

They went past the bar, which was on their left. Across from the bar was a courtyard dining area. Dick had spent a fair amount of his time and money at the bar looking out to the courtyard. This was his old home court.

They were seated in the main dining room. There was a viewing kitchen at the back of the room. They were with the West LA/Beverly Hills crowd. It included movie and TV types, from actors to producers. There were well-heeled businesspeople and entertainment people, the gawkers and the wannabes. Dick had seen them all over the years, as he had been brought up in the area.

"A half bottle of Billecart-Brut Reserve Champagne to start with." As the waiter left, Dick suggested to Coleen that it went well with the

Roasted Chino Farm's Beet Layer Cake. "It's a salad to die for, both in taste and presentation."

For a main course, Coleen ordered pan-roasted leg of young Sonoma lamb. Dick ordered a favorite of his: the pan-roasted liberty duck breast. He decided that a bottle of Brunello de Montalcino 2001 wine would go well with their dinner.

As they were eating, Wolfgang Puck strolled up to the table to chat, something he always did when he was in town. After all, this was his flagship restaurant.

"Mr. Hartmann, how are you this evening?"

"Just fine, Wolfgang. I'd like to introduce you to Coleen Ryan, a friend of mine."

"Nice to meet you, Coleen. Are you enjoying your dinner?"

"The beet layer salad was unbelievable. My lamb is perfect. It's a perfect dinner!"

"I am so glad to hear that. Dick, don't be such a stranger."

Following their gourmet meal, Dick, with Coleen on his arm, went into the kitchen and thanked the chef and Wolfgang again. He always did this at the restaurants he frequented. Then they headed back to the hotel.

Dick and Coleen stood in front of the door to her room just looking at each other.

"You want to come in?" she asked.

"Do you want me to?"

"I would like that very much."

As soon as the door to the room closed, they grabbed each other and kissed. Then they separated for a moment, and each removed their weapon and handcuffs. They were quickly placed on the table in front of the sofa, where they sat close together.

He asked, "Did you enjoy today?"

"It was the best day I've ever had. You're fun to be with."

"I liked being with you, too."

She pulled her legs up under her and turned a little sideways so she could see him better. He turned a little too, until they were facing each other from a foot away. He thought to himself, *This is a very nice package.* The shape of her ears, the color of her eyes, the legs all belonged to a model; her figure was great. There was nothing wrong with Coleen. Nothing at all. That was for sure.

She smelled great. Subtle Ysatis perfume. He leaned forward and kissed her, just lightly, on the lips.

Her mouth was open a little and was cool and welcoming. He slid his free hand under her hair to the back of her neck and pulled her closer. They kissed harder. She placed her hand behind his head and pulled him toward her. They kissed over and over again.

Their tongues moved quickly. He felt her warm skin. He slid his hand under her skirt. She grabbed his shirt and pulled it out of his waistband. He felt her nails against his skin.

He said, in a stupid way, "I don't do this—not with people who work for me."

"We're not working now," she said. "Besides, we're consenting adults. We're celebrating being alive."

Dick pulled her sweater upward and she raised her hands over her head so that he could get it off. She was wearing a white, lacy bra. He reached behind her back and unclipped it. Her breasts were just as good as he'd imagined on the first day he met her.

She unbuttoned his shirt and he raised his arms in turn. She leaned over and lifted his shirt over his head and then did the same with his T-shirt. Her hands moved over his chest, touching his nipples for a few seconds. She moved down to his belt, which she unbuckled and slid off. He slid off his pants and undershorts as she slid off her skirt and panties. They both were naked. He kissed her breasts. He picked her up and carried her to the bed.

The next morning, Dick woke up next to Coleen, who was still sound asleep. He looked at his watch. It was eight in the morning.

That was a great evening. Feel great this morning. No, fantastic. But I need a shower.

After slowly sliding out of his side of the bed so as not to awaken Coleen, Dick went into the bathroom. He closed the door behind him and found an unwrapped bar of bath soap, shampoo, and conditioner in a basket on the counter next to the sink. He turned on the shower and got it to the temperature he wanted and then slid in behind the shower curtain. He took a long, hot shower. It felt great. Particularly when he was washing his hair.

He got out of the shower and found Coleen's hairbrush in a bag on the counter. Thank God. If he didn't brush his hair immediately after a shower, it took on a wild look of its own. He put on one of the two hotel white, terry-cloth bathrobes located on the back of the bathroom door and exited the bathroom feeling very refreshed.

He was greeted by Coleen, who said, "You look like a Cheshire Cat. What's with that big grin on your face?"

"Oh, good morning. Look who's awake. My look is because I was feeling guilty when I snuck out of the bed to take a shower, but in the shower, I thought of J. Edgar Hoover and his very close aid, Clyde Tolson. They were rumored to be gay lovers. My guilt suddenly was gone."

"I was hoping for another answer. You sure know how to make a girl feel good. Not really a romantic, are you?"

"Oh, sorry. Didn't we have this conversation last night? That didn't sound too good, did it?"

"Not really. In fact, it sounds downright weird. Do you really think Hoover and Tolson were homosexual partners?"

"I have no idea and really don't care, but it's been a great rumor for years. I guess I'm not cut out to be a romantic. That's another reason why I'm still single."

"You sure come up with a lot of excuses for being single. We'll see what we can do about that."

"Exactly what are we talking about? Romanticism or the bachelor thing?

"Now you look worried. I can read your face like a book. For now, let's just try romance."

Dick bent down and starting picking up his clothes and folding them.

"What're you doing?" she asked.

"Folding my clothes so I can take them back to my room."

"Why would you want to do that?"

"So I can change into some clean underwear and clothes to wear to the airport."

"You're leaving?"

"Relax. I'll be back in an hour. You need the time to take your shower and do whatever you do before going out. Why don't you order us breakfast from room service for an hour from now?"

"I like the sound of that. What do you want to eat?"

"Surprise me."

Dick returned in an hour and knocked on the door. Coleen opened it and, with a half bow and an outstretched arm, indicated a feast of food on a portable hotel table with a white tablecloth. The shiny, metal lids had been removed to display the food.

"Holy shit. What did you do, order everything on the menu?"

"Not quite. There were some things on it I didn't like. Eat up. We have a plane to catch."

35

Fresno, California

Coleen glanced across the lobby of the Piccadilly Inn and saw two familiar faces. "Hey, Tom and Sharon, what're you guys doing here?"

"My God, Tom, it's Coleen from our academy class. Coleen, what're you doing here?

"I'm working on a case here in Fresno."

"By some chance, it wouldn't involve the local IRS center, would it?"

"It sure does."

"We're part of the crew here to help you interview the Hispanic IRS workers. We're meeting four more agents here in the lobby and we're going over to the Center together. We all checked in last night. What're you doing here at this hotel?"

"We've been staying here while working on this case. That's Dick Hartmann over there. He's the lead special agent on the case. Come. I'll introduce you to him and the rest of my squad. Hey, everyone, this is Tom Oken and Sharon Webster from my class at the academy."

Following introductions, they all drove over to the IRS Center. Something felt different about the Center as they walked to the Security Office. It was quiet, and everyone was staring at them.

Dick stuck his head into Mark Stevens' office. "Good morning. How's it going?"

"Well, it could be said we're busy. Based on the info you guys provided and the worries of our IRS special agents, we're planning to rescreen all of the Hispanic employees working here."

"I brought help with me for the rescreening process."

"Thanks. My staff has taken all the personnel files down to one of the big bays in the processing area. Come. I'll show you."

The squad and six additional agents followed Mark through the maze of halls that led to one of the large tax-return processing bays. There were twelve IRS special agents already seated at desks ready to begin interviewing the Center's Hispanic employees. The FBI and IRS special agents were paired up for the interviews.

During breaks between interviews, Coleen had opportunities to talk with the two members of her academy class. Tom had just finished an interview, and Coleen walked over to where he was sitting.

"Hello again, Tom. How's it going?"

"Coleen, it sure is good to see you. I could ask you the same question. I must admit, I was surprised to see you here. I thought you were sent to the San Francisco office."

"I was. I'm in a violent crime squad at the San Francisco field office. Our squad was assigned to investigate the murder that occurred at this IRS Center."

"Oh, yeah. They clued us in about the murder. You, apparently, are one of the lucky ones. I was sent to the Albuquerque field office, and Sharon over there was sent to Salt Lake City. We had dinner together last night, and it seems we're doing about the same thing. They have us doing security checks on applicants for various government agencies. I can't believe you're actually participating in a murder investigation."

"I'm not sure why I was so lucky. I'm part of a great squad, and our leader is Dick Hartmann. You probably know his name. It seems he's kind of famous in the bureau."

"I sure do know his name. He teaches a special advanced course at the academy."

"That's the guy. Anyway, how's it going here with the interviews?"

"I find it kind of touchy. First, we're only screening the Hispanic employees. The IRS agent I'm working with takes the lead. They bring us their personnel files and we ask questions to see if the information in the file is correct. Of particular interest is where they currently live, have they ever been a gang member, and do they have any relatives that are gang members. Also, have they seen or heard anything suspicious here at the IRS Center. If they're wearing long sleeves, we ask them to roll them up so we can look for gang tattoos. Boring. Boring."

"What happens if they have tattoos or you don't like the answers to your questions?"

"They're sent to that office over there, where they're questioned further by more senior special agents from both the bureau and the IRS. I understand several have been temporarily suspended and had their passes to the Center taken away."

Just then, Sharon walked over. "Coleen, good to see you."

"Hi, Sharon. Jim was just filling me in on what you guys are doing here. How long is the gig?"

"My guess is a couple of days."

"We should have time to catch up at the hotel."

"I'd like that. It's weird. They have us on some special floor with local police security."

Coleen smiled. "Then we're neighbors. I'll explain about that over drinks tonight at the bar."

"Boy, is that mysterious. I'll look forward to that explanation. We'd better get back to our interviews. It's a slow process, as many of the staff here seem to be more fluent in Spanish than English."

"I'm sure this process is going to slow down tax-return processing this year."

36

Fresno, California

The Spanish Language Unit employees were surprised to be greeted by agents Coleen Ryan and Brian Brooks when they opened the door to their work area.

Each employee's name was struck off a list as he or she entered. They were instructed to sit in one of the chairs lined up against one of the walls of the unit. As they sat, they watched IRS special agents and auditors at their workstations, combing through their papers and accessing their computers.

Once everyone had checked in, Coleen spoke to the seated group. "We're going to question each of you about the day Mr. Shaw was murdered. You aren't under arrest, but you are considered persons of interested in this investigation. Also, please don't talk to each other until you've been questioned."

"Ma'am, what is a person of interest?" one man asked.

"It just means we believe you may have some pertinent information about what happened to Mr. Shaw. You may not even realize it, but we've identified certain criteria that make you a person of interest."

At nine thirty, the entire group of SLU employees was escorted to a conference room in the main building, where they again waited in silence. In an adjacent conference room over the next three hours, Dick and Harriett questioned them one by one. Many of the questions asked were the same as those the FBI agents asked them in prior days. Then there were the new questions. Did you know that Edison Shaw was investigating what you did? Did Mr. Shaw ever question you? Are you familiar with this form letter? Did you know this letter is not an approved IRS form? Do you know where this letter may have come from? Do you know anything about missing checks that were included with correspondence you reviewed?

After the three hours of questioning the SLU employees, all except one were advised by IRS Agent Larson that they and the SLU were under investigation. The SLU was temporarily closed down, and the employees were advised that they were on paid leave from the Center until the investigation was concluded. Their ID cards were taken, and they were instructed not the leave the Fresno area.

Chris Martinez was purposely the last to be questioned. His fingerprints were found on all of the bogus IRS form letters. After Dick and Harriet concluded the routine initial questioning, Chris was taken back into the now-empty large conference room and left alone.

Dick gathered the squad outside the conference room. "Okay. I read this guy as a nice guy that got in over his head with the Bulldog gang. I don't want him to lawyer up before we can get anything out of him. He's been given his rights. I'm going to let him cool off for a while and then apply the nice guy, 'oh, by the way,' conversational approach."

Coleen asked, "What's that?"

"Coleen, just watch. This will be a learning experience for you."

An hour later, Dick and the entire squad returned to the conference room with sandwiches, chips, and soft drinks. "Oh, hi, Chris. It's lunchtime. Why don't you join us?"

Agent Lee had been selected as the "nice guy" and began talking randomly with Chris about his job at the IRS center, where he went to school, and what his favorite courses were.

Then, in between bites of his sandwich, Agent Lee asked in a nonchalant way, "Chris, just curious, why your fingerprints are on all of these letters?" He slid a number of the SLU letters they had found toward Chris.

"You know, don't you?" Chris replied.

"Yes, we have things pretty well figured out."

That's all it took to get things started.

In the next few minutes, a video camera was set up to record the questioning. It became a team effort, with a constant flow of questions. After two hours, Chris had detailed the entire SLU scam. Yes, the Bulldog Gang was involved in the operation. They obtained checks from individuals who they'd previously billed for bogus unpaid taxes. They felt safe in what they were doing because the taxpayers they were dealing with were always referred back to the SLU. He talked about the trips to San Francisco and the "company" credit cards and who had them. He included information on Jimmy Sanchez and Jorge Garcia, but when asked about Shaw's murder, he said that he didn't know anything about it.

As Chris was led away, Dick commented, "Well, that went well. Nice work, people. Time to get arrest warrants for Jorge Garcia and Jimmy Sanchez, and a search warrant for Chris Martinez's residence.

37

East Los Angeles, California

The Santa Ana winds were blowing, creating a warm afternoon in East Los Angeles. The three of them were sitting at a picnic table under a shady, covered area of Jorge Garcia's uncle's house. The house was small, so Al Gomez and Ed Abramson ended up sleeping on the back porch.

"We need to get outta here," Al said to Abramson.

"You're right about that. Jorge, did you see your uncle's face this morning? He wants us to leave."

"Fuckin' A, he does. We've worn out our welcome. Things should've cooled down by now. We need to move on."

"It's time to head down to Mexico. It'll be safer, and we may be able to pick up some money from the computer data files we have with us. They'll pay big time for the information on those files." Al commented.

Al replied, "You're right. Let's head to San Diego tomorrow and cross the border there. To play it safe, I think we need to split up. There's no question the cops are looking for us. They probably have some pretty good pictures of us by now. Two Hispanics traveling with a white dude makes it easier for them to spot us. Sergeant, you're my friend, but it's time to break up the relationship, at least for now."

"I'm gonna need some money," Ed replied.

"Understand, my friend."

Al went into the house and returned with his backpack. He reached inside and pulled out packs of hundred-dollar bills. "That's ten thousand. It should take care of you until we can get back together. Call Jorge's uncle here for messages. I've given him a burner phone, just for our calls. Here's the number."

"Okay. I'll stay in touch. If we're going to split up, I'm taking off today. I'm tired of sleeping on this porch; slept outside enough in the marines."

"Certainly understand that. A good night's sleep without your snoring will be good for me too. Good luck, my friend."

Thirty minutes later, Ed left the house, freshly showered and wearing clean clothes. He wasn't sure what to do after splitting from Al and Jorge. He had ten thousand dollars in cash but no plan. He suspected that he'd probably never see his marine buddy Al again, but that was life.

He walked onto a main street near the house and spotted a bus pulling up to a bus stop. He ran for it and jumped on just before the driver closed the doors. Al was right about splitting the group up. He was the only white guy on the bus, which headed west from East LA toward the civic center. He got off near city hall and started walking. Within a few minutes, he was in Chinatown. He found a small Chinese restaurant, went in, and had war won ton soup and an order of sweet and sour pork with steamed rice. He laughed to himself after opening the fortune cookie, which read, "You have great wisdom." He doubted that.

After walking a considerable distance west, Ed ended up at Sunset and Vine in the heart of Hollywood. Might as well be a tourist. He walked down Hollywood Boulevard and stopped in front of

Grauman's Chinese Theatre. He checked the size of his hands and feet against those of the stars in the theater's concrete courtyard. Tiring of that, he looked around to find something else to do to kill time. He spotted the Kodak Theatre and thought, *I've watched the Academy Awards presented from this place.* He walked to the far side of the theater, and a huge sign in the form of a bowling pin caught his attention. Lucky Strike Lanes.

Ed loved bowling as a kid and did a lot of it in the marines. He wandered in. It took some time for his eyes to adjust to the dimmed lighting, but they he did, and he realized this did not look like any bowling alley he'd ever seen before. He pulled up a stool at a very fancy bar, which had to have at least twenty-five barstools. The place was more like a disco lounge than a bowling alley. It was ultra-modern, which gave it the appearance of being too swanky to be a bowling alley. Most of the lighting was neon. They didn't have Dos Equis, so he ordered a Corona, which came with a lime stuck in the long neck of the bottle. The first swallow went down very easily.

"Do you like that Mexican beer?"

Ed turned to his right. On the barstool next to him sat a hot-looking, short, dark-haired gal wearing a blue T-shirt with an Australian flag on the front. To compensate for her height, she had on five-inch heels.

"As a matter of fact I do. You Australian?"

"Very perceptive," she said as she grabbed the front of her T-shirt on either side of the Australian flag and pulled it forward.

"I know. I'm so smart. If you're Australian, why are you drinking Bud?"

"When in Rome, do as the Romans. The Bud is all right, but I do prefer my Foster's better. I'm Kelly and this is Trish. What's your name?"

"I'm Ed."

"You live here?"

"No. Just a tourist like you."

"We've been in the area for a week. Did Disneyland, Universal Studios, Rodeo Drive, and on and on. How about you?"

"Just got into town. Do you like bowling?"

"Never tried."

"How about trying? I used to be pretty good at it."

"Trish, what do you think?"

"Why not?"

Ed pulled out a wad of bills and paid the bar tab for all of them. He then led them to the front desk. They were assigned lane seven and provided with bowling shoes.

As they sat down at their alley, Ed tried to explain the game and was happy to assist each of them in developing the proper stance. After numerous gutter and lofted balls were thrown, frustration set in on the part of the two Aussies. They decided they'd drink while they watched Ed bowl. Once he got into the groove, he hit a number of strikes in a row.

A waitress brought over a menu and they ordered a round of Foster's and some snacks. Ed was in heaven. Ten thousand bucks in his pocket and two beautiful Aussies on either side of him who were rooting him on to bowl strikes. *What else could you ask for?*

Over the next hour, the gals decided they liked Ed. He was funny and an American. They invited him back to their hotel in West Hollywood. Trish drove the rental car down Sunset Boulevard and pulled into the hotel driveway, which was located right across the street from the House of Blues. The valet parking attendant recognized the girls and gave them a friendly hello and Ed a thumbs-up. They went up to the room, cleaned up, and decided to head across the street to close down the House of Blues.

Ed found he was on the older side of the crowd at the House of Blues. The place was packed. It was standing-room only, with the bar backed up three deep. They tossed down a number of drinks and feasted on lobster tacos. Kelly and Trish were feeling no pain as they started dancing together, with their heads whipping their hair around. They lasted until closing time, when they staggered arm-in-arm across Sunset back to the hotel.

The drinks and adrenaline flowing through his body that day had taken their toll. Ed collapsed on the couch in the girls' room and began snoring—a terrible, drunken snore. Kelly pushed him a couple of times, and he rolled over. The snoring decibel level was successfully lowered, at least in the short term. She then flopped on the bed next to Trish, who was already sound asleep.

The next morning, they all woke up at noon, totally hungover. They were moving slowly and the gals suddenly realized that they had to check out at one in the afternoon. To Ed's absolute delight, they ended up sobering up together in the shower. They rationalized that there was only time for one shower, so it had to be a group shower.

"Ed, do you want to join us in San Diego? We have a hotel reservation there for tonight."

With their luggage and his backpack in the trunk of their rented convertible, they headed west on Sunset toward Beverly Hills. Just after passing the UCLA campus, they entered the Interstate 405 Freeway heading south toward San Diego.

Kelly was driving, with Trish in the front seat next to her. Ed spread out across the backseat, enjoying the sun. He quickly went back to sleep. Traffic on the 405 was terrible until they passed the off ramp to LAX. When the freeway opened up, Kelly decided she'd crawled along enough and pushed down on the accelerator. She was cruising along at eighty-five miles an hour. A CHP officer spotted the car and followed in behind until he got a speed reading. After a couple of miles, he turned on the car's flashing red lights and briefly hit the siren.

Kelly looked in the rearview mirror and shouted in a definite Australian accent, "Fuck me dead!"

"Kelly, what is it?" asked Trish. "Oh, fuck."

Ed heard the siren. His mind was in a daze. He knew there was a problem coming. He sat up and looked behind him. His face turned white, and the heavenly feeling he'd felt with the girls evaporated. He reached down and unzipped the small travel bag he had thrown on the floor. He found the gun and slid it under his jacket on the seat beside him.

Kelly moved from the fast lane of the freeway to its shoulder and finally came to a stop. The highway patrolman got out of his car and walked to about six feet behind the convertible and shouted, "Lady, turn off your engine."

Kelly, shaking, complied. The patrolman then walked up to the driver's door and leaned over it and asked, "Do you know why I pulled you over?"

"Because I was going too fast?"

"Yes, miss, because you were going too fast. May I see your driver's license and vehicle registration?"

"Officer, I'm Australian. I'm just visiting your country. I'm so very sorry. I didn't realize how fast I was going."

"Welcome to the US of A, miss. May I see your Australian driver's license and your rental-car agreement?"

It took awhile for Kelly to find her driver's license in her over-stuffed travel purse. Trish located the rental agreement in the glove compartment. This took several minutes, during which time the officer's eyes took an interest in Ed.

With the driver's license and rental agreement in hand, the officer returned to his patrol car. Ed watched him the entire way. He wasn't looking at the license or the rental agreement. He was looking at something else in his car and then got on the police radio. The cop was watching something in his car. Ed guessed it was a computer screen. The officer then looked quickly at the driver's license and rental agreement and started heading back to the car. His stance was different, and his right hand was sitting on the top of his gun holster. Again, he stopped six feet behind the car. This time, he shouted, "I'm going to have to ask you all to get out of the car."

"Why?" asked Kelly.

"Ma'am, you all need to get out of the car right now, and I need to be able to see your hands."

Kelly and Trish opened their doors and got out of the car. Ed stood up in the backseat with his jacket over his arm. He fired two shots; one hit the officer in the head and the other in the chest. Either one would have been fatal.

The Australians screamed. Ed jumped into the driver's seat, started the car, and drove off.

38

Los Angeles, California

E d knew he had to get off the freeway and dump the car. He took the first off-ramp, going north on Sepulveda. As he entered Culver City, a patrol car spotted the red convertible driving at a high rate of speed. It matched the one that had just been reported over their radio as being involved in an officer-involved shooting.

The patrol car followed the speeding convertible. The officer radioed headquarters and then hit the switch for the lights and siren. The red convertible sped up, and the chase was on. Within a few blocks, two other Culver City PD cars joined the hot pursuit.

Ed had no idea where he was going. The streets in this area seemed to go at strange angles. He made a partial right onto a small street and then a couple more blocks down, turned right again. He was going up a hill on a steep and winding road. He'd entered the part of Culver City known as Culver Crest. This was the neighborhood of many local mid-level executives and movie-magic technicians at MGM Studios. The area was an upper-middle-class residential neighborhood with nicely maintained houses and beautifully manicured front lawns.

As he turned one of the corners, Ed realized he was trapped. At the far end of the street was a patrol car blocking the road. He slammed on the brakes and the car came to a screeching halt. His mind raced as he pushed the button that popped the trunk. He jumped out and quickly retrieved the backpack. Then he ran across the lush, green lawn and pushed open a wooden gate that led to a backyard where a young boy was playing in a sandbox.

Ed grabbed the boy around the waist and lifted him to his side. The kid was screaming as Ed and the boy entered the house through a sliding glass door. He found himself in a family room. A woman entered from a distant doorway. Sternly, she shouted, "Who are you?"

Ed pulled out his gun and pointed it at the boy's head. "Shut up and listen to me."

"Oh, God. Don't hurt Billy!"

"Lady, shut up and lie down on the floor."

"Why do you want me to lie down?"

"Lady, I'm not going to hurt you or your Billy here, if you follow my directions. There are going to be a ton of police around your house in a couple of minutes. I can't waste my time worrying about you, but I need to keep you here in the house, understand?"

Sophie Winestock complied and lay down on the floor. Billy kept struggling in Ed's arms, not fully understanding the threat of a gun. Ed noted a small bathroom. He glanced in. There were no windows—a perfect place to keep the kid out of the way. He deposited Billy in the bathroom and shoved a large chair up against the door to keep him in.

Back in the family room, Ed locked the sliding glass door, pulled the drapes across, and ripped the cord from one of the other window drapes. He tied Sophie's hands behind her back and then tied her feet.

"You brute. Why are you doing this?"

He stood over her and put his index finger up to his lips. "Shhhhh. Just keep quiet, lady, and everything will be fine. Understand?"

There was a small nod of her head, indicating she understood.

Screams and pounding kept coming from the small bathroom.

God, kid, would you shut the fuck up? I can't think. Ed pounded back on the door.

"Shut up, kid, or I'll hurt your mom!"

Billy became quiet.

Ed kept his profile low as he crawled to the front door. It was locked. He tucked the gun into his belt and then pushed a large living room chair up against the front door. Other furniture was stacked against the windows. Returning to the family room, Ed sat down next to Sophie Winestock with his backpack next to him. He felt defeated.

Things remained calm for a while, but then Ed noticed a cop moving toward the sliding glass door. He could hear the sirens of other cars approaching.

Ed shouted, "I'll kill this lady and her kid if you don't back off!"

The Culver City patrol officer thought for a moment and then retreated. Staying low, he backtracked along the side of the house to the street. Now there were four Culver City patrol cars in front. Officers, guns drawn, were watching from behind their service vehicles. An unmarked car pulled up with two detectives inside.

The first responding officer advised the two detectives of what he had seen. "The suspect entered the house from the backyard. He'd seen the suspect sitting next to a woman tied up on the floor of the family room. The suspect spotted him and threatened to shoot the hostage."

The detectives requested further backup, now knowing they had a hostage situation on their hands. The house sat high on a cliff that backed up to Holy Cross Cemetery. It couldn't be reached easily by the roads in the area. Two units were dispatched to the rear of the cemetery to seal off any possible escape attempt at the back of the house.

As the patrol officers waited for backup, they were advised by dispatch that the suspect was Edward Abramson. He was considered armed and dangerous. He was wanted for shooting a CHP officer, and the FBI had issued a federal arrest warrant for him.

"Do not proceed with apprehending the suspect until further backup arrives," they were instructed.

39

Culver City, California

Hartmann was enjoying the cool San Francisco weather following the heat of Fresno. He was surfing the Comcast TV guide,
looking to see if there were any sporting events on that might interest
him. He heard his cell vibrate on the table, and then it rang. The
discussion was short. He texted his squad to meet him for a flight to
LA. Ed Abramson was holding two hostages and had communicated
to the hostage negotiators that he'd only talk to Hartmann.

The FBI flight touched down just a few miles from Culver City
at LAX. In less than twenty minutes, they traveled from LAX to the
hostage scene.

Dick spoke with the hostage negotiator. He filled him in on what
he knew about Abramson's personality and his previous meetings
with him. The negotiator suggested Hartmann call the house phone
that he'd been using.

"Hello."

"Hello, Ed. How're you doing?"

"That's a dumb question, Hartmann. How the hell do you think
I'm doing? Fuckin' terrible. I shot a cop. Didn't really mean to do
that, but it happened."

"You wanted to talk to me?"

"Yeah. You seem like a straight shooter, and you already know me. I want to strike the best deal I can. I think you're the person who can get it done. I don't want to die."

"Okay, Ed. The first thing you're going to have to do is release the hostages to show good faith."

"Come on, Hartmann. You fucking think I'm nuts? I'm not going to release either one of them until the deal is worked out."

"What's the deal you're looking for?"

"I'll give you the info you need about what's happening at the IRS center and let the hostages go, if you make sure I get out of here alive, and no death penalty."

"Okay, Ed. Give me some time to check what I can do."

"I've got all the time in the world. You should see what's in the refrigerator here."

"Okay. Let me make a couple of phone calls. You just stay calm."

Dick hung up and looked at the hostage specialist, who advised, "Sounds like he's rational and realistic. I'm not sure how you want to play this, but the cop he shot isn't federal. The death penalty thing is probably up to the state attorney general. He killed a CHP officer."

"Yeah, I agree with your assessment. Let's get one of our attorneys here and have them contact their friends in the state attorney general's office. My gut feeling is that the state is not going to want to give in on the death penalty."

While Agent Daniel Lee contacted the FBI General Counsel Office, Dick and the rest of the squad met with the Culver City detectives and local FBI agents. The officer who went into the backyard recounted what he'd seen. Mrs. Winestock's husband arrived at the scene. He was advised of what had occurred and provided the officers with information about the layout of the house.

Two alternative plans were made. The second, only to be used if it appeared the hostages were in immediate danger, involved the use of the SWAT team. The first was more passive. Dick's team members were going to take the lead. Dick was going to continue his communications with Abramson and try to get him to move into the living room at the front of the house.

Daniel and Harriett were going to be hoisted by a man-lift up the side of the cliff from the cemetery at the back of the property into the backyard. They were to move up against the back of the house and place listening devices and scanners through one or two windows. Brian and Coleen were going to the yards of the neighboring houses to see if they could cross between the yards to get up against Winestock's house.

Twenty minutes later, everyone had made it to his or her assigned location. The listening devices and scanners where placed through two windows. They showed the family room and one of the three bedrooms.

Ed had moved his hostages into the living room at the front of the house. He could see Dick through the front window while he was talking to him on the phone. Brian was up against the right side of the house, crouched down below a window.

Coleen was on the left side of the house, next to the wall of the garage. She saw a door that led into the laundry room. She knew Abramson was in the living room, so she rose up and looked through the door's window. The room had a second door that led into the rest of the house. She tried the door handle, and it easily and quietly turned. Slowly, she opened the door and slid into the small laundry room. Suddenly, the other door burst open and knocked her backward in the confined space. She was standing face to face with Abramson. His right hand held a gun that was pointed straight at Coleen's face.

"Lady, what the hell do you think you're doing?"

Her gun was wedged at her side against the small room's wall. A false move or kick to the guy's groin would probably result in his gun firing at her head. *God, this was a major screw-up.*

"Drop your gun before I blow your face off!"

Coleen thought for a moment and then complied. Abramson backed away, with the gun pointed at her head. He was smart enough to keep some distance between them. He ordered her into the living room.

"See that lady over there? Lay facedown next to her."

Mrs. Winestock, who was sitting against a wall of the room, moved over to give Coleen room.

"Do you have handcuffs?" Ed asked.

"Why do you want to know?"

"Oh, come on, FBI agent, I recognize you now. Why do you think I want to know? Forget about the question. Yes, you do have handcuffs. Reach behind your back and put them on yourself."

Once the handcuffs were on, Ed walked over and pushed them tighter. He then frisked her and, to his surprise, didn't find a backup weapon.

Oh, God! This is a nightmare! How could I put myself in this position? Stupid, stupid, stupid, Coleen thought.

When Dick's conversation with Ed was cut off in mid-sentence, he knew something was wrong. The SWAT team commander, who was standing next to Dick, quickly ordered option two into motion. The SWAT team sharpshooters, who were already in position, released the safeties on their weapons. Six team members prepared to storm the house.

Ed was back on the phone. "What the hell are you trying to pull? Now I have another hostage. One of your female agents."

Dick put his hand over the phone. He grabbed the communications mic and clicked the button. "Harriett, Harriett, what's your position?"

As soon as she responded, he asked, "Coleen, what is your position?" The lack of response told him what he wanted to know.

"Ed, I suspect that you have Agent Ryan. Let me talk with her."

"No way, but nice try. Just get me what I want, and no more tricks. I thought I could trust you."

"Is she all right?"

"Yes. She's all right."

"You can trust me. I'm working on it. It takes awhile to get something like what you want approved."

"Hartmann, as far as I'm concerned, the trust part is gone. If I don't get what I want, your agent is the first to die. I've got nothing to lose now. You can't fry me twice."

"Okay, okay."

The hostage negotiator leaned over to Dick and said, "Change the subject. You don't want him thinking that way."

"Hey, Ed, now that you've got our agent, how about letting the kid go?"

"No way. I'm keeping them all. That should speed up your approval process. Otherwise, you'll try and wait me out for days. That's not gonna happen. They all die in an hour, and then we'll have a shootout that'll shame the OK Corral. I would just as soon die now than wait on death row. It's your decision as to the outcome."

"Okay, okay. We're getting close," Hartmann replied.

Dick looked over at the FBI associate deputy general counsel. "What's the decision?"

"The state guys don't want to let him off the hook. The best I can do is give you an agreement that covers federal prosecution, which is worthless for him. It won't protect him from the state death penalty. How smart is this guy?"

"I don't know, and the way things are going right now, I don't care. Give me your agreement."

Dick got back on the phone, "Ed, I've got your agreement. I'll bring it in to you."

"Not that I don't trust you, but I don't. Give me five minutes, and then you come up to the front door with only your pants on. Come through the door, and I'll tell you what to do next."

Dick picked up the tactical headset. "Daniel, how's the reception on the fiber-optic cameras?"

"We have pretty good views of the kitchen and one bedroom."

"All right. Keep me posted on anything you see. Abramson is apparently going to be moving things around. I need to know what he's doing."

"I'll keep you posted."

"Harriett and Brian, I'm going to need you two to back me up. Brian, work your way around to the side of the house where Coleen was located. I want both of you to get to either side of the front door of the house without being seen."

"Got it."

"Me, too."

"Which one of you is the better shot?"

After a pause, Brian said, "Harriett is. She always beats me at the range."

"All right, Harriett is the first through the front door of the house. I'll go through the front door of the house. You two come up on either side. If I say to Abramson 'Here's what you want,' Harriett comes through the door first to take him out. I'll drop to the floor to my right to give you a clear shot. If I don't say that, stay put. I want you both to repeat this plan to me."

Dick listened as they repeated the plan.

Daniel's voice came over the tactical headphones. "Abramson moved the chair away from the front door. Abramson and the hostages are now in the kitchen. I have a clear view of them. Mrs. Winestock and her son are sitting tied up against some kitchen cabinets on the left. Abramson has Coleen standing in front of him, with his gun to her head."

Dick added another signal to the plan. "If I use the phrase, 'Nice to talk to you in person,' you two are to crawl through the front door of the house."

Dick hadn't counted on Coleen being used as a human shield.

Ed was ready and made the call to Hartmann.

Stripped down to the waist with the worthless agreement in his right hand, Dick started walking toward the house. He could see Harriett and Brian crawling along on either side of the front of the house toward the door he was going through. He entered and Ed shouted out, "We're in the kitchen! Bring the agreement in here and set it on the counter near the doorway."

Dick walked over to the kitchen door. Ed was standing against the back wall of the kitchen with his left arm around Coleen and his gun pointed at her head.

Ed looked into Hartmann's face as he placed the agreement on the counter.

Dick calmly commented, "Nice to be able to talk to you in person instead of over the phone."

"Did you get the agreement I wanted?"

"Just as you requested."

"It's not, is it? I'm screwed. I know it."

Coleen could feel Ed's body tense up and his trigger finger starting to move. All in one motion, she ducked her head out of his grip, jabbed him in the ribs with her elbow, and raised her cuffed hands to hit the gun.

Dick dropped to the floor and shouted, "Harriett, take him out!"

A single shot rang out. Blood splattered everywhere. Dick looked up from his prone position on the floor and saw Ed drop. Coleen was standing there, wiping blood from her face.

Harriett stood in the doorway with her weapon unfired.

Abramson was bleeding from the head, where he'd shot himself.

It took Dick's brain a couple of seconds to realize what had happened. He quickly got up from the floor and handed Coleen one of the kitchen towels. He kicked Ed's gun away from his body and bent down, checking his neck for a pulse.

"He's alive. It looks like the bullet just grazed the front of his forehead. Coleen's movement must've spoiled his aim." Dick grabbed another towel and held it to Ed's forehead.

"Get the EMTs in here. I don't want to lose this guy."

Dick turned his attention to Coleen, who was shaken by the incident. She'd suffered no injury but had Abramson's blood all over her.

"Coleen, that wasn't one of your smartest moves. Thank God, everyone but the perp is okay. That's important. Sorry about your clothes. Don't ever do something like that again."

Dick thought back to his army days when he saw the beautiful Diana, the love of his life gunned down in front of him. His mind seldom drifted back to that day, but when it did, the pain was unbearable. *God I can't lose another one. Don't get involved.* His face briefly turned ashen as he felt the pain. Then the incident at hand regained his attention.

"Oh, my God, look at me! I'm not sure I can even justify remaining on your squad. It seems like I need to buy new clothes every other day." Coleen paused and then added, "Dick, I don't feel so good."

40

Westwood, California

Hartmann and his squad watched as the EMTs bandaged Abramson's head, loaded him onto a gurney, and rolled him out to the ambulance.

Dick checked with one of the EMTs about Abramson's condition. He was advised that the head wound appeared superficial. "My guess is that he'll have a serious headache and Frankenstein stitches going across his forehead. The docs will have to put him under, and it's doubtful if he'll be able to answer any questions until tomorrow."

"Where are you taking him?"

"The trauma center at UCLA Medical Center in Westwood."

Dick arranged for agents from the LA field office to babysit him for the night. He called his office to make reservations for the squad at the W Hotel in Westwood, a place both he and Coleen had come to know very well.

The two local agents who drove them to the house took one of the Suburbans and left the other one for the use of the squad. Within an hour, they'd checked into the W Hotel. As they were heading upstairs, Dick asked if there was any interest in barbequed steaks with baked potatoes. He got a resounding, "Yes." They all agreed to meet in the lobby at seven for a barbeque dinner.

As soon as Dick got to his room, he called his parents. "Hi, Mom. Your long-lost son is in town."

After the "how are you's" and updates were done, Dick asked, "Have you and Dad eaten yet?"

"Of course, dear. You know we eat at five."

"Do you think I can bring some of my FBI friends over for a barbeque tonight?"

"Oh, my goodness, tonight? Richie, of course you know you're always welcome, and of course, bring your friends."

"Thanks, Mom. I have a favor to ask. I'm going to pick up steaks on the way and we'll barbeque them, but do you have any potatoes around that you could throw in the oven?"

"Of course. I suppose you want me to make a salad?"

"That'd be nice, Mom. I'll pick up some pie and ice cream when I get the steaks."

"Richie, how many friends are you bringing?"

"Four."

"That'll be fine. What time?"

Looking at his watch, Dick responded, "Eight, Mom."

"Richie, you have to start eating earlier. That's not good for you."

"I know, Mom."

Dick and the Animals drove down Wilshire to his parents' house in West Hollywood. A good-looking, gray-haired man opened the door before they even got to it. Dad had to have been looking through the cracks in the venation blinds, as he usually did when he was expecting company.

Coleen looked at the man standing there. *Now I know where Dick got his good looks.*

The Spanish-style home had a white-stucco exterior, red-tile roof, and a heavy, brown, wooden front door with wrought-iron hardware.

They entered directly into the living room, which had a high, rounded ceiling and a large front window with numerous square muntins. The furniture was arranged to take advantage of the large fireplace. There were four comfy chairs and a couch.

"Mom and Dad, these are my FBI friends. We work together. This is Harriett, Coleen, Brian, and Daniel. Guys, these are my parents, Frances and Charlie."

"Richard, the barbeque is going in the backyard. Why don't you take your friends out there? You'll find beers and soft drinks in the old galvanized tub."

Everyone found the large galvanized tub filled with ice and assorted beverages. It was quickly depleted of beers. Dick took charge of barbequing the steaks after finding out how everyone wanted theirs cooked.

Mr. Hartmann Sr. loved to tell a good story. He decided to provide a little history on their house. "This place belonged to my parents, Richard's grandparents. My dad had it built in 1926 for six thousand dollars. Like me, my father was a movie-studio still photographer. My job is to take the vitally important photographs of film sets, or studio shoots, which are used to create the press and publicity for feature films. See that addition to the garage over there? It's a darkroom my dad built to process the pictures he took. Follow me. I want to show it to you."

The FBI agents looked into a small room that had dozens of black and white photos of movie stars. Dick's dad pointed and said, "My father took those pictures on that wall, and I took the ones over on this wall."

Coleen asked, "Who's in those two pictures that are showcased differently than the rest?"

"Oh, that's Jane Russell, who played in a movie called *The Outlaw*, and that's Howard Hughes, the billionaire who owned RKO Pictures, where the movie was made. The Howard Hughes picture is interesting because it was shot for a *Time Magazine* cover but was never used. Quite a story to that one. My dad worked on retouching the Hughes photo. They say when it was done, it didn't look like him, and *Time* refused to use it."

"I know about Howard Hughes, but I'm not sure who Jane Russell is."

"She was a very beautiful movie star who was made famous by Hughes's picture *The Outlaw*. They say Hughes bought RKO just to make that movie with her. I'm not sure that's true, but it's a good story. He apparently had affairs with a lot of the Hollywood stars. He designed a special bra for Jane Russell to use in the movie that showed off her assets, if you get my drift."

"Steaks are done," Dick interjected.

Dick placed the steaks on a large platter supplied by his mom, and they headed back into the house. The formal dining room was set up for their dinner. It was located between the living room and a breakfast room that was off the kitchen. The dining table was formally set for the five of them.

There was a big, wooden salad bowl filled to the brim with a Caesar salad, sitting on top of a three-legged stand located next to the dining table. Dick's mom brought in a platter with five baked potatoes. The famished group dove into their meal.

When the main course was gone, Dick's dad offered everyone a glass of port in the living room. Fifteen minutes later, Mom announced that there were heated apple and cherry pies on the dining room table. A vanilla ice cream container was sitting in a bowl with a proper metal ice cream scoop sitting on top of it. Both Mom and Dad joined the group for the dessert, which they ate in the living room.

Harriett and Coleen volunteered to help clean up. They were quizzed on how they liked the FBI. What was the training like? Did they have to do the same things as the male agents? How was it working with her son Richie?

Richie? Where did Richie come from? I'm going to give him such a bad time about "Richie." Oh, that's going to be fun, Coleen thought.

In returning to rejoin the men in the living room, they passed through the breakfast room. Coleen noticed a large, brightly colored mural of birds and trees on the wall near the ceiling. In the center of the mural was a distinctive, almost real, parrot.

"That's a beautiful mural."

"Oh, yes, it is. Ritchie's sister, Rosalie, painted it. It's an oil. My daughter is now a famous artist in Hawaii. She's lived there for many years."

"She does beautiful work."

"Did you know Richie can sculpt and paint?"

"No. I never would've suspected that."

"He's actually quite good. It seems to run in the family."

They stepped into the living room and joined the men, who were talking about the Dodgers and the Giants. Dick's dad was giving him a bad time about changing his allegiance from the Dodgers to the Giants. He couldn't believe his son would do such a thing.

"Dad, don't give Richie such a bad time. It's only a game."

"Frances, it may only be a game, but he was raised a Dodger fan. You can't change teams like that. He was brought up in LA on the Dodgers."

"Oh, Charlie, you both were brought up in LA on the Rams. You don't even like them now."

"That's a different story. That lady should've never been allowed to take over that team."

"That's old news now, Dad."

"I know. But how can LA not have an NFL team? I don't understand the times."

"Mom, Dad, we've got to go. We need to get up early tomorrow and need some shut-eye. It's been a long day," Dick told his parents.

"You're right, Richie."

"Mom, Dad, thanks again for having us. I do appreciate it. Love you."

"Love you too, Richie."

Good-byes were said all around. Dick hugged his dad and kissed his mom.

41

Westwood, California

The morning sun was shining brightly through the palm trees as Dick walked past the W Hotel's swimming pool. He was seated at table in the Backyard, the hotel's outdoor restaurant. He was soon joined by the other squad members. They were protected from the sun by a large, canvas umbrella as they sat drinking their coffees.

"By the way," Coleen said, as she and the other Animals loudly greeted him in unison, "Good morning, *Richie!*"

"The name is *Dick*, thank you very much. Or, maybe from now on, you should call me Special Agent Hartmann."

Harriett responded, "Okay, Special Agent Hartmann, what's the plan for today?"

Before he could respond, Coleen glanced at the squad and offered, "Before we get started, we'd all like to thank you again for a great dinner last night. We definitely enjoyed meeting your parents."

"You're all welcome. I can report that my folks liked all of you too. Now, down to business. I spoke to the general counsel's office before coming down and was advised that because Abramson murdered a highway patrol officer, the state is going to take the lead on the prosecution. They'll probably seek the death penalty under the special circumstances provision of California law. Because of the importance of our finding out what happened at the IRS center, and the possibility that Abramson may have been involved in the murder of Shaw, we'll be allowed to interrogate him. He's lawyered up, so I'm not sure if he'll say anything of value."

"So, what's the plan?" Brian asked.

"Brian, I want you and Harriett to go play nice with the Culver City PD. Determine what they have found out and take a closer look at the car Abramson was driving. Go through the house where we captured him and see if you can find anything that'd be helpful."

"On it."

"Daniel, you get to play nice with the CHP. Find out anything you can about the shooting scene where the patrol officer was murdered. Coleen and I will go over to UCLA Medical Center and see if we can convince Abramson's attorney to let us talk to him."

Brian asked, "What do we do for transportation?"

"I've taken care of that. The LA field office is located here in Westwood, not too far from here. I'll drop you guys off. They're expecting you and will provide you with a car. Daniel, you'll be joining up with a local agent who has a rapport with the CHP."

After the drop-off at the LA field office, Dick and Coleen returned to UCLA Medical Center. They were directed to the third floor, where they met two Culver City detectives in the waiting area. The detectives introduced them to the attorney representing Abramson.

Dick started the conversation. "Mr. Harris, the FBI has an interest in talking with your client about an investigation we are conducting concerning the IRS service center where he worked in Fresno. We don't have a direct interest in what happened yesterday."

"Agent Hartmann, against my advice, Mr. Abramson is willing to speak with you, but only you. I'll be in the room with you. You may not ask any questions about yesterday, but you may ask questions about what happened in Fresno. You may not record the meeting, nor take any notes, but I think what Mr. Abramson has to tell you will be helpful to you. Is that agreeable with you?"

"Yes, it is."

The California Highway Patrol officer standing guard at Abramson's room allowed them to enter the room after he closely scrutinized Hartmann's FBI ID. They found Abramson sitting up in bed with his head bandaged above his eyes.

"Well, hello, Agent Hartmann. Can't say it's good to see you again."

"Hello, Ed. It looks like you're going to survive."

"Yeah. I'll survive this, but I doubt if I survive the lethal injection they're going to give me."

"Ed, don't talk about that. That's not why Agent Hartmann is here," his attorney advised.

"Yeah, I know. He wants to know how bad things are back at the IRS center. Well, they're pretty bad."

"You want to tell me how bad?"

Ed sighed, looked at the ceiling for a moment, and then responded, "Yeah. I'm hoping you'll put in a good word for me. Not sure what good it'll do, but that's the only hope I have now."

There was a period of silence as Ed took a drink of water from the glass on the tray next to his bed. His movement was hampered by the handcuff on his other arm that chained him to the bed.

"Well, first, the Bulldog gang has infiltrated that IRS center. Shaw was killed by one of them. Until you guys arrived, there were two scams going on. One involved identity theft. The gang found a way to capture thousands of taxpayers' information, including names, addresses, social security numbers, and in some cases, bank account and credit card numbers. Most were being sold for three to five bucks a name, but Gomez was keeping a couple of hundred names that had credit card numbers for himself. He was setting up a whole scheme to buy merchandize over the Internet with the cards. Apparently, a few days ago, they hit the jackpot. Somehow, they tapped into a single database that included millions of files. Gomez told me he spent $1,500 to get the largest flash drive available. His techie downloaded tons of information from the IRS database to it."

"Oh, man. Do you know where that flash drive is?"

"Gomez showed it to me here in LA. He has it taped to his computer, which he's hauling around in his backpack."

"What's the other scheme?" Hartmann asked.

"It's been going on for a little over a year. The gang controls the Spanish Language Unit, or SLU, where all the calls and correspondence are conducted in Spanish. They'd send out letters billing Hispanics for back taxes or additional taxes. Any checks sent back to pay the fake taxes, they would pull out and cash for themselves. Because all of the Hispanic calls and correspondence were forwarded to the unit for processing, they could get away with it. If someone complained, they simply told that person that the letter they'd sent for the taxes was in error. It was a very profitable operation."

"What a great scam. Do you know which gang member murdered Shaw?"

"Yes. It was Jorge Garcia. He worked in the mailroom," Ed explained.

"Do you know where he is now?"

"The last time I saw him, he was here in LA. My guess is that Jorge and Gomez are headed to Mexico to sell the IRS information."

"How were they able to tap into the IRS computer system?"

"Through me."

"Through you? Care to explain that?"

"I was the principal player in that scam. That's why I got to know Mrs. Shaw. The information was retrieved using Shaw's computer. The audit guys were the only ones who had passwords that could get into just about all of the IRS systems. I got the passwords from Mrs. Shaw. She got them out of his little notebooks, and then a couple of the Bulldogs who were tech savvy would use Shaw's computer to get into the IRS systems to retrieve the information that was needed."

"What do you mean, you used Shaw's computer?"

"Just that. We used Shaw's computer. Otherwise, we couldn't get into the systems."

"How did you get to Shaw's computer?"

"When he went to lunch, I'd use my master key to let Chris Martinez into Shaw's office. He'd use the computer with Shaw's access codes to get the information. Shaw always went to lunch in the cafeteria and read a book during lunch. He always took an hour's lunch, but I watched him from the security monitoring room. I played chess with the guy that watches the monitors to make sure Shaw didn't cut his lunch break short."

"Do you know where in Mexico Gomez was headed?"

"I have no idea. I believe he has family there."

"What exactly was Mrs. Shaw's role in this?"

"She was a lonely woman, just looking for attention. Long before meeting me, she had fallen out of love with her husband. I believe she actually fell for me. It took me awhile, but I convinced her to copy the access codes from Shaw's little books. She had nothing to do with his murder, but when I broke it to her, I don't think she was that surprised. It was kind of a strange meeting. I think she was happy that he was dead. She wanted us to run away together. She knew that I didn't murder him, because we were together at the time of the murder."

"Is there anything else you can tell me?"

"I would get that flash drive back if I were you. Gomez bragged that it contained information on three million people.

"How many?"

"Three million."

With a big sigh, Dick loudly said, "Oh, man! Anything else?"

"Not really. I think you've gotten quite a bit of information from me. Please remember that."

"I will, and I do appreciate your help, but there's no way I can condone or forgive your murdering a fellow law-enforcement officer, nor the murder of anyone, for that matter."

With the meeting concluded, Dick quickly went back to the lobby area and found Coleen.

"Let's get back to the car."

"What did you find out?" Coleen asked.

"A lot. I need to make some phone calls that can't be overheard by anyone else. We're going back to the local FBI field office."

It was a short drive to the field office. Dick and Coleen used a small meeting room where they could make calls.

Dick's first call was to Robert Larson at the IRS. He detailed the problems at the Fresno Service Center and told him that there was a flash drive headed to Mexico with three million names and critical information on it. They agreed that Larson should take a team back to Gomez's house and see if they could locate any other flash drives or anything else that might have IRS information on it. They agreed that the next day, they'd serve arrest warrants on those who worked in the SLU and try to get more information on where Gomez might have gone in Mexico.

Dick headed up a conference call to Mark Gambirasi in the San Francisco field office and several senior staff members in DC headquarters. He filled them in on what he'd learned from Abramson and explained that the IRS records were now probably in Mexico. He was asked to prepare a written report to present to the director as soon as possible.

Dick and his squad flew back to Fresno that afternoon. On the flight, Dick, with the help of the squad, drafted a written report to be sent off the DC headquarters. It was finished by the time they landed.

42

Los Angeles, California

G ood morning. I understand your trip to Los Angeles was successful. I read your report," Robin said.

Dick responded, "Scary, isn't it? Three million IRS files out there
somewhere."

"Yeah, and we need to find them pronto."

"The info we got from Abramson certainly will help. Now it's
down to some grunt work. Any way I could meet with the agents who
interviewed the arrested gang members and their families today?"

"It's already set up."

Robin led Hartmann and his squad to a conference room. "Here's
a list of agents who'll be joining you. They had quite a time of it. Not
fun trying to question gang members. I understand a couple of agents
expanded their vocabulary from the interviews."

"I bet. By the way, we picked up some doughnuts on the way over.
There should be enough for everyone to last through the process. Is
there a chance of getting some coffee to go along?"

"There are already a couple of coffee carafes in the room. Just dial
674 if you need more."

"Thanks."

Shortly after Dick and the squad were set up in the conference room, the first of the agents arrived. Within the next ten minutes, all were present, and introductions were made.

By comparing interviews, they might be able to develop something of value. Each of the interviewing agents went over the interviews they thought would have relevance to the case.

Just as the third agent started, Robin entered the room and said, "Dick, you have a phone call that you need to take in my office."

As Dick walked down the hallway with Robin, he asked, "Who's the call from?"

"Deputy Director Summer."

"Oh, this should be interesting."

Dick picked up Robin's phone. "Hi, Tom, how are you?"

"I'm doing fine, Dick."

"To what do I owe this honor?"

"Your report on the IRS investigation stirred up a hornet's nest here in DC. The director included a summary of it in his briefing to the president this morning. Apparently, the president is concerned about the effect on the American public if they find out the IRS has allowed the information for three million American taxpayers to get into the hands of a gang."

"I can understand his concern."

"Well, there's so much concern that the president has asked his chief of staff to conduct a meeting in the West Wing tomorrow morning. You're to attend that meeting. It's at ten a.m. DC time. One of our planes'll be at the Fresno Airport within the hour. Get over there. Sorry for the short notice."

"I'll pick up my toilet kit and a change of clothes and head to the airport. Will I see you tomorrow?"

"That you will—the director and me. This is a big-time meeting. I don't need to tell you this, but review your report on the plane. There'll be a lot of questions. And get some sleep on the plane."

"See you in the morning."

As Dick was boarding the FBI Gulfstream for the trip to DC, he asked the crew, "Hopefully there's some chow on board?"

"Of course. We figured you'd be hungry at this hour, and we need to eat, too. It's going to be a cross-country trip. We have turkey and roast beef sandwiches, a big bucket of fried chicken, mashed potatoes, coleslaw, and chocolate chip and oatmeal raisin cookies. Sorry. No wine or liquor service on this aircraft. Uncle Sam won't allow it. So fasten your seat belt and get ready to dine." The captain called back.

A little after takeoff, Dick had a turkey sandwich with a Coca-Cola while rereading his report.

43

"A gent Hartmann, Agent Hartmann. Wake up."

Dick's eyes opened to see the young co-pilot.

"We are just about to land at Washington National."

"What time is it?"

"It's four a.m. Eastern time, sir."

A bureau car drove him to a Marriott Hotel, which was within walking distance of FBI headquarters. He caught a couple hours of real sleep, showered, shaved, and dressed. When he arrived at headquarters, he was taken to the deputy director's office.

"Good morning, Tom."

"Hey, Dick, good to see you in person. How's the golf game?"

"Improving. Take you on anytime."

"Love to, but not this trip. You ready to go?"

"Ready as I ever will be. Anything I should know before the meeting?"

"Just that the FBI is taking the lead on this thing. Treasury wants to keep this as hush-hush as possible, so they won't be using their agents for any of the field investigations. They want this classified as a murder investigation, with no mention of any lost IRS information.

Here; read the highlighted section of this Treasury Department report on the IRS computer system. As you will note, the report is two years old."

"Okay. Let's go."

As they walked down the hall, Dick read the highlighted section of the report just handed to him.

> It is the opinion of the Treasury Inspector General for Tax Administration that the IRS's computer system has inadequate controls and could make confidential taxpayer information vulnerable to hacking and theft. This lack of monitoring could allow a disgruntled employee, or a hacker, to disrupt computer operations and steal taxpayer data.

"I can see why Treasury wants to keep this quiet," Dick responded.

"Their own report has set them up for a fall if this gets out to the press. By the way, the new executive assistant director of criminal investigations and the executive assistant director of law enforcement will be going with us. We'll pick them up down the hall. The director is already at the White House doing the daily briefing with the president. He'll also attend the meeting."

They continued walking until they came to Mahogany Row. Before entering, they had to go through another security checkpoint. Tom knocked on a door down the hall. Jesse Holden opened.

"Jesse, good to see you. Congratulations on your promotion. It's well deserved."

"Thanks, Dick. You staying out of trouble on the Left Coast?"

"Of course not. You wouldn't expect me to."

With a sigh came the response, "You're right there. Just try to keep the waves a little lower than you usually do. I just got this job and would like to keep it for a few more minutes."

"Do my best."

"You ready for today?"

"I know what's in my report, and I believe it to be accurate."

"Okay. Let's go knock 'em dead."

A little further down the hall, Ted Bruce, executive assistant director of law enforcement, was waiting for them in front of his office.

"Dick, you sure know how to draw an important crowd."

"That's why I never tried working undercover," Dick replied.

"Interesting report you wrote. I hope you can catch those guys before they start using the IRS info."

"I do, too."

They were driven to the White House in a bureau Suburban. Once they cleared the main gate, they drove over to the West Wing and were let out near a side entrance. A marine guard led them to a conference room where they met up with several other familiar faces. While everyone was drinking coffee, Dick looked at the placards set out on a long, rectangular table.

Jackson C. Wallace – Chief of Staff for the President
of the United States
Jennifer Ann Thompson – Secretary of Treasury
Robert S. Muller Ill – Director, FBI
Thomas V. Smith – Deputy Director, FBI
Robert T. Eriksson – Commissioner of IRS
Jesse R. Holden – Executive Assistant Director, FBI,
Criminal Investigations
Theodore M. Bruce – Executive Assistant Director,
FBI, Law Enforcement Services
Adam Mills – Senior Special Agent, IRS
Richard A. Hartmann – Supervising Special
Agent, FBI

Quite a gathering to review my report, he thought.

Jackson Wallace walked into the room with Jennifer Thompson. They walked directly over to Dick.

"Buddy, how're you doing?"

"Been doing great. Who's this beautiful lady?" Hartmann asked.

"Jennifer, please meet Special Agent Dick Hartmann. As you can tell, he thinks he's a ladies' man, and as secretary of treasury, I'd be very careful of him. He knows everything there is to know about money laundering."

"Nice to meet you, Agent Hartmann, and why are you such an expert on money laundering?" Jennifer asked.

"It's nice to meet you, Secretary Thompson. What I know about money laundering, I learned in conjunction with Mr. Wallace here. He used to be a pretty good investigator before he got into politics. But if I told you more, I'd have to kill you."

"My, my. You do sound dangerous. It sounds like you two have history together."

"We do go back a ways," Wallace replied.

"Jack, how is POTUS doing?" Dick asked.

"You know how he is. He's doing as well as can be expected as the president. It's a tough job. He's aged more than shows up in the press photos. By the way, he said to say hello. He still remembers how we helped him out when he headed up the CIA."

"How's the younger son doing?"

"You mean Junior? He's doing fine. Off the juice. Works here in the White House. Barbara keeps him under control."

"Sounds like you two gentlemen have had some interesting times together. Hopefully, we can get together for cocktails or dinner sometime. I'd love to hear more of these stories," the secretary interjected.

"Jennifer, let's get the meeting started."

The president's chief of staff took Jennifer by the arm and led her to her seat, which was next to his. In a commanding voice, he said, "Madam Secretary and gentlemen, I would like to start the meeting."

With that announcement, everyone sat where their place cards dictated at the table. "I believe everyone is now acquainted. We're here because the president is concerned that what is contained in Special Agent Hartmann's report could have an adverse impact on the public's trust that the IRS can keep their financial security and privacy protected. The IRS doesn't need another black eye. You've all received copies of the report, and I will assume you've read it. The report indicates that there's information on three million US taxpayers in the hands of a Fresno, California-based, Hispanic gang. It appears that one of the gang members is trying to take the information into Mexico. We have recent reports from various sources that Mexican cartels are now involved in identity theft. These facts do not bode well for the IRS or our tax system. We're here to fix this problem."

Having completed his opening remarks, the chief of staff looked at Dick and asked, "Special Agent Hartmann, how confident are you that the facts in your report are accurate?"

"The information included in my report is principally from an interview I conducted of a former security guard at the IRS service center in Fresno. He was working closely with the Bulldog gang's leader. They had served in the military together. Based on my interrogation experience, I believe what he told me is credible."

"Thank you. This meeting isn't the time to place blame for the release of the information, but rather to see how we can quickly fix the problem that currently exists. I'll add, though, that the lack of security at this IRS center will present another major 'blame' problem in the near future. You can count on it."

FBI Deputy Director Tom Smith added, "To confirm what was said earlier, recent intelligence indicates that the drug cartels in Mexico are expanding their activities to include focusing on US identity theft.

This doesn't require them to physically get drugs, guns, or people across the border. They just use a computer and the Internet."

Looking around the table, Jackson continued, "The FBI director, secretary of Treasury, and I discussed this with the president during this morning's briefing. The conclusions are as follows: the FBI, and specifically, Agent Hartmann, will take the lead in this case. He's already on the ground running, and from personal experience, both the president and I firmly believe he has the credentials to get the job done. Director, your comments?"

"Thanks, Jackson. We're ready to take the lead. The reason for the two FBI deputy directors being here is to ensure that Agent Hartmann and his squad receive all of the FBI's resources needed to successfully conclude this case. As we discussed this morning, the case will be referenced as a murder case to keep the real objective as quiet as possible—that is, retrieving the stolen IRS information. Hopefully this is accomplished before it is put into use. Jennifer, you're up."

"While the FBI is trying to resolve the information-leak problem, Treasury, and specifically the IRS, will be developing contingency plans in the event the information goes into play. To assist the FBI, Treasury is funding a hundred-thousand dollar reward for information relating to the apprehension of Jorge Rodrigo Garcia and Alejandro Gomez, who remain the prime suspects for the murder of an IRS special agent. There will be no mention of missing IRS files. We recognize there is a slim chance that this operation will work out well. To achieve success, we must literally retrieve the IRS files before they're used. It does us no good if the files are lost or destroyed. We must retrieve them and confirm that we have all of the copies, to reassure the material never affects the American taxpayers."

The secretary of Treasury looked directly at Hartmann and said, "Good luck, Agent Hartmann."

Jackson stood up and asked, "Any other questions or comments?

Agent Hartmann, as the secretary of Treasury said, we all wish you good luck."

Tom Smith and Dick decided to walk back to FBI Headquarters. They exited the side gate from the White House and headed east on Pennsylvania Avenue to the J. Edgar Hoover FBI Building five blocks away. They walked through the courtyard entrance, past the bronze sculpture of "Fidelity, Bravery, Integrity," which is the FBI motto. The three figures in the sculpture are placed against a backdrop of a large American flag, which appears to wave in the breeze. "Fidelity" is female, seated on the right side and looking up at the male figure of "Bravery." To the left of "Bravery" is "Integrity," who kneels on one knee, with his left hand on his heart. The bronze figures are simple with little detail.

On their way, they discussed the case and how to handle it. After they'd gone through the screening process to enter the building, Tom suggested they meet with Deputy Director Duran, who was responsible for coordination with foreign law-enforcement agencies, and the FBI's extensive network of legal attachés located in embassies and consulates around the world.

Duran was in his office with Deputy Director Tom Summer. After brief hellos, Duran gave Dick a folder with the name of the FBI attaché in the Mexico City Embassy. He advised Dick that someone from the DEA with contacts in Mexico would be getting in touch with him.

Duran told Dick, "The Director's instructed me to make sure you have everything you need. So if you need any assistance, any assistance at all, give me a holler."

"I second that comment," said Summer, who was responsible for all FBI criminal investigations. His unit had historically been the heart of the FBI. It was charged with investigating everything from bank robberies to corporate misdeeds to mob bosses. There were well over a hundred federal laws it was responsible for upholding and investigating.

His friend Tom Smith added, "Thanks for what you've found out. It's a feather in the cap for the bureau."

"It's time for you to get back to work. I've arranged for a car to take you to National Airport, where you'll be flown to Lackland Air Force Base. Your squad will be waiting for you when you get there."

Dick boarded the FBI Gulfstream and quickly figured out pretty quickly that it was the same aircraft that had flown him to Washington. The same crew manned it.

"By any chance, did you restock the chow?"

"Sure did." The captain called back.

"How long is the flight to Lackland?"

"You'll have plenty of time to check out the food. The flight will be five hours and twenty-three minutes from wheels up to wheels down."

"Okay. Let's sample some of that food."

44

Los Angeles, California

The day after Ed Abramson had left them, Gomez and Garcia were driven to the Greyhound bus depot in Los Angeles by Garcia's uncle, where they caught the first bus to San Diego.

They sat in the next to the last row of the bus. Garcia took the window seat and watched the scenery pass by. Los Angeles was one continuous sprawl. The bus turned onto Interstate 5 Freeway toward San Diego. Just past General Hospital and Cal State LA, Gomez fell asleep. Garcia listened in on the conversation between two young, white dudes in the seat in front of them.

He guessed they were in their late twenties. His ears perked up when he heard the word *grass*. They were discussing the taste, smell, and affect of Northern California grass from Garberville compared to the stuff from Mexico. In their opinion, the California stuff was much higher grade. Garcia thought to himself, *They're probably right*. In Fresno, he'd tried both, but from a business standpoint, he preferred the Mexican stuff—not because it was better, because it wasn't. In the United States, you had to deal with naïve Northern Californians who grew their marijuana in groves in the middle of forests, up near the Oregon border. They were usually high on their own stuff and, having smoked it for so long, their brains were fried. *Not something I'm going to have to worry about for a while,* he thought.

The trip to San Diego took two hours. As soon as they got off the bus, they walked to the Old Town Trolley Center and caught the bright red Tijuana Trolley that took them to the border between the United States and Mexico. With their backpacks securely and nonchalantly in place on their backs, they simply walked across the border with hundreds of other people going to Tijuana for fun. They walked down Avenida Revolución, the main downtown tourist thoroughfare. They decided to kill some time in a strip club. Following three Jell-O shots, they switched to drinking beers. After a couple of hours, they were feeling no pain and decided it was time to find a place to stay.

Gomez had been to Tijuana many times before. He guided Garcia to the Zona Norte, where he found his favorite bordello. They met with the madam, who led them to the lineup of girls. They each selected one for the night and made arrangements for two adjacent rooms. After they paid the madam, the four of them, laughing, headed upstairs for an evening of pleasure.

Midway through the night, Garcia heard Gomez shouting. There was a massive thud against the wall that separated their rooms, followed by a girl's scream. Garcia sprang out of his bed, knocking the prostitute to the floor in the process. He ran, naked, into the hallway. He pounded ferociously on the door to Gomez's room. After a few minutes, Gomez opened the door and let him in.

The girl was lying on the floor. She wasn't moving. Her face was bloody, and an arm looked like it'd been dislocated.

"What happened?"

"She was trying to steal the backpack with the computer in it. I caught her just as she was opening the door," Gomez replied.

"Is the flash drive still taped to the computer?"

"It should be. I grabbed the backpack first. The strap was wrapped around her arm. She literally went flying through the air when I grabbed the pack and swung her with it. She hit the wall. When she started to get up, I hit her. I hit her hard."

"We'd better get outta here."

From the doorway, they heard a loud voice exclaim, "*Señors*, what the fuck is going on in there?"

Al and Ed looked toward the doorway, where the madam and two huge bodyguards were standing.

Al shouted at her, "She tried to steal from me!"

"Is she alive?"

"I don't know."

"Carlos, see if she's still alive."

"*Si*, madam."

Carlos entered the room, kneeled down next to the prostitute, and put his fingers on her neck.

Looking at the madam, Carlos said, "She has a pulse."

"All right, you two, I want you out of here right now, and you owe me a thousand dollars to clean up your mess."

Al glanced again at the bodyguards. He reached into the backpack and counted out ten one-hundred dollar bills from a bundle of bills that was sitting next to his gun.

"Madam, you have a deal. Here's the thousand."

"Be out in ten minutes. Pedro will stay with you until you leave. Carlos, take the girl downstairs," the madam instructed.

With that, Carlos picked up the prostitute, threw her over his shoulder, and walked out of the room. Pedro moved back into the hallway and took up a position where he could see into both Al's and Jorge's rooms. He said in a gruff voice, "Leave the doors open."

Jorge, still nude, walked past Pedro to his room to dress and pick up his backpack. His prostitute had ditched him during the confusion.

Al, now concerned about the flash drive, pulled the computer out of the backpack. He looked carefully at it and breathed a sigh of relief.

It hadn't been damaged. He dressed and readjusted the items in the backpack and met Jorge in the hall. They both stared at Pedro as they walked past him, but they didn't say a word.

Once they were on the street in front of the bordello, Jorge asked Al, "Where to now?"

"Let me think. God, what time is it?"

Jorge looked down at his wrist. "Shit. That little bitch took my watch."

"You sure it's not still up in the room?"

"I'm sure. I placed it on the bed stand next to me. I'm positive it wasn't there when I got dressed."

"Do you have your wallet?" Al asked.

"Yeah. It's right here. See? Oh, fuck. My money's gone."

"Welcome to Tijuana. The first time I was here, some gal lifted my wallet at a bar. Here's a couple hundred. It should hold you over for a little while. Put it in your pants pocket, not your wallet, and put your wallet in your backpack."

"Thanks for the *dinero* and the advice. Let's blow this town."

"Maybe we're in luck. Isn't that an empty cab over there?"

They walked over to a cab parked down the street from the hotel. The driver was snoring in the front seat. Jorge knocked on the half-rolled-down window and said, "Wake up. Wake up. We need a ride."

"No on duty. *Dormer*, sleeping. No on duty," the driver replied.

"How about a hundred US dollars to take us to Ensenada?" Al asked.

The cabby woke up and said, "No go to Ensenada. Too far."

"Two hundred?"

"No. Long way. It takes at least an hour."

With that answer, Jorge pulled the gun out of his backpack and started playing with it.

Al said, "Two hundred fifty dollars, and you get to live."

"Señors, get in. I take you there fast. Less than an hour."

The cabby proceeded south on Highway 1D, passing through Rosarito Beach and a tollgate just before the town of San Miguel. As the cab approached the outskirts of Ensenada, the driver shouted into the backseat, "We're just about there. Where do you want me to take you?"

Al was half asleep and Jorge was sound asleep when they heard the cabbie. Suddenly wide-awake, Al said, "Hotel. Take us to a hotel."

"Si. I will take you to a nice hotel."

Ten minutes later, the cab pulled up to the Hotel Ritz. They paid the cabbie the two hundred fifty dollars. He drove away, happy for the money and relieved to still be alive.

45

Ensenada, Baja, Mexico

The desk clerk seemed very friendly, considering their grubby appearances and their arrival at six in the morning. Al selected a second-floor room with a balcony and two double beds. They walked up the stairs to the room, locked the door, and put a chair up against it. They dumped their backpacks on the floor, opened the sliding door to the balcony, and climbed into their beds with their clothes still on. Their bodies didn't move until two that afternoon.

Al got up first and took a long shower and then shook Jorge awake. While Jorge was showering, Al took everything out of his backpack. He carefully wrapped the laptop in a hotel towel and placed it back into the backpack, surrounding it with the remaining money. It wasn't going to get out of his sight until they'd made a deal to sell the information it contained.

They found a bus schedule in the lobby and determined they'd missed the last bus to San Felipe for the day. They were going to have to stay another night in Ensenada.

They hadn't eaten since yesterday, and their growling stomachs told them it was time to find a restaurant. They ambled down side streets toward the ocean and then headed to the waterfront, which was made up of docks and warehouses. There were hundreds of fishing boats docked at the pier. They decided to head south from the pier area and found an outdoor taqueria right on the beach. The beach in front of the taqueria was full of young Americans who'd come down to drink, find drugs, and have sex.

They mounted tall stools at the taqueria's stainless-steel bar. The bar was unique. It was supported by two tall palm trees, part of a palm-tree grove along the beach. They welcomed the shade from the steamy afternoon sun. Both ordered fish tacos and beers from the old lady behind the bar. The tacos were served along with a giant, glass goblet containing all kinds of condiments. Al and Ed spread the condiments heavily over their tacos. The shade, the beers, and best of all, the tacos, were a great combination. They started to relax again.

"Jorge, it's time to go. I need to find an Internet café," said Al when they were finished eating.

As they walked through town, a sign that said "Shit for Sale" caught Jorge's eye. It was a typical small shop, cluttered with tourist junk.

"It's hot down here. I'm going to get a T-shirt," he said to Al.

They entered Shit for Sale and looked around at the junk. Stapled on one of the walls were a number of T-shirts. Jorge spotted one with "One Tequila-Two Tequila-Three Tequila-Floor" printed on it.

"I'll take that one."

Al laughed. "That one suits you."

"Jeff, the bartender at Dos Amigos, would agree with you."

Al signaled the shop owner to give him the red T-shirt that had "Mexico" printed across the front. "How much do I owe you?"

"Ten American dollars."

"Here you go," Al said, and then, in Spanish, he asked, "Is there an Internet café around here?"

The owner walked outside and pointed. "Café Internet that way. Toward Boulevard Cardenas."

Following the pointed finger, two blocks from Shit for Sale, they spotted the Internet cafe on Boulevard Cardenas. They rented a laptop station that was tied to a wireless network. Jorge pulled the laptop out of Al's backpack and untapped the flash drive. With Al sitting next to him, he first checked the files on the flash drive that contained the IRS information. Click, click, click—there they were.

Al patted Jorge on the back and said, "Money, money, money. Bring up the Fresno Bee website."

They scanned through numerous articles about the gang activity in Fresno and the crackdown mounted by local, state, and federal authorities to shut down their operations. Their pictures were included in one of the articles about two gang leaders that'd fled the city, and it said that they were being sought by the FBI for major criminal activity. The article indicated that they may have fled to Southern California or crossed the border into Mexico, where they had family.

Jorge then texted his favorite cousin in Fresno to see what she could tell him. He was in luck. She was online and responded immediately. She texted back that the FBI had visited his family. His picture was on all of the local TV stations. Many members of the gang were being held on various charges. She wanted to know what he and Al had done, because the FBI was offering a hundred-thousand-dollar reward for information that would secure their apprehension. Jorge responded that he didn't know why they would be offering such a reward. His cousin ended the message "Jorge, I love you. Be safe."

Jorge looked over at Al, who was watching the screen with him, and said, "What's with the hundred-thousand-dollar reward?"

"I suspect it's because of the IRS identity-theft breach. Move over and let me on the computer."

Al took over the computer and sent an e-mail to his contact in the Gulf Cartel, which was located in Apatzingan, Mexico. This cartel had supplied the Bulldog gang with many of the drugs they sold in Fresno. Al communicated with them by e-mail on a regular basis.

Jorge thought to himself, *The Mexican drug cartels want to expand their operations from drugs. The drug market has become saturated, and the prices are dropping because of the competition. Americans are hooked on drugs and business was constant, but it was doubtful if there are any expansion opportunities left.*

The Mexicans had also gotten into running guns from the United States into Mexico. They were also moving Mexicans and now foreigners such as Russians, Chinese, and South Americans into the United States.

Identity theft is the next product line!

In his e-mail to the cartel, Al indicated that things had gotten too hot for him in Fresno. He was now in Ensenada. He wanted to set up a meeting. He had something the cartel might have an interest in buying. Within minutes, there was a response. They were to travel to La Paz, where they'd be picked up by a yacht named the *Cuidado* at the Marina de La Paz. When they arrived in La Paz, they were to contact the cartel and let them know.

Back at their hotel room, Al spoke to Jorge as they lay on their beds. "We need to get to La Paz as soon as we can. I'm not so sure it's safe for us to be this close to the border. The feds have all kinds of agents down here helping the Mexicans stop the drug trafficking. If they have a hundred-thousand-dollar reward out for us, they must want us real bad."

Jorge responded, "I have family in San Felipe. Maybe we should go there."

"We need to get to the gulf side of Baja, so San Felipe it is. But I don't think you should contact your relatives at their home. The feds may be watching."

"I know what my uncle looks like. I'll get a message to him, and we can meet him away from his house."

"All right. Let's take a look at that bus schedule again," Al replied.

"Here it is. The bus leaves here at eight in the morning and arrives in San Felipe at noon."

"Let's get some chow and get back here for some shut-eye. We need to get up early tomorrow to catch that bus."

They found a burger place named Einstein's a short distance from their hotel. The thought of a juicy burger washed down with a cold beer sounded great to them. They took their time enjoying their cheeseburgers and beers and then headed back to the hotel and collapsed. Sleep came quickly. They were both tired from their travels and the constant rushing of adrenaline flowing through their bodies. Being on the run and looking over your shoulder all the time took its toll.

46

Lackland Air Force Base, Texas

It was a little after seven-thirty in the evening when Dick's flight landed at Lackland Air Force Base, just west of San Antonio. The Gulfstream pulled up to a hangar, where a sister FBI Gulfstream was parked. The aircraft's stairs were lowered, and Dick was directed into the adjacent hangar. Waiting for him in an office was the rest of his team, who had arrived an hour ahead of him.

"Hello, Animals! Good to see you."

Daniel asked, "Why are we at this air force base?"

"Because this is where we catch our flight to Mexico City."

Dick proceeded to explain what'd happened in DC. Lackland seemed to be the best meeting spot for the flight to Mexico City.

"Have you guys had a chance to eat?" he asked his team.

Brian responded, "The air force has treated us pretty well. We ate at the Officers' Club. The food was excellent."

"Excellent. Grab your bags, and let's load up. We can catch some sleep on the plane."

47

San Felipe, Baja, Mexico

The bus was traveling on Mexico's Highway 3 over the Sierra de Juarez Mountains. The view out the window was bleak as the landscape changed from sand to dirt and then back to sand. It was desolate. There was an occasional stubble of ocotillo cactus, some mesquite and scattered cardon cactus, and mile after mile of rocks. No water in sight.

Al was considering what the future would hold for him. *My life will be different from this point forward. I'm no longer the leader. I'm no longer the boss. I'm no longer going to live in Fresno, or for that matter, any part of the United States. Yes. Life is going to be different.* He glanced at Jorge in the seat next to him. Jorge was still young, but he had already seen a lot with the Bulldogs.

Drops of sweat were running down Al's forehead, as the bus's air-conditioning system was no match for the 115 degrees outside. It didn't help that the bus was crowded. It definitely didn't help that he'd drunk far more in the past few days than at any time in his life, and he was tired of running. He felt down. He knew that things were not going to get better anytime soon, if ever. In all likelihood, both he and Jorge would be killed. They'd done bad things in Fresno, but that was the way it was for them. That's how they survived in their society. They were never part of Fresno's "white people's" society. They lived in Bulldog society.

The bus traveled slowly across Baja from Ensenada to San Felipe. They were traveling from the shores of the Pacific Ocean southeast to the shores of the Sea of Cortez. First on Highway 3, and then at the town of Crucejo La Trinidad, the bus turned south on Highway 5 toward San Felipe. To get between the two coasts, the bus traveled through a pass that divided the Sierra de Juarez and Sierra de San Pedro Mártir ranges.

Once they were through the mountains, the bus headed past the crusty salt marshes that led into the town of San Felipe. Just before arriving in town, there were numerous campgrounds with names like Campo Los Amigos, Pete's El Paraiso, Campo Hawaii, and Club Live and Let Live. During the season, these camps were filled with off-road motorbikes and dune buggies operated by North Americanos. The trip had taken more than the four hours indicated on the bus schedule. It was almost one o'clock when they arrived at the bus terminal on the south end of San Felipe.

San Felipe, initially a fishing port, now embraced the "snowbirds" who spent their winters in their mobile homes, driving in from all regions of the United States and Canada. Then there were the visiting anglers, off-roaders, and RVs down for a week or two.

A cab took Al and Jorge from the bus terminal to the waterfront promenade called the Malecon, where they picked one of the outdoor tables at Rosita's Patio & Grill for a late lunch. They were both sweating in the hundred-plus-degree heat. Jorge'd been to this restaurant twice before with his parents when visiting his relatives.

"My friend, you're about to eat the best fish you've ever tasted. It comes from that bay right in front of you," he told Al.

They wolfed down the local rockfish with rice and beans and topped it off with cold Corona beers with limes in the bottles' necks.

Setting down an empty Corona bottle, Jorge rose from the table. "I've got to take a pee, and I'm going to see if I can find my uncle down at the docks."

"Okay. I'm good here. I'll watch our backpacks."

Jorge headed down to the docks in front of the restaurant. He had two uncles in San Felipe. His Uncle Carlos owned a water truck called a *pipas*, which filled the water tanks of shacks located on the outskirts of town where there was not yet running water. He remembered, as a small kid, riding in the truck as his uncle delivered the water. He remembered the fun he had sitting next to his uncle as the great, lumbering truck with its huge, sloshing water tank went down the dirt roads on the outskirts of the town. Those were good times.

The uncle he was looking for, Enrique, owned a *pangas,* or fishing boat, that was usually tied up at the dock. He asked other pangas owners about his uncle and found out that he'd taken a party out fishing that morning and would probably return around three in the afternoon. He headed back up to the restaurant, knowing he had time for a couple more beers with Al before his uncle returned.

Suddenly, his head instinctively turned, and he stared at a young, pretty girl with long, blonde hair sitting on a low wall under a shade tree. She was listening to her iPod and had a professional-looking camera hanging from her neck. She wore a pair of ripped jean shorts, cut fashionably high; so high, he could see her left buttock peeking out. The white tank top was protruding nicely, with the help of her large breasts. He guessed she was about seventeen or eighteen. He walked over and sat next to her.

"You from the States?"

She looked at him for a minute and then pulled the earphones from her ears. "Why do you want to know?"

"Just interested. You know, you're very attractive."

"You trying to pick me up?"

"Don't know yet. You from Southern Cal?"

"Burbank."

"A Valley girl."

"I hate that phrase," she replied.

"Sorry. Just popped out."

"Where're you from?"

"Fresno."

"A Central Valley Boy."

"Got me. Want a beer?" he asked her.

"Why not? I'm bored here."

As they walked up to Rosita's Patio & Grill, Jorge asked, "Why were you sitting on the wall? There have to be better things to do around here!"

"My parents love to come down here and fish. I hate fishing. I hate most of the things my parents do. I was down here taking pictures. I love photography. In fact, you look like a good subject," the girl replied and then took three pictures of Jorge from different angles.

"Nice camera. I'm Jorge, and that's my friend Al over there. I'm here to visit my family."

"You're Mexican?"

"My parents were born in Mexico. I'm American. I was born in Fresno. Is that okay with you, or do you have something against Mexicans?"

"No, no. I like you. You seem nice, and you're kinda cute."

"What do you mean, 'kinda cute?' I'm a handsome dude with hot, Latino blood. What's your name?"

"Leslie."

They walked over to the table, where Al was just finishing another beer.

"Al, this is Leslie. She's down here from LA. She's going to have a beer with us."

"Hi, Leslie. Have a seat right here," Al replied as he patted the seat right next to him.

Leslie sat between Al and Jorge as they drank beers and found out about each other. Leslie's digital camera became a topic of conversation as they looked and laughed at the pictures she'd taken. They took turns taking pictures of each other with the camera.

While Leslie was taking a picture of the port, she noticed that the fishing boats were starting to return with their fishing parties. She spotted her parents through the camera lens and ducked down so they wouldn't see her.

"What're you doing?" asked Jorge.

"I don't want my parents to see me. They don't like me drinking, and I'm not ready to go back to the condo yet."

Jorge spotted his uncle's boat among the others. He had a party of two guys onboard. They were in the process of unloading their catch and walking back up to the dock toward the restaurant. His uncle was washing the boat down. "Hey, guys, I need to go say hello to my uncle. I'll be right back."

Jorge walked down to the dock to his uncle's boat. "Uncle Enrique. Cómo está usted?"

"Jorge, what're you doing here?" his uncle responded.

Jorge'd never lied to his uncle, and his uncle knew about his gang connections. It wasn't that unusual for those that went to the United States to get involved in gangs.

"I'm in a little trouble in Fresno and need to hide out for a while," he told him.

"I already know. Your father called. He thought you might show up here. We also had a visit from *la policia*. They were asking about you."

"I thought that might happen. Is there some place we can stay tonight? There are two of us. My friend Al is up there at the restaurant. We'll be heading to La Paz tomorrow. Any suggestions on the best way for us to get there without la policia spotting us?"

His uncle thought for a moment. "I have an idea. At six o'clock tonight, meet me and the family down on the beach, just south of town. Here. I'll draw you a map. It's quite a walk, but I think my idea will work. You're going clamming with your relatives tonight. After that, there's a boat-parking facility nearby to that particular beach where a number of Americanos park their boats until they come down. I know of a boat where the Americanos have returned to the United States. You'll sleep in that boat for the night. Then we figure something out."

"Gracias, uncle. See you tonight."

Jorge found Al and Leslie still talking at the restaurant.

"Leslie, Al and I need to talk in private. It's been great to meet you, and I really hope we get to meet up again," Jorge told her.

"You're not getting rid of me that easily. I'm going to the bathroom to get rid of some of this beer, and I'll be back."

"Jorge, you have to get rid of her. We don't need any more problems," said Al.

"Okay, okay. I understand."

"What did your uncle have to say?"

"The cops have been to his place. It's not safe to go there. We're going to meet him and some of my family tonight at a beach south of town. They'll have dinner on the beach, and my uncle says we can sleep on one of the boats stored there."

"Better than anything I can think of. Let's head to the beach."

Just as they started to get up from the table, Leslie returned and asked, "Where are you guys headed?"

"Leslie, you need to leave us alone."

Looking disappointed, Leslie started walking back up to the main part of town. Several times, she glanced back at Jorge, who was walking from the restaurant down Avenuda Mar de Cortez. She had a crush on him. *God, he's good looking, and nice,* she thought.

They weren't used to walking in the heat of San Felipe. After half an hour of hiking, a Jeep Grand Cherokee pulled up alongside them and a voice shouted out, "You boys want a ride?"

"Leslie, what're you doing here?"

"Trying to give you a ride. Get in."

"Oh, shit. Come on, Al, I'm dying out here." Jorge got in the front seat next to Leslie, and Al climbed into the backseat next to a container of chilled, plastic water bottles.

"Looking at you two, you need to drink some of that water. You guys wouldn't have made it another fifteen minutes in this heat. Where the fuck are you guys going?" Leslie asked them.

"I'm meeting my relatives at a beach down this road. It's here on the map my uncle gave me."

"Do you realize that spot is another five or six miles from here? Why are you going there?"

"Leslie, this is going to sound real weird. We're going to a clam bake," Jorge replied.

"Actually, it's not that weird. Clamming is popular here, and that's the right beach for it. So I'll join you for clamming."

Al broke her off. "Leslie, I don't know who you think you are, or who you think we are, but I can tell you that you should drop us off at the beach and go back to your parents. If you stick with us, you're going to find out that we're not the nicest guys in the world."

"My fucking world is boring. Boring. I'll take my chances. There's nothing for me back there with my parents. I want to experience life. My parents live in a small, comfortable world. Maybe someday, I'll want a similar world, but I don't want that now. Let's go clamming," she responded.

Leslie drove on, past the small Aeropuerto San Filipe and the town of Playa El Fargo. She turned left onto a dirt road. Suddenly, they could see wide expanses of wet sand with an occasional large rock jutting out. The tide was out, and there was a quarter mile of damp sand. It was perfect for clamming.

Jorge pointed down the beach and said, "Drive over there. That's my Uncle Carlos's water truck next to that pickup truck. He delivers water to the houses that aren't connected to the public water system."

Leslie parked the Jeep next to the water truck. The three walked toward the blankets spread out on the beach in front of the trucks. There were cardboard boxes loaded with food and utensils spread around the blankets. A few older people were sitting on the blankets, but most were in the water below.

Jorge found his uncles standing together drinking beers and watching the people in the water. Introductions went on for some time as Jorge introduced Al and Leslie to his uncles, who in turn introduced them to their wives and kids.

Everyone on the beach was in a festive mode. Even Al began to chill. They watched as several of Jorge's young, male cousins prepared the clambake-cooking pit. Shovels of sand were flying as they dug a large pit about three feet deep. The pit was lined with small rocks the younger kids had collected from the beach. Stacks of dry driftwood were placed on top and set on fire.

Uncle Enrique shouted to the kids to grab their buckets and shovels and head down to the water. The three new arrivals joined the kids in the clamming fun. Leslie apparently had done this before, as she showed Jorge how to harvest the larger white clams from beneath the wet sand.

The clamming lesson soon ended and Leslie led Jorge by the hand behind a large rock, where they sat on the sand. They kissed and talked and kissed some more.

After an hour, everyone started to head back to their blankets with their buckets of clams. Jorge and Leslie, barefoot and beaming like little kids, ran their bucket of clams back to the blanket area.

The ladies, including Leslie, who had been adopted by Jorge's relatives, washed the clams first in a tub filled with saltwater and then in two big tubs that had been filled with freshwater from the water truck. The sand from the clams slowly filled the bottom of the tubs. Once they were cleaned of sand, they were stacked on a plywood sheet next to the pit.

The same young men who'd prepared and ignited the fire were now clearing away the pieces of wood from the hot rocks that had not completely burned. The exposed hot rocks were thickly lined with wet seaweed and layered with clams, corn still in its husks, and then some more seaweed. The pit was covered, at the direction of Jorge's uncles, with a tarpaulin, weighted down with more rocks, and then left to steam. It was a labor-intensive way to cook clams, but the results were fantastic.

The adults drank beer and tequila. The kids drank the sweet Mexican Coca-Cola. While waiting for the clams to bake, they had fish tacos. For the visiting Americans, they had taco chips and salsa.

After an hour, the tarp was peeled off the pit, revealing a steaming heap of clams and corn. The cooked clams had opened and were placed on big, white platters that were placed on a table. There was a stack of paper plates, a roll of paper towels, and all types of condiments on the table. At the end of the table was a container that held warm, soft tortillas.

Jorge's uncles seemed to have an instinct for how long to cook the clams, since they were not tough or rubbery. They were cooked just right—moist, slightly chewy, and delicious.

The two coolers were refilled with beer and Cokes from the trucks. Paper bags filled with bottles of tequila and plastic cups were under constant attack. There was a happy, carefree mood in the air. The party lasted late into the evening. Al had fallen asleep on one of the blankets. Jorge and Leslie had settled in on another blanket down the beach, closer to the water.

Uncle Enrique walked over to the blanket where Jorge and Leslie were laying. "Jorge, we're going to be packing up soon. I need to tell you about the boat I mentioned. Your friend can drop you off near there. I'll draw you a map."

"Uncle, it's all right to talk in front of Leslie. She knows about my problem and about me. She'll help me find the boat."

"Leslie, is that right?"

"Si, it's all right. I'll help."

"Do you know the big storage area up by the airport?" he asked her.

"Yes. I know it well. My parents store their boat there when they're not here."

"There's a boat there called *Pains & Gains*. It's on a trailer. You shouldn't have any problem finding it. The hull is painted a light blue, and the top is white. It's twenty-four feet in length, with funny-looking twin keels. I've never seen another one like it. An American couple owns it. I know they've left for several weeks. You can sleep on it tonight and then maybe hire one of the fishing boats tomorrow to take you south. Be careful. Here's a key to the gate at the storage yard."

Leslie interrupted, "Thanks, Enrique, but I have a key to the storage area in my parents' car. You can keep yours."

Jorge looked at his uncle with true gratitude. "Thanks, Uncle. I appreciate all of your help. The clamming was fun. Hope to return soon. Say hello to my dad for me."

Al was talking with Jorge's relatives when Jorge and Leslie walked back to the group.

"Al, it's time for us to take off," Jorge said.

Leslie drove them to the storage lot by the airport, and at the gate, she asked Jorge to open the glove compartment and take out a small, manila envelope with a key to the gate in it. They drove up and down three aisles before they spotted the funny-looking, blue and white boat with stubby twin keels. Jorge lifted the tarp covering the front of the boat to reveal the black lettering that read, *Pains & Gains*.

Jorge climbed into the cockpit and found the cabin door locked with a small padlock. "Leslie, is there a tool kit or tire iron in the back of your folks' car? I need it to break the lock on the cabin."

"My dad has a tool kit behind the backseat."

She opened the back of the Jeep and pulled out a toolbox. "Will a screwdriver and pliers work?"

"They sure will. Hand 'em up."

It was tight quarters in the cabin, but there was a small bunk on either side. A small galley area included a sink and stove. There was a hand-pump potty down below in front. All the comforts of home, if the boat was in the water. Leslie and Al climbed up to take a look.

They were sitting crunched together in the cabin when Leslie said, "You're not going to be that safe trying to hire a boat from one of the fishermen. The Jeep has a trailer hitch. Why not just sail this boat down to La Paz?"

"Leslie, we're Mexicans from Fresno. There isn't a lot of sailing done there. We have no idea how to sail a boat." Staring at the mast across the top of the boat's cabin, he added, "Let alone figure out how to put this thing together."

"Ah, you macho Hispanics from Fresno. Let Captain Valley Girl help you. I've been sailing since I was a little kid. You guys stay here. I'm going into San Filipe and pick up some food and beverages for our voyage. Got fifty bucks?"

Al looked at Leslie long and hard and then handed her a hundred-dollar bill. "I'm beginning to like you."

The first thing Leslie did was drive to her parents' house. Quietly, she snuck into the house, filled a small bag with some clothes, and, for safety, left her camera on the dresser. Then she headed to the local grocery store.

As soon as she returned, they hooked the boat trailer up to the back of the Jeep. The groceries were deposited in the cabinet. Leslie had picked up a Styrofoam cooler and filled it with ice and beers as well. At the same beach where they'd been clamming, Leslie backed the Jeep and trailer down to the beach and assumed the role of captain; she told Jorge and Al how to mount the mast and attach the rigging located under the seats of the cockpit. They launched the boat and tied a line from the boat to a large rock on the beach.

Leslie drove the trailer to the most remote section of the beach and backed it as far into the water as she could. To hide the trailer, they let the air out of the tires and pushed the trailer as far as they could into the water. In this part of Mexico, no one should bother with the trailer for months.

Leslie put her arm around Jorge's neck. "It's beautiful and peaceful here. The sun rises over the sea out there and sets over the mountains."

They left the Jeep parked on a hill above the tide. Jorge and Al took out their backpacks. Leslie reached back in and pulled out two black, plastic trash bags from a box. "Put your backpacks in these. I know you have things in there that you don't want to get wet."

She did the same with her small bag, which held her limited wardrobe. She felt naked without her camera. It'd played an important role in her life.

She thought, *That's all right. I'm going to be living a far more interesting life from here on out.*

They waded out to the boat and climbed aboard.

48

Sea of Cortez, Mexico

Leslie was in heaven. She was, at least for now, in total control—total control of two men. It was a feeling she'd never had before.

As captain of the boat, Leslie taught Jorge the basics of how to work the lines to change the sails. Al, usually with a beer in hand, watched the instructions as he steered. They sailed for hours, wanting to get as far away as possible from where the boat was launched. Al eventually headed below and fell asleep on one of the small bunks.

Dead tired, Leslie steered the boat into a small inlet and dropped anchor. Al continued to sleep below. Jorge and Leslie made themselves a spot to sleep in the cockpit. They didn't take up a lot of space, as they fell asleep nuzzling close together.

"Caaaa-Caaaa." The high-pitched, screeching cry of seagulls woke them up the next morning. There was a strong wind coming down over the mountains. The boat was rocking, and spray was coming into the cabin. At Leslie's recommendation, they decided to wait until the wind died down before raising the sail.

The swells died down enough for them to heat water and make instant coffee. Leslie served the granola cereal she'd bought.

Al sat at the table staring at the description on the box: "whole-grain oats, wheat, and rice mixed with golden brown sugar and almonds, baked into crunchy clusters."

Al growled, "What the hell is this shit?"

"It's good for you. It'll make you healthy."

A quick response came back. "How long's it gonna take to get to La Paz?"

"My guess, and it's just a guess, is that in this boat, somewhere between six and ten days."

"Fuck! You mean we have to stay on this fuckin' boat for ten days?"

"Unfortunately, yes," Leslie replied.

Finally, the wind lessened to the point where they could pull up the anchor and set sail. The wind continued from the east. It was fairly strong and constant, so the sailboat clipped along at a good pace.

Leslie looked down into the cabin and noticed Al cleaning a gun he'd taken from his backpack. *What've I done? You're committed now, sister. Just make the best of it*, she thought to herself.

She hollered down into the cabin, "Al, I know you think breakfast sucked, but hopefully you're not planning to shoot me. I'm doing my best to get you to La Paz as fast as I can."

"Relax, kid. You're doing fine."

As time passed, they learned that dawn signaled the start of an oven-like heat that would clamp down on them. To provide some shade in the cockpit, they rigging an extra sail to cover part of it. Occasionally, one of them would jump overboard and ride behind the boat, hanging on a towline to cool off.

On the fourth day, they moored in the small community of San Francisquito, where they ate in a local restaurant and restocked their food and water. The shoreline was desolate. The next afternoon, they pulled into an inlet for a break. They found a small fishing community snuggled at the base of the cliffs. Except for this small beach, the mountains came down to the shore. Why this fishing village was located there was beyond them. There was scarcely room among the rocks below the cliffs for the fishermen's huts. They enjoyed an extended lunch as a building breeze and a band of clouds provided some relief from the scorching sun.

The three sat on the ground with their backs against a rock and believed they'd figured out why the local fisherman had selected this site. The high cliffs provided shade in the afternoon, which helped cool them. Al suddenly got serious and looked over at Leslie and asked, "Leslie, have you ever thought of killing someone?"

"Al, it may shock you, but everyone has thought of killing someone at some point. I think what you mean is, would I kill someone?"

"Would you?"

"Maybe. The easy answer is yes. If a close family member were in jeopardy of being killed by someone else, I think I could kill that person."

"How about just killing someone for the sake of doing it?"

"I don't know. Why do you ask? You going to ask me to kill someone?"

"Maybe someday. Jorge has. Everyone in the Fresno Bulldogs has. It's their way of jumping into the gang."

"Jorge's told me about the Bulldogs and his life in Fresno."

"It's not a lifestyle approved of by the white society you grew up in, but it is an important part of the Bulldog society, Jorge's society. It's funny; after awhile, you don't even think about it or the consequences of the inner society's behavior."

Jorge looked at the two of them, got up, and headed down to the beach. He looked back and shouted, "I have to go pee, and I'm going to climb up that cliff and look around. Your discussion is getting too deep for me."

"What do you mean 'the inner society?'"

Al scooted around on the ground to get into a more comfortable position. He pulled a Ziploc bag out of his backpack that contained marijuana and cigarette paper. He rolled himself a joint, lit it, and took a couple of drags.

"How long have you had that weed?"

"Since Fresno. Want some?"

"Of course. Now you should be a great philosopher."

"When I was in the service, I had lots of time to think. I was brought up in a devout Catholic family. For some reason, my thoughts took me to developing what I call the 'circle of people.' Not a lot to do when you're in the service besides training, obeying, and thinking, unless a war comes up. In boot camp, my lieutenant took an interest in my shooting ability. I was pretty good. He stressed my getting every shot within the target's bull's eye. 'That's the only way you can become a sniper,' he would say. It became an obsession with me. I would dream about the target, with its bull's eye, and the rings going away from the center. The bull's eye was perfect. To be in a ring away from the center was bad. The further out the ring, the less perfect you were. I've applied my dreams of the target to life. It's kind of like the Catholic religion. I look at people in the world as belonging to certain rings of a circle, with fences at various points."

Al leaned over and picked up a stick that was lying on the ground. He drew a large circle in the dirt and then used the stick to make points about the circle. "The closer you get to the center of the circle, the more God-like you are. The closer you get to the outer rings of the circle, the closer you are to the devil. The middle, or bull's eye, is God.

"Each ring or fence of the circle has its own rules, or lack of them. Each has its own leaders and followers. For example, you come from a society where the president of the United States is the leader. My society is made up of gangs that live in your society but couldn't care less who is president. Our leaders are prisoners in Pelican Bay State Prison in California, or they are like me, the leader of the Bulldogs in the Fresno Dogg Pound."

"What part of the circle do you think I'm in?"

"Leslie, I suspect you were brought up closer to the center. Jorge and I were brought up somewhere in the middle, but we have moved closer to the outer ring. My guess is that you're on the brink of joining Jorge and me in one of the outer rings."

"Why haven't you tried to fuck me?"

The question caused Al's head to jerk back, and a smirk came across his face. "What?"

He took a long drag on the joint and then crushed it out.

"We're out here alone. You haven't had a woman in awhile. Why haven't you tried to fuck me?

"Do you want me to rape you?"

"No. Of course not."

"Then why are you asking the question?"

"I'm not sure. I guess because I'm curious," she replied.

"You have a fucking strange curiosity. Did you ever think I may not like you? Or, there has been no opportunity? Do you ask questions like that to everyone?"

"No, not everyone. But, I tend to ask a lot of questions of people who interest me."

Al thought for a moment, looked up into the air, and then continued. "There's no reason I have to tell you this, but I will. No, I haven't been with a woman for several days. But I don't just go around raping girls. As the leader of a gang, I have had sex with a lot of girls. They were like groupies who would have sex with just about anybody. I've been with prostitutes. And yes, I've had a couple of girlfriends. Leslie, I hate to burst your bubble, but you're not my type. You're too young. I like a woman, one who takes charge and will give me a bad time. The other reason I haven't tried to have sex with you is that Jorge is my best friend. He really likes you. I don't screw the girl of my best friend, particularly a fellow gang member. One of the most important things to gang members is loyalty, particularly when it's a Mexican gang."

Jorge came walking up. "What're you two talking about now?

Al responded, "Just trying to knock some sense into your girl-friend's head. Let's go back to the boat."

Leslie understood what Al was saying but didn't offer any com-ment. They all walked back to the boat in silence, but it was a good silence. Leslie thought to herself, *The outer rings seem more fun than the one I come from.*

It was the sixth day when they pulled into Santa Rosalia, where they were able to pull up to a small dock and tie up the boat. The brightly colored, wooden buildings looked more European than Mexican, but the papaya trees lining the streets told them they were still in Mexico.

They found a cafe on the corner of Avenue Obregon and Calle 5, where they ordered hamburgers on a nice, open patio. After all the fish they'd eaten on the trip, they wolfed down the hamburgers. In fact, the hamburgers tasted unbelievable. Their server told them there was an Internet cafe just down the street at Calle 1. With Al looking over his shoulder, Jorge advised the cartel that they were in Santa Rosalia and should be in La Paz within the next two days. The response was, "Fine, but we thought you'd be there by now."

In the evening of the eighth day of their voyage, they spotted the lights from La Paz. They sailed the boat to a beach north of the city and grounded it.

49

La Paz, Baja, Mexico

After eight days on the *Pains & Gains*, they were glad to leave it behind. Their sunburned faces looked back at the boat. They all laughed when Al declared that the boat was correctly named for their venture—definitely more pains than gains.

Al swore, "I never want to get on a fucking sailboat again."

With their backpacks in place, they headed toward the lights of La Paz. Eventually, they set foot on the Alvaro Obregon, the main street along the waterfront. They found a rustic-looking hotel a block off the main street. They figured the establishment didn't care that much about who checked in.

They walked around the hotel lobby area while waiting for two Canadian backpackers to check in. It looked newly painted, but for some reason, there were old, faded paintings rehung on the walls and undusted bric-a-brac placed back on the tables and shelves around the lobby in the same locations they were before the paint was applied.

Some of the paintings were original oils with a European look to them. Others were copies of paintings from famous artists that gave the place a kind of bohemian look. Al paid cash for two rooms.

He was startled when he was given two padlocks with keys to secure their rooms.

Leslie commented, "This place is weird. What's with the padlocks?"

Their rooms were next to each other off an interior courtyard. Each room had a heavy, wooden door with a wrought-iron hasp for the padlocks. The rooms were dark. On the inside of each door, there was a slide lock for use when inside.

They peeked into the first room. It was very dark. Leslie hit the light switch, and fluorescent lights that lit the room started blinking. When the lights warmed up, they revealed bright-blue and yellow walls—a "south of the border," cheerful feel.

They found their rooms to be identical in layout with two double beds, ceiling fans, closed Venetian blinds, and fluorescent lighting. Best of all, there were clean showers with hot water. The towels supplied were not the best in the world, but they were far better than what they'd used during their sailing voyage.

Jorge and Leslie agreed to knock on Al's door in the morning when they woke up. Showers removed days of caked-on sea salt. They slept peacefully as their bodies relaxed on dry, warm beds that didn't rock up and down like the boat.

Jorge slept in a separate bed after his shower because he didn't want to wake Leslie. Early in the morning, he lifted the covers on Leslie's bed and lay next to her. Their bodies touched, and the love-making began.

It was mid-morning and Leslie took a shower, while Jorge lay on top of the bed, watching her. She picked through her now-worn and salty clothes. "God, I hate to put any of this stuff back on."

"That's okay with me, but it limits us to staying in the room."

"Ha, ha, ha. Get your buns out of that bed. We need to wake Al and find some new clothes."

They walked arm in arm, with Leslie in the middle of her two male friends. They found a coffee shop in a very upscale hotel on the

Malecón, a waterfront street with a wonderful walking path along the harbor. Bloody Marys were ordered, and then they ate traditional American breakfasts: bacon and eggs with real, hot coffee made from bottled water.

Following breakfast, they continued their walk through the harbor. On a street named 16 Septiembre, they wandered into Dorian's, a large department store. They found it had an extensive selection of stylish clothing, shoes, lingerie, and jewelry. Finding new, dry, and clean wardrobes was the objective. Over a two-hour period, they advised each other on their selections. In the end, each chose several new, lightweight cotton and linen outfits, underwear, and dressy leather sandals, and Leslie added some sexy lingerie.

Everyone changed on the store's premises and ditched the salt-encrusted clothes in a nearby trash container. Leslie stopped at a makeup counter, where she picked out several items to support her ladylike appearance. Al paid for everything. The three felt human again.

As they were walking back down the Malecón, Jorge suddenly stopped and said, "I have to go back for something. I'll catch up."

Al and Leslie continued walking slowly, taking in the sights, when they spotted an ice cream parlor called La Fuente. It wasn't hard to notice, since it had a huge, polka-dot tree sign and a line of people out the front door. Leslie got in line, while Al kept an eye out for Jorge. By the time she got to the front of the line, Al and Jorge were standing next to her, ready to order. Leslie ordered guava, Jorge, tequila with almond, and Al, for some reason, decided to try elate, or corn ice cream.

When their ice creams were finished, Jorge stopped, reached into his pocket, and pulled out a locally made silver necklace with a beautiful silver crucifix attached. "Leslie, this is for you. It'll keep you safe. If it's all right with you, we will get it blessed."

"Jorge, it's beautiful. Thank you so much. I'm not very religious, but yes, let's get it blessed," she replied.

Al interrupted, "Jorge, when in the hell did you get religion? Come on, you two fuckin' lovebirds. We need to find an Internet café."

Leslie stopped a young American couple walking down the street toward them and asked if they knew of an Internet café. The young man said that they'd just passed one a few blocks away, inside the Plaza Cerralva.

Jorge fired up the computer and made contact with the cartel. He was advised to meet a member of the cartel at the Plaza Constitución at six. The instructions were to stand at the entrance to the Catedral de Nuestra Senora de La Paz, located on the western side of the Plaza, where a man wearing black slacks and shirt with a Panama hat would meet them. They would be transported to a yacht, where they would meet with a senior member of the cartel.

Back at their hotel, they showered again and changed into clean underwear and sporty-looking, upscale clothes. When they checked out at two in the afternoon, the desk clerk informed them that the Plaza Constitución was just two blocks away. With backpacks and bags of clothes in hand, the three headed down toward the Malecón and found a restaurant right on the water called the Kiwi. Sitting at a table on the terrace, Al ordered a bottle of champagne to celebrate their arrival in La Paz.

Al raised his glass and said, "Leslie. This is a toast to you for getting us here safely."

The decision was mutually made to enjoy the relaxed Mexican atmosphere and spend the rest of the afternoon on this terrace before heading to their meeting. They drank, ate, and talked until five o'clock and then walked over to the Plaza Constitución.

The plaza was quite sizable and crowded with people, many of whom were sitting on benches under the shade trees, watching others pass by. As they walked past a bandstand, they noted the majestic Cathedral of Nuestra Senora de Ia Paz on the far side rising in front of them. The cathedral had two large bell towers on either side of the main structure. It wasn't ornate, and the architectural design resembled California Mission churches.

Jorge asked Leslie, "Do you know what 'Nuestra Senora de Ia Paz' means?"

"I suspect it's something like 'Lady of Peace.'"

"Very good. It means Our Lady of Peace. Let's go in for a minute. We need to get your crucifix blessed."

Hand in hand, the young couple walked through the massive, ornate main door, which was topped by a round arch supported by two columns.

Jorge knelt down in a pew at the back of the cathedral. Leslie followed him. He crossed himself, like he'd done so many times as a boy. He made three wishes, just as his grandmother had told him to do when he was very small. He wasn't sure it was really part of the Catholic faith, but he loved his grandmother, and her belief that you got three wishes when you visited a new church stayed with him. He made his three wishes, crossed himself again, and rose.

Leslie felt out of place as Jorge led her to the front of the church. The priest arranging objects on the altar noticed them and spoke in Spanish.

"Bienvenido a la Catedral de Nuestra."

Jorge replied in Spanish, "Father, we'd like to have this crucifix blessed."

The priest smiled while looking carefully at the couple. Then he replied in English. "Ah, you're Americans. I'll happily bless your crucifix."

As they walked down the steps at the front of the church, they saw Al talking with a man dressed in black wearing a Panama hat. As they approached the two men, they heard the stranger say, "I have a car near the entrance to the Plaza. Please to follow me to it."

Parked at the entrance to the Plaza was a very well-maintained, older Cadillac limo. Its driver, wearing a traditional chauffer's cap, got out and placed their backpacks and bags in the trunk. The man in the Panama hat sat next to the driver in front, and the three of them settled in the backseat. They were driven to the Nuevo Vallarta Marina, eight miles north of the city.

The limo pulled up to a gate near a docking area, where the driver removed their belongings from the trunk and placed them on a small cart. They followed the man with the Panama hat and the cart down a walkway and onto a dock, where there was a speedboat waiting for them. One of the boat's crewmembers loaded their belongings onto the boat. The man with the Panama hat helped them board, sat behind the steering wheel, and pushed a button that started the powerful twin outboard engines.

50

Sea of Cortez, Mexico

The speedboat wove its way through the marina, passing slips on both sides that were filled with pleasure crafts of all types. Eventually, they left the main marina, heading toward the large yachts. They motored toward a large yacht with a helicopter sitting at the back of the upper deck.

The speedboat tied up to a large opening in the yacht's hull. The base of the opening was just a foot above the boat's water line. A section of the yacht's hull acted as a canopy above the opening. None of them had ever seen anything like it before. They were able to step directly onto what looked like a lounge area on the second deck. Sleek lounge chairs and tables were strategically placed along the deck, which was approximately twenty feet across. There was a similar opening on the other side. The canopies were heavy, metal panels that could be raised and lowered by huge hydraulic pistons. It was like an overhead garage door opener, except the construction of the door was similar to that of an aircraft door. When it closed, it became part of the yacht's hull.

After helping them aboard, the man in the Panama hat returned to the speedboat and headed back toward the marina. Two of the yacht's crewmembers picked up their bags and disappeared. The yacht's captain introduced himself and then looked at Leslie and politely asked, "We weren't expecting the lady. How many rooms will you require?"

Jorge responded, "Just two. The lady will share my room."

"Thank you. Please follow me."

The captain led them up two decks, where they entered a wide, well-lit hallway with three doors off each side and a set of double doors at the end. "Your rooms are these first two across from each other. Make yourselves comfortable. Cocktails will be served in the main lounge, two decks above, at eight. Señor Ramirez and his daughter Juanita will be your hosts. We'll be pulling up anchor and moving out to sea shortly."

Jorge and Leslie entered their cabin. Their belongings were waiting for them. The cabin was very modern in style: sparkling clean, with a queen-size bed with a beautiful red bedspread and white, fluffy pillows. Furniture included a couch and a glass coffee table with polished stainless-steel legs. There was a small bar with two very modern-looking stools. The cabin was very bright because of the large floor-to-ceiling window looking out to sea. A door led to a full bathroom featuring white marble, glass, and chrome. White towels embroidered with *Cuidado*, the yacht's name, hung from chrome rods.

Leslie asked Jorge, "Does cuidado mean anything in English?"

"Yes, it means 'caution.'"

"Jorge, this is unbelievable. Look at this bathroom. It's like something out of a decorator's magazine. Who is this guy Ramirez?"

"He's the leader of the Central Michoacan cartel. They call him 'EI Chapa,' or 'Shorty' in English. You'll see why at dinner. Al and I have been doing business with him for a couple of years now. Hey, Les, there's a bottle of champagne in the fridge. You want some?"

Stripping off her clothes and stepping into the tub, she replied, "Sure. Bring two glasses in here and join me for a bubble bath. This tub is big enough for both of us." As they lay across from each other in the tub, they noticed ripples in the tub water as the yacht started to move away from its mooring. This was nothing like their recent sailing trip.

Al surveyed his cabin, which was identical to that of his travel companions' across the way. He took a shower and lay on the bed drinking a beer. *Not a bad lifestyle. I could get used to this,* he thought.

At eight, Al knocked on Jorge and Leslie's cabin door. Jorge answered, dressed in light-tan, linen slacks and a white, open shirt. Standing behind him was Leslie, looking very sultry with her tanned body in a short, white, peasant-style dress with a low neckline. They walked together to the main lounge. As they moved up the stairway, they could hear someone playing classical music on a piano.

The top of the stairway opened onto the yacht's main salon, which featured a curved bar with six bar chairs, a round coffee table with a curved sofa on one side, and three cloth chairs on the other. To the left, as they entered, was a white grand piano being played by an attractive Hispanic lady. She appeared to be in her early thirties and was dressed in a black cocktail dress. Standing next to the piano, listening attentively, was her father, Carlos Ramirez.

Carlos greeted his guests in English, but with a strong Mexican accent. "Welcome friends to my yacht, the *Cuidado.* I'm pleased to introduce you to my daughter Juanita, who, as you can tell, is an accomplished pianist."

"Hello, Juanita. I'm Alejandro Gomez, but my friends just call me Al. Your father has spoken about you often. It's a pleasure to finally meet you." *She certainly doesn't take after her father. Her mother must have been a looker,* he thought.

Juanita responded in English, with just a slight Mexican accent, "Nice to meet you, Al. Who're your friends?"

"This is Jorge Garcia and his friend Leslie."

"Nice to meet you, Jorge and Leslie. Padre, we should move to the bar and offer our friends a drink."

The bar was tended by one of the crewmembers, who took their drink orders. He was dressed in a white sailor uniform. Leslie understood why they called Carlos "Shorty." He was only about five foot, three inches tall. He was stocky, with Mexican features. Carlos suggested they try the margaritas, and they all agreed. The bartender served them in crystal margarita glasses.

"Alejandro, it's good to see you again. I understand things have changed in Fresno," said Carlos.

"Yes. I suspect you know more than I do as to what is happening there at the moment."

"You're probably right. My friends at the Pelican Bay Prison in California inform me that they've replaced you with one of their amigos from Los Angeles. Right after your battle with the policia, my shipments of drugs to your Bulldogs went down, but as usually happens, that only lasted for a few weeks. Now they're returning to normal. Just another bump in the road, as they say."

"Señor Carlos, you've confirmed what we've been hearing from our contacts over the Internet."

"Then, amigo, welcome to Mexico, apparently your new home. I understand you have a proposition for me."

"I do."

"Let's discuss it during dinner."

Carlos joined the bartender on the other side of the bar. In a proud and authoritative voice, he described his yacht. "My amigos, let me tell you about the *Cuidado*. The Spanish shipyard Astondoa built her specifically for me. I spent a month there during her design. She's fifty meters, or, to you Americans, 164 feet in length. The hull consists of steel, with an aluminum superstructure. My cabin is on the top level behind the bridge. You're staying in two of the six guest cabins. Our top speed is 15.6 knots, and we can sail for five thousand miles at 12.5 knots. There are two Caterpillar diesel engines and ten crewmembers on board. I'm sure you've noted the helicopter on the upper deck that will fly us from the *Cuidado* to my estate. How about another margarita? Then we'll have dinner."

While being served their second margaritas, Juanita returned to the piano and started playing "*La Cucaracha.*" They all left the bar and stood around the piano laughing as they sung together, with Juanita leading.

> "La cucaracha, Ia cucaracha
> Ya no puede caminar
> Porque no tiene, porque/e falta
> Marihuana que fumar"

They sang it over and over again. Then Juanita stopped playing, looked at Leslie, and asked, "Do you know what you've been singing about?"

"I know. It's about a cockroach."

"You're right. I've been leading you in singing one of many improvised versions of that song."

Laughingly, she added, "It's my padre's favorite, as it has to do with his business. 'La Cucaracha' is a folk song that became popular during the Mexican Revolution, and the verse I've led you in translates in English into something like, 'The cockroach, the cockroach can't walk anymore because it doesn't have, because it's lacking, marijuana to smoke.'"

While trying to hold back his laughter, Carlos announced, "Follow me to the dining salon. I believe it's time for dinner."

They entered a large room with a long, rectangular table, four chairs on both sides, and one chair on each end. It was set for a party of five. Carlos sat in one of the end chairs with his daughter on his right and Leslie on his left.

"Let me tell you something about my daughter. Her mother died of cancer when she was four, and her brother was killed last year by one of my enemies. She's the only child I have left. I've raised her to replace me when I die. While she plays the piano extremely well, she can also shoot the center out of a target with a pistol or rifle. She played field hockey at the University of Arizona, where she went for two years. She continued her studies at the University of Mexico in Mexico City in the Faculty of Accounting and Administration. Juanita can move money around the world with great ease. I make sure the money is made so that Juanita can manage and move it."

Having said that, Carlos proudly looked at his daughter. "Juanita, Señor Garcia has a proposition for us."

Al, somewhat surprised, hesitated for a moment. He then proceeded with his presentation. "Señor Carlos and Señorita Juanita, in Fresno, we did very well selling your marijuana, methamphetamine, and cocaine drugs, but we had, as they say, hit a plateau. I realized that some of the new Bulldog members were coming to us with college degrees. The world is changing. Who'd have thought of gangbangers with college degrees? Several of them went to work for the government tax center in Fresno and wanted to get involved in white-collar crime rather than selling drugs on the street."

Carlos interrupted. "I've studied this. The mafia did the same thing. I believe we can grow in white-collar crime."

"You're right, Señor Carlos. There'll be as much money in white-collar crime as there is in selling drugs. We'll grow in influence and control of our areas."

"Go on. Go on. What do you have for us?"

"We have computer files in our possession that have information from the US government tax agency—the IRS. These files contain the names, dates of birth, social security numbers, addresses, and some credit-card information on three million American taxpayers. I'll sell you this information for three dollars a name."

"You want me to pay you $9 million for this information? I doubt if I'll do that. Juanita and I will talk this over and let you know our answer in a day or two. Now, let's enjoy our dessert and some very fine port wine."

51

Pacific Ocean, Off the Coast of Mexico

After two days in the Gulf of California, the *Cuidado* left the gulf's calm waters and headed south to tip of the Baja peninsula and then west into the Pacific Ocean.

It was late afternoon when the yacht headed toward a large cargo ship flying a Chinese flag. The ship was rigged with cranes, allowing it to load and unload its own cargo at small ports. The yacht closed to within a hundred yards of the ship and stopped. A launch, with three people aboard, was lowered from the side of the ship.

Carlos ordered the captain to open the hull doors so the lounge deck was open at the water level. The huge hydraulic pistons hummed as they lifted the heavy, metal panels from the hull. The launch tied up to the sea-level deck. A Chinese gentleman jumped from it onto the *Cuidado* deck.

"Mr. Rui, how are you? Welcome back to the *Cuidado*," Carlos said.

"Mr. Ramirez, it's good to see you again.

"Let's go up to the main salon for refreshments."

Carlos led Mr. Rui up to the yacht's main salon. Juanita, Leslie, Al, and Jorge rose from their bar seats and introduced themselves.

Mr. Rui ordered a gin and tonic, while the rest continued drinking their margaritas. After Carlos and his Chinese friend's second drinks were served, they moved to a table away from the rest of the group.

Mr. Rui pulled some papers out of his jacket pocket and laid them on the table so Carlos could review them. "Here's the chemical delivery schedule for the next three months. This should keep you in the methamphetamine business for the balance of the year. May I assume the usual payment terms?"

"You may. I'll give you the money before you leave. Eight hundred thousand, right?"

"Correct, and we'll deliver the merchandise to the usual dock. Now, do you want to see what I've brought for you?" Mr. Rui asked.

"Si, si. I've been looking forward to this for weeks. Does it work as well as you told me?"

"Even better."

Carlos shouted across the room. "Juanita and everyone, we need to go down to the lounge deck. Mr. Rui has something to show us. You can refresh your drinks, since it'll take a little time to get the item over from the ship."

Ten minutes later, with drinks in hand, they went down to the lounge deck and looked across at the ship as a crane was dropping something over the side.

When the item was just above the water, Al commented, "That looks something like a boat."

"Good eye, Al. Actually, it's my first submarine," shouted Carlos as he jumped up and down.

"It's a what?"

"A Chinese-made submarine, built specifically to my specifications."

Now in the water, the submarine motored under its own power over to the *Cuidado*. The launch was untied and moved away from the yacht to make room for the sub to tie up. A Chinese sailor stuck his head out of the top of the sub and guided it to the yacht.

"Mr. Ramirez, here is your first sub." Said Mr. Rui.

"It looks great. Now, everyone, I'll tell you the details of my submarine."

"Padre, please do. I didn't know anything about this."

"It was supposed to be a surprise, Juanita. It'll replace many of the mules we use to take drugs into the United States. I personally thought of it and designed it. It's my disposable drug submarine. Thirty-eight feet long and made of fiberglass. As you can see, the fiberglass is colored light-green to match the color of the ocean. It's designed to travel just beneath the water, leaving almost no wake. It has a small diesel engine that'll power it for two weeks. Only one person is needed to make it work. The plan is to ground it at night on a remote beach and unload the drugs. Then it's turned around and set out to sea, where, a mile offshore, a valve opens, and the submarine sinks, leaving no trace. The crewmember then goes off with those picking up the drugs."

"Padre, what does one of these cost?"

"Juanita, the cost for each one is less than the cost of an American SUV. Is that not right, Mr. Rui?"

"Correct, Mr. Ramirez. Forty thousand dollars for each, including delivery."

"Padre, you're so smart. Forty thousand is less than it costs us to use mules to move the drugs across the border," Juanita replied.

52

Michoacán, Mexico

The sub was personally tested by Carlos and members of the *Cuidado's* crew over the next two days, and then the yacht headed west toward Acapulco, its homeport.

One hundred and fifty miles before the *Cuidado* reached Acapulco, the Bell 407 Helicopter lifted off the back upper deck and headed east toward the mainland of Mexico. Its seven seats were filled. In the front seats sat the pilot and co-pilot, who also acted as bodyguards. The passengers sat behind them in two rows of seats facing each other.

The testing of the sub and playing with the toys aboard the *Cuidado* had kept them all busy. Juanita and Leslie proved to be better swimmers than Al and Jorge. Carlos was more an observer than a participant. The yacht's WaveRunners were used to go scuba diving, snorkeling, fishing, and water skiing. The meals on the yacht were like those found in a five-star restaurant. Each night, they watched a movie before going to bed. Carlos and Al were becoming good buddies, as they both liked the old-time gangster movies. Now they were returning to the real world, all knowing each other much better.

Carlos leaned across his daughter, who was sitting next to him, and said in a loud voice so he could be heard over the helicopter's engines, "Juanita and I have discussed your proposition. We've decided not to pay you for the information on your computer."

Juanita interrupted, "Padre, let me explain."

"I will, my daughter. But first let me explain why. Amigos, this is something new for us. We have an interest in getting into, ah, what do you call it? Oh, yes, the identity-theft business. What you have is too much. We may be able to work with a thousand names, but three million? That's too many. How do we know we'd be able to use them all before we were stopped somehow? We don't have the capability to use them all right away. Now, my daughter, you explain our offer."

"We're offering you a partnership. We'll set up a computer center and a network of people to access the information you have and other similar information we obtain. You cannot go back to the United States, so you'll stay here with us. We'll split the profits, 40 percent for you and 60 percent for us. This is our offer."

Al and Jorge looked at each other. They weren't sure how to respond, so Al suggested, "We'll think about it and let you know by tomorrow. It's hard for me to believe we can't go back to the United States, but you're probably right. Let us think about it."

Carlos responded, "You have until tomorrow. From where I sit, it's a good deal for you. Your life here would be very nice, and we would make a lot of money."

Carlos looked down out of his window and then leaned across the seat in front of him and touched the pilot on the shoulder and spoke to him in Spanish. Then he turned to his guests and said, "We're approaching my estate. I've asked the pilot to circle. I'll point out some of the features of my estate."

After flying over a mountain range, the helicopter dropped lower and hovered over an especially striking area. It was quite green, with forests filled with native oak, cedar, and pine trees. Carlos proudly pointed out aspects of the estate as it appeared in front of them.

"There's the Aguililla River, the reason for the lush vegetation.

It flows all the way to the Pacific Ocean. Oh, and there's the town of San Rico. It has a population of about five thousand. They're very friendly to us, and many of them work for us. San Rico's about 240 miles southwest of Mexico City. My estate is just five miles west, up the Aguililla River.

"Ah, there it is, over there. That's my casa. It's where Juanita and I live and work. There's four bedrooms and our two offices. Across the drive from my casa is our private, nine-hole golf course. Juanita and I play it all the time."

Leslie said, "It's a beautiful estate. What're those two buildings in the middle of the golf course?"

Juanita responded, "Those are the two guest houses. They each have six bedrooms. You'll be staying in the one that's closest to the main house. We're going to convert it to the computer center you need."

Al asked, "What're those buildings over there?"

"That's the housing for the servants and bodyguards, and the maintenance buildings."

Carlos then asked the pilot to fly past the maintenance area. "My estate ends at the barbed-wire fence. You see that building over there? It's a mile from the estate. That's the methamphetamine-processing building. Over there is the landing strip where we fly in cocaine from Colombia. In addition to their regular food crops, the farmers in the area raise marijuana, our other major product. We pay them well for it. Tomorrow, we'll give you a tour of our little section of the world."

53

Michoacán, Mexico

The helicopter landed on a helipad next to the estate's main casa. They exited and gathered on the dirt driveway in front of the casa. There were jeeps at either end of the driveway—each with a fifty-caliber machine gun mounted on it. Two bodyguards sat in the front seats. Behind one of the jeeps was an older-model, white Chevy Bronco.

"Welcome, my friends. Mi casa es su casa. I'm sure you'll want to settle in at the guesthouse and clean up. The Chevy Bronco over there is yours to use while you're my guests. Just follow that jeep. It'll lead you to the guesthouse. We'll be serving cocktails and dinner at six tonight."

Jorge was elected driver of the Bronco. He followed the jeep toward the two-story, Spanish-style guesthouse with a red-tile roof, similar to the main house. The house overlooked the golf course. Lush trees surrounded it, offering shade from the hot sun. The three entered the large entryway, admiring the spiral staircase with its wrought-iron railing. Arched doorways on either side of the entryway led to a dining room on the right and a large sitting room on the left. Off the dining room was a small kitchen. A lady, dressed in peasant clothes, greeted them in broken English. In Spanish, she instructed the two bodyguards from the jeep to help take the luggage upstairs.

Al started to take the first bedroom, located to the left at the top of the stairs. He was stopped by the peasant lady. She beckoned him to the end of the hallway, where there was a much larger room with a huge bay window that faced directly out to the sixth tee of the golf course. He thanked the lady and made himself comfortable in his new, elegant surroundings. Jorge and Leslie selected a similar room at the other end of the hall.

A half hour after they'd settled in, the peasant lady knocked on each of their doors and led them downstairs to the dining room. Lunch was already laid out. They were hungry and gorged themselves on a steamy stew of rice and chicken, accompanied by a big pitcher of lemonade.

After lunch, they were escorted to the large sitting room, where Juanita was waiting for them. "Welcome to your new home. If you agree with our proposition, tomorrow we'll start to convert this room into our computer center. Then we'll see what we can do with the information you've brought with you. I've already ordered the computer equipment. It should arrive in the next few days. We'll also start to find people to help us. There are a number of people in the village who've returned from working in the United States that may have developed some computer skills and understand English."

Al put his arm around Jorge and, in a low voice, said, "I think we should take their offer."

"I agree."

"Juanita, you can tell your father we're going to take his offer. So tomorrow, let's start converting this to a computer room," said Al.

"Padre will be pleased."

"Now that we're partners, just how big is your organization?"

With pride, she responded, "Quite sizable. We're in the Pacific range in west central Mexico, in the state of Michoacán, which is like one of your US states. The closest civilized town is the rural village of San Rico. There are farms between the village and us. Including the town, the farms, and the estate, there are probably fifteen hundred to two thousand people working for us. The family estate here is our headquarters. We have ties to many gangs in the United States, who have thousands of members who distribute our drugs. As father says, thank God for the Americans. Without their cravings for drugs, we wouldn't have a business. You know, I have my university degree in economics. One time, I spent hours thinking about our size. You must remember, we don't pay taxes. Our labor costs are very low. Protection and lost merchandise are our most costly expenses. But, based on my calculations, that cost is still less than if we had to pony up for American welfare benefits. Considering all of this, I determined we'd be in the top 30 percent of the Fortune 500 List. Our cartel's sales are in the billions of dollars each year."

"Don't you worry about security or being arrested by the police?" Juanita said.

"It's something we think about all the time. Our concern isn't with the police; we can buy them off. Our greatest concern is with the other Mexican cartels. Any time you have billions of dollars, you're a target. As you can see, we're isolated, and the roads to get here are narrow. The people in the local village and on the farms protect us. The village is small enough where everyone knows everyone else. It's impossible for strangers to enter our area without being noticed. The police and army in this area work for us, not the government. We know what they're going to do beforehand so that we can counter their plans, or many times, they just don't follow through with their orders. We're safe here. I will admit that Padre and I spend most of our lives here on the estate or on our yacht, the *Cuidado*. We use to travel more, but it gets harder every year."

Juanita pushed her chair back from the table, stood, and said, "Let's take a ride around the estate."

Behind the wheel of the Bronco, Juanita headed down a dirt road toward the maintenance area they had seen from the helicopter. A concrete block wall surrounded the area, which was topped by strings of electrified wires. Two armed guards sat on lawn chairs by the gated opening in the wall. The maintenance facilities were sizable, with a barracks building, a large, metal building, and a low, concrete-block building with a heavy, metal door.

"Let me tell you a little about our security. As I said previously, we don't worry about the local police. They actually work for us. Here on the estate, we have guards known as Zetas. They're part of our security network, made up of former Mexican soldiers and gang members. They have a better spy network in the government than the federal government's Center for Investigation and National Security."

The Zetas guards saw Juanita and waved them into the compound. She took her visitors inside the metal building, where there was a tracked armored vehicle with a gun turret on top. Al walked over and climbed up into the turret. It was equipped with a 20mm cannon and a machine gun. A plate inside indicated a German company named Henschel had constructed it in 1964.

"Where'd you get this?" Asked Al.

"Padre says it belonged to the Mexican Army. It ended up missing during a field exercise they were doing near Mexico City. Padre won it in a poker game from an army general."

The facility also housed four white Chevy pickup trucks with .50-caliber machine guns mounted on the back, four older, army-type jeeps, also with .50-caliber machine guns, and six Humvees. Several spaces for other vehicles were empty.

Next, Juanita called over to the guards. One of them walked over and knocked on the steel door of the concrete building. A little window in the door slid open, and the guard said, "Juanita is here with visitors."

A man holding the barrel of a machine gun slowly opened the

door. Four feet inside the door was a heavy, wooden table, where a man dressed in a T-shirt and military fatigue pants was cleaning a military-style rifle. There were tools spread over the top of the table. The building was an armory, filled with weapons and ammunition of all types. There were military-type pistols, machine pistols, rifles, machine guns, grenade launchers, hand grenades, and handheld anti-aircraft and anti-tank rocket-propelled launchers.

Juanita, with pride on her face, said, "As you can see, we're well protected. Our weapons are the best in the world. They're better than the Mexican military's weapon supply. Of course, we have more money to spend than they have."

Al walked down one of the aisles in the building, looking at the weapons. "This is unbelievable. Absolutely fucking unbelievable."

54

San Rico, Michoacán, Mexico

"Cock-a-doodle-doo! Cock-a-doodle-doo!"

"What the fuck?" Al's head lifted from the bed's covers. He looked out the window and saw the rooster's cocked head as it continued to crow. He wandered downstairs and found the table set for breakfast.

The rooster's crowing had the same effect on Jorge and Leslie. They went downstairs, yawning, shortly after Al. The Americans dug into their breakfasts of eggs, tacos, fresh fruit, and coffee. Halfway through, Juanita came through the front door. She was wearing light-cotton, khaki-colored military pants and shirt. The pants were tucked into high, black riding boots. Her hair was down.

Al looked up from his plate and thought, *Now, that's a woman.*

She sat across from Al at the table.

"Yesterday, you saw our security. Today, you'll see our production facilities and the village of San Rico."

Juanita instructed the guard in front of the house to take her horse back to the stable. She climbed behind the wheel of the Bronco. Her first stop was the security area they'd visited the previous day, where she spoke with one of the guards. A few minutes later, a jeep with a mounted machine gun, manned by two guards, pulled in behind the Bronco.

Al noted that most of the guards had big, gold rings on their hands. "Juanita, what's with the gold rings the guards are wearing?"

"Very perceptive, my friend." She asked one of the guards to show Al his ring. With pride, the Zetas guard held out his hand.

"The ring is good luck to them. It has the icon of Saint Death, or Holy Death. It's based on Santa Muete, who has a growing following here in Mexico. There are chapels throughout Mexico to honor her. Some claim she is the Grim Reaper, and they pray she will bring death to their enemies. The Zetas believe that the grim reaper figure on the ring protects them. A Mexican novelist, Homero Aridjis, has written a book about her. He counts narco-traffickers, corrupt cops, and politicians among Santa Muerte's followers."

With the jeep following them, they exited the well-guarded estate and headed down a dirt road toward San Rico. After a mile, they turned right onto another dirt road and drove for a mile through barren terrain. The road ended at a large building with thick, bright-white adobe walls and the traditional red-tile roof.

They pulled up between the building and a shed that was loaded with drums and boxes of chemicals. As they exited the Bronco, they smelled noxious fumes coming from the building. There were two sizable white trucks being unloaded next to the shed. The drums and boxes had both Spanish and Chinese, or at least, Al thought, Asian writing on them.

Acting as tour guide, Juanita pointed to the shed. "The Chinese provide us with most of the raw materials we need to produce meth-amphetamines. We order them just like you'd order any type of raw material. The drugs are shipped by sea on Chinese- operated ships into Acapulco. The trucks you see there are unloading one of the raw materials we use, pseudoephedrine. They just picked it up from a ship that came in from Hong Kong. We also get some equipment and material from the United States that we pick up at the border. Follow me inside."

They entered the building. The noxious fumes were even more intense. The building was filled with commercial lab equipment being watched over by a number of workers wearing white smocks.

"We have to be careful with the operations in this building. The process is very dangerous. The chemicals used are corrosive, and the cooking process can result in an explosion. We use what is called the Birch Reduction Method in the reduction of ephedrine. It's a relatively simple process, but as I said, it's also very dangerous. We're able to produce a kilo every eight hours. The profits on the crystalline meth produced in this building are in the millions and millions of dollars each year. All that money comes from the United States, thank you very much."

Al was impressed. He'd set up two houses in Fresno to do a similar process, but the equipment he used consisted of glass jars and coffee carafes, not the stainless-steel vessels and pipes in this building.

"Okay, everyone, let's get out of here. The smell is getting to me."

The vehicles returned to the main road and headed toward San Rico. They had only driven a short distance when Juanita turned onto a narrow dirt road that curved around and ended up next to the river. They drove along the bank of the river for a ways, when suddenly, a Jeep with a machine gun pulled out in front of them, and six armed men came out of the nearby vegetation.

Juanita rolled her window down and spoke to them. Her entourage continued toward their destination. A few minutes later, they came to a spot where the trees and vegetation had been cleared and graded along the river for about a half a mile. The clearing acted as a landing strip for small aircraft. A Cessna 303T Crusader with twin engines was parked adjacent to a runway under some trees. Next to the plane was a small, wooden building with a small front porch and an antenna sitting on top of its roof. Power was provided by a gas generator located next to the building.

"Welcome to our airport. It may not look like much, but it gets considerable traffic. We're connected to a Columbian cartel that flies cocaine into this location. Then we consolidate the cocaine with other drugs and fly it to the US border, or sometimes even across the border into the United States."

Juanita pulled onto the runway and parked next to the wooden building. She waved to the two men sitting on its porch. "Those are two of our pilots. They're Americans."

The tour resumed as they continued down the runway to another dirt road at the other end. It curved through the rough terrain and thick vegetation. A small farmhouse appeared on their right, and Juanita slowed the car. "You'll note the corn fields surrounding the house, but tucked away over there are several fields of marijuana plants.

"The farmers deliver the marijuana to the airport, where we either fly it out directly or sometimes bring in trucks to take it out. There are twenty-three farmers from this area who supply us with marijuana. They all grow crops of corn, wheat, potatoes, beans, and oats and raise cows, horses, pigs, sheep, and goats. They supply most of the food for the village and the estate, but their main cash crop is marijuana."

The road continued to wind around through pine-covered mountains, past similar-type farms, and eventually connected with the road to San Rico.

Leslie asked, "We've been going up and down quite a bit. What's the elevation here?"

"We're in the Sierra Madre Mountains. In this area, the elevation ranges from three thousand to 7,100 feet. I know the airport back there is at three thousand feet, but San Rico is at five thousand. We're in a tropical climate zone, but because of the altitude here in the mountains, the weather is much cooler than in the lower-lying jungles and coastlands."

The Bronco slowed at the top of the hill. "That village down there is San Rico."

They looked down on a village with cobblestone streets that divided a number of one-story adobe or plaster-over-brick buildings, all of which had red-tile roofs. It was like the Old West, with a number of people riding horses and donkeys. The locals were wearing clothing that was representative of a small village, not the big city. Many of the men dressed in white and wore sombreros; the women were in colorful, long skirts with beautiful shawls. They stopped at the main plaza, which was surrounded by tall pine trees. The centerpiece of the plaza was a fountain, and set off to one side was a small stage.

Juanita pulled up to the Blue Star Café that faced the plaza. "It's time to get some lunch."

As they walked up to the café, they could hear classical music playing from the stereo system. The food being prepared in the kitchen had a pleasant aroma. Juanita ordered for them. Servings of roast pork from a pig that had just been roasted that day, along with fresh vegetables and tortillas, were set in front of them.

Following lunch, they walked up one of the streets off the main plaza. They passed a church with an adjacent cemetery and continued walking for another block, and then they turned back toward the plaza.

"There're only four prominent buildings in San Rico: the church you just passed; city hall, or presidencia municipal; the casa de cambia, or currency exchange center. There's no bank, as you know it. Cash is king here. The last large building is the comisaria de policia, or police station, over there."

Juanita noticed a familiar car with one of the protective jeeps parked behind it. "That's my padre's car over there. I must go talk with him. I'll be right back."

She talked with one of her padre's guards, who was leaning against a wall smoking a cigarette. She entered the building and returned a few minutes later, motioning to the group to join her.

"Padre's Zetas guards captured five soldiers from a patrol headed toward our village last night. They're being questioned inside. You're welcome to watch our interrogation methods. I think you'll find them quite efficient."

She looked directly at Leslie. "Leslie, you may not want to join us. We don't question nicely, and they'll all be dead by the end of the day."

Leslie thought for a moment and said, "Juanita, if you can do it, I can too."

Juanita looked down from the top step at the three of them. *Leslie is proving to be an interesting person. I think that I'm going to like her. I have no idea why she likes Jorge. He's a loser; Al's a different story,* she thought.

The front wall of the building was windowless. A guard opened the heavy, wooden door. The walls were made of adobe that was at least three feet thick. There were a few small windows high above on either side that allowed small beams of light to enter. The building had an ominous, dark feeling. Their eyes took time adjusting from the bright sunlight to the very dark, small entry room, where a guard sat at a heavy, wooden desk. Juanita spoke to the guard, who opened the door to his right. It led into a sizable room lighted only by oil lamps mounted along the walls. Sitting on a bench to their right were three soldiers with ski masks turned backward over their heads so they could not see. Otherwise, they were naked and slumped over from the beatings they'd taken so far.

The wall opposite the soldiers had six openings into small rooms. As they started walking toward the first opening, they could hear a bloodcurdling scream from one of the openings further down the wall.

Juanita led the group toward the opening, where two of the Zetas guards were standing over a naked soldier who was sitting on a specially designed chair. The chair's seat had been removed and replaced by a toilet seat. Two thin electrical wires with alligator clips were attached to the soldier's testicles. The wire ran across the floor to a small table with a control box. Another set of cables ran from the box to a car battery located underneath the table. One of the Zetas guards was sitting in front of the control box, manipulating the switches. He hit a button, and the soldier's body jerked violently. The soldier screamed in excruciating pain from this electrical zap to this sensitive part of his body.

A Zetas guard standing over the man shouted, "What base are you from?"

Leslie looked at the others. "This is terrible. How can people do this to each other?" she said.

Al and Jorge didn't respond, since they'd used the same types of torture techniques themselves in Fresno. Juanita looked at Leslie and, responding like a teacher, answered her question. "This is just part of our business. Padre had this facility built and is very proud of it. It's just business. I've squeezed the balls of some of these scum with pliers myself just to get information."

Al thought to himself, *God, she's beautiful, but dangerous. Don't get on the wrong side of her.*

A scream for help came from the opening at the end of the wall. Juanita led them to it. Carlos was standing next to a table where another naked soldier was strapped down with leather straps. Duct tape covered his eyes. A plastic tube was taped to one side of his nose. The tube was connected to a hospital IV setup and controlled by a Zetas guard. Liquid was spurting out the other side of the soldier's nose and running down his face. Two fingers were missing from the soldier's right hand, and blood was dripping on the floor. The Zetas stopped the flow of liquid. After a few seconds, the soldier, in a state of panic, screamed in Spanish, "Stop! Stop! Please stop!"

The Zetas leaned over and, in a whisper, said something to the soldier. He responded back with a whispered answer.

Carlos walked over to them and said in a low voice, "Welcome. We're getting the information we need from these scum. I believe in the United States, you call this 'waterboarding.' We've added a Mexican flavor to it. We add the juice from jalapeno peppers to the water. Not only do they think they are going to drown, but their sinuses burn like hell."

The soldier's body went into a spasm, and then all movement ceased.

Carlos paused as they watched, and then added, "We also learned from your CIA not to torture too much. If you do, the resistance to it actually increases. You want to induce 'learned helplessness' and 'debility, dependency, and dread,' aiming to destroy their minds. Effective torture takes time. It's not the pain created by what you do, but rather, the effect on the mind."

"Padre, why were they coming here?"

"They were stupid soldiers. They were a scouting party that drove too far toward the village. I've learned that they were supposed to sneak into our compound in preparation for a raid on us by the police and federal troops. We'll now respond and let them know that they do not want to come here."

"Oh, Padre, you're so smart. I love you."

"I know, Juanita. You're a wonderful daughter. Enough business here. We're just about finished. Take our friends back to the estate. I'll join you for cocktails as soon as I'm done here.

"Si, Padre."

As they walked back to the vehicles, Leslie asked, "How often is that place used?"

"I'm not sure. I suspect a couple times a week. As Padre says, part of our business is to maintain fear. Without fear, we could not continue to exist. Al and Jorge, I'm sure you found fear worked well for you in Fresno, didn't it?"

"It can be effective." Jorge said.

"Juanita, do you enjoy going to that place?" Leslie asked.

Juanita put her arm around Leslie comfortingly. "Leslie, I don't mind it. Because of my brother's death, I'll take Padre's place someday. I have to be prepared to continue the business. I cannot appear weak. I think Americans place too much importance on life. We Mexicans don't, nor do I think most of the rest of the world places that much importance on it."

Parked next to the Bronco was a pickup truck. In the back were four mutilated bodies. Leslie, whose stomach was already nauseous, asked Juanita, "Are they being taken to be buried?"

Juanita laughed. "No, Leslie. I'd think they're being taken to be butchered and cooked. Padre doesn't want the bodies found."

"What do you mean, butchered and cooked?"

"Sometime, I'll show you, but not now. By the look on your face, I think it's time to return to the estate."

56

Michoacán, Mexico

Two electric golf carts with clubs secured in the back were parked in front of the guest casa. Juanita got into the front cart on the driver's side, and Al sat next to her. Jorge and Leslie took the other.

At the first tee, Juanita asked, "Have any of you played golf before?"

Leslie responded, "Yes. I've played with my father."

Both Al and Jorge indicated they'd never touched a golf club.

"Okay, Al. I'll help you. Leslie, see what you can do with Jorge."

Juanita'd arranged for two buckets of balls to be placed at the first tee and for two staff members to be located out on the fairway to retrieve balls as they were hit. After half an hour, the two buckets were empty.

Juanita looked at Al and Jorge and commented, "Well, this should be an interesting afternoon. Al, why don't you start us off."

Al shanked a ball off to the left about ninety feet. Jorge swung at a ball three times before he hit it into the fairway. Leslie hit one straight down the middle of the fairway, and Juanita hit one ten yards in front of Leslie's. Juanita and Leslie were enjoying the game, while Al and Jorge were getting more and more frustrated with their errant balls.

At the par-three fifth hole, they finished putting and sat at an umbrella-covered table. There was a small bar adjacent to the hole that was attended by the two staff members who'd shagged the practice balls on the first tee. The location provided a view of the river situated at the back of the estate. As they were talking, Leslie suddenly interrupted the conversation.

"Shhhh. Do you hear that?"

They listened and Juanita said, "Oh, that's just the zoo animals."

"What do you mean, the zoo animals?" asked Leslie.

"My padre had a zoo built for me. I loved *The Wizard of Oz* and was always saying, 'Lions and tigers and bears, lions and tigers and bears, oh, my.' Padre thought I liked wild animals, which I do, so he built me a zoo."

"Can we go see it?"

"Leslie, sounds like a good plan to me. It'll give the guys a break from their game. Or should I say, their lack of a game."

Jorge responded, "A trip to the zoo sounds great to me."

The golf carts wound down a dirt path to a building with rock exterior walls. It contained a large party room and a single bedroom for the zookeeper. They walked out a sliding glass door to the back and stood on a raised deck that looked down on a huge, man-made pond, surrounded on three sides by large boulders. At the right end of the pond was a dirt enclosure, where a hippopotamus was looking up at them.

Juanita led them though a gate, and as they walked down a path, Leslie ran around a corner in front of them and let out a scream. As the rest turned a corner, they came face to face with a gorilla gripping its cage's bars. He was just a foot away from Leslie, staring directly at her. She backed into Juanita, who was laughing. They could tell this wasn't the first time this had occurred.

"Okay. Let's go see the other animals." Said Juanita.

They continued down the path toward the river, passing four

separate natural cages with wrought-iron fences. These cages housed two adult African lions, several albino tigers, and two black panthers. Finally, they arrived at a cage similar in structure to the one that housed the gorilla, but this one housed a large brown bear.

"That's my zoo. What do you think?" Juanita asked the group.

Leslie responded, "It is unbelievable."

"Padre is so good to me. Now, let's go back to our golf game."

As they played hole six, which was next to the guesthouse, they noted several men unloading computer equipment. After three hours on the course, including the zoo break, they holed out on the ninth, located just adjacent to the left side of the main house. Carlos was there to greet them.

"How'd you like my golf course?"

Knowing her father's absolute love of the course and his temperament, Juanita responded for the group. "Padre, they loved it. We're going skinny-dipping now."

The water was cool, which felt good after playing golf in the heat. After an hour, they dried off and sat on white, fluffy towels in chairs next to the pool. Al wrapped a towel around himself, slid on pool sandals, and headed toward the guesthouse.

"Where're you going?" Asked Juanita.

"I'll be right back. Just need to get something from my room."

Ten minutes later, Al returned with his baggie of marijuana and prepared a joint. Jorge picked the bag up off the table where Al had tossed it and made another joint. He took a couple of hits and passed it on to Leslie.

"You know, the last time I did this was with Al in that small fishing village on Baja. Al got very philosophical that evening, didn't you?"

Juanita responded, "Al, philosophical? I want to hear about that."

"He must've been talking about the target with the bull's-eye. Too deep for me."

"Jorge, how'd you guess?"

"I've heard that story many a time."

"Well, I haven't. Al, sounds interesting. Let's hear your philosophy," said Juanita.

They were all mellowing out from the marijuana, and Al felt talkative. He repeated the story he'd told Leslie at the fishing village. When he ended, Juanita commented, "You know, the people in the rings toward the center of your bull's-eye think gangs and their members are stupid. Padre and I have been dealing with gang leaders for years, and I can tell you, most are far from stupid."

"Juanita, thanks for that comment. I don't think of myself as being stupid, and I can tell you that many of the gang leaders I deal with at Pelican Bay, Tijuana, and the cartels here in Mexico have higher IQs than most of the population."

"We can't be that dumb. Gangbangers run Pelican Bay, not the guards. From what I've seen, Fresno, Tijuana, and most of Mexico are run by the drug cartels, which, to me, are forms of gangs. In fact, just think about Columbia. That's a country run by drug cartels. Sure, many of the gang members aren't that smart, but isn't that true of most of society?"

Juanita interrupted. "You know, I handle the money for Padre's business, and I can tell you from my dealings that our industry probably controls 20 percent of the world's economy. Oh, my God, Leslie, see what you got started?"

"Leslie, where do you think my gang in Fresno got its money? From people like you. We made more money on the Fresno State campus than the rest of the city. We basically controlled the Gamma Beta Sigma Fraternity. Those kids were our principal suppliers and users on campus and in the city. My guess is, it was probably the same where you attended college. By the way, where did you go to school?" asked Al.

"UC San Diego."

Juanita smiled at the answer. She knew that college was one of their best customers.

"Okay. Enough. Al, for a gang leader you are very philosophical," she said.

"An old marine sergeant buddy of mine used to say the same thing."

"Leslie and I are going upstairs so she can try on some of my clothes."

Leslie followed Juanita up a stairway to the second floor of the main house to her old bedroom. Her suite included a sitting room and large bathroom, designed for a movie star. Dolores was standing next to the bed. They took showers and then Juanita and Dolores went into the large, walk-in closet and brought out dresses, skirts, pants, and blouses for Leslie to try on. It was literally a fashion show with Leslie the model, Dolores the dresser, and Juanita the critic. It was surprising how close they were in size. They both finally decided on six outfits for Leslie.

"Dolores, take these over to the guesthouse and hang them in Leslie's closet." Juanita said and turned toward Leslie. "Leslie, I want to show you something. It kind of has to do with the stories at the pool."

They went back down the stairs to a basement area where there was a hallway that slanted downward about ten feet. At the end was a heavy, wooden door. Juanita knocked on the door and a small window in the door opened, and someone peeked out to see who was on the other side. After a few seconds, a man dressed in black opened the door.

They entered a room with a long, rough, wood table sitting in the center, where two more men dressed in black were sitting playing cards. They both were armed, and they immediately rose when Juanita walked toward them. Leslie noted there were three cots along the left wall and assumed there were always three guards in this room at all times.

"I want to show my friend the vault."

"Certainly."

"Leslie, you need to look back at the door while I open the vault."

Leslie joined the three guards at one side of the table. They all looked away from the large vault door. Juanita glanced back at them to make sure they weren't watching as she entered the combination. When she heard the proper click, she turned the handle and opened the vault.

"Leslie, come join me in Padre's counting room. Only he and I can open it. He tells me it was replicated after a vault in one of the Las Vegas casinos."

The vault door actually led into a huge room with a modern, steel table. There were four rows of shelves on top of narrow counters. Each row had metal slots that went from the top of the counter to within a foot of the ceiling. The slots held currency. Most held US dollars, but there were also some pesos, British pounds, Swiss francs, and euros. Each slot was designed for a specific domination. There were painted marks on the slots as they went up to indicate how many dollars or pesos or euros were currently stacked in that slot.

Leslie walked over to one of the slots that contained US twenty-dollar bills and noted that based on the current height of the stack, there was approximately $450,000 dollars there.

"The markings are not totally accurate, but close enough when you're talking about $400 million. We take in, on average, more than a million dollars a day. To protect us, Padre pays out about a million each week in bribes to Mexican officials, police, and Mexican Army officers."

As they walked back to the guesthouse, Juanita said to Leslie, "Don't tell Al and Jorge about what I showed you. Let's keep it our secret."

57

Mexico City

The FBI Gulfstream was approaching Runway 23 Left at Benito Juarez International Airport, east of Mexico City. It'd been cleared to land, and the captain announced that they'd be wheels down in five minutes. Dick and his entire squad were sound asleep, and the announcement woke them up.

They looked out their windows, only to see haze that covered a sprawling, densely populated city, with an occasional mountaintop sticking out. The plane touched down on the runway, taxied for some time, and finally stopped in front of the cargo terminal located on the far side of the airport, away from the passenger terminals. The FBI agents grabbed their belongings and headed down the aircraft stairs. A black GMC version of a Suburban with tinted windows was parked a hundred yards away. Instinctively, they walked toward it, still groggy from the flight.

Dick recognized the agent standing next to the vehicle. "Ron, what the heck are you doing here?"

"Hi, Dick. Greeting my friends. Boy, you all look beat and in need of showers."

"The last time I saw you, you were at headquarters in DC. What're you doing here?"

"I came here just about two months ago. Part of a joint task force with the DEA and CIA. There're even some army and navy guys involved. Come on and get into the car. I'll fill you in on the way."

They loaded their gear into the back of the vehicle and found places to sit. Dick sat in the front seat next to Ron and turned around to face his squad. "Ron here probably will be a deputy director of the FBI in the near future. We worked together on a number of cases in the DC office."

Turning toward Ron, Dick asked, "So what's so important that you got transferred here?"

"The National Security Council is seriously worried about the stability of Mexico. Basically, the drug cartels are in control of this country. Chavez from Venezuela is starting to gain some control over local dissidents, and the Chinese are sending agents across the US-Mexico border. There're more than a hundred people in the embassy here in Mexico City working on this. Plus, we have people in Guadalajara, Hermosillo, Mazatlán, and Monterrey. We have the blessing of the Mexican president. Do I need to say more?"

"No, I think you've said enough."

"I'm going to drop you and your crew off at to your hotel, which is a block from the embassy. You can shower, change clothes, and then meet me at the embassy at two. The ambassador wants to talk with you before you do anything."

"Sounds like a plan."

Ron left the airport and immediately hit traffic congestion. "The traffic is always like this during the day. It's worse than New York City. I understand it rivals Rome in regards to the driving. We have a special permit that allows us to drive in the city at any time. Private vehicles can only drive in the city every other day, depending upon their license-plate number. They're serious about this. The fine is like $1,500 dollars if they catch you driving on the wrong day."

They turned onto Paseo de Ia Reforma Avenue. After a few minutes, they were facing a large statue. Ron explained, "That's the Angel of Independence. Your hotel is over there on the left, and the embassy is the next block past it. See over there?"

Dick had been to Mexico City on an army assignment many years before, but it'd changed a lot. This was a first-time visit for the rest of his squad members. They looked across at the embassy. It was huge. In fact, it occupied an entire city block. There was an eight-story, fortress-like building situated behind an ornate, twelve-foot-high, spike-topped, wrought-iron fence.

Ron spotted them looking at the embassy. "Impressive, isn't it? It's the largest American Embassy in the western hemisphere and boasts a larger staff than only a couple of other of our embassies. Tells you something about our interest in and ties with Mexico. This embassy is literally the listening post for all of Central and South America. If you look closely at the top of the building, you'll see antennas of all types."

As the bellmen set about unloading the squad's bags, Ron reminded them that he'd meet them at the embassy's main entrance at two. "By the way, this isn't the safest city in the world. Even if you are FBI agents, stay together when you walk over. The bad guys would just love to kidnap one of you. Don't worry about carrying your weapons here. In this town, I think everyone is armed. The local police have automatic weapons. If you do run into a problem, call me on my cell. Here's my card with the number."

Based on their walk through the hotel lobby, it appeared that the hotel catered to American businesspeople that were scattered throughout the lobby. Most were on their cell phones or using their computers. Some were in groups talking to each other, either with fellow Americans or with their Mexican clients. Mexican-American commerce was at work. They passed a sizable lobby bar and found the registration desk. The hotel was comprised of two separate buildings, the older main hotel and the newer tower section. The extensive hotel lobby connected them.

Harriett walked up to the registration desk first. "I believe you have a room for Harriett Foster. Here's my credit card."

The man behind the desk keyed information into the computer in front of him. After a moment, he responded in perfect English, "Oh, yes, Ms. Foster. We do have a room for you. The American Embassy arranged for it. You have a woman's room on the fifteenth floor."

"What's a woman's room?"

"Oh, I understand. The fifteenth floor is designed specifically for women travelers. The rooms are furnished a little differently than the other floors. It's safer, and I think you'll like it."

"Sounds interesting."

"Here's your key. Will you need any assistance with your bags?"

"No, thank you. Which way to the elevators?" Harriett asked.

"They're over there, to your left."

With that, Harriett stepped away from the registration desk and waited for Coleen to register. The process was done in a few minutes. Coleen walked over Harriett asked, "May I assume you have a woman's room on the fifteenth floor?"

"Sure do. Aren't we special?"

Dick interrupted the conversation to advise everyone to meet at the same location in the lobby at one thirty.

58

American Embassy, Mexico City

Refreshed from their showers and once again in clean clothes, the squad met in the hotel lobby at one thirty.

The noise from the traffic on the Paseo de Ia Reforma was unbelievable. Half of the vehicles passing them were green and white VW taxis. From across the street, the eight-story American Embassy looked like a fortress. Its entrance was right on the street, protected only by a massive concrete planter.

Brian commented, "I have to assume that when they built this place, they weren't too worried about security. I can't believe the building is not set back farther from the street with a fence or wall in front of it."

They all shook their heads in agreement. Harriett brought their attention to a small, dead-end side street just before they got to the embassy. It was blocked with metal barricades and covered with a sheet-metal canopy that protected a long line of people waiting to get into the embassy.

They showed their IDs to the marine guard at post one, who was expecting them. He pointed them in Ron's direction. He was standing across the lobby waiting for them. Harriett asked the marine, "Why're all those people lined up to get into the embassy?"

"They're Mexican nationals, ma'am. They line up on Rio Danubio every morning to apply for US visas. We probably process two thousand requests every day. We erected that metal canopy to protect them from the sun. It can get very, very hot here."

"Thank you, Corporal."

Ron greeted the group. "Hello again. You guys look much better. Is the hotel to your liking?"

"From the little time we spent there, it seems great." Commented Harriett.

"The ambassador is waiting for you in his office. I'll take you up."

Ron led them into the waiting area of the ambassador's office. "Hi, Jane. I believe he's expecting us."

"He is. I'll take you in."

The ambassador stood behind his desk, and he walked around to greet them. "Welcome to Mexico. I know your mission is of the utmost importance. The president's chief of staff called me last night and told me you'd be coming and why you're here. We've anticipated your arrival. We've set up a meeting that should be helpful to you.

"I must advise you that Mexico is a powder keg. The present government fully welcomes our support, and as you'll find out today, we're giving them all the help we can to keep the lid on. There are situations brewing that could push Mexico into anarchy. We don't want that to happen, or we could literally be fighting a war on our entire southern border.

"The US press is reporting on the drug war and the Mexican drug cartels. I'm not sure they fully realize what it could lead to. The Mexican drug cartels are being supported by the Colombian cartels that use them to transport and distribute drugs into the United States," the ambassador continued.

"On top of that, there're local dissidents who'd like to overthrow the current government. There're foreign governments, such as Venezuela and, believe it or not, China, who are exerting influence over segments of the population. We just learned that one of the drug cartels has an operation that smuggles Mexican nationals into the United States and also has agreed to smuggle in both Chinese nationals and Muslim terrorists as well. We can only guess why either of these groups want to get people into our country.

"I fully understand that none of this is why you're here, but we don't need the wrong people getting hold of the information you're after. From what I understand, if they do, it's possible we'll be fighting not only illegal activities, but a possible economic war.

"I've said more than I should have. More importantly, I have another meeting scheduled that'll be a lot more fun than this. I'm getting my picture taken with eighty students and professors from across the United States who are beginning their Fulbright fellowships here in Mexico.

"Ron will introduce you to a number of people that may be able to help you. They don't know exactly why you're here, and if I were you, I wouldn't tell them. It's time for you to get to work. I wish you all the best. If there's anything I can do, don't hesitate to call," he concluded.

They thanked the ambassador, and Ron led them to a conference room down the hall. He opened the door, and inside were nine people sitting around the table.

"Everyone, this is FBI Special Agent Dick Hartmann and his team from San Francisco. You've all been asked to assist them in a mission here in Mexico. As you know, they're after two Hispanics gang members from Fresno, California, who have classified information in their possession. We can't disclose the nature of the information, but it's critical that it be recovered as quickly as possible.

"To speed up this initial meeting, I'll do the introductions. Jim over there heads up the Office of Defense Coordination. His group manages all US Department of Defense security-assistance programs here in Mexico. There are a lot of them. He's good to know because of the contacts he has with the Mexican military.

"Eleanor is head of our DEA operations in Mexico. John is the local spook. You won't believe how many other CIA operatives there are here in Mexico. Now, let me introduce the Defense attachés. You'll recognize their affiliations by their uniforms. Orville over there represents the army. Next to him is Cooper with the air force, Franklin with the Department of the Navy, Michael, the marines, and David, the coast guard. Yes, even the coast guard has an attaché here. Oh, I'm sorry, I left out Marty, who is our FBI attaché."

Opening his briefcase, Dick thanked Ron for the introductions. "What I'd like to do is brainstorm about how we locate these two men. Here are their pictures and descriptions."

Eleanor, with the DEA, spoke first. "When I first received the info on your mission, I spotted one item that made me laugh. A $100,000 reward may be big money in the states, but it's nothing here. The cartels make payoffs in the millions of dollars. In order for us to get a lead on a drug dealer here, we'll have to offer a half-million, million, or even a $2 million reward. I spoke to the ambassador about this, and he contacted Washington. Your reward for these two guys is now $2 million. You can thank me later.

"Next, I'll get these pictures and descriptions out to our agents in the field here and see what they can come up with," she finished.

Marty, the FBI attaché, then spoke. "I'll have my staff develop a Spanish-language flyer to be distributed to the Mexican military and police. It'll also be posted on the embassy's website, and it will include the increased award amount."

Dick asked, "Any other ideas?"

There was no response.

"Okay. Thank you all for your help. If you get a hit on anything, give Ron or me a call. We need to get these guys ASAP."

Ron suggested that Dick and his squad join him and Marty for dinner that evening. Eleanor overheard the conversation and asked if she could also join them.

"Eleanor, you're more than welcome to join this FBI bunch. Your help and input today is greatly appreciated. Why don't we all meet in the lobby of your hotel? Is it okay if we eat early, and somewhere close to the hotel?"

"Dick, with your reputation for fine dining, I can't believe you're even asking that question. Of course we can. Actually, your hotel has a great Italian restaurant called Ristorante Amici. It has an extensive wine list, and, being an Italian restaurant, I suspect they may even have a Brunello di Montalcino."

"You have a good memory. I'll go for that. How about six thirty?"

"See you there."

59

Mexico City

Harriett and Coleen rode down in the elevator and headed to the lobby bar, where everyone had agreed to meet. They sat at a small table and ordered Diet Cokes while they waited for Dick and the rest of the squad to show up.

An American and a Brit sitting at the next table were trying to pick them up. The American was carrying on a conversation with Coleen and the Brit with Harriett. The American worked for an insurance broker in New York, and the Brit was with Lloyd's of London. Coleen and Harriett indicated they were in Mexico City from San Francisco on business. Several other people from their firm were meeting them in the bar before heading off to dinner. The American indicated that he frequented San Francisco and asked for Coleen's phone number. After his considerable insistence, she gave him a number just before Dick and the rest of the squad showed up.

They all started walking to the Ristorante Amici in the hotel when Harriett leaned over toward Coleen. "You should be ashamed of yourself. What's the guy going to think when he calls that number and the operator answers, 'San Francisco FBI Office?'"

"Serves him right for being so insistent."

"You know he's going to be telling his Brit buddy all night how lucky he was."

"No. It's probably going to be more like he's going to be saying, 'Who's the stud? Who's the stud? I'm the stud!'"

"You do know men," Harriett replied wryly.

Dick turned and asked, "What're you two talking about?"

"Oh, nothing. Just girl talk." Harriett replied.

The maître d' asked, "May I help you, sir?"

"Yes. We have a reservation. It should be under Ron Bashkim," Dick replied.

"Oh, yes, sir. Mr. Bashkim and the rest of your party are already seated at Mr. Bashkim's usual table. Please, follow me."

The group followed the maître d' across the restaurant to an outside terrace. The table had a great view of a monument with a gold angel on top, who was looking down on them. Their table was situated so that it was separated from any of the other tables on the terrace. Ron was seated at one end, with his back to the angel. Marty and Eleanor were also sitting at the far side of the table with their backs to the angel. Dick assumed they'd taken these seats so he and his squad could face the angel.

Ron and Marty stood to greet the group.

"Welcome, all, to one of the best views in Mexico City. As you probably know by now, that is the Monumento de Ia Independencia. The angel on top will be watching over us while we eat."

Dick responded, "We'll accept any help we can get. May I assume that you frequent this restaurant often?"

"I do. Mainly because the embassy is located just down the street, and this table is somewhat isolated from prying ears. Best of all, the chef's from Italy," Ron replied.

The maître d' handed each of them a menu and gave Ron a wine list, who passed it on to Dick.

"Dick, go to the pages with the Italian reds. About halfway down on the second or third page, I believe you'll find a Poggio all'Oro Brunella di Montalcino. It's absolutely fabulous," Ron recommended.

"I love this restaurant. We're going to have a good meal tonight, or, at least, good wine. What do you recommend from the menu?"

"My favorite is the seafood ravioletti. It has lobster and vermouth sauce topped with fresh basil. Unbelievable!"

"Works for me. Coleen, what're you ordering?" Dick asked.

"I'm going for something that looks very different. The chicken breast on a creamy ragout of tiger prawns with rice looks interesting to me. Different combination. I'm giving that a try."

The discussion of the menu went on for some time as they waited for the wine, and beers for Daniel and Brian. The waiter arrived with their beverages and then took dinner orders.

Prior to being served, and while they were eating dinner, most of the group's conversation concentrated on what it was like to live in Mexico City and what was happening in Mexico.

After dessert and coffee, they all headed down together in the same elevator. As they walked across the hotel lobby, Coleen heard lively Latin music. She asked Ron, "Where's that music coming from?"

"The Jorongo Bar. It's a Mexico City institution. Great live music and dancing."

"Hey, Dick, it's still early. How about some music before we head to our rooms?" she asked.

They all turned to hear what Dick would have to say. "Let's give it a go. I'm still wide-awake. I have no idea why, but a little entertainment will do us good."

The entire group entered the bar and found two tables next to each other. After being served drinks, everyone started dancing, freestyle, to the Latin beat. Dick's dancing included some interesting moves across the floor; they weren't necessarily to the same beat as the music. Suddenly, Eleanor added an unexpected jump to her dancing and collided with Dick in the middle of the floor.

Dick shouted, "Sorry, Eleanor!"

Eleanor shouted back, "It wasn't your fault, Dick. My cell phone is on vibrate. It went off and startled me. I'll take it out in the lobby, where it's quiet."

Dick continued his strange dance steps, now across from Coleen, who was laughing. The music stopped, and they all returned to their drinks at the tables.

Eleanor returned. "We all need to return to the embassy. Things have happened faster than I thought they would."

60

American Embassy, Mexico City

It was late in the evening, and the embassy was quiet. Eleanor led them to a conference room where John, the local CIA spook, was sitting behind a table with a file and some papers in front of him.

"Have a good dinner?" he asked the group.

"It was great, John, but let's get to work and not rehash the dinner."

"Understand, Eleanor. Let's get to work."

Dick started the conversation. "What've you guys got?"

John took over the conversation. "When you put up $2 million, things seem to happen. There was a phone call here to the embassy first. Then I got calls from one of my DEA guys in Tijuana. Our two friends were noticed there because of the money they were spreading around. Two of our female undercover agents actually talked with them in a bar. They were spending money like crazy and the agents thought it might be drug money, so they took an interest in them."

"Okay. Let's hear about the call to the embassy."

"It came in about an hour ago. It was from the father of a missing girl. He reported her missing two days ago from San Felipe. They have a house there. It's a popular spot for Americans to settle during the winter."

John showed them the file folder. On the left side was the picture of a young girl seventeen or eighteen years old.

"That's Leslie Anderson. From what I understand, her father's been checking the embassy website every night to see if there's any news about his missing daughter. He saw our reward bulletin tonight and recognized the pictures of our two subjects."

John turned a page in the folder. The page had two other pictures on it. One was of Leslie with Jorge Rodrigo Garcia sitting on a wall. The other was of Jorge sitting at a table with Alejandro Gomez, drinking beers. "Her father uploaded these pictures from a camera his daughter left behind."

Dick looked through the rest of the file and didn't find anything else of importance. "Eleanor, can you arrange a flight for me to San Felipe tomorrow?"

Before she could respond to Dick, John piped up. "Mind taking a CIA flight? I can set it up for you right now for tomorrow."

Dick agreed, and John made the call. While on the phone, he looked over at Dick and asked, "How many will be on the flight?"

"Just two. Myself and Brian."

John checked with his contact on the phone and said, "I know you're in a rush, but the best I can do is a one o'clock flight tomorrow afternoon. You can return at any time. The plane will wait until you're done."

"Thanks. That'll work," Dick replied.

"I'll have a car pick you up in front of your hotel at eleven tomorrow morning and take you to the airport."

"Okay, everyone. It's late, and you'll be able to sleep in. Tomorrow's Sunday, a day of rest for you and a day of work for Brian and me. Let's head back to the hotel. Eleanor, can you arrange for my squad to use an embassy conference room on Monday?"

"Dick, consider it done. See you Monday."

61

Mexico City

Dick turned off his cell-phone alarm, washed his face, and put on his workout clothes. He headed down to the fitness center for a strong workout. Twenty minutes into his run on the treadmill, Brian and Coleen showed up, said hello, and started their workouts.

During her workout, Coleen checked out Dick's physique. *He does have good pecs*, she thought.

Next, Harriett walked in wearing her workout gear, followed a few minutes later by Daniel. Dick thought to himself, *I picked the right Animals. They're staying in shape, physically and mentally.*

"What're you guys doing today?" he asked.

"Sightseeing. Franklin, the navy attaché, has agreed to show us Mexico City."

"And which one of you ladies does he have his eye on?"

"Harriett made the arrangements."

"Have a great time. Probably see you later tonight." Dick offered

Refreshed from his workout and shower, Dick headed to the lobby, where he met up with Brian. As soon as they walked out the front door, a man approached Dick. "May I assume you're Agent Hartmann?"

"Yes, I am."

"I'm your driver. You look exactly like John described you."

In a little more than half the time it took Ron to drive them from the airport, this driver had them back at the same hangar. There was a nondescript CIA twin-engine, turbo-prop plane waiting for them.

Ron greeted him. "My friends, welcome to Air America. I'm your captain, co-pilot, and cabin crew."

Climbing into the plane, Dick commented, "You didn't mention you were flying us."

"Must have slipped my mind."

There was enough room for six passengers, plus a pilot and co-pilot. Dick sat next to Ron in the co-pilot's seat, and Brian sat in the back.

"Buckle up, my friends. I like to have fun when I'm flying. That's probably why I'm working for this airline and not a real one. CIA couldn't care less how I fly, just as long as I get there and back," said Ron.

"I can see the CIA is getting their money's worth out of you," Dick replied.

After takeoff, Ron pulled the stick back, and they almost headed straight up. Brian was glad when they started their descent a little more than two hours later. It'd been an interesting flight, somewhat like a roller-coaster ride, which wasn't Brian's favorite amusement-park ride. The plane set down at the Aeropuerto International in San Felipe. Though it possessed a grand name, there were no commercial flights in and out of this airport. Ron taxied over toward a section of the fence that had a gate. He parked the plane and got out with them.

"I'm also your driver. We have a car parked over there. Don't ask. It's a CIA thing," he said.

Dick opened the case file. They looked up the address for their destination.

Ron responded, "I haven't the foggiest idea where that is, so I'll need to ask at the airport office."

They drove over to the office and learned that they didn't have far to go.

"Señors, that address is in a condo complex a mile toward town from here." A man in the office advised them.

Five minutes later, they pulled up to a condominium complex. Dick and Brian found the unit where Mr. and Mrs. Anderson lived and knocked on the door.

An older gentleman with a gray beard answered and said, "You must be the FBI agents. About time you took an interest in my daughter's disappearance."

"May we come in?" asked Dick.

In a low, somber voice, the man replied, "Yes, you may. Please hold your voices down, as my wife's asleep. It's been a hard time for both of us."

They entered a two-bedroom unit with a small kitchen. There were three barstools facing the dining/living area from the kitchen. A balcony with outdoor furniture looked out over the beach. The man motioned for them to sit on a white-leather couch in the living room. He sat facing them on a lounge chair made of matching leather. Tables on either side of the couch contained family pictures.

"That's my daughter in those pictures. You'll note, she's quite the athlete. Plays tennis, golfs, and swims like a fish. She loves to take pictures. That camera around her neck is a Nikon D4S. The same type of camera used by professionals. She was always taking pictures."

There was a period of silence, and then Mr. Anderson asked, "Do you know anything about where my daughter is?"

Dick responded, "No, we don't, but we understand you may have some information that will help us find her."

"I do. Last Tuesday, she didn't come home. I wasn't too worried, as she's kind of a free spirit. But when she didn't turn up by the afternoon the next day, I started looking for her."

Taking a breath, the father continued. "I found her camera lying in her room, and that, in itself, was strange. She always has it with her. As I mentioned, my daughter loves to take pictures. The camera is digital, and I checked out the last pictures she took. There were several that included two Mexican-looking men that I didn't know. The other night, while I was checking the US Mexico City Embassy website, there were the two guys in the pictures. Is my daughter in danger?"

Dick answered in a calm voice. "I'm not sure if your daughter is in danger; however, the two guys in those pictures aren't the best people for her to be with. We have a great interest in finding them. You indicated that you don't know them; is that right?"

"I've never seen them before. They're new to this area. I know this because I went down to the restaurant in this picture and the owner told me they weren't locals."

"May I take your daughter's camera with me? I'd like our lab professionals to see if they can determine any other relevant info from it," Dick asked.

"If it helps get my daughter back, take it. Do you know anything about those two guys? Is my daughter safe?"

"Mr. Anderson, I'm not going to lie to you. These two are tied to a gang in Fresno. We have reason to believe they're dangerous. It doesn't seem like your daughter was kidnapped, but rather, went with them willingly. That's a good thing. We'll do our best to bring her back to you."

"Appreciate your coming. Leslie's our only child. We greatly miss her. Please bring her back to us."

"We'll do our best."

They returned to the car with Leslie's camera in-hand.

62

Mexico City

On the way back from Mexico City Airport, Dick called Daniel Lee to tell him he had a digital camera with shots of Alejandro Gomez and Jorge Garcia in San Felipe. When the car pulled up to the hotel, Dick was greeted at the entrance by Daniel. "Hey, Boss, what've you got for me?"

"Good to see you, Daniel. How was the sightseeing?"

"It was great—quite a city."

"Yes, it is. Here's Leslie Anderson's camera. There are a number of pictures of the two suspects on it. Send them off to our lab for analysis, and dust the camera for prints. It looks like some of the pictures were taken by somebody other than Ms. Anderson. I want to know everything they can find out about these guys: what they have with them, what they're reading, who they're talking to. You know the routine. Hopefully, we'll have the info back tomorrow."

Daniel replied, "I'll get right on it, Boss. No reason why we shouldn't have blowups of the pictures and the info back tomorrow. I have a digital big-screen TV in my room, which should provide a pretty clear picture of the images from the camera. I'll see if I can spot anything before the lab gets back to us."

"Sounds great. Any dinner plans for tonight?"

"Yeah. Coleen checked with the hotel concierge and selected some place to go. She made reservations for all of us at seven thirty tonight."

"Love it. My crew is a bunch of Animals who like to be with each other and like to eat. What more could I ask for?" Dick replied.

It'd been a hot and tiring trip to San Felipe. Dick needed a shower and some time to fill out his report, call Washington, and fill them in. The message light was on in his room. It was Coleen advising him that everyone was meeting in the lobby at seven o'clock for dinner, and that she'd made a reservation for them.

There was also a voice mail message from Harriett indicating that they didn't accomplish much at the embassy concerning the case, but that they were learning a lot about Mexico, the cartel problem, and were making needed friends with the embassy staff. They were planning to return tomorrow morning for a meeting with Eleanor and the CIA guy.

63

Mexico City

The Embassy had arranged for a car and driver for the visiting FBI squad. The SUV drove into the Polanco District, which proved to be a very fashionable neighborhood with beautiful designer boutiques, formal dress shops, fine jewelers, and leather-goods stores.

Dick turned to Coleen. "Coleen, just how did you decide on this restaurant for tonight?"

"I asked the concierge for the hottest restaurant in town. This is what she recommended."

Daniel commented, "Look at the shops out there, and the people walking around. I think we've just found the Rodeo Drive of Mexico City."

Brian chimed in, "This is definitely an upscale neighborhood. The only thing I knew about Mexico was Tijuana. This is definitely not Tijuana."

Their black SUV fit right in cruising down the boulevards in the Polanco District. The streets bustled with the sons and daughters of Mexico's elite. They were teeming with young, hip people who appeared to love brand-name merchandise. The young men sported slicked-back hair and wore designer shirts with the top three buttons open. The young ladies held their expensive Gucci handbags, and Ray-Ban designer glasses framed their chicly made-up faces. The agents' trained eyes noted that many of these kids were subtly being followed by black SUVs, packed with armed bodyguards.

Brian observed, "This's a very vibrant city with its street vendors and throngs of people. I had no idea how immense it was. I'm very impressed, but there does seem to be a lack of urban planning. Mexicans like bright, vibrant colors, and from what I've seen, orange is the most popular. From what I see here and noted elsewhere, there seems to be a great divide between the wealthy and poor."

After passing a few more blocks, their SUV pulled up to a very sleek and modern-looking restaurant named Pujol. It had a glass facade and was relativity small. The walls ranged from beige to stark black.

Dick let Coleen take the lead. They were welcomed by the maître d', who escorted them to their table halfway back in the dining room. It was covered with a white tablecloth and elegantly set with fine cloth napkins, crystal glasses, and silverware.

Harriett commented, "Very chic, very chic. I think I'm going to like this place."

"Just remember who selected it," replied Coleen.

The maître d' introduced them to their waiter, who greeted them in English with a slight Mexican accent.

"I understand you're from the American Embassy. Let me tell you something about our chef and his menu. The chef owns the restaurant and is a graduate of the Culinary Institute of America in New York City. The dishes are based on traditional Mexican fares, except he uses creams and foams based on contemporary Spanish cooking instead of the sauces usual to Mexico. Since this is your first time to our restaurant, I'd suggest the seven-course tasting menu. It includes four wines paired to the courses."

The squad checked out the menu. After some discussion, they all decided to take the waiter's advice and order the tasting menu. During dinner, they discussed the case. Dick filled them in on the meeting with Leslie's dad. They at least had confirmed that their subjects were in Mexico. Now it was just a matter of time until they found them and took them down.

After finishing the meal, Daniel wiped his mouth, replaced the napkin in his lap, and told the table, "That was one of the best meals I've ever had."

Brian agreed and turned to Dick. "What'd you think of the wines?"

"They were very good. I noted from the bottles that they were all Mexican. They aren't yet quite up to the standards of good French, California, or Italian wines, but they are very pleasant. I agree. That was a great dinner."

Over the next three days, the squad worked out together in the hotel fitness center each morning and walked across the street to the embassy. At noon, they'd return to the hotel and take a jog together and then return to the embassy. It was that waiting period common to most cases, but this case had a critical timing element to it. Dick was getting frustrated, as was Washington. The workouts and jogging relieved some of the tension. They were now well known by the embassy staff, and they were all learning the intricacies of Mexico City and finding great restaurants in the evening—although none of the meals during the next three days matched the meal at Pujol.

64

Mexico City

It was Wednesday morning. Dick walked with his squad from the hotel to the embassy. He knew they needed to get a break on the case before the identities of so many American taxpayers were illegally put into use. Time was of the essence. Just a few minutes after they'd settled in at the Embassy conference room, Eleanor and John entered together.

"We've got good news for you guys," Eleanor said as she placed three glossy photographs on the table. It was obvious that the photos had been taken at a distance with a telephoto lens. The pictures were of people boarding a yacht. "Recognize anyone in these pictures?"

Daniel, who'd been looking for three days at the pictures taken by Leslie Anderson, now turned one of the pictures toward himself. "That's our two subjects, and there's Leslie Anderson with them."

"That's your two Fresno gangbangers boarding a yacht, or should I say, ship, owned by Carlos Ramirez, head of one of the largest cartels in Mexico."

Coleen picked up one of the pictures. "That's a hell of a yacht. Who took the pictures?"

John answered, "Those are CIA photos taken two days ago. The short version of a long story is that apparently Carlos Ramirez has expanded his business partners to include the Chinese. Initially, they were just supplying chemicals needed by Ramirez to produce meth, but one of our CIA operatives got word that the Chinese intelligence community was taking over the chemical sales. The rumor is that the Chinese minister of state security plans to expand their arrangements with Ramirez to include the transport of Chinese intelligence agents into the United States through Mexico. We followed a senior intelligence officer from China to the yacht. We've been taking pictures and trying to pick up verbal conversations since he boarded the yacht. It was at this point that your guys showed up with the girl."

Dick looked up to the ceiling in thought. "Man, this case couldn't get any more complicated. We have a Mexican cartel running drugs into the United States to be distributed by American gangs. We have stolen IRS computer files with personal information we need to retrieve taken into Mexico. We have Chinese intelligence agents being smuggled across the US border to pursue some espionage project, and last of all, we have a murder suspect to catch."

"That pretty well sums it up. By looking at the way this girl is smiling and clad in the photos, you don't seem to have a kidnapping on your hands." John offered.

"Agreed." Dick responded. "Given the time sensitivity involved, let's sit down and figure out our plan of action."

After two hours of reviewing options and strategies, it was agreed that the first priority was to get the computer files back, along with the two gang members. These suspects needed to be interrogated about who else had access to the information on the computer files. The second was to make sure no Chinese espionage agents got into the United States. Lastly, they would put in place measures to disrupt the drug cartels' ability to transport drugs into the United States.

They had just started working on the details of how they were going to accomplish these priorities when John's cell phone rang. He looked to see who was calling and then took the call. When he concluded the call, John announced, "The yacht's left La Paz. It's heading out to the open sea."

Dick asked, "What do you make of that?"

"The DEA's been watching Carlos for a couple of years now. John's interest is much more recent. Based on past history, I suspect that Carlos's yacht is headed to Acapulco, where he'll fly his helicopter back to his place in Michoacán," John replied.

"Is that good or bad for us?" Dick asked.

"I suspect good. There isn't much we can do while everyone is on the yacht, but when they get on land, and isolated at his estate, I believe we'll be able to make our move," Eleanor added.

John added, "Eleanor, I agree with you. I suspect this isn't going to be a CIA operation. You and Dick'll need to consult with the ambassador and get some agreement with the Mexican government before any action can be taken. I also suspect you'll need to line up some additional assets for this mission. I can provide you with some help—actually, quite a bit of help. Meet me in my office at two o'clock, but for now, go enjoy a good lunch."

"I suspect that I should wait until after the meeting with you before seeing the ambassador," said Dick.

"I would."

65

Mexico City

Back at the hotel, Dick called Washington and filled them in on what he'd learned. He agreed to get back to them as soon as the afternoon meeting ended. The squad met in the lobby for a short run, after which they had a quick lunch. At one thirty in the afternoon, they walked back to the embassy and checked in at the reception area. To their surprise, the marine guard at station one advised them they were going to be escorted to the meeting with John.

Dick asked, "Why do we need an escort? You know us, and we certainly know our way around."

"Sir, this place is bigger than you think."

A few seconds later, a smartly dressed marine walked through a nearby door. In a commanding voice, he announced, "Please follow me. We have a ways to go."

They walked down corridor after corridor and started to realize just how enormous the embassy building really was. After ten minutes, they took an elevator down two floors into a basement area. The elevator door opened into a small lobby, where another marine guard was sitting behind a desk. Behind him, to his right, was a secured door.

"Sergeant, these are the FBI special agents that have a two o'clock with Mr. Hampton."

"Thank you, Corporal. I'll take it from here and call you when they're ready to leave."

Looking up at the group from behind his desk, the sergeant asked, "Which of you is Richard Hartmann?"

"That's me."

"Please have each member of your group sign in. I'll give you badges for this secured area. If you have weapons, I must ask you to place them in the lockers on the other side of that partition, and take the key with you."

They all signed in and placed their guns in the lockers as instructed. When they returned to where the sergeant was sitting, he used the phone and told John they were ready. A few minutes later, the secured door was opened, and John invited them to follow him in.

The agents walked down a short hall, where there was another guard station manned by a marine. Next to it was a door. John used his security card to gain entrance. They entered a large room with dozens of cubicles, most of which were occupied by people either on phones or looking at computer screens. There were glass offices around the room. They passed by one large office, where they recognized many of the participants from their very first meeting at the embassy. Over the door to the office was a sign that read "Defense Attaché Office." Another office had a sign that read "Office of Defense Coordination (ODC)," and a third, "Drug Enforcement Administration (DEA)," where Eleanor was standing in the doorway, waiting for them.

John asked, "Eleanor, should we show them what we have?"

"Yes. I just checked on the room, and they're waiting for us."

John and Eleanor led them down another hallway, which led to a large, secured room with several desks and six large, flat-screen monitors that were mounted high on the room's walls.

"Welcome to what is referred to as the 'Mexico City Country

Office,' better known as MCCO. Eleanor is our leader. Eleanor, why don't you tell them what we do here," said John.

"This unit has quite a history. It was formed during the Cold War era and was the central location for monitoring military, economic, and political intelligence activities throughout Latin America. As you may remember, the Russian Communists were quite active here in Mexico and, for that matter, throughout Latin America and the Caribbean. We still have major concerns over Chinese, Cuban, and Venezuelan activities in the area, but our main concern now is the Mexican drug war. We believe that further expansion of these activities could take down Mexico and present a major danger to the United States. Because of the prevalence of this drug war, the DEA spearheads the MCCO, while the CIA and your FBI and military attachés provide backup support. John and I will show you what we have for you, and that will also help you understand this facility's capabilities."

John led them over to a cubicle, where a technician was sitting at a computer screen. "This is Mike. He handles satellite surveillance for us. We have a portion of one of our spy satellites dedicated to what we're doing here. Mike, these are FBI special agents. We've agreed to provide them special assistance."

"Nice to meet you guys. Eleanor and John have filled me in on your mission. We've been monitoring that large yacht you have expressed an interested in. Look at that screen. I recorded this activity about an hour ago."

It took a couple of seconds to figure out what they were looking at, and then Dick commented, "Isn't that Carlos Ramirez's yacht?"

"It is. Now watch."

After a few seconds, they watched as a helicopter took off from the yacht and headed in the direction of Central Mexico. "I'll show you where it landed, and we'll be able to take a look at the people onboard."

The screen went blank for a moment and a new picture appeared showing a helicopter flying around a large estate next to a river. "I suspect they're giving their visitors an aerial tour of the place." After a few minutes, the helicopter set down on a landing pad next to a large building.

"That's Carlos's house," Mike explained.

They continued to watch as seven people got out of the helicopter. "Now, take a look at that big screen on the wall over there. I've enhanced the images of the people."

Mike picked up a laser pointer from the top of his workstation. "These two are crew. There's Carlos, and this is his daughter, Juanita. She's a true Mexican beauty. Here are your subjects, Gomez and his sidekick, Jorge Garcia. This cute little lady is Leslie Anderson, your missing person."

Dick looked closely at the screen. "I'm impressed, very impressed. I understand the expanding problems in Mexico, but I'm curious as to why you singled out Carlos."

"About three months ago, Carlos was included as a target in a directive from Washington, which designated six Mexican companies and ten individuals under the 1999 Foreign Narcotics Kingpin Designation Act. Carlos is at the top of the list, as he heads up the Central Mohoacán Cartel. His organization produces and distributes methamphetamines, cocaine, and marijuana throughout the Western United States. He also seems to be branching out into transporting guns and illegals across the border, including possible terrorists and foreign spies." John responded.

"Quite the crime boss. What can you tell us about the estate?"

"Lots. Mike, you want to fill them in?"

"Sure. Let's move over to that table, where we'll have more room." The swivel chairs at the new table allowed people to turn to look at the various large monitors on the walls around them.

Mike brought a box from his cubicle and sat it on the table. "I'm going to do a little show and tell to fill you in. Here's a map of the estate. It shows you the buildings and other features within the estate's boundaries. I'll begin with the fun stuff. In front of the main house is a golf course. It has nine holes and is used quite often by both Carlos and his daughter—both good golfers. If you take a close look at this area over here, that actually is a zoo containing all kinds of wild animals.

"The two buildings adjacent to the golf course are guesthouses. This building over here and the shed next to it are the weapons-storage area, and over here are the barracks for Carlos's private army. He actually has a German-made tank parked there. The story is, he won it in a card game from a Mexican general.

"Now to the pièce de résistance. In the main house, there's a vault in the basement where hundreds of millions of dollars in cash are kept."

Dick, in his usual inquisitive way, asked, "You didn't get all of this information from these aerial photos, did you?"

John cut Mike off from responding and said, "No, we didn't. As you can imagine, everything you see and learn today is totally confidential."

"Agreed."

"We have successfully infiltrated an operative at the estate. We developed a fake background and credentials for our operative that Carlos's daughter could not pass up. Our operative has been there for two months now and feeds us information."

"Well, this briefing's been quite thorough and is more than I could have ever hoped for. Mike, I want to thank you very much. Eleanor and John, we're going to have to get onto the estate to retrieve the computer files and our two Fresno subjects."

"Dick, you're right. But it's not going to be easy. Carlos has his own army, and many of them are former Mexican Army members. They're called the Zetas. In addition, Carlos controls the town that leads into the estate. It's not going to be easy to get onto the estate.

This is going to have to be very carefully planned and executed, and don't forget, we're in Mexico, not the United States, so we could have diplomatic problems." Eleanor offered.

"Okay. It's getting late. I suspect that we'll have a few days before we can, or have, to do anything. Let me contact Washington and advise them of what we've learned and see what they want us to do next."

"Dick, I think that's a wise approach. In the meantime, we'll keep gathering intelligence on the estate and your two subjects."

"Appreciate it, and thanks again, Mike. You do great work. Animals, let's go back to the hotel and rest our brains for tomorrow. By the way, John, can your operative at the estate let us know what our guys are doing with the computer files? That's our real target."

"Will do."

66

Mexico City

The squad crowded together in Dick's room eating the breakfast he'd ordered for all of them from room service.

Dick briefed his team. "I e-mailed my report to Washington last night and followed up by telephone this morning. We're to proceed with planning a visit to Carlos's estate. In case we need them, the Critical Incident Response Group is dispatching the Hostage Rescue Team (HRT) from Quantico to San Diego. Generally speaking, they don't work outside the United States, but it was decided that they'd be better accepted on Mexican soil than a Navy Seal team. Nobody trusts the option of using any Mexican military units."

"Boss, what do you want us to do?"

"Brian, we're all going to go back to the MCCO unit and learn everything we can about the estate, where the computer is located, and where our two subjects are staying. I suspect John's been advised by now to assist us. Everyone finished with breakfast?"

Coleen walked next to Dick to the embassy. "I'm beginning to think this is home. Since joining the squad, I've spent more time away from San Francisco than in it. Is this usual?" she asked him.

"I hope not. We've been away from the city for quite a while now.

I'm missing San Francisco myself. This has been an unusual case. It just seems to keep changing directions, but I think we're getting to the end. It'll be good to get back home."

"I would love to just be able to unpack my suitcase and make a home." She added, in a low voice, "And to get to know you better."

"Oh, yeah. That sounds good to me," Dick replied.

Harriet's voice came from behind them. "What're you two whispering about?"

"Nothing of great interest. Just missing the city," Coleen replied.

"I'll agree with you on that. I love to travel, and Mexico City is a great place to visit, but I'm ready for some fog and my local restaurants."

Dick repeated what he'd said to Coleen. "I suspect we're getting to the end of this case, hopefully. But we'll be here for a few more days."

They arrived at the embassy and repeated the same procedure with the marines to get into the MCCO unit. When they arrived at the unit, John and Eleanor were standing together, talking.

"Good morning. Anything new?" Dick asked.

"Well, you guys certainly have clout. We've been advised to help you get anything you need to complete your assignment. Before we determine what else you need, we're to go up and see the ambassador. I don't know if you were advised, but the president made a phone call last night to Mexico's president to seek his assistance. That's what our visit with the ambassador is about."

"I was advised by Washington that POTUS was going to make that call, but I didn't know it had been made already," Dick replied.

"Ready to go upstairs?"

"Lead the way."

Dick followed John and Eleanor from the MCCO unit to the elevator. As they rode down in the elevator, John updated Dick on recent developments. "I got word last night from our mole at Carlos's estate that your two subjects were staying in one of the guesthouses, and it looks like they'll be there for a while."

As soon as they walked into the ambassador's waiting area, his secretary walked over and greeted them. "He's expecting you. Go on in."

The ambassador was standing next to a window talking with Jim Abrams, head of Office of Defense coordination, and Ron Dillon. "Come on in, come on in. We're just talking about your assignment and situation."

Following greetings, the ambassador continued. "I was briefed last night by the president's chief of staff before and after a phone call was made by our president to Mexico's president concerning your assignment. The magnitude of the problem was explained. We'll have the full cooperation of the Mexican government with these stipulations: one, you're cleared to take the lead on extracting the two subjects from Fresno. Two, neither the Mexican military nor the local police are to be involved in any action to apprehend the subjects, as there was concern by both presidents from past history that there are too many possible information leaks here in Mexico. Three, once the subjects are apprehended, they are to be briefly turned over to the Mexican Army and transported to a judge, who'll approve their extradition to the United States. This is more for favorable local publicity than anything else, and you four are on your own here in Mexico. Carlos controls his estate and the town that leads up to it. You can't expect any help from the Mexican military."

Jim jumped in. "Our assumption is that Gomez and Garcia will remain on Carlos's estate for a while, based on the CIA information. Dick, have you been updated on that info?"

"Yes. John's filled me in."

"Good. Then our plan is to extract our two subjects from the estate, along with the computer and related data. The mission will originate from a navy ship off the coast of Mexico. The strike team will be comprised of the FBI Hostage Rescue Team members." John looked at his watch. "They should be landing with their equipment in San Diego just about now. If necessary, there'll be some assistance provided by Navy Seals, as well as marine air support."

Ron added, "Dick, as respects the raid, your squad will be involved only to make sure that we get the IRS information back. The Hostage Rescue Team will take the lead and apprehend the subjects. Your team will follow up to get the computer files and anything else related to it. You also have the assignment of taking the subjects to the Mexican Army, who, in turn will take them to the local Mexican judge. We want to keep the Mexican president happy but control the dissemination of any information related to our interest in these subjects and how we got them. Nothing is to be said about the IRS information."

The ambassador concluded the meeting in his office. "Thank you, everyone. I don't think there is anything more I can add at this time. I have another meeting in three minutes, so be careful and keep me posted."

They all returned to the MCCO unit to take another look at the satellite videos of the site and work with a mapping expert to prepare a strategy for entering it. Toward the end of the meeting, John looked at a message he'd been handed by an assistant. He read it and passed it on to Dick, who also read it.

"Dick, you want to give them the news?"

"Why not? But first, Mike, where'd you go to school?"

"Where did I go to school? What has that got to do with anything?"

"I'm a graduate of Oregon State."

"Aha. A farm animal. But, nevertheless, an animal mascot. You'll fit right in."

The squad got it, but John and Mike thought Dick was going nuts.

"Okay, Animals." Brian leaned over to Mike and quickly explained what the animal reference was all about. "Tomorrow morning, we'll be leaving Mexico City and heading to Coronado, California. Hopefully, no one gets seasick."

67

Coronado, California

It was ten thirty in the morning when the FBI aircraft, carrying the squad and their new compatriots, landed on the runway at the Naval Air Station North Island in Coronado, California. The group was in a good mood as they deplaned.

A sizable, gray, navy passenger van was waiting for them. Standing next to the van was a young female petty officer, who greeted them. "Welcome to Coronado. I'll be your driver for today."

They loaded their luggage in the back of the van and found a seat inside. "I'm to take you to Naval Special Warfare Group One. Some other FBI personnel are already over there. After you're finished with your meeting, I'll take you to your quarters."

The petty officer drove expertly through the post's gates and past a golf course and then into the community of Coronado. They turned onto Ocean Boulevard, which became Strand Boulevard. It was well named. On their left was San Diego Bay, and on their right, the Pacific Ocean. Coleen thought to herself, *What a peaceful day,* as she sighted seagulls wandering over the sand, picking at anything that looked like food.

The van hadn't traveled very far down Silver Stand Boulevard before it turned left into another naval installation. Signs on either side of the entrance read "Naval Amphibious Base, Coronado." After passing several buildings, the van pulled up to a building with a sign designating it as Naval Special Warfare Group One.

They walked up the steps of the building and into a small lobby, where Dick shouted out, "Look who the cat dragged in. Roger, did you draw the short straw and end up with us?"

"That I did, Dick. And how the hell are you? I haven't seen you in a couple of years, though I sure hear a lot about you. The press loves you."

"Got to make up for the bad publicity you guys got us. Ruby Ridge. Waco."

"Low blow. We've learned a lot since those fiascos, but we can't talk to the press about them. Just like this mess you're getting us into," Roger replied.

Hartmann had met Roger when they had worked together as young field agents and remembered when he applied for the Hostage Rescue Team. It took him two years after going through the grueling assessment and selection process. Hartmann remembered how proud Roger was of making the team and always espousing the unit's motto "Servare Vitas" – Latin for "To Save Lives." There was no question in Hartmann's mind that Roger was dedicated to saving American lives.

"Touché." Responded Dick.

"Dick, I need to talk to you in private before we have a group meeting."

Roger led Dick to a room down the hall while the rest of the squad waited outside the building enjoying the late morning sun.

"Dick, I've been filled in on the plan, and I've read your reports to Washington. I protested against part of the plan but lost. It seems Washington wants you and members of your squad to go to the raid site with us. What kind of physical condition are you and your squad in?"

"We're all in pretty good condition. We work out daily."

"Okay. You know that the Hostage Rescue Team has never had a woman qualify. I would prefer if we eliminated the two women on your squad from this mission."

"Look, Roger, I suspect we aren't going to be part of the initial raiding party. Harriet was regular army before she joined the FBI. Coleen just graduated from the academy. Both are highly trained, physically strong agents."

"All right, here's what I'm going to do. We have at least three days before this mission begins. I want your squad to work out daily with my guys. I have the right to scrub anyone who I believe might be a detriment to this mission."

"I'll agree to that as long you're honest in your assessment," Dick replied.

"Oh, come on. You think I won't be honest?"

"You can be an asshole on occasion. You need to be honest in this analysis."

"Agreed. One other thing: everyone is going to be confined to the base until we leave for the mission. We don't need someone being overheard talking about the mission, and your ugly puss is well known to the press. This'll also assure that everyone is in good shape for the mission. Navy grub and workouts at a Navy Seal base—what a combination to get, or keep, everyone in condition," Roger responded.

"Okay. Let's give everyone the bad news."

As they started walking out to find the rest of the group, Dick commented, "The petty officer who drove us over here mentioned you've been here before."

"Every couple of years, we have a joint training session with the Seals stationed here. I'll tell you, we're pretty good at what we do, but boy, those guys are unbelievable."

"That's what I've heard."

"Well, you'll get to see firsthand. They're going to assist us in this mission, and we'll be working out with them. That's where we're going to head from here. Seal Team Five is located just down the street. Get your people and follow me."

At the top of the stairs leading out of the building, Dick called down to the group talking below to follow Roger and him. They walked together to a building with a sign indicating "Naval Special Warfare Group One–Seal Team Five." Roger led them to what looked like a planning room and introduced them to the leader of Seal Team Five.

"Welcome to Navy Seal Team Five. I'm just here to greet you. If necessary, I'll offer advice if I think it'd be helpful. Roger, take over from here." Said Naval Special Warfare Office Athan Poveda, the leader of Seal Team Five.

Roger and Dick stood up in the front of the room and explained to everyone what they'd talked about and agreed to minutes before. There was no mention of women not serving on the mission. What was mentioned was that they were to stay on the base and go through training until they left for the mission. The training would include jumping out of helicopters while they were hovering several feet above ground.

Roger outlined the mission. His people would be in charge. They'd capture the two subjects and secure the area. Dick's squad would then be dropped in at the site to find the computer and any other items they believed contained the missing IRS information. If necessary, the building and equipment would be demolished by explosives. The subjects would be turned over to the squad, who would take them by helicopter to a site where they would turn them over to the Mexican Army. The army would accompany them to a courthouse, where a Mexican judge would approve their extradition to the United States.

"Our platform for the mission will be the naval ship *Bonhomme Richard*. It's named after John Paul Jones's famous ship. It's ideal for our mission. It's an amphibious assault ship, designed specifically for marine landing-force assaults by helicopter."

During the next three days, Dick's squad trained with the FBI Hostage Rescue Team and Navy Seal Team Five. They started at five thirty each morning by running five miles around the base. Following the run, they'd do calisthenics, maneuver through obstacle courses, perfect their shooting skills at the firing range, and jump from helicopters. An hour each morning and afternoon was devoted to the classroom, where Brian, with the help of Mike the map guy, would go over maps and aerial photos of Carlos's estate. All their meals were at the base galley, and they were in bed at the bachelor officers' quarters by nine. Dick thanked God that his squad kept up and thought to himsef, *If they weren't a team before, they certainly are now.*

68

Coronado, California

It was four in the morning, and the squad was getting into the same gray navy van with the same driver that'd picked them up when they landed at Coronado Naval Air Station. They were dressed in military coveralls with no identification markings. Each had a sports bag with clothing and other items they'd need for the mission.

The petty officer announced, "I've made arrangements to send your luggage to your office in San Francisco. I'm not sure what you mission is, but I wish you luck."

The van followed two other vans carrying the HRT members. They left the Naval Amphibious Base, drove through Coronado, and crossed over the Coronado Bridge toward San Diego. After thirty minutes, they drove onto Naval Base San Diego and wove their way around the base to a pier where the *USS Bonhomme Richard* LHD-6 was docked. Coleen looked up at the ship and thought, *It looks like an aircraft carrier.*

As they were boarding the ship, Roger announced, "We may not be too popular with the crew. Their liberty was cut short for our mission."

They walked up a stairway that took them to a deck in the middle of the ship. The officer who met them at the top led them to a ready room two decks higher. Just below the bridge, they were greeted by the ship's captain, executive officer, and master chief.

"You can use this room to plan your operation. Let the chief here know if you need anything. We'll be getting underway in two hours. It'll take us two days to get into position for your operation."

"Thank you, Captain. Appreciate your assistance. I suspect Mike and Brian'll need some help setting up their electronic gear," Dick replied.

"Chief, see what they need, and find the right crew members to help them."

"Aye, Captain. I'll take care of it."

While Brian and Mike set up their equipment with the assistance of two of the crewmembers, the rest of the team followed the master chief to a large bay just below the flight deck. They checked out the three helicopters they'd be using for the operation. They were freshly painted a light-tan color and had no identifying markings on them. They found their equipment and loaded it onto the choppers. Finally, they rejoined Brian and Mike, who were playing video games on one of the computers.

"Hi, guys. We're all set up here. We can pick up the satellite images from the estate. Checked out the radios we'll be using. How about some grub?" Asked Brian.

Over the next two days, they checked and rechecked their gear, worked out, ate, and waited.

69

Pacific Ocean, Off the Coast of Mexico

It was three in the morning and there was very little light in the sky when the helicopter lifted off the deck of the *Bonhomme Richard*.

The operation's participants watched as they passed over the shoreline and dropped down low over the Mexican terrain. The pilot had studied the maps well, avoiding populated areas, flying through desolate valleys, and skimming over the mountaintops. The chopper sat down on a barren field two miles south of Carlos's estate. The initial scouting mission was on.

The four FBI agents dressed in camouflage outfits jumped out and picked up the gear they'd already tossed to the ground. Quietly, Roger and Dick headed toward the western end of the estate. Two hostage rescue team members headed toward the eastern end of the estate.

Within an hour, Roger and Dick located a viewing spot directly across from Carlos's airstrip. Roger set up a scope, and Dick looked across with binoculars. All was quiet. Occasionally, a pickup truck with a machine gun mounted on the back would patrol the strip. Using the satellite radio, Roger checked in with his other team members. They indicated they were looking at a cabin with a couple of sheds adjacent to it. Roger radioed the ship that they were in position for their two-day stay.

The morning sun was just beginning to come up when Roger got a call on his radio. "Roger, you should see this. There're three guys at the cabin over here. They drank some coffee, went over to one of the sheds, and pulled a guy's body out of the back of a pickup truck. They proceeded to hang it up from the overhang of the shed's roof, and now they're gutting him—I mean. literally gutting him. They're stuffing his innards into a fifty-five-gallon drum. These guys are crazy." Paul said.

"I'm glad I'm not at your location. It's still quiet over here. Oh, I take that back. A light just went on in the building at the airstrip. You'll get a chance to take care of those three crazies in a couple of days," Dick replied.

Two hours later, Paul called back to Roger. "They've now gutted four people and are heating a fifty-five-gallon drum on a burner. When we do attack, there's no need for concern about gunfire being heard by the other guards. They get up early and take target practice on dead bodies tied to trees next to the cabin. These guys are butchers."

Each night, the two teams moved from their viewing sights, crossed the river, and wandered through the estate, canvassing specific aspects of the terrain, the buildings, and activities taking place. There were patrols, but they were able to remain undetected throughout their surveillance. By the end of the second night, they knew the estate by heart, and they headed for their helicopter ride back to the ship.

Everyone met in the ship's ready room. The two teams had taken dozens of pictures, and they constructed a more detailed map of the estate. Notes were made about the types of construction, entrances to the buildings, patrols, problem areas, and numerous other things they had noted during their two days of surveillance. They were now ready to implement the mission.

They hit the sack early, wanting to be physically and mentally prepared for the next morning's mission.

70

Pacific Ocean, Off the Coast of Mexico

It was still dark as the three helicopters lifted off the *Bonhomme Richard* deck. Roger and his FBI Hostage Rescue Team members were on the first two choppers. Dick and his team were on the third. The pilots headed to the same landing spot they'd used before. As soon as they landed, Roger used a satellite phone, called the CIA operative, and simply said, "On our way. Any problems on your end?"

Roger got a favorable response. His team headed for the estate. Dick and his squad remained in their helicopter at the landing site. Their helicopter would land at the estate's golf course next to the guest cabin after Roger's team had captured Al and Jorge and secured the site.

When the HRT reached the river, they split into two groups—one led by Roger and the other by Paul. Roger's group headed toward the landing strip. Paul's group headed toward the "Butcher's" cabin. They would eliminate the patrols, and then both teams would concentrate on the guesthouse, where their targets were located.

Roger looked across the river through the night scope. He gave the command for his team to cross. They spread out on the landing strip. As Roger had noted from their previous surveillance, the patrolling pickup truck with two armed cartel guards inside always stopped in front of the airport building, where they took a break. Two of the HRT members took out the guards with little or no noise. Once that was done, the team kicked in the door to the building and captured two sleeping cartel members. They were all secured in the building and guarded by one of the HRT members. Following this action, Roger contacted Paul and gave him the "go" on taking over the Butcher's cabin.

Paul and his team crossed the river. They were approaching the Butcher's cabin when the door swung open and one of the Butcher's sons came out. He headed toward some trees at the edge of the clearing to the cabin, unbuttoned his pants, and started taking a pee. He was surprised when he felt a gun placed against his temple as he was doing his business. A gloved hand was placed over his mouth. The team gagged and tied him to one of the trees that'd been used to prop up bodies for target practice. Paul and one of the HRT team members entered the cabin through the front door. The Butcher looked up from his bed and attempted to reach for his gun on the table next to him. Paul fired just as his hand touched the gun. The Butcher died immediately. *You deserved that, you bastard. Only wish you'd lived a little longer so you suffered. You got off too easy,* Paul thought. The other son apparently had too many tequilas the night before. He just sat up in his bed and raised his arms in the air. He was secured to a tree next to his brother.

Paul called on the radio. "Roger, we're secured here and heading toward the guesthouse."

"See you there."

Paul and one of his team members drove the Butcher's pickup truck to the front of the guesthouse, while the rest of the team moved on foot toward the house, surrounding it from various locations, based on the prior day's planning.

A guard in front of the house approached the pickup and saw

immediately that it was not being driven by the Butcher or one of his sons. He was raising his rifle to fire when a member of the team came up behind him and grabbed his neck in a secure chokehold. He was quickly gagged and bound.

Roger tried the front door to the house and found it unlocked. He and six of the HRT members entered. They didn't find anyone on the ground floor. As they headed upstairs, they saw a girl coming toward them. Leslie saw the team heading upstairs and screamed. She quickly ran into Al and Juanita's bedroom, which was closer than hers, and locked the door behind her.

"Juanita, Al, wake up! Wake up! There're men coming up the stairs!" she screamed.

Juanita reached over to the nightstand next to the bed and grabbed a small transmitter. With a steady hand, she pushed the button on it that triggered an alarm in the main house and in the guards' barrack. *Thank you, Padre. You're always trying to protect me.* Then she opened the drawer on the nightstand and took out a gun.

Al's first reaction was also to grab a gun from the nightstand on his side of the bed. He then rolled onto the floor and pointed the gun at the door, ready to fire. He could hear movement in the hallway outside the bedroom.

Al shouted, "Juanita, get the shotgun out of the closet!"

She crawled to the closet, pulled out the shotgun, and handed her handgun to Leslie. They sat, waiting for help to arrive.

Roger was the third HRT member heading up the stairs; three others were behind him. He thought to himself, *Fuck, fuck, what a fucking screw-up.* He waved two of his guys to check out the rooms that had open doors. They signaled back "all clear."

He looked down at the diagram provided by the CIA informant. It identified who was staying in each bedroom. Roger thought for a moment. *Jorge should be alone in that bedroom. Leslie ran into the other bedroom, occupied by Al and Juanita. The CIA informant is in the bedroom over there.* Roger slowly turned the handle to Jorge's bedroom and pushed the door open. Jorge was still half asleep as his head turned from the pillow and stared at Roger. Jorge began to reach for the gun on his bed stand, but he was not quick enough. He was subdued by Roger and another team member, who subsequently took him downstairs.

Now Roger's attention moved to the other bedroom. The HRT members had taken positions outside the room, one lying on the hallway floor and the others up against the walls outside the locked bedroom. Roger called through the door. "Alejandro, we're with the FBI. We have you surrounded."

He then gave hand signals to other team members to attach an explosive charge to the door and get ready to throw a couple of flash-bangs into the room as soon as the door was blown open.

Al's mind began to clear. He thought to himself, *What the fuck is the FBI doing here in Mexico?*

He fired three shots though the door and shouted, "You aren't going to take me alive. I'm not going to prison!"

Crawling on his belly, he headed to the window. He had one foot outside on the window ledge when the bedroom door blew open and the flash-bangs exploded inside. A combination of surprise and the blast from the flash bangs caused him to fall backward from the window ledge. He hit the ground hard; his ears were ringing, but instinct took over as he rolled over, crouched upward, and began to run.

The hostage-team members outside were just as surprised by the explosion from the house as Al. The distraction gave Al the opportunity to run toward bushes located adjacent to the golf course. He crawled into a sunken sand trap and lay quietly for several seconds, trying to recover from the ringing in his ears. Then he headed in the direction of the zoo. A rescue team member at the back of the house spotted Al and ran after him.

The flash-bangs stunned Juanita, who dropped the shotgun she was holding. The first HRT member through the bedroom door grabbed her. She fought like the devil but was quickly subdued by a stronger FBI agent, who lifted her off her feet and started the descent down the hall toward the stairs.

Just before the blast, Leslie, by instinct, dove into Juanita's closet and pulled clothing down over her. In the rush to capture Al, and in the fight put up by Juanita, the agents hadn't noticed her. She still clung to the gun Juanita had handed to her. After a few minutes, Leslie peeked out from under the clothes through the opening in the closet door. She didn't see anyone in the room and, deafened by the blast, stood up and headed for the bedroom doorway. She looked down the hallway and saw Juanita being carried away by a man toward the stairs. Raising the gun, as Juanita had taught her, she aimed at the back of the agent holding Juanita.

Once it quieted down, Dolores opened the door to her room, holding a gun in her hand. Roger looked at her and gave the thumbs-up sign. He'd remembered her picture.

"How are you doing?" he asked.

"I'm fine. How's it going?"

"Ran into—"

"Get out of the way!" Dolores raised her gun and fired down the hall. The bullet went through the middle of Leslie's forehead, causing her gun to point upward and fire a bullet into the hall ceiling. *God, I didn't want to do that. She was such a nice girl; just picked the wrong guys to hang with,* she thought.

Juanita struggled with her captor to see what was happening behind her. She screamed, "You bastards! Padre and I will get even with you for this!"

Roger, now standing outside, spotted vehicles and guards heading their way. He evaluated the situation and made two calls on his headset. "Dick, get your chopper over here as quickly as possible. Things didn't go as expected. I'll buy you some time, but the way things are going, your team may not have much time to get the job done."

Dick tapped the pilot on the shoulder and gave a hand signal to take off. "We're headed your way."

Heavy gunfire was now coming from the direction of the main house. Roger's team took up defensive positions and returned fire. After a few minutes, he received a call from one of the HRT members, indicating that a tank was headed his way.

"Okay. We have help on the way that should take care of most of our problems." Roger said over the communications link.

Roger had already situated snipers in strategic locations. They'd come from the group that'd taken over the Butcher's cabin and were now kept busy picking off the Zetas who were manning the 50mm machine guns in the back of the pickup trucks. Other team members were maintaining a field of fire to keep individual Zetas from getting through to them.

The helicopter with Dick's team inside landed on the golf course. They rushed to the guesthouse. Roger and Dolores met them at the front door and filled them in on what'd happened. Based on their information, Dick, Brian, and Dan quickly went into the first-floor office and started looking around the newly constructed computer center. Coleen and Harriett took charge of Jorge and Juanita, marching them back to the helicopter.

Brian walked through the computer center. He determined that the IRS files had been downloaded to a server, as well as to the computers in the cubicles. There were too many computers to take back with them, so they decided to take the server and destroy everything else with explosives. Dan ran past Coleen and Harriett, who were marching the prisoners to the helicopter. He grabbed a bag of C-4 explosive packs and detonators from the back of the chopper and ran back to the house.

Dick was standing at the doorway to the house when he heard on his headset that one of the subjects in the house had escaped through a back window and was heading toward the zoo. He responded to the HRT member in pursuit that he'd head toward the zoo to back him up.

"Copy that. Suggest that you head toward the Butcher's cabin on the far side of the zoo. I'm behind him and will either catch him or drive him that way."

Dick ran at full speed toward the Butcher's cabin. Halfway there, he spotted a navy fighter jet, which flew right over his head. It took out one of the Zetas' pickup trucks with its 25mm GAU-12 Equalizer cannon. *The cavalry has arrived,* he thought to himself. *Don't know where the hell they came from, but the help is welcome.* After taking out the pickup, the fighter plane turned and fired missiles into the German tank and weapons-storage building.

The explosion from the weapon stash lit up the landscape. Dick spotted Al running up the walkway from the zoo. In turn, Al spotted Dick heading toward him. Dick was just a few seconds behind him as Al ran into the shed next to the Butcher's cabin. Dick wasn't anticipating the slippery, slimy floor that was covered with old blood, and who knew what else, and his feet went out from under him. He slipped along an aisle between the Butcher's cooking drums. Suddenly, he was on his back, looking up at Al.

Seeing Dick coming toward him, Al had grabbed a meat hook that hung over one of the cooking drums. He swung it downward toward Dick's head. *Oh, God.* Dick instantly moved his head to the right and kicked out and upward with his right leg. By the luck of God, his boot caught Al in the middle of his groin. Al's body staggered back about four feet. The meat hook, which had almost connected with Dick's head, hit the ground hard next to them and then went flying in the air. It hit one of the fifty-five-gallon steel drums used by the Butcher to stew people. Al's body slumped over forward. Both his hands went down to protect his groin. His eyes were crossed as he stood there in a daze. Just then, the HRT member ran up.

"What'd you do to him?"

"Kicked him in the balls. Wasn't that part of our training at the academy? It certainly worked well," Dick replied.

"I'm sure it does, but I can't remember what we called it."

"How about a 'ball buster?' Grab him by the other arm, and let's get him down to the helicopter. I don't think he's going to be able to walk any distance on his own at the moment."

They dragged Al back to the chopper and dropped him next to Jorge and Juanita.

Coleen looked at Dick. "What the hell have you got on your uniform? It stinks something awful."

"Thanks for the friendly greeting."

Brian and Daniel stuck their heads in the chopper. "Hey, guys, watch this." He pushed the trigger button on the detonator switch, and the guesthouse exploded into pieces.

A second later, another, larger explosion occurred just off the estate, lighting up the sky.

"What was that?"

Dick responded to Brian, "I have no idea, but let's get outta here."

Brian and Daniel climbed into the chopper. Daniel was holding the computer server, and a number of the flash drives were in his pocket from the computer center. The door closed, and Dick signaled the pilot to take off. Then he called to Roger, "We accomplished our mission here. Thanks to you and your team for the help. Time to go home."

All three choppers headed west toward the Pacific Ocean. Just before reaching the coast, the chopper with Dick's team and the prisoners onboard left the others and headed south toward Acapulco. It set down on a landing pad at the Icacos Naval Base, located on the beach in Acapulco Bay.

71

Acapulco, Mexico

The door to the helicopter opened. Dick looked out at Marty, the FBI attaché from the embassy in Mexico City, and John Hampton, the CIA station chief. Behind them stood a unit of the Mexican Naval Infantry. Both the Mexican and American authorities had great concerns about Carlos's cartel trying to retrieve their own, particularly as his daughter had been captured.

Once the FBI squad and the prisoners were off the chopper, the helicopter took off for the *Bonhomme Richard*.

"Good job, Dick. Are you all right? You look and smell terrible."

"John, it's just the clothes. All I need is a good, long shower and some clean clothes."

"Well, you don't have far to go. We're the guests of the Mexican Navy, or Armada de Mexico, tonight. For security reasons, we're going to be staying on that frigate moored at the end of the pier. It's the *Allende*. You and your team can shower, and then we're having dinner on the ship with the captain. As I understand it, he's the base commander."

"John, you know how I love to eat a good meal. But, I'm ready for a quiet meal back in San Francisco," Dick replied.

"I can understand that. But duty calls. FYI, this base is the headquarters for the Mexican Pacific Command. A Mexican judge and two US attorneys from the American Embassy will interview the prisoners. Everything's set for them to be transferred to you by the Mexican authorities at the airport tomorrow morning. A bureau plane will then take you and your two gangbangers back to San Francisco. By the way, I brought your team a change of clothes from the *Bonhomme Richard.*"

The Mexican Naval Infantry took charge of their prisoners, escorting them to the *Allende's* brig. The team climbed up two decks to their quarters for the night. After a shower and donning fresh clothes, they made their way up two more decks to the ship's wardroom, where the captain was waiting at the doorway with a vice admiral.

The captain led them into the wardroom. "Welcome again to the ARM *Allende.* Let me introduce Vice Admiral Jose Mora. He is the commander of this navy base."

It was tight quarters in the wardroom. They all sat around a long, narrow table. Dick and his team feasted on an excellent meal of sea bass. They learned that in the morning, the prisoners would be taken by a convoy of navy vehicles to the Acapulco Airport, where the two American gang members would be returned to them for transport back to the United States.

As the dinner progressed into small talk, Dick leaned over toward John Hampton and said in a whisper, "John, thanks for your help with the capture of Gomez and Garcia. What was the deal with the arrival of the cavalry? I assume you had something to do with it."

"Oh, you mean the air support. It was agreed by the Mexican authorities that we could use some air support if things got bad. I suspect they didn't want to have to explain why there were dead or captured US military personnel in their country. I have a hunch they hoped we would have to use the air support, since they gave us two targets to wipe out if the support was needed. Besides saving your hides, the two

Harrier attack planes from the *Bonhomme Richard* destroyed Carlos's weapons stash and the meth lab."

"Why the meth lab and not the main house?"

"Good question. The meth lab generates cash flow for Carlos. The Mexicans want to lessen his access to cash. The main house is full of cash, which they'd love to capture to help fund their war on the cartels. Dolores, our mole, estimates there's at least $40 million stashed away in the vault. With much of Carlos's fighting capability destroyed and his cash flow lessened, the Mexican military may be able to finally launch a successful physical assault on his estate."

Vice Admiral Mora stood at the head of the table and raised his glass in a toast. "To our American friends, thank you for your assistance trying to rid our country of the drug cartels."

Well fed, and having been unexpectedly toasted, Dick and the team gladly found their way back to their quarters. Their exhaustion took over. As soon as they hit their uncomfortable navy bunks, they fell sound asleep.

72

Acapulco, Mexico

It was early the next morning when the three prisoners were escorted down the gangplank of the *Allende.*

The convoy was led by two Humvees mounted with 7.62mm machine guns, followed by two armored personnel carriers, each with twelve naval infantry onboard, and then a military sedan. This parade of vehicles was followed by two more armored personnel carriers and two more Humvees. The Mexican Navy wasn't going to take any chances in transporting the prisoners to the airport. The navy vehicles were followed by two black Suburbans for the Americans, who would take charge of the prisoners at the airport.

Dick was sitting in the passenger's seat next to John Hampton in the first Suburban, with the balance of his team seated behind them. The second Suburban was filled with embassy staff, including two attorneys. They watched as Al, Jorge, and Juanita were placed in the sedan in the middle of the convoy.

The convoy started out slowly and then picked up speed as it entered the divided highway, heading to the airport fourteen miles away. The early-morning traffic was light. The convoy traveled south on Boulevard de las Naciones and was entering an interchange half a mile from the airport when suddenly, two large semi trucks entered the highway, heading toward them from the southbound lanes of the interchange. The semis, traveling at a high speed on the wrong side of the highway, were headed straight toward the convoy. The first Humvee slammed on its brakes, skidding sideways. The other vehicles skidded left and right, trying to avoid hitting the vehicle in front of them. The semis turned across the road, effectively blocking it off.

In the confusion, a number of dirt bikes came up from either side of the highway. Two picked up the drivers of the semi-trucks and sped off around the trucks and back down the highway. Eight dirt bikes surrounded the sedan holding the prisoners. Their riders threw smoke grenades in a circle around the sedan. They used a sledgehammer to break the sedan's windows and then shot the navy driver and the guard sitting next to him. The freed prisoners mounted up behind three of the dirt-bike drivers. All of the bikes drove out through the smoke at breakneck speed and headed back down the interchange toward the ocean; bullets flew all around them. The army-trained, cartel-paid Zetas managed to outsmart the navy infantry, at least this time.

John Hampton slammed on the brakes of the Suburban. It came to a stop facing down an embankment toward the ocean. He looked over at Dick and then shouted out, "Hold on!" as he punched the accelerator and followed the dirt bikes, which were now traveling at full throttle.

Dick thought to himself, *Give me a break. I can't believe this case; it's turning into a lifetime assignment.*

"Come on, John. Catch these guys!" Dick shouted.

They were on Reforma Acupulco Lomas de Chaputepecc, going at least ninety miles an hour toward the ocean, trying their best to catch up with the bikes. Suddenly, the bikes turned onto Ave del Mar and into the driveway of a very large condominium complex. The Suburban followed as they wound through streets within the complex and ended up at the beach. The Suburban couldn't follow the dirt bikes across the sandy beach, so its doors flew open and John, Dick, and his squad took off on foot. They ran across the sand after their suspects, but they were too slow. All they could do was watch as they slid their dirt bikes down on the sand at the edge of the beach and jumped on waiting WaveRunners, which they rode out to sea.

"Shit. I don't believe this!" shouted Dick as they walked back to the Suburban. As they drove to the airport, the decision was made to fly back to the embassy in Mexico City to see what, if anything, could be done to salvage this case.

73

Sea of Cortez, México

The WaveRunners pulled up alongside Carlos's mega-yacht, and the riders walked onto the opened lower deck. Crewmembers pulled the WaveRunners onboard as Juanita ran to her father.

"Thank you, Padre."

"Juanita, you are my daughter, my only child. It is my responsibility to take care of you. I'm not going to lose you like I lost your brother. Come. Let's go upstairs. I have a lot to tell you."

As they started up the stairs, Carlos looked around at Al and Jorge and said, "I want you two to fly back to my estate on the helicopter. It isn't safe for you to be here. I have no idea what the Americans will do next."

When they reached the top of the stairs of the cabin deck, Carlos turned to Juanita and said, "Why don't you take a bubble bath? I know you love to do that, and it will relax you. Meet me afterward in the main lounge. We have much to discuss."

Two hours later, Juanita walked into the main lounge. Carlos was sitting at the bar drinking a margarita.

"Come, Juanita. Come over here and have a margarita. Orlando, please fix us a pitcher of margaritas, and then I must ask you to leave us for a while."

"Si, Señor Carlos."

"How did the police and Americans treat you?"

"Not badly," Juanita replied.

"Did they question you?"

"No. There was no time for them to really question me. They were planning to fly me to Mexico City. I think they believed they'd have plenty of time to question me there. Thank you again, Padre, for getting me away from them."

"My pleasure. Now we need to talk about other things. I'm afraid Al and Jorge are expendable. They have to be done away with. They brought the Americans here, and I don't think the Americans will leave us alone until they're gone. I can't hand them over to Americans because they know too much about what we do. When they land at the estate, the Butcher's sons will meet them. The sons blame them for their father's death. I suspect their deaths will not be nice. I'm sorry about Al, because I know you liked him."

"It's all right, Father. I was starting to tire of him, and he wasn't that great a lover. The one I will miss is Leslie. She was becoming a great lover."

"Oh, I see. We don't need to continue on this subject."

"No, Padre. I'm fine about Al. You made the right decision."

"Juanita, the helicopter has been flying back and forth from the estate to the yacht since the invasion of the estate. I've moved a little over $20 million from the estate to here for safekeeping. It's in cabin three. I want you to do what you do best: take care of the money. I trust our crew, and they respect you. Sail first to Cayman, and then on to Europe. I'll tell everyone you are taking the yacht back to Spain for an overhaul. See our friends in Cayman and Europe, and hide the money until we can get together again."

"Padre, what're you going to do?"

"I need to return to the estate and get operations back to normal. During the raid, they destroyed our stash of weapons, and for some reason, they blew up the meth lab. I need to calm our people down and repair the damage."

"Oh, Padre, I'll miss you."

"And Juanita, I will miss you, but we're strong people and things will turn out all right. Please play me something on the piano, and then let's have dinner."

74

Mexico City

Dick was in the hotel lobby rereading the case report he'd written the evening before. He took a sip of his coffee and thought, *I didn't think I'd be in the lobby of this hotel again.*

Coleen walked up with a paper and a cup of tea in her hand. "Good morning. What're you working on?"

Looking up, Dick responded, "Oh, hi, Coleen. Good morning. Sleep well?"

Coleen pulled up a chair across from Dick. "Great, but I'm ready to go home and try sleeping in my bed in my new apartment. Since joining your squad, I've only slept in it once. What are you working on?"

"The case report for Washington. I'm having a problem with where we go from here. We have the IRS computer data back, but it would be good to be able to question our two subjects to see if there's something we're missing. And we still have a murder warrant out for Jorge Garcia. Do we stay and try to track him down in Mexico or just leave that up to the system?"

"Hey, Boss, Coleen, you guys ready to walk over to the embassy?"

"Good morning, Harriett, Brian. Let's go," Dick replied.

Dick folded up his file and they walked down Paseo de Ia Reforma to the embassy. The marine guard greeted them as if they worked there, and they headed to the MCCO area, where they were greeted by John and Eleanor.

John said, "Let's go over to Mike's desk."

Mike was looking at a computer screen with images on it. "Welcome back. Sorry to hear the story of what happened yesterday. Once I heard it, I started monitoring Carlos's yacht and estate. Your guys rode the WaveRunners to the yacht. There seems to be a lot of activity there. The helicopter's been burning fuel like crazy, going back and forth between the estate and the yacht. Let's look at some of the images I have up on the large screen over there."

They watched the images of people getting into Carlos's helicopter. "This was taken after the WaveRunners arrived at the yacht. If you look closely at these two, you'll see they are your suspects, Alejandro Gomez and Jorge Garcia. The chopper took them back to the estate."

Mike then pushed another button on the screen control. Up popped a picture of Carlos and Juanita, nicely dressed on the deck of the yacht, talking to each other. "This was taken about two hours after your suspects were transported to the estate by chopper. We now know where all of the players are located. Now let me show you what happened to the estate."

Mike pushed the button again. A satellite image of the estate appeared on the screen. "This crater here is where the guesthouse was, and where your guys and the computer center were located. Your air support has put some new sand traps in the golf course, and they still haven't cleared up the heap of destroyed vehicles. This is the weapons-storage area. I don't think we will have to worry about Carlos's weapons stash for a while. This huge crater over here was the meth lab. That's all I have for the moment."

Eleanor continued, "My contacts with Mexican drug enforcement have told me that they plan to raid Carlos's estate within the week.

Your activities softened up their target. They weren't able to even get close to the estate before, but they believe they will be successful this time. My guess is that you'll have your two subjects back in the States shortly, assuming they survive the raid."

Dick responded by thanking everyone for the update. *Well, that pretty well tells me how to finish up my report,* he thought. "Okay, Animals, it looks like it's time to head home."

John looked over at Eleanor and suggested to Dick and his squad that they have dinner with Eleanor and him at the hotel that night.

"I'll arrange for a car to pick you up for the ride to the airport in the morning," he said.

75

Mexico City

The next morning, a white Chevy van pulled up to the front of the hotel, where the squad was waiting to be taken to the airport. To their surprise, John Hampton was driving.

Dick opened the front passenger side door and shouted in, "John, what the heck are you doing driving us to the airport?"

"Well, we're going to take off from a different airport. It's a little farther away," John replied.

"What's happened?"

"Load the baggage and get in. I have a surprise for you."

"Hopefully it's a good surprise."

"Well, it will at least be interesting and will conclude your case report."

John drove out of Mexico City, entered a tollgate, and paid the toll for Highway 15 Northwest. "Your flight will be leaving out of Morelia, located in the state of Michoacán. As you may remember, Carlos's cartel is called the Central Michoacán cartel. You can all relax. We have a four-hour drive ahead of us."

After an hour, they started climbing into the mountains between Mexico City and the Pacific Ocean. The temperature dropped to a pleasant level. They opened the van's windows to enjoy the fresh air. They left Mexico City's smog behind them as they continued to climb. After three hours, they exited onto Highway 43. John followed the signs to downtown Morelia.

It was a sizable city, located in a valley surrounded by high, rocky mountain peaks. From the van, the city looked picturesque, with a Roman-style aqueduct running down the center of one of the streets the van drove down. They passed a large shopping bazaar, old, Spanish-style buildings, statues, monuments, fountains, parks, sidewalk cafes, and food stands.

Coleen commented, "What a peaceful, pretty city."

They were driving east down Avenida Madero Poniente when they hit a roadblock manned by soldiers wearing ski masks. Humvees lined both sides of the street behind the soldiers.

John spoke to one of the soldiers in Spanish, who called over an officer. After further discussion, they were waved through. John parked the van about halfway down the street. The officer John had spoken with followed their van, and once they got out, he led the group toward a very large building.

John spoke to the group. "That's the Palacio Federal, which houses government offices and the post office. We received a bulletin this morning from the Mexican Army about what you're about to see."

They rounded a corner and walked toward the main entrance of the building. Before they got there, Coleen cried out, "Oh, my God, are those what I think they are?"

"I'm afraid so. Dick, you can close your case files. Carlos apparently has taken care of your problem. I have pictures, which I'll forward to you electronically. The Mexican Army has provided us with DNA samples for you to match up in the States."

They walked closer and stared at two poles located on either side of the path to the Palacio Federal. On top of the poles were the heads of Alejandro Gomez and Jorge Garcia. Signs were taped to the poles, which read, "No ayudar a la policía estadounidense," which translated to, "Don't Help American Police."

76

San Francisco, California

Coleen rolled over in the bed, leaned her head on her right hand, and looked over at Dick, who had just sat up and was looking out the window.

"You know I still have only slept in the bed in my apartment once," she said.

"So, is that a problem?"

"Not at all. I like this arrangement. I hate making beds."

"Oh, I see. You only stay at my place so you don't have to make beds?" Dick asked.

"Well, no, there are other reasons, but I owe you for having to make the bed. How 'bout I fix you breakfast?"

"You're on."

Coleen headed to Dick's kitchen as he headed to the bathroom for a shower. She knocked on the bathroom door to announce breakfast was ready.

Coleen sat a plate of bacon and scrambled eggs in front of Dick at the dining room table.

"Sorry about the eggs. I think I used too much milk, and that was the last of the eggs. Actually, they're the same consistency as my mother's eggs. Eat up."

Dick looked down at runny eggs and burnt bacon. Irish cooking. It must run in the family.

Got to remember to have breakfast out, he thought.

Dick's cell phone rang. He was happy for the excuse to get away from the plate in front of him. He headed to the bedroom, looked at the phone, and noted it was Daniel.

"Daniel, what's up?"

"You remember Mike, the techy guy at the embassy in Mexico?"

"Sure do."

"Well, we hit it off, and he just called to let me know that Carlos's estate was raided by the Mexican military today. Carlos was captured. They found $20 million in his house, so they're very happy. Also, his yacht entered the Panama Canal yesterday. Apparently, his daughter's onboard, probably headed toward Europe."

"Thanks for the info, Daniel. See you Monday in the office. Enjoy the rest of your weekend."

Dick returned to the dining area to find that Coleen had finished her breakfast and was cleaning up in the kitchen. He took his plate and dumped the food left down the toilet and returned his clean plate to the kitchen.

He put his hands around Coleen's waist and gave her a big hug. "Thanks for the breakfast. It's my turn for lunch. How about walking over to Sausalito? I'll buy you lunch at Scoma's. On the way, I'll fill you in on the phone call."

Epilogue

On June 11, 2001, Richard Albert Hartmann and Harriet Marie Foster were among thousands of taxpayers who received the following new IRS form letter.

Dear Taxpayer:

We recently learned that that there was an attempt to secure and compromise your taxpayer information.

Our special agents have taken action to secure the information before it could be used. However, in the event that you believe your identity and personal information has been compromised, please contact us for assistance.

Our toll-free telephone number is listed below. Our representatives are available to assist you in resolving any problems. We have made arrangements with a private firm to assist you with identity theft repair.

Sincerely,

Denise Kennelly
Chief Security Branch

A second new form letter was sent to more than one thousand Spanish language taxpayers.

Dear Taxpayer:

This letter is to advise you that our audit staff is reviewing your 2000 tax return. To assist us with our review, you will need to provide us with evidence that you paid the balance indicated below.

The evidence can be either in the form of a canceled check, or a copy of your bank statement, listing the payment made to the IRS. Confirmation of payment should be returned to us in the enclosed self-addressed envelope.

Sincerely,

Denise Kennelly
Chief Security Brancy

Keep reading for an excerpt from the next novel
about FBI Special Agent Dick Hartmann and his
San Francisco-based squad by Richard V. Rupp.

DEATH
ON THE
HIGH SEAS

COMING SOON

I

Acapulco Harbor, Mexico

The slight rocking of the yacht moored at the far end of the Acapulco Yacht Club made Emelie's workouts in its gym more interesting. Over the months, she'd gotten used to the deck slowly moving under her. The *Cuidado* was a mega-yacht, but it still moved with the rhythm of the bay.

Emelie Björk was beautiful. She was nearly six feet tall, with platinum-blonde hair and icy-blue eyes. Her 140 pounds were properly divided into her 36D bust, twenty-five-inch waistline, and thirty-seven-inch hips. Her body was toned, not like a model's, but rather like an athlete's. And for good reason. She was faithful to a lengthy and vigorous daily workout.

She grew up in a beautiful small village in northern Sweden that was surrounded by endless forests. There was a surplus of solitude, as the physical space was endless and lacked for people. For three months of the year, her village was essentially dark twenty-four hours a day. As Emelie grew up, the village got smaller. Her friends, of which she had few, left as soon as they finished high school.

Why does this place even exist? she wondered to herself.

Her father was fun and boisterous. He made good money, as he was one of the few locals to land a job as a driver for a car-testing company. Their clients included German manufacturers such as BMW, Porsche, Mercedes-Benz, and Volkswagen's Audi. The extreme cold temperatures of their village were perfect for testing a car's ability to handle winter driving. Winter temperatures hovered around minus-four degrees Fahrenheit most days, making ice on the local lakes consistently thick enough for driving. This year, BMW was focusing on fuel efficiency in cold weather and optimizing their anti-spin capabilities.

Emelie would take the cross-country ski trails at the back of the village to reach the lake. She'd sit on a snow-covered hill to look down and watch her father work. She had fond memories of the silence being broken by the roar created as her rough and unpretentious father drove a V8-powered BMW across the frozen lake, north of her village. He would spin the tires and slam on the brakes. Sometimes, the car would spin around and around. She deeply loved her father, who had spoiled his only child rotten.

She'd been born out of wedlock, which was not unusual in Sweden. Her mother and father cohabitated for a few years; then her mother left the village, and she never saw her again. Emelie never understood why her mother left. Her father was a great person and had treated her mother well, but her mother seemed to want more than her father or their small village had to offer.

The Swedish social system provided a safety net for her, and her father did the best he could to raise her. Good meals were provided at school, and her father cooked wonderful meals such as yellow pea soup, dumplings, and prepared meat stewed with onions. He cooked elk burgers and smoked reindeer meat. They'd go fishing together and bring back perch for dinner. She loved the blueberries and cloudberries when they came into season. She was a good student and loved to read. In fact, she spent hours and hours alone reading.

Her beauty limited the number of girlfriends she had in school.

Her strange personality limited the number of boys interested in her, and her father was often away at work. Studies suggest that people are affected by long spells of darkness. This prolonged darkness, combined with loneliness, had an effect on Emelie.

When she was eleven, one of the family cats scratched her as she petted it. She watched the blood flow down her arm. Slowly, she put her hands around the cat's neck and squeezed. She stared into the cat's face for several minutes as its legs flailed back and forth in an attempt to resist death. Then its legs went lifeless. She buried it in the endless forest before her father could discover what she'd done. During her high school years, numerous small animals disappeared from the village. The overall population of lynx, red squirrels, and rabbits from the surrounding forest seemed to mysteriously decrease. All were buried in the endless forest—some with severed heads, as the art of killing was perfected.

Emelie had just finished her workout. The gym door opened, and the lover she'd first met in a London restaurant entered.

"Ready for some kickboxing?"

"Let's get to it."

After thirty minutes, the session was over. They stroked and kissed each other before going through the gym door. Her lover shouted back, "Got an assignment for you. You're going on a cruise in two weeks. It's from Los Angeles to San Francisco. I'll tell you more about it at dinner."

Her lover's statement had piqued her interest. When Emelie got back to her stateroom, she set the dummy up and mounted the new head she'd designed on it. It was still constructed of rubber, so she'd inserted a thin, plastic tube, the size of a larynx, in the neck of this head. It was more realistic.

While the test did its job, it wasn't yet what she wanted. *I'll have to make a new head tomorrow. Practice makes perfect,* she thought.

2

San Francisco, California

FBI Agent Dick Hartmann headed back toward his usual barstool. He was twelve dollars lighter, having lost that amount to Willie Brown, "da Mayor," and Wilkes Bashford, San Francisco's upscale haberdasher, playing boss dice at the back corner of the Le Central bar. Dick followed behind them as they headed toward their favorite table at the front window.

Just as he was about to sit down on the barstool, he heard a familiar voice call out, "Hey, Dick, why don't you join us over here?" To his amazement, his friend Gordy was sitting at a table across from the bar with two other guys.

"What the hell you doing over there?"

"Toni wouldn't let us sit at the bar with these bottles of wine in front of us," Gordy replied.

"Okay. I can understand that. Why do you have six bottles of wine in front of you?"

"Meet Jack Fernald. He's a wine wholesaler." Gordy turned his head and called out to the waiter. "Louie, we need another wine glass for Dick."

"Okay, I'm a professional sleuth. I can figure this one out. Jack here is a wine wholesaler. Hello, Fredrick, my friend. Why are you, the sommelier of another restaurant, tasting wine at Central?" Dick asked.

"I'm slumming it and trying to help Jack out here. He's trying to convince Toni to buy some wine from him. Sit. Sit and try the selections," Fredrick replied.

"I see your attempt to convince Toni to buy some of your wines is going well. She's isolated you guys over here."

"Well, at least she didn't throw us out," Jack replied.

"I bet she'll charge you corkage."

"Shhh, God, knowing Toni, she might," said Gordy.

Hartmann slid across the back bench next to Gordy and joined the tasting.

"What've we got here?" he asked.

Jack responded, "We have a pinot grigio, chenin blanc, chardonnay, pinot noir, zinfandel, merlot, and finally, a cabernet."

"Any particular winery?"

"Each is from a different California specialty winery. Here. Try the pinot grigio first."

Dick looked at the wine in his glass, swirled it, placed the glass under his nose so he could smell the aroma, and then took a taste. "Nice."

"Dick, your friend Gordy here just turned down my offer of a free cruise," Fredrick said.

"Gordy, I don't believe that. You've been drinking too much of this wine."

"Believe me, I'd love to go, but I've got to be at my home office in Switzerland for a meeting. Hey, Fredrick, why don't you offer the trip to Dick? I'm sure he'd love to go."

Facetiously, Fredrick replied, "Yeah, I'm sure my boss'll buy into that one. *You* were invited because you handle the reinsurance for our program. Dick here is an FBI agent. Sorry, Dick. Don't take this wrong, but I'm not sure there's a fit."

"No offense taken, but out of curiosity, what kind of cruise trip is this?"

"Our restaurant buys its insurance through a captive insurance company that was set up in the Cayman Islands. This particular company is set up to insure upscale restaurants like ours. You know our owner, Daniel Scott. He's in the restaurant all the time, but I'm not sure that you know that he owns six other upscale restaurants. There's one in Washington, DC, London, Paris—you get the idea. He joined this captive-insurance company thing with a number of other upscale restaurants several years ago. The company is located in Cayman for tax reasons.

"They are prohibited from holding their annual meeting in the United States. If they do, they are subject to US taxes and laws. Most of the meetings have been held in Cayman, but this year, it was decided to hold it on a cruise ship. The cruise ship is going to sail one hundred miles out to sea from Los Angeles while the business meetings are held, and then return three days later here in San Francisco. Apparently, the insurance company has been doing very well. They've offered to cover most of the cost of the trip. Each of the participating restaurants has agreed to provide gourmet meals and wine during the trip. The best chefs in the world will be competing with each other. With this group, the cruise is going to be out of this world."

"Sounds like quite a trip," Dick replied.

The conversation waned as the wine-tasting group ordered lunch, and they each settled in with the wine they liked. Hartmann selected the A. Rafanelli Zinfandel. Jack, the wine wholesaler, wandered over to the bar while the others talked to see if he could convince Toni to order a case or two of his wine.

With cappuccinos and espressos in front of them, Fredrick turned toward Hartmann. "Dick, you know what? Daniel Scott really likes you, and he digs that you're an FBI agent. I'm going to give him a call and see if you can fill in for Gordon."

Dick leaned back, laughing. "Yeah! Yeah! Yeah!"

Frederick, following the Central "no cell phone" policy, walked outside the front of the restaurant to make a lengthy call. He returned to the table with a big smile on his face.

"Hartmann, you've got yourself a gourmet cruise trip, but Daniel insists that you bring your friend Coleen along, or no deal."

"You do know she's also an FBI agent and reports to me."

"Yeah, and Daniel and I both know she's with you every time you come into Ultra."

Dick rose from the table and said, "This is going to be interesting," as he headed outside and made a call. Five minutes later, he returned.

"Okay. Coleen and I are taking you up on your offer."

About the Author

Richard V. Rupp is an internationally recognized lecturer, writer, and published author on the subjects of insurance and risk management. He was born in Santa Monica, California and grew up within a Hollywood movie industry family. He served in the Army Reserve where he was assigned to the Army Finance Corp. His business career led him to the commercial insurance industry, where he became as executive that specialized in developing new insurance products and risk financing concepts. His forte was research, writing, and designing risk management and risk funding products to be used by major corporations. His positions allowed him to travel the world including frequent trips to London, Bermuda, and Cayman.

Dick and the love of his life Coleen, now split their time between Los Angeles and Palm Desert, California. Coleen encourages Dick's passion for writing, and serves as the primary editor for his creative endeavors.

Printed in the United States
By Bookmasters